'What do you mean?' Isobel looked up. Surely Furio had not betrayed himself and her.

'This morning, early, I received a proposal of marriage on your behalf. A note was delivered by hand. It asks,' Alessandro lifted a sheet of cream paper wearily, 'that I should give my consent.'

'What did you say?' Isobel licked her dry lips. She didn't know how she felt. She had never thought of marrying anyone.

'Thus far, I have said nothing. I shall write, however, and say that the power of giving or withholding permission does not rest with me. You are not my daughter,' Alessandro met her eyes, 'I'm sorry to say. . . .'

Alessandro took Isobel to the airport. Before he left her at the barrier he gave her the drawing which he had kept locked in his desk.

'Whatever happens, *carissima*, whether you come back or not, you should consider this. You have a gift. Cherish it or it will slip through your fingers.'

About the author

Born in the West Riding of Yorkshire and educated at the same school as Charlotte Brontë, Rosemary Enright studied in Paris and Wales, then worked as a fashion model before becoming an officer in the Women's Royal Army Corps. She has also worked in a variety of industries including jewellery, printing, construction and, most recently, advertising. She has spent much of her adult life in the Middle East and North Africa, but has now settled in Harrogate with her daughter.

Signed by the Artist

Rosemary Enright

CORONET BOOKS
Hodder and Stoughton

Copyright © Rosemary Enright 1993

First published in Great Britain in 1993 by
Hodder and Stoughton Ltd
First published in paperback in 1994 by Hodder and Stoughton
a division of Hodder Headline PLC

A Coronet paperback

The right of Rosemary Enright to be identified as the author of
the Work has been asserted by her in accordance with the
Copyright, Designs and Patents Act 1988.

10 9 8 7 6 5 4 3 2 1

British Library Cataloguing in Publication Data

Enright, Rosemary
Signed by the Artist. – New ed
I. Title
823.914 [F]

ISBN 0 340 60705 X

Printed and bound in Great Britain by
Cox & Wyman Ltd., Reading, Berkshire

Hodder and Stoughton Ltd.
A Division of Hodder Headline PLC
338 Euston Road
London NW1 3BH

For my friend, C.C.

PART I

ONE

"**M**ilan!"

Isobel Jefferson's palms met with an audible snap as the Trident jet's wheels skimmed the runway. Her fellow passengers glanced at her with mild, affectionate amusement. This was the first great journey of Isobel's life and she had left none of the English and Italian businessmen who surrounded her in any doubt of its significance.

In the bare two and a half hours since leaving Heathrow, soberly suited textile and furniture manufacturers along with representatives of every allied trade had seen the familiar airborne sights anew through Isobel's eyes. Books, papers and company reports had been put aside with only formal sighs of regret. Isobel's odyssey, it became plain, was to be celebrated by all.

Charming frowns from middle-aged brows, this rangy, duffel-coated Devonshire parson's daughter won herself an audience. Nothing escaped her eye or lacked for fresh minted description. And by the time the slowing aircraft taxied to a halt, a half dozen men would never be able to look upon Lake Maggiore again except as a long glass button fastening Switzerland to Italy. Isobel had read her maps.

Now, through the window, her turquoise gaze devoured nearby blades of grass for satisfying symptoms of foreignness. Whatever their mundane appearance, the underlying substance of things here must be different. Italy, breeding ground of genius, would surely nourish its creatures with a magic elixir present in the very soil.

"Well," the man who had willingly surrendered his window seat to Isobel pressed her tense, expectant shoulder. "Good luck with the au pair job." Abandoning her contemplation of the scene outside, Isobel turned to him with a wide arcing smile.

"How kind you are. I suppose my babbling on means you'll have to do your homework on patent bedsprings tonight when you should be enjoying yourself . . ."

Laughingly, the man disowned the inconvenience and offered Isobel a lift into the city centre. His Milanese customer was sending a car for him. It would be a pleasure, he said, to see her safe to her new employers' door . . .

"No thank you," Isobel declined primly. She was suddenly remote. "Nina, Frau Fischer, is coming to collect me. It's all arranged. I shall be fine. It's so very nice that we met."

Isobel spared a moment to watch her temporary knight retreat down the cabin, bulging briefcase in hand. The set of his neck, lodged far back into its collar, seemed to express offence. A pity, Isobel reflected without guilt. Friendships formed between one place and another naturally lasted for the duration of the journey – throughout its trials and pleasures. When they were done, so was the friendship. A small work of art completed. Done, but not destroyed. A picture to hang in the memory.

Isobel frequently thought in these terms. Looking at pictures, attempting to make or imagine them occupied most of her waking hours. But just now, more urgent matters claimed her. Nina, her new employer, had told her what to do. So it was with a surprisingly confident step that Isobel met the snow-cold breath outside the aircraft and followed the crowd streaming into the airport building. *Benvenuto a Milano*, its green neon letters grinned. A good beginning.

Bagagli. Baggage reclaim. It was written up in French and German too. Quite a help that, Isobel acknowledged. There was the safety of her precious combined easel and materials storage unit to be thought of. A present from a deceased great-aunt who used to dabble, it was her most prized possession. She waited for its appearance beside the luggage conveyor, her eyes sharp with anxiety. A thing like that would cost fifty pounds now and could never be replaced.

Other passengers from the same flight, mostly men, reached for their smart, streamlined cases and marched away with a quick smile and slight wave in Isobel's direction. Intent on immediate concerns, Isobel hardly noticed them go. Nina must be waiting for her in the Arrivals concourse, perhaps already impatient. The easel came, undamaged, thank heaven. But before Isobel's battered leather suitcase wobbled along to join the easel, thirteen infuriating minutes crawled by. She would be late. Four thirty in the Arrivals concourse, that's what she and Nina had agreed. Local time.

Passing through Immigration, Isobel had no time to savour the officials' interesting uniforms. Staring forcefully into their peaty, appraising eyes, she willed them to agree that she was who her brand-new passport said she was. Not one of them, as it turned out, was disposed to argue.

Miss Jefferson's eyes were certainly blue, as her thick plait of hair was undeniably blonde and her stature, at just under five foot eleven inches, removed any imagined identity problem. Milanese officialdom saw no reason why one more English au pair girl should be refused admittance. There were many such girls. This one, crane tall, was a passing wonder. No more.

Nina was not there.

In all the gleaming space of clean linoleum and pale grey paint, Isobel recognised nobody. Patiently, she examined every feminine face, measured each willow wand figure, peered into eyes that were every colour but emerald and, therefore, not Nina's. Isobel stood motionless for a few moments, out of consideration. If she could not see her employer, whom, after all she had met only once in London two weeks back, perhaps Nina could see *her*. Being tall had its few, unglamorous advantages, Isobel thought wryly. Nothing.

Deflated, she collapsed on to a seat. Something must have gone wrong. The digital clock on the wall said it was 1705 hours. Isobel worked it out. Too late. Angry or puzzled, Nina had given up and gone home.

Thoughts of finding a taxi occurred to Isobel's exhausted mind. She had Nina's address. Expensive, but lateness imposed its inevitable penalties. *How* expensive? That was the problem. How far was the airport from the city? Would there be such a thing as a bus? No, she decided. If there was, it would surely mean taking more than one. That was too ambitious a project with three pieces of luggage and scarcely a word of Italian. She could telephone, of course. She had the number. But would the operator speak English? And were Italian public call boxes like English ones?

Obstacles which would have been as molehills only a few hours ago, loomed like cliffs. Milan was an awfully long way from Plymstead Magna.

Nothing, Isobel concluded, would be lost by waiting another twenty minutes. Canon Jefferson frequently advised his children and rapt congregations alike, that agitation was the enemy of resolution. The Lord's own answers to problems were brought by angels. They preferred a steady shoulder upon which to alight. Isobel, the Canon's youngest child and only daughter had often thought the notion a touch sentimental. Flavoured with Pre-Raphaelite romance rather than common sense. But in the present emergency, it would serve. Whether or not the rustle of angelic wings was to be counted on, there was much of solid human interest to observe here. Paticularly the women.

Isobel watched them cross and recross the concourse with the naturalist's unabashed curiosity. Clad in furs flowing from neck to ankle, the grand *signore* stalked with sinuous grace. Two legged

11

cheetah, cougar and jaguar prowled past Isobel's seat . . . placing their immaculately booted feet with fascinating exactitude. There, there and *there* . . . and on, until magazine vendor, boutique or exit door was reached. No hesitation.

As they walked, slim, sculptured knees broke free of the furs, with the glint of gilded buckles slung on narrow, swaying hips. Magnificent. Faces, deeply tanned and cameo sharp looked to the front unwaveringly, balanced on long, smooth stems. There was not a single head of boring brown hair to be seen here. Thick, languorous locks that were primrose pale, garnet red or petrol glinting black swung aside to reveal ears embellished with knots of gold and cheekbones carved from coral.

Isobel forgot about the time.

* * *

Josef Fischer, Swiss industrialist and Chief Executive of Stylo Fischer, received an outside call in his office at precisely twenty minutes to six. The caller was his wife, Nina. The ensuing conversation concerned the collection from Malpensa Airport of Isobel Jefferson.

"*Liefste,*" she wheedled him huskily, "I would go, I've been trying to go. But I've had a migraine all afternoon, I'm sure I'm not fit to drive. Estella's got earache, remember. It's too cold for her to go out . . ."

"What time is her flight due?"

Josef's secretary brought him his coat at a silent signal. The Signora Fischer's wants were unending. Dutch born, like her naturalised Swiss husband, she had made few friends in Milan since she came to join him. Perhaps the English girl would help her settle. Josef's secretary hoped so. Her boss's concentration on business matters was too often distracted by domestic crises. That sort of thing was frowned on in Milan.

Tight lipped in the outer office, the secretary dialled four numbers and rescheduled Josef's next meeting, at 7.15, for 9.00 p.m. at the Excelsior Gallia. A dinner there should soothe irritation.

"Oh, I don't know. I think it was four o'clock," Nina responded languidly to her husband's question about the flight. ". . . No, half past. Yes that was it." Since the Fischers were thinking of the English girl, they spoke in English.

"But Nina," Josef expostulated, half standing to shrug himself into his town coat, "it's going up to six *now*! She'll have taken a taxi. Gone to an hotel . . . or back on the next flight home . . ."

"Oh no," Nina had interposed calmly. "She won't have the

money, so she'll wait. Poor people always do. Anyway, she's placid. Like a Bavarian milkmaid . . ."

"I thought she was English?" Josef dragged his fingers through his crimped wire curls as he always did when Nina worried him. She wandered off the point so often.

"Oh yes, she is, of course. English. Like marmalade is English. Isobel. Isobel Jefferson. That is her name. You'll go, won't you?"

Josef had never thought of refusing.

"Vittoria," he called his secretary. "Try and get Miss Isobel Jefferson paged at Malpensa. Say I'm on my way. *Ciao.*"

A maid, a good reliable maid who could double as a nanny, would be just the thing to persuade Nina to relax and get out more. Meet people. It had been Josef's own mother's suggestion to recruit an English girl if at all possible. English servants were the very best. She had telephoned her opinion from Geneva. Of course, they had become rather expensive, even before the war. But what they delivered in terms of honesty and reliability offset their wages. You could leave a child with an English housekeeper and have an easy mind.

These were the thoughts which preoccupied Josef Fischer as he accelerated his Ferrari through Milan's spreading industrial outskirts and on to the Laveno road, heading north to Malpensa Airport. He pinned great hopes on Isobel Jefferson and prayed that he would not be too late. Even the words 'English maid' had a clean, sweetly wholesome sound. She would bring peace and contentment with her. Lately, they had been sadly lacking at the Fischer apartment in the Viale Majno. Isobel Jefferson was essential.

In all Josef's discussions with his wife and his mother regarding the girl's appointment, the expression 'au pair' had never been mentioned.

Parking the Ferrari outside the Arrivals concourse, Josef shouldered his way past a knot of lounging chauffeurs, through the plate-glass doors and into the impersonal expanse beyond. Where was she? He glanced at his watch. Half past six. The girl had waited, *if* she had waited, two whole hours. Oh Nina, Nina, Josef inveighed inwardly, why do you do these things?

There was an announcement about a delayed arrival from Buenos Aires.

A woman at a distance of twenty metres or so, spun impatiently on her heel. Fanning her ocelot coat behind her, she walked imperiously away. The movement caught Josef's eye and brought it to rest on Isobel whose attention was focused on the same woman. She sat bunchily on a seat, leaning forward with her knees together and ankles widely separated. There was a pad on her lap and a pencil or something like it, in her hand. She looked up from time to time, revealing a nose that descended vertically from her brow bone. A student perhaps? Not Italian, anyway. It must be her. She corresponded to Nina's description. Certainly, she had the resigned air of one who had been nowhere recently and had no expectation of going anywhere soon. The navy duffel coat and shabby luggage were additional evidence.

"Excuse me," Josef ventured. "Are you by any chance Miss Jefferson?"

"Isobel. Yes!" Isobel sprang to her feet and extended her hand letting go of the pencil which fell to the floor as did the pad. "I'm sorry I didn't recognise you. I was expecting to see Nina . . . No, I didn't get a message . . . It was probably my fault. I do daydream . . ."

Josef took the hand she offered and found himself looking into wide, friendly eyes, the colour of northern seas in summer. Isobel's lips parted to display a set of even, white teeth and a disarming dimple in her left cheek.

There were apologies and edited explanations. Admissions that since they had never met, there could be no question of recognition on either side.

"Nina . . . my wife, is . . ."

"I'm so looking forward to seeing her again. And you mustn't mind about my waiting. I hardly noticed. Everybody here is so beautiful, I've been having the most wonderful time."

Josef's glance bent towards the sketchpad. For that is what it was, he realised, stooping to retrieve it. On it, he caught a glimpse of just three crudely eloquent lines: the woman in the ocelot coat. The swirling marks conveyed the energy of monied annoyance . . . even upside down.

"Oh, thank you! Oh no. Don't look, please," Isobel snatched the pad hurriedly and stuffed it into her untidy holdall. "I really can't draw for toffee, though I love to try. That's what I hope Nina will be able to teach me. Just basic draughtsmanship. What Sister Augustine at school could never get it into her head that I wanted. Needed. You can't spend your life tinkering about with cowslips and bladder campion, can you?"

Startled, Josef agreed that you could not, although he had no idea what bladder campion was. Some vaguely aquatic vegetable? Miss Jefferson was an extraordinary girl.

Once clear of the airport, he thought his wife's new maid more extraordinary still.

"What a fabulous car you have," she volunteered. "It's a

14

250 GT. Lusso V12, isn't it? Three litres, double camshaft, twin carburettor and aluminium engine casing. Nought to sixty in five to six seconds. That's miles of course. I don't know what it would be in kilometres. How fast does it go?"

Josef told her.

"Hmm," Isobel remarked sincerely, "I think you should get a little more out of her than that. She may need tuning."

"Do you think so?" Josef enquired supinely. "Perhaps I should see about that."

He was quite at a loss. So much for Nina's poor, placid English girl. What had they spoken of during their interview at London's Carlton Towers? Cars? Drawing? How was it that this amazingly clumsy, self-confident girl knew anything about either? As the Ferrari raced down the flat, black miles into Milan, he learned a little more.

Isobel knew about Stylo Fischer. It was a relatively young design subsidiary of Fischer Textiles. The parent company was based in Switzerland. She knew also that Nina sometimes did design work for the company. Office interiors, hotel refurbishments and so forth.

"She must be terribly talented," Isobel added.

Josef bit his lower lip. It was months now since Nina had produced as much as a sketch for Stylo Fischer. That outlet for his wife's restlessness had proved a blind alley. The rather casual art training she had received in Paris during her late teens had never prepared her for the tight technical disciplines of large-scale interior design. So she had lost interest in working for the company very quickly. Nina had never learned to deal with criticism.

"Of course," Isobel assured her companion, "Milan is the hub of the design universe."

Josef found the affirmation ludicrously reassuring. There was something to be said for Miss Jefferson's invigorating certainties. Bowed down by the weight of thirty-five serious minded years, Josef felt the corners of his mouth lift involuntarily.

"We're going to work together, Nina and I," Isobel went on without pause. "Well, she's going to work properly and I'm just going to tag along and pick up what I can," she amended. "It's really very decent of her but of course, the chance of working for a real, practical artist is what attracted me to the job. Oh how heavenly! Was that really a Lamborghini?"

Gravely, Josef confirmed Isobel's identification of the car which had fled past them on the opposite side of the carriageway. Isobel had never seen one before she said, except in pictures. She had an impressive amount of information concerning the Lamborghini's inner workings, however. But, she believed, for sheer visual poetry the Maserati carried the palm. Not that she'd seen one of those actually in the tin, so to speak, either.

Flicking his glance sideways, Josef noticed that Isobel had circled the thumb and forefinger of her right hand and was vibrating it in an oddly passionate gesture. This was not so English. The moment passed.

A shantytown of cardboard, corrugated iron sheets and canvas shot by on Isobel's right. Poverty stricken hovels in a vacant space between towering suburban apartment blocks, their squalid interiors illuminated by storm lanterns. On open ground, camp fires glowed orange and blue on thin featured faces. A small child played with a broken scooter in the dust, cuffing aside a three legged dog. Isobel had never seen such degradation in her life before. Could nothing be done?

"Gypsies," Josef answered her shortly. They lived by thieving. Big cities attracted such dross.

Sobered, Isobel was silent for a while. This was indeed another, older world. Destitution here was not clothed in romantic platitudes or hidden away in institutions. The poor were not blessed, after all. At seventeen, travel broadens the mind with dramatic immediacy.

"I did think of going to France," Isobel reverted to her former, artistic topic, "because they have the Impressionists, you know. But they're mostly in Paris and once you've seen them, you've seen them. In Italy, virtually every town has a collection. And the Renaissance began here. So it seemed best to begin at the beginning and get to the root of things. Learn my drawing from the ground up."

Josef was confused. He had picked up an art student at Malpensa, not a maid. Isobel Jefferson had everything more or less mapped out. During the three ten day holidays she had negotiated for herself during her year with the Fischers, she was going to Florence, Rome and Perugia . . . or possibly Venice. And she was not sure in which order yet. First, she hoped to get to grips with the Italian language. Josef began to feel acute sympathy for the Italian language.

"And you don't think working for us will distract you from all of this?" Josef applied the pin to Isobel's ballooning enthusiasm as delicately as he knew how.

"Not at all. I think I'm very lucky. Nina's a fantastic person and Estella and I are going to get along famously. I'm pretty good with children. It's what comes of being immature," she added drily.

Intrigued, Josef asked who considered her to be so.

"Oh, just about everyone. But particularly the nuns at my school. I went to an Anglican convent, you see. My father's in the

Church so I suppose he wanted to give them some business. Actually, calling me immature was just their way of saying they couldn't answer my questions. When I was little, anything I wanted to know was a red herring according to them. In my last term it had become prurient curiosity. Naturally they couldn't put that in my report. Much too near the bone. So they put immaturity instead. That covers a multitude of sins. And the very last thing my parents ever wanted me to be was grown up, so it suited them down to the ground. Made everyone happy."

Josef digested that slab of autobiography in silence. He knew little of English clerical families other than that servant girls were rarely recruited from their ranks. Governesses, maybe. A long time ago. But all that was Nina's affair.

There was only one thing further he felt he should know. Perhaps it would have been better to know nothing at all. But it was too late, now. Isobel had seduced his mind away from its beaten tracks. No, seduced was the wrong word. She *hauled* in attention like a fisherman with a teeming net.

"Why didn't you go to art school? I don't wish to intrude but . . ."

"Not at all," Isobel dismissed the tentative caveat airily. "Two things. My brothers' education cleaned my mother out. She was the one with the money, you see. Being boys with proper livings to earn, they had to come first. And on top of that, I've absolutely no talent at all."

Josef started to demur, partly out of courtesy and partly out of conviction. The three sketched lines he had glimpsed briefly at the airport gave the lie to Isobel's statement. But she cut across him.

"No, really. I have to work frightfully hard for every single thing I achieve. And there's never been anyone to help me, you see. Poor old Sister Gustie couldn't think of anything but flower drawings. She was jolly good at them herself. But plants are pretty anaemic, don't you think? Except trees. Anyway, you don't get into art school with a portfolio cram full of bluebell woods and tulips in a bowl. No portfolio, no student's grant," Isobel concluded succinctly.

"And you intend to make yourself one of these, er . . . portfolios? Won't it be very hard with, as you say, no talent and no teachers?"

"Possibly," Isobel responded austerely. "But I have to do it. Nothing else will ever make me happy. I say, are we here? What a street!"

The Viale Majno was a glittering residential thoroughfare in 1965, as it is now. A broad triumphal way, it is lined on either side with mansions of brooding magnificence, stern monuments to private wealth gathered over centuries in peace and war alike. But on that chill November evening, Josef Fischer wished the great boulevard three times as splendid. There was a largeness to Isobel Jefferson's appreciation which dwarfed all on which she bestowed it.

* * *

Josef left Isobel with Nina and went straight to his meeting at the Excelsior Gallia. He kissed his wife before leaving the apartment and spoke to her in Dutch. He would not be home before midnight, he said, and Miss Jefferson, of whom he had formed a favourable first impression, would surely be hungry.

"Whew!" Isobel smiled broadly as soon as the lobby doors had swung closed behind Josef's departing figure. "I suppose you do this all the time, but I'm such a novice traveller I feel I've circumnavigated the world. I'm so glad to see you . . . I suppose Estella's in bed?"

It seemed obvious to Isobel that Nina's initial, perfunctory greeting would be enlarged now that her husband was gone. Confining her glance to Nina's ineffable face, Isobel waited for that expansion.

Inwardly, she longed to exclaim over the geometric glories of the Fischers' elegant lobby. Walls lined with stretched zebra skins framed in walnut panels and, on the floor, hexagons of matte black tile, each rimmed with chrome. A miracle. But this was a private home and no comment could be made until invited. She had gone quite far enough with Mr Fischer's Ferrari, Isobel knew. Her mother would not have approved.

Instead, Isobel chatted on, guessing that Nina was taking time to readjust to her height. They had joked about it during the interview. The long and the short of it . . . What a pair they would make. Because Nina was diminutive. A tiny, flame haired gazelle of a woman with a skin as opaquely cream as the Devonshire kind. It reflected every colour purely.

As she talked, Isobel absorbed the impact of Nina's beauty all over again. Only the smile, warm enough to ripen pomegranates when seen in London, was missing. Regarding her with the same eager optimism with which a picnicker scans cumulus clouds in the sky, Isobel waited to be asked to remove her duffel coat. She was tired. It would be nice, too, to be taken to her room, allowed to unpack . . . to be offered the use of a lavatory. She felt grubby and wanted to wash.

Isobel ran her entire stock of small, pleasant things to say down to the bottom. For a moment, there was a dense pause in which Nina's eyes restlessly quartered the space surrounding Isobel's stationary figure.

"Well," she announced finally in her faintly metallic English accent, "it's a good thing you're here at last. I'll show you round the apartment."

"Oh, thank you," replied Isobel, grateful that the burden of conversation had now been taken up and transferred. "It's so lovely and warm in here, I wonder if I might just take my coat off."

Nina regarded her directly. "Yes, I suppose so. You can hang it up through there for the moment. I don't like clutter in the lobby."

Surprised, Isobel passed through the door indicated and helped herself to the facilities she found beyond. The wash basin faucets foxed her at first until she realised that the rough surfaced silver sphere stood for 'cold' and the smooth golden one for 'hot'. Sun and moon. Pretty.

Drying her hands, Isobel remembered that poor Nina had been suffering with a migraine all day. Mr Fischer had said so. No wonder she was so unsmiling. Not at all herself. The pain. It always made Isobel's mother ratty.

Isobel gave her reflection in the looking glass an indifferent glance as she tightened the elastic band on the end of her pigtail. A dab of compressed powder and she was ready. With any luck, food would not be too long delayed.

"Don't use that cloakroom in future," Nina said, turning from an arrangement of orange orchids as Isobel emerged. "It's for guests."

Isobel blushed and apologised while Nina looked her plaid kilt and hand knitted jersey up and down. They *were* rather juvenile, Isobel thought, uncomfortably conscious of Nina's scrutiny. But her mother chose her clothes. Why was good taste always so appalling? She envied Nina's feral looking leopard-print slacks and matching skinny-cut shirt.

A tour of the apartment followed. The rooms were huge and there were many of them. Groups of lean, attenuated furniture made from precious woods were disposed about the cool tile floors like sculptures. Little here was for ornament alone. Most items had at least a notional function. Decoration was supplied by surface texture and by beams of concealed lighting which Nina demonstrated as she led Isobel from room to room. The few pictures were monochromatic and represented the mathematical possibilities inherent in unemotional triangles, cubes and cones. The work, Sister Augustine would have said, of charlatans.

Isobel did not agree but kept her interest in the steel framed prints to herself. The account Nina gave of her palace and its contents did not invite interruption. In any case, Isobel found herself very nearly speechless. She had never seen such a home as this.

It was like a dazzling machine, momentarily at rest. Nothing in her considerable imagination could have been less like the rambling, creaky floored Queen Anne parsonage house in Plymstead Magna. Least of all the bathrooms.

There were four in the Fischer apartment and Nina's own drew an unguarded squeak of excitement from Isobel. The bath itself was of grey-veined marble, its broad rim fitted flush with the floor tiles so that it looked like a miniature swimming pool. Sublime luxury.

"You must be careful how you clean that," Nina cautioned. "There's some special marble paste in the cupboard and you must *never* use anything else. Do you understand?"

Isobel nodded. Nina had said rather a lot about cleaning. There was a small room full of electrical gadgetry specifically for the purpose, the correct use of which Isobel was instructed to master. And the surrounding shelves were filled with neatly organised detergents, pastes, polishes, spirits and waxes. Again, Isobel was to familiarise herself with their various uses. And now the bath.

Isobel fought off an engulfing wave of despair. She was just hungry and tired. That was all. Everything would look brighter once she had eaten. Bed would be welcome, too. It had been a long day.

"That's everything," Nina said as she switched off the lighting in the bathroom. "Except for Estella's nursery and we can go over that in the morning. I'll show you your room. You can bring your things in from the lobby."

"How's your headache?" Isobel asked. Nina appeared not to have heard the question. Wearily, Isobel humped her suitcase, holdall and easel from the lobby and followed in Nina's wake. She felt a little light headed.

Isobel's room lay behind the vast, gleaming kitchen, between the nursery bathroom and Estella's own quarters.

At first, Isobel's eyes refused to convey what they recorded to her brain. There was no window. All the other rooms had enormous windows looking out on to the bright lights of the Viale Majno. Here, there was none. The electric lighting was in sharp contrast to the sophisticated arrangements in the rest of the apartment, too. A single naked light bulb hung spiritlessly from the dingy ceiling. No bedside lamp. There was a painted chair and a narrow divan with child's printed cotton bedlinen on it. A Formica veneered hanging cupboard and a chest of drawers with one leg propped on a folded wad of newspaper completed the appointments. They rested on a concrete floor stained with a dark red paint. The colour of dried blood.

It took Isobel less than ten seconds to absorb all this. There are moments when a lifetime's training in tolerance and good manners goes for nothing. Isobel swung round to face her hostess. The torrent of furious words banking behind her teeth froze as she saw a flicker of fear in Nina's green eyes. She needn't think I'm going to hit her, Isobel thought resentfully. But the tremor of rage which had passed through her subsided.

Even so, this was not what she had been promised. She had never been used to luxury and had not expected it. But no au pair girl that Isobel had ever heard of had been required to sleep in a windowless kennel. She had Nina's advertisement in her shoulderbag, cut from *The Lady*. It said quite plainly, "Au pair girl to help in artistic household and live as family."

Isobel had no need of words. The outrage etched on her features was enough for Nina. She joined her jewelled hands before her breast and twisted them together. A curiously servile mannerism. Isobel, unnerved by her own power to produce this effect, was sorry for her. There had been a misunderstanding.

"It looks a little bare. We'll go out tomorrow. We can go shopping for some nice things to make it look pretty . . ."

"I can't paint in here," Isobel said starkly.

Nina stared up at Isobel blank faced, as if she had never heard that Isobel painted . . . Had never offered her help in that direction or proposed the sisterhood they were to have enjoyed. Nina had done what she always did. Listened to what she was told and responded with the currency that seemed to buy most at the time of dealing. The transaction agreed, she forgot its terms. Painting?

"Well," she murmured vaguely, "perhaps in the kitchen, then. Goodnight. You must rest. Estella wakes early."

Nina made as if to close the door but Isobel grasped it firmly.

"Look, Nina. I'm hungry . . ." Flecks of temper sparked in Nina's eyes. Mentally, Isobel shook herself. That was another mistake. But Isobel's own dizziness and the pain growling in her stomach was not.

"Oh," the exquisite matron looked back at the tall, fair girl. "Are you? Well, there's some milk in the fridge in the kitchen . . . and some bread. Help yourself. Don't forget to wash up the glass."

Before she went to sleep that night, Isobel said her prayers out of long habit. The prayers of intercession, as her father called that phase of the operation, were the longest bit. And tonight, since she was absent from home for the first time, making the effort seemed a crucial act of loyalty.

So many things for God to attend to. Daddy's rheumatism . . . it had been getting worse lately. Mummy. Well yes, Mummy. She

21

didn't seem to need much unless it was a new bicycle pump and a good turnout for her forthcoming jumble sale. She gave the best ones in the diocese. Simon, Isobel's younger, favourite brother, about to take his final exam in air navigation at Hamble. And Rupert's first film directing job in California. He was bound to do well. Rupert had never needed much help from God. The poor gypsies ... How lucky she was in comparison. A good subject, though, if only she could do it ... Those triangles of light in the tent openings ... And Nina's headache. Migraines were utter hell ...

Young and healthy, Isobel fell fast asleep before "Amen" was ever uttered. She dreamed of bees humming in and out of her father's hives in the orchard at home. Actually, what throbbed in her head was the noise of the central heating boiler in the cupboard adjoining her room. It was very warm.

TWO

Several days passed in which Isobel struggled to find her feet in the Fischer family circle. There were no guidelines. Nina's moods fluctuated, up and down, like a barometer glass in equinoctial weather. For a space, she recovered all the sunny cordiality that Isobel had warmed to in London.

"We have so *many* things to talk about . . . Don't you think a new friendship is like a parcel, all done up with thrilling, knotty string?"

But too often, the smile that beckoned Isobel to Xanadu led only to a deserted pleasure dome, stirred by aimless winds. Round and around.

"You're working too hard, Isobel." Nina tripped, one afternoon, into the dining room where Isobel was buffing the rosewood table on her most recent orders. "Come on. I have made coffee and we'll guzzle some of the pastries I bought in Peck's this morning. Leave that. No one ever died of dust."

It was the second full day and the first occasion on which, seated at the kitchen table, Isobel raised the matter which chiefly vexed her.

"I really must register with the *Questura* soon, Nina. You have to, by law, I think. And anyway, I can't enrol in a language class until I do. You have to show your residence permit."

No sooner had the words fallen from Isobel's mouth than Nina's face closed. Her eyes, normally light emerald, darkened to forest green and her tightened lips went pale. Isobel watched, more fascinated than afraid. These strange moments came and went. They were unnerving, but so far, unattached to any significant result.

"But Isobel . . . *lieveling* Isobel," Nina's shadowed countenance cleared, "you really don't need to speak any Italian. I speak English, don't I? Estella's not very good yet, but that's part of the reason you're here, isn't it? And I do all the shopping . . ." Nina patted Isobel's hand reassuringly.

It was impossible just then, or so it seemed to Isobel, to remind Nina that whilst what she said was true, the fulfilment of her own purposes was part of their arrangement. Light domestic tasks, companionship to the child in exchange for pocket money and time off to attend Italian classes . . . But Nina was already talking about something else.

She had a new design project to begin. Perhaps Isobel would care to look over her shoulder. Nina would be glad to teach all she knew of perspective. It was really terribly easy once you understood it.

"I know, we'll start tonight, after you've put Estella to bed. Oh no, I can't. We're taking some people to the opera. Business. Tomorrow, then. Yes, tomorrow. We'll do some drawing, *liefste*."

The hint that this part of their bargain might soon be honoured, made Isobel wary of promoting any disharmony between herself and her employer. Nina possessed the treasure which Isobel craved. Technique.

And so it went on.

Isobel had seen little of Josef since the night of her arrival. He left the apartment early after a hurried cup of coffee which he drank standing up in the kitchen, immersed in papers spread on the table. He would glance up abstractedly as Isobel ushered Estella in, dressing-gowned and fractious, to eat her breakfast cereal.

"I won't like this," she invariably said of the cereal whilst banging her spoon on the table. "It's bad. Papa, tell this girl I *not* eat this."

"But sweetheart," Isobel coaxed, "it's what your Mummy wants you to have because it's so good for you . . ."

At this point, Josef took off his horn-rimmed spectacles and swept up his papers without comment. He dropped a kiss on his infant daughter's abundant wiry curls, flashed a sweet, commiserating smile at Isobel and was gone. His voice, clear and light, was heard in the lobby calling to his wife in Dutch. There was never any audible reply. Nina had taken to sleeping late.

"Papa work," Estella announced complacently as she heard the automatic security mechanism on the lobby doors click into place.

And indeed, Josef seemed to work all hours. If he came home for the informal evening meal, which Isobel shared with her employers, he returned to his office afterwards or disappeared into a little study, in which, Nina informed Isobel, her husband must never be disturbed.

But Isobel liked Josef. He was kind in his absent minded, pre-occupied way and teased her gently about her love of fast cars. She told him over dinner one evening that her brothers had spent their pocket money on car magazines. When she was at school, she had cut out the pictures of the cars for their lovely, racy shapes and put them in a scrapbook. Inevitably, she had absorbed some details of their anatomy.

"I thought little English girls had a love affair with horses," Josef smiled, ignoring his wife's fidgets as he offered Isobel another escalope of veal.

"Well, I was different," Isobel stated simply, accepting the second helping.

"*E vero,*" Josef had muttered to himself with one of the lightning changes of language that often occurred in the Fischer household. Different, certainly.

Estella, an ethereally built four-year-old with her mother's refinement of feature and her father's dark colouring, was a child of obdurate temperament. The Swiss breakfast cereal was the sticking point over which she and Isobel fought the day's first battle. Nina said quite categorically that, like it or not, it was Isobel's responsibility to see to it that Estella ate at least 75 grammes. It was nutritious and that was the end of the matter. Isobel ate toast.

Towards nine o'clock, Nina, misty in a cream satin *peignoir* with her red hair tousled gloriously over her shoulders, made an appearance in the smartly equipped nursery where Isobel dressed Estella. Estella greeted her mother querulously and always in Dutch.

What followed sounded like a catalogue of complaints from the child against Isobel which Nina met with clucking responses, smoothing her daughter's hair. Suspecting injustice, Isobel was powerless to protest. She understood no word of what passed between mother and daughter. At any rate, she thought, it was discourteous of them to speak in a language she did not know. She was not exactly a servant, after all. But the manners of Plymstead Magna were not those of Milan. That could hardly be expected.

When Nina took Estella, seraphic in her fine, smocked alpaca and velvet collared coat, to join her pre-school group, Isobel commenced the day's duties. Surprised though she was not to escort the child herself, she was kept too busy to propose any alternative programme. Nina's continual, curiously hollow sounding endearments purchased her submission to endless piles of ironing and the thrice weekly cleansing of the apartment's broad empty balcony. Unlike neighbouring ones, it boasted neither pot nor palm.

Task followed task. The worst of these was washing down the tile floor and lacquered walls of the nursery with disinfectant every day. It seemed so pointless.

"No, no, Isobel," Nina had said on the very first day. "You mustn't do it with a mop. Not in the child's room. You must get down on your hands and knees with a cloth. That is the only way to be sure every germ is killed."

25

Startled by Nina's dictatorial choice of words, Isobel laughed. "Poor germs," she reproached obliquely. Were there some rubber gloves? The disinfectant solution was making her hands raw.

"No. They are not efficient. This is important. You must do it without gloves," came the older woman's staccato reply.

Must and *must not* were the most frequently used words in Nina's extensive English vocabulary. Isobel swallowed her dislike of them and excused Nina. Her English, after all, was excellent. It was unreasonable, Isobel mused, to expect her to be sensitive to every nuance of polite form. Nina spoke four languages, whereas Isobel, impressed by the power of knowledge, spoke only one. She would teach Nina, gradually, by example. That was the best kind of sermon . . . as Canon Jefferson maintained.

On the fifth day, a Friday, Josef returned unexpectedly to the apartment during the morning when Nina was out. He found Isobel engaged in the hated, daily disinfection of Estella's nursery. She always did it first, to get it over with. Hearing a key turn in the lobby doors, Isobel assumed it was Nina, back from dropping Estella off at her nursery school. She wrung out her cloth again for the umpteenth time and prepared to clean the next square metre of spotless tile.

"What are you doing, Miss Jefferson?" Isobel swung round to see Josef in the nursery doorway. He had taken off his street shoes at the door as he usually did and wore only socks, a sheaf of papers in his hand. "Why don't you use a mop?"

Isobel sat back on her heels glumly and laid the backs of her stinging hands briefly against the cool of her cheeks. She was doing, she said with a shrug, as she had been told to do. Every day. The ghost of something, surprise or possibly embarrassment, passed over Josef's rather plump features. It was enough to encourage Isobel to confide in him.

"Well," he said cautiously, "it does seem rather a waste of time . . . Perhaps if you did this every other day it would be enough. I will speak to my wife. And the other thing, the *Questura* . . . I will check. If it is necessary to register, you can do it after the weekend. *Ciao*."

Josef waved the papers in farewell. He had forgotten them that morning. After a moment, the lobby doors clicked shut.

There was silence in the apartment again. Only the faint hooting of traffic horns penetrated the sound insulated windows. They were never opened to admit the clanging noise and fumes of the city. All that was excluded. A system of fans and air ducts ventilated the apartment. Very different from the rattling, draughty sashes at Plymstead Magna.

Missing them a little, Isobel reminded herself that at the Parsonage, there were only mooing cows to hear and the harmless odours of hay or rain soaked earth to smell. Her parents' perfect, storybook world. Isobel shook herself. Frankly, it had all been very boring.

And a modern flat, Isobel told herself firmly, in this modern block, could not possibly feel eerie.

Josef's reminder of the approaching weekend was sufficient in itself to cheer Isobel. There had been no drawing session yet, and none of the promised improvements to Isobel's accommodation, but now surely, she would be able to get out and see Milan. She must have some fresh air. Begin to know the sights, sounds and scents of the place. So far, she had seen only what was visible from the apartment's windows. When cleaning them, mostly.

There were four other apartment blocks that Isobel could see through the bare-branched trees. Brown or lemon yellow stucco with noble pediments and blue-painted shutters. There was a slight but distinctly Alpine pitch to their roofs. One, more modern, was faced with green marble . . . there was a lot of marble in Italy. And they all had uniformed commissionaires to sweep back doors for opulent women carrying minuscule dogs or pale, tired faced men wearing suits or topcoats cut with scalpel precision.

Twice a day there would be schoolchildren, squirming in and out of chauffeur-driven cars with adorable complaining faces and petulant gestures. Much like Estella's. Once, Isobel recognised an English nanny's uniform. Schoolgirly and cosy. Its wearer passed by, pushing a pram, unaware that she was watched from above. Involuntarily, Isobel waved. She felt foolish but would not have minded being able to say hello.

"Hello," was what Nina said when she erupted into the apartment an hour after Josef's departure. Isobel was peeling celeriac in the kitchen.

"Is that for this evening? You needn't bother with it." Nina let fall a profusion of packages on to the kitchen table. "We're going to the country for the weekend. You can do Estella's packing and help me with my husband's. We're collecting him from the office and going straight from there. I shall scream if I don't get out of this place," she added, echoing Isobel's earlier thoughts.

Isobel's surge of excitement was short lived, however. It was soon apparent that she was to be left behind, alone. The prospect was deeply alarming. She had never been quite alone anywhere before. There were other things, too.

The refrigerator was all but empty. Nina had not gone shopping the previous day. All her present packages contained clothing. A cashmere sweater, a silk scarf, a fox fur hat and a pair of silk

27

lounging pyjamas. Emilio Pucci. Nina displayed them to Isobel with a parakeet stream of chatter. Milan was the best shopping town in Italy, possibly in all of Europe, did Isobel realise? It must be thrilling for a little English country mouse to see such things.

"Not so little, eh?" Nina pinched Isobel's cheek playfully. It hurt. Sweeping up her purchases, she skipped away to her own room, crooning to herself in German.

Isobel calculated swiftly. She had less than fifteen pounds in traveller's cheques and a few lire. She had spent nothing since she arrived, having had no opportunity to do so. But she would need to buy food for the weekend. Nina would not do it. Not now. And she had made no mention of Isobel's little honorarium. Isobel determined to have it. It was embarrassing to ask for money but she had earned it. Nina was very good at forgetting things, but at least she should not be allowed to forget this. How very clever of her to be collecting Josef from the office. No appeal to him would be possible.

Instantly, Isobel put the mean thought from her. Nina was not bad. Just thoughtless. Everything would be sorted out on Monday. Josef had promised.

Nina paid Isobel four days' money, counting the notes and coins out on to Isobel's open palm. As she pointed out, Isobel had not worked at all on the Monday of her arrival. The value of the lire was somewhat less than three pounds sterling. It was the going rate for an au pair.

"There's no food in the fridge, Nina." Isobel thought she might as well draw attention to the fact. It was a shame that she should have to spend her own money on eating.

"Then you'll have to go out and buy some, won't you," Nina said crisply. Before Isobel could interrupt she went on to give a list of instructions.

Isobel need do no work and she could go out. The Duomo was worth seeing and maybe she could find herself some English friends. But she must be back in the apartment by seven o'clock on Sunday evening as the Fischers expected to return themselves by eight. She was on no account to meddle with the central heating thermostat. Isobel should be perfectly comfortable. Most important of all, Isobel was not to open the apartment door to anyone or allow anyone inside. Nobody.

"Yes, all right," Isobel said, taken aback at this barrage of emphatic prohibitions. "But why?"

"People round here," Nina snapped, "they won't mind their business. We don't want anyone to know you're working for us. You understand?"

"Not really," Isobel admitted. "Why does it matter?"

Nina took a step forward and thrust her face close to Isobel's who looked down at her, amazed.

"These Italian *shmucks* . . . So cureeious . . ." Nina lengthened the word, her lips curled back from her teeth in a snarl. "*Jealous.* Jealous of my Isobel. They will try to make trouble for Josef and me. So, nobody eh?"

Once again, Nina pinched Isobel's cheek. She stepped back and seemed to recover from the weird spasm which had distorted her features.

"If you must go out," she reiterated, hours later in her normal tone, draping a yellow cashmere coat about her shoulders, "try not to be seen. Not coming, not going. That is best."

Shaken, Isobel helped Nina to the lobby doors with her luggage and Estella with hers. The *portinaio* or caretaker would collect it from there and take it down to the subterranean garage.

"*Arrivederci, cara.* Enjoy yourself." Nina's departing smile was warm as toast.

Half an hour later, Isobel began to shiver. A chill? The heating, like the ventilation, came through air ducts. There were no radiators to cling to and no other form of heating in the apartment. It was normally so effective. Isobel went and put another sweater on.

Feeling hungry, she looked at the celeriac and threw it out. Horrible, turnipy stuff. She made do with dried pasta and cheese that night. There would be some shops open at that hour but she did not know where they were. All commerce was banished from the Viale Majno's plutocratic purlieu. Nor did she care to go out in the evening alone. Not at first. It was dark.

In the deserted apartment, the silence billowed, magnifying the hollow rattle of lone domesticity. Isobel winced at the ring of her fork on the plate.

After washing up her supper things, Isobel fetched some drawing materials and settled to making a sketch of one of the kitchen chairs. They had interesting, flowing lines. Work was always company, too.

Knowing none of the rules of perspective, Isobel had found an effortful way around the problem. If you stared long enough at a thing, planing from your mind all the everyday assumptions about depth and direction, the image would finally reduce to a flat, two-dimensional shape which could be transferred to paper. Once there, the image would spring to life again. The system was hard work and made the eyes ache. But at least it filled the mind.

Long before her eyes began to strain, Isobel's fingers stiffened. It really was too cold to work. The only recourse was bed.

She lay there for an hour, listening to the self-generated high frequency whines in her sound starved ears, attempting to take stock of the day. Jealous, Nina had said. Why should people be jealous? All the people round here were enormously rich. They could have au pairs if they wanted them. They probably did. It made no sense at all. How nerve rackingly illogical Nina could be. As for being left alone here . . . Well, a little privacy was quite restful.

Isobel tried to look on the bright side as she had been taught to do at home. Things could be a lot worse. She drummed her heels on the bottom sheet energetically. Anything to generate warmth.

Tomorrow, Isobel promised herself, she would think very carefully about what to put in her first letter home. There was no point in worrying them all in Plymstead Magna yet. Less than a week had gone by. It was too soon to draw conclusions. The Fischers and Milan deserved a fair trial. They had so much to give her.

Sleep would not come. Eventually, Isobel rose and pulling on a robe, went to look at the central heating boiler in the cupboard next door. She had been told not to touch it, but there were limits to obedience. It was terribly cold.

The thing was silent. No hum or buzz. There was no central heating at home in Plymstead Magna and Isobel studied the contraption before her with apprehension. There were knobs, dials and levers. What did what? If she manipulated any of them, she might damage the entire system. Defeated, Isobel closed the cupboard door. It looked as though the heating had broken down . . . or been switched off. Deliberately. How *dared* Nina?

Emboldened by anger, Isobel made a decision. The Fischers slept in twin beds and Nina's had an electric blanket. A luxury unheard of at the Parsonage. On cold nights there they managed with bedsocks and stone hot water bottles.

Marching into her employers' bedroom, the only room with a carpet, Isobel switched on the electric blanket and slipped between the satin sheets. Bliss. Even the guilt was luxurious . . . as was the residue of Nina's gardenia perfume. If Nina didn't like it . . . Well, she might not be told. One really had to look out for oneself, Isobel thought grimly as she switched off the light. In the morning she would consider what to do. There would have to be changes – and soon.

* * *

She woke to a thunderous knocking.

At first, Isobel was muzzy with sleep and did not connect the distant hammering with the outer doors of the Fischer apartment. Nobody would come here. Except them.

Sitting bolt upright among Nina's pillows, it came to her that there might have been a change of plan. The Fischers had come back early from wherever they had been. Well, so much the better, they would *all* have some explaining to do.

Scorning, now, to disguise her trespass by making the bed, Isobel got up and put on her shabby kimono. A jumble sale find. Quite nice, if faded. The hammering continued unabated.

"I'm coming," Isobel called down the empty, echoing bedroom corridor. "Please, just wait a moment while I find my slippers." The tile floors, normally kind to the touch of naked feet, were icy.

Reaching the lobby, she heard voices outside the door. Loud masculine voices speaking in Italian. Not Josef. What could be the matter? A fire? Suppose it was. She wouldn't even know the word. There was a dictionary in her room. Should she get it? Nothing else could justify her disobeying Nina's orders. Nobody was allowed into the apartment.

"Who is it?" Shuddering with cold, Isobel approached the doors. "Please, who is there? I can't open the doors . . ."

Among the answering avalanche of Italian words, Isobel heard her own name. Who wanted her? Who in this whole city knew that she existed? The thundering resumed. Isobel, unable to stand it longer, snatched up the key from the console table and, fumbling, drew back the sliding locks and bolts.

A man pushed past her, flinging some direction to another who remained outside.

"Who are you?" Isobel stepped back, vulnerable in her night-clothes. "I'm not allowed . . ."

The man, dressed in a belted leather trench coat, withdrew a card from an inside pocket and waved it under her nose. Isobel glanced at it. It meant nothing. It seemed to Isobel that the man harangued her in his own language for many minutes. The swallow-swooping cadences of this tongue were suddenly full of menace. So was the violent looking leather coat. Tears of simple fright pricked at Isobel's eyes.

"*Parla Italiano?*" the man demanded when his first volley of words was exhausted.

Isobel shook her head miserably. No, she didn't speak Italian. Not one word. Only please and thank you.

The man touched her shoulder kindly, all fury spent.

"Why did you not tell me so?" he said in perfectly grammatical if heavily accented English. "I am not a . . . how would you say . . . a lion, am I?" He pulled a comical face.

"You roared enough," Isobel flashed back at him accusingly, ashamed of her tears.

It was all perfectly explicable, Isobel discovered. The man introduced himself as Silvano Crivelli. He was an official of the *Questura*. Immigration had notified him of her entry into Italy and she should have registered within the first forty eight hours of her arrival. Why had she not done so? And why, moreover, as her entry permit said au pair, had she not attempted to enrol in an Italian language class? The schools all sent returns to the *Questura*. All foreign nationals intending to work or study in Italy were made aware of the requirements. Was that not so? Miss Jefferson had known of the regulation, had she not?

The questions were shot as if from the mouth of a machine gun.

Isobel attempted to explain that she had had no opportunity. The Fischers were very busy people. Mr Fischer had honestly intended to attend to the matter on Monday. He was a foreigner himself, so they were all a little at sea.

The man from the *Questura* regarded Isobel narrowly.

"The responsibility is yours, Miss Jefferson. This exploitation must be stopped. Monday, you come to the *Questura*. Yes? And then you begin to learn our language."

With that he left, leaving the radiance of a gold toothed smile behind him. Isobel found she liked him.

Yes, Monday. There was no need now for Josef to check on anything. All was plain. Au pairs had rights.

Glad that things were coming to a head at last, Isobel took the electric blanket from Nina's bed and put it on her own. That was fair.

After changing Nina's sheets, she spent the rest of the weekend admiring the spiny splendours of the Duomo. Third largest church in the world, said the English leaflet. Outside it looked like a black porcupine, half hidden by its protective reed screens. Cleaning was in progress. Within, there were many sombre diversions. Isobel went back twice.

Gazing at gruesome Saint Bartolomeo, coquetting in his flayed skin as if it were some gorgeous garment, Isobel heard a throaty giggle behind her. A group of American nuns stood in the candle pricked gloom. One of them caught her eye.

"Just plain excruciating, isn't it, honey?" the gothic gowned lady said in twanging New York tones. "Plain pornography. You here on holiday like us?"

Isobel was delightedly shocked.

She fell into conversation with the party of nuns. In spite of her half-sincere demurrals, they insisted on taking her for a cup of chocolate in the Galleria Vittorio Emmanuele. And cold as it was, they all enjoyed sitting at a table on the mosaic floor beneath the lofty glass vaulted arcade watching the large nosed, self-appreciatively handsome Milanese go by. Isobel drank deep with her eyes. There was no one here to tell her not to stare. How could one remember if one did not look? It was good to be in physical touch with the city, at last.

Isobel asked the nuns many questions about their lives, saying that since her father was in the Church, she took a professional interest in how the other, 'Catholic' half lived. The nuns roared with laughter and Isobel enjoyed their salty, good-humoured wit. There was no one, they agreed, half as Catholic as the High Anglican party. Had her father never been tempted to 'go over' to Rome?

"What? And lose the Parsonage at Plymstead Magna?" Isobel replied naughtily. "It's Daddy's pride and joy. He knows which side his bread's buttered. Right on the English side."

This promoted another gust of hilarity.

Isobel parted from the nuns with many mutual good wishes, having said nothing of her own troubles. They were small and as good as solved, anyhow. Dodging the clashing, rumbling, orange trams in La Scala piazza to find a Number Five, she thought it must be a wonderful thing to be a *real* nun. Or any person who recognisably embodied a great idea. Then you wouldn't have to worry about yourself at all. You were simply the vessel that carried something of infinite value to the world. Recognition. It was the only garment that really counted.

Isobel would have it when she was an artist. Once that thing which scorched inside her had been squeezed, somehow, to her fingers and released on to paper, board or canvas . . . only then would she be complete. Acceptable to herself.

Blind and deaf to anything but her own thoughts, Isobel nearly missed her stop.

She was late. Only half an hour until the Fischers were due back at the apartment. Well, as it happened, Isobel meditated, unlocking the lobby doors, she *had* made some friends. None of them permanent and none of them English. But that didn't matter.

* * *

Isobel tackled the question of the central heating first. Of course, it probably *had* just stopped of its own accord. And she made a clean breast of her action concerning Nina's bed. Nina drew her upper lip down in a quiver of fastidious disdain.

"Well, what on earth did you expect me to do?" Isobel was stung. "I'm not a leper. And I changed your sheets . . ."

33

"Are you menstruating?" Nina asked coldly. Isobel's face drained.

Still in his tweed travelling coat and cradling the round-eyed, thumb-sucking Estella in his arms, Josef regarded both women in consternation. He went straight to the boiler cupboard. In a moment, the familiar throb was heard again. Josef returned to the lobby and, releasing Estella into Isobel's care, spoke to Nina in Dutch. Without a word to the English girl, husband and wife withdrew to the study.

"Did you have a nice time, darling?" Isobel enquired of the child as she started undressing her.

"I rided a horse," Estella grudgingly confirmed.

"How *wonderful*," Isobel enthused. "I always wanted a pony. Did you go fast?"

Racking her brains for additional questions so that the intermittently raised voices emanating from the study should be muffled, Isobel switched off and removed Nina's electric blanket from Estella's little bed. The child, at least, had done nothing to deserve a freezing reception.

"Come on, sweetheart. No bath tonight. Just a cat-lick and then jump into bed while it's warm. Brrr."

Whatever disagreement had taken place between Estella's parents, it was now at an end. They came together, ruffled but composed, to their child's bedside. No, Josef said, Isobel could not read a story tonight. It was too late. Was she warm enough? Estella, nearly asleep, replied that she was.

"Thanks entirely," Josef muttered in German, "to Miss Jefferson's forethought."

"I'm sorry, Miss Jefferson," Josef apologised directly in English, "that you've had such a wretched two days. My wife intended to isolate only the rooms you would not use in our absence, and to reduce the quantity of hot water available as the requirement would be less . . . Very sadly for you, she made a mistake."

Whatever the rights and wrongs of the matter, Isobel was convinced that some sort of justice, albeit concealed from her, had been done. Of course, Nina's obscenely hostile question could not be mentioned to her by Josef. But out of gratitude to him, she would have liked to delay reporting the *Questura* man's visit till the following day.

Better, perhaps, to have it all out than in.

"You couldn't help it," Nina greeted the news of the official's forced entry with uncharacteristic blandness. "These Italians," she shrugged. "Fat mouths and feeble memories. He was only trying to frighten you, Isobel, *liefste*. Trust me, they'll forget the whole thing. It's all noise and hand waving with these people. They never finish what they begin."

"But I *want* to register," Isobel was exasperated. Talking to Nina was like throwing darts at a slate.

She turned to where Josef had been standing a moment ago, but he had disappeared. And he remained elusive for the next few days. Isobel found herself trapped in the apartment again by a series of 'emergencies' and 'unforeseeable circumstances', all explained by Nina with a hair raising winsomeness which bristled the back of Isobel's neck.

Helplessly, she awaited the outcome. None of Daddy's problem-solving angels, Isobel cynically assured herself, would ever bust their way in here.

Nor did they. Instead, less than forty eight hours later, two plain clothes arresting officers from the *Questura* arrived at the apartment to take Isobel away. Police. Fortunately for Estella, Nina was there although she was of little use either to the child, Isobel or the *Questura* men. All she could do was scream abuse of spectacular foulness in every language she knew except English. The men shouted in response, shaking their fists. Estella threw herself on the ground and yelled a steady, one note accompaniment. Isobel could not calm her. It was a desperate, gut churning scene.

Isobel remained stoical as she was helped, quite courteously, into the waiting Fiat below. Large, wet flakes of snow were falling and she had forgotten her duffel coat. What would happen now? Banishment? If that was what they had in store, Isobel devoutly hoped it would be free. She had no money for the fare home. Nina had paid for her plane ticket to Milan. After a year, it had been agreed, she would also pay for Isobel's ticket home. Not before.

In a quiet street, the official Fiat came to rest. Isobel was hustled inside an ochre washed building with bars on the street level windows. Finding herself in an enclosed square, open to the leaden sky and colonnaded on every side, Isobel considered that the *Questura* wore a grimly gladiatorial aspect. She was about to be thrown to the lions.

At least it was a lion she knew.

Looking up from the papers on his desk, Silvano Crivelli emitted an introductory roar . . . in Italian. Impatiently, he dismissed the escort and signed Isobel to be seated. He proceeded to subject her to a fusillade of reproaches and questions, at the meaning of which Isobel could only guess.

How many hours a week did she work in that place? What was she being paid? She was not fit to have a passport. Italy was a civilised country. Why should Isobel allow this stain upon its name?

More than half of it was in Italian. As before, Silvano ventilated his feelings vigorously and at length. Isobel broke down.

"I have been patient with you. Kind. And this is how you reward me . . ."

On and on.

"You have your passport?" Silvano demanded finally, in English.

Assuming it was about to be confiscated, Isobel extracted the document from her shoulderbag and handed it across the desk. Would there be some sort of trial?

"Sign here, Miss Jefferson."

"For my possessions?" Isobel supposed that she would have to don a prison uniform. Striped . . . or with arrows? One never knew in Italy. Thinking a doleful pleasantry better than none, she asked.

Silvano Crivelli's well thatched scalp shot back from his brow, stretching his eyes wide.

"Miss Jefferson . . . I thought you young . . . I thought you inexperienced. I did not," he tapped his own forehead in a hurtful gesture, "dream that you were crazy! This here is your permit." Crivelli paused to stamp the document with pounding downward force. "Do not lose it. You are now, at last, at vast cost to the Municipality of Milan, *registered*! Go, and let me see you no more."

Relieved, Isobel wiped her tear stained face with her fingers. Silvano handed her his handkerchief with a grimace of mock disgust.

Isobel took it and trumpeted fiercely into the square of dark silk. If one had to blow, she believed, one had better blow hard. Snivelling was despicable. Half-hearted. Being well brought up, she rolled the handkerchief into a discreet ball and putting it in her shoulderbag, assured Signor Crivelli that it would be returned to him when laundered.

"A souvenir of Milan, Signorina," Crivelli's tone hovered between gallantry and sarcasm. "I am allowed certain expenses."

The Municipality of Milan appeared to bear one further expense. Isobel was sent back to the Viale Majno in a taxi. Actually, the fare was paid out of Silvano Crivelli's private pocket. The crazy girl had no coat. And, if you could ignore her so-called clothes, as Silvano remarked deprecatingly to a fellow functionary, she was *molto bella*. In her barbarous, northern way. Those wide square jaws and definite chin . . . Some day she would grow into them. Truly, a warrior queen. If somewhat lachrymose.

Isobel re-entered the Fischer apartment in dread. But everything had returned to its usual, brittle normality. Nina spoke of domestic matters in a quiet, injured tone of voice which left Isobel feeling she had been in some way responsible for the unseemly events of the morning. Estella, she was told, had been afflicted with an attack

36

of breathlessness. Isobel could do nothing less than express her sorrow and, in so doing, appeared to accept the blame.

Nina celebrated her victory by saluting the fridge several times. Warily, Isobel laughed. The joke, whatever it was, was too subtle for her. She felt rather slow.

More days passed and still the freedom to enrol in a language class was denied. It was always tomorrow . . . When this event or that was over. Silvano Crivelli did not come again to the rescue. He was an overworked man with a thousand infringements of the labour laws to attend to.

From time to time, Isobel's eye would catch on the lobby telephone and the directories beside it. A lifeline? Perhaps if she could manage to contact Signor Crivelli . . . but she feared his contempt. And what could he do but send her home like a parcel? Cash on demand, presumably. An ignominious ending to the Italian venture that would be. She had been here less than a month. Too early yet to think of giving up. Too soon to risk writing home and asking for the money to leave Milan. All parsonage spending was condemned as frivolous until absolutely unavoidable. That didn't include Daddy's claret, of course.

Isobel's normally buoyant spirits grew heavy.

To keep them up in the evenings, when her domestic chores were over, she worked on a drawing with which she was, at first, modestly pleased. The American nuns in charcoal and chalks. She had thought it might work. The lines of the robes, so splendidly vertical, were simple enough to do . . . with the merry pink, shield shaped faces mounted in their identical white linen frames. Isobel couldn't get the half-remembered features quite right, but that wasn't really the point of the thing. What mattered was the grouping of black, white and soap-and-water pink around that table in the Galleria. A pair of rimless round spectacles on one face and a squiggly grin on another did the rest. And big, bold crosses on the flattened, virginal breasts.

As the drawing took shape, it began to recall the happiest afternoon Isobel had spent in Milan. She kept it pinned to a board, propped up on her easel which stood in her room. Cleaning, preparing vegetables, listening to Nina's incessant, contradictory monologues, Isobel fed on the drawing. It became the whole focus of her existence. She was glad to get back to it at the end of the day. Like going home to someone she loved.

Nina saw the drawing only once when Isobel brought it out to look at the flesh tint in the light of the kitchen. She gave it a cursory glance.

"Oh dear," she said. "Poor Isobel. You do need some lessons. I must do something about you some time."

37

Flinching from the words, Isobel knew that they lied. The drawing – *American Friends* she had titled it – was good. A fluke, of course . . . but good enough for her portfolio. Something worthwhile had come out of this fearful frustration.

More than that, in making this drawing, Isobel had felt for the first time that certainty every artist knows. The crackle of divine creative current that passes directly from the object pursued to the hand. A species of vision. Nina's insult was powerless to harm it.

A few days later, Nina got up earlier than usual and watched Isobel cajole cereal into Estella's mouth while she ate her own spartan breakfast. Isobel had never been able to eat much in the morning.

"What are you doing?" Nina looked up from her paper as Isobel inserted another slice of bread in the electric toaster.

"Making more toast . . . Do you want some?" Nina usually preferred the rich, sugary pastries which she bought for herself.

"Take it out," Nina snapped. "Put it back. You eat like a pig. Great, fat pig."

Her face flaming with anger and mortification, Isobel rose unsteadily from the table.

"Peeg, Peeg!" Estella chortled ecstatically.

Isobel fled from the room and stood in the lobby, lips compressed and arms squeezed tight around her own body, breathing hard. She knew she was big . . . tall. But *fat*? Were two slices of toast too much to ask . . . ?

Josef found Isobel staring at herself in the looking glass above the console table. Her attitude of catatonic distress went to his heart . . . which was a pity, he sighed to himself, as he had a great deal to do. But poor Miss Jefferson needed cheering up.

"I think," he said, pausing on his way out to the car, "that you don't have enough recreation. Why don't you," he asked, placing his hand shyly on her back, "go out some evenings? The Via Solferino. That's where the young people go . . . And your English Church is there . . . I will speak to my wife."

That was Josef's self-protective answer to everything. However, the following Sunday evening Isobel was sent off with directions and the numbers of trams. The pastor and his wife, Isobel remembered, were nominal acquaintances of her parents. She would not be quite a stranger.

Outside in the streets there was a cheerful, winter's eve bustle. A hint of Christmas already in the air and a bitter wind blowing off the Alps. Lights, glossy displays in the shops, handsome couples sauntering arm in arm . . . or uncoiling from the interiors of sleek, beautiful cars. Bursts of laughter as restaurant doors swung open and closed. Fleeting, spicy aromas.

Isobel passed like a ghost through this world, powerless to join it. A prisoner in transit, aboard a clattering, whistling tram.

She quite enjoyed the service in the little yellow church. It was Evensong. Predictable, elegiac and intimate.

Dear Lord and Father of mankind, Forgive our foolish ways ... The hymn always brought a lump to her throat. Afterwards, it said on the printed service sheet, there was to be a 'social' in the chaplain's house nearby. This took place every Sunday so that English au pairs could meet each other. There seemed to be a lot of them here.

Isobel went. She introduced herself with a diffident smile as Charles and Margaret Jefferson's daughter to the chaplain's dumpy wife. She looked approachable ... motherly, almost, in a powder blue twinset and pearls. But Mrs Smallwood, like Martha, was troubled by many things, a paucity of paper napkins in particular. She effected tepid introductions to Lucy, Miranda and Joan. They were all doing so well with their Italian. Talking like natives. Looking a little like them too, Isobel noted as she toyed with something non-alcoholic. Very smart in their neat tailored dresses which exactly bisected the knee. Milan had rejected the mini-skirt. Then came the conker smooth leather boots. The girls sized each other up cautiously, as English girls do, at home and abroad.

The Reverend Smallwood came over and haw-hawed hospitably about holidays recently taken by some of the girls. Joan was just back from Bologna. A nice, cool time to go. It was good to see Isobel in church at last. They *had* been expecting her. Charles Jefferson had dropped the Smallwoods a line, over three weeks ago now. 'Not got his bishopric yet?' Ah well, the 'Bells and Smells' persuasion weren't in favour just now.

The vicarage bunfight banter was somehow strained. Isobel munched a cube of cheese from a cocktail stick that had been stuck in a cabbage. She felt ill at ease. A thousand questions occurred to her mind. 'Help', was the word that teetered on the tip of her tongue. But the expatriate glances were coldly appraising. Isobel felt aware of her low heeled, rough brown shoes. They weren't lace-ups, at least. But nor were they boots.

"How long have you been here? I haven't seen you before. Which class did you say that you go to?" the girl called Miranda piped through her pouting, pearlised lips.

It was the opening Isobel needed. She began to ask the other girls about their pay and conditions. Hers, she said, were not terribly good ...

"Now, now," Mrs Smallwood, passing with a tray of sausage rolls, reproved sharply. "None of that. We have to remember that we're guests in this country."

Isobel went away and never came back.

There was one further humiliation. Nina had a dinner party. She demanded to view the whole of Isobel's sparse wardrobe on the previous afternoon. Very foolishly, Isobel believed she was to be of the party. She always did eat with the Fischers, although, apart from Josef's occasional asides, Isobel was allotted little share of the conversation these days. She ate very sparingly now, hating to be thought greedy or fat. That accusation had drawn blood.

"Well, I suppose this isn't too bad," Nina looked at a green tweed skirt with distaste. "What have you got to wear with it?"

There was a Viyella blouse in roughly the same colour. It would do. Nina gave Isobel's drawing a passing glance as she left her room.

"Nuns. That's what *you* would think of. Fascist. Millions of my people died because of people like you . . ."

Isobel was shattered. What people? What did Nina mean?

Nina waggled her gem laden fingers irritably, glancing away.

"Oh *Isobel*! Why do you take everything I say so seriously? I tease and you whine . . . We're Jewish. Didn't you know? What a silly little fool you are."

Jewish? Isobel had known nothing of the sort. What difference did it make? She couldn't connect herself with the genocidal mania, arrested three years before her birth. And how could anyone speak of *teasing* in the same breath as all that . . . ? Once again, all the links were missing.

The rest of the day passed in jangling silences. Mistrusting her own every step and word, Isobel begged off supper and went early to her bed. So far, that had proved an unconfusing refuge.

*   *   *

At the dinner party the following evening, Isobel was made to act the part of parlourmaid or waitress. Expressing her revulsion at this duty, she proposed a compromise. She would stand by in the kitchen and do all the washing-up as each course was removed. Then she would go quietly to bed.

"Waitressing isn't what my parents brought me up to do," she added with spirit. "I know nothing about it."

"You're here to work," Nina countered in a monotone, as if she had not heard. "Not skulk in your room." With her face averted, she produced a muslin, bibbed apron from a drawer in the kitchen. "When you have served our guests, you wash up and tidy the *sala da pranzo*. Then you may go to bed. Here, starch this and iron it," she finished, throwing the apron at Isobel. Seething, Isobel obeyed. She hated the apron and its absurd great bow at the back. An overt badge of enslavement.

She took her revenge without counting the cost, playing her publicly subservient role with comic, consummate skill. Serving to the left, removing from the right. Bending and swaying. Height can lend deference a satirical flavour if you know how to do it. And Isobel did.

"If you require me further, madam," Isobel spun around to close the double doors of the room, "just rub the lamp. Or perhaps your guests would care to see me perform selected solo sequences from *Les Sylphides*?"

Between them, Isobel figured, Nina, Josef and their guests knew enough English for that.

Josef retired to his study as soon as the guests were seen to their cars. Recriminations between Nina and Isobel would be bad for his nerves. Perhaps Nina expected too much. The girl was only seventeen and untrained.

There were no immediate repercussions. And no bare-fist confrontation with Nina. Estella was her mother's chosen weapon of retaliation. Isobel could not have foreseen it.

Whilst she was in the bathroom the next day after breakfast, the child trotted into Isobel's room and tore her drawing of the nuns from the board. In the nursery she scored it over with wax crayons. An intricate, indelible, multi-coloured scribble. Mama had said that Isobel's picture was too dull and dark. It needed some red, some purple, orange, green and yellow. It would be nice, wouldn't it, if Estella could help?

When Isobel discovered the fate of her work, she knew at once that Estella was innocent. She had to think that. Or she might hit the child. If she started she would not be able to stop. Already her right palm itched with death dealing rage.

"Good, now." Estella held up the ruined portrait group with its torn corners and grotesque decoration. The child put her head on one side consideringly. "Why not your Mama buy *you* crayons?"

Isobel sat down on Estella's bed, very dangerously quiet. A hatred for Nina, Estella and even Josef breached the flood defences in her mind, leaking its poison so that it showed in her face.

Estella ran screaming to her mother. Isobel locked herself in her room and grieved for the only thing she had loved in that place. A dull, flat, heavy feeling that weighed her down bodily. The unforgivable sin of despair. Going to hell would make no difference to anything. She had been there for weeks.

Isobel lay on her side, in the dark, staring at the thin line of daylight under her door.

Nina made no comment on Isobel's strike action and finished dressing Estella herself. When they left for the nursery school, Isobel emerged from her room. She used the Fischers' telephone to ring her home in Devon. Reversed charges. It was easier to get through than she thought.

"Oh, dear," Margaret Jefferson's voice sounded flat and remote. "It's fearfully expensive . . . reversing the charges. I thought you must have had an accident . . . Couldn't you have written? Are you sure you've really given things a chance? I don't know that you'd be much better off at home at the moment. Dismal weather . . . Daddy's rheumatism is really quite bad . . ."

"My drawing, Mummy. It was deliberate . . . The best thing I've done."

A thousand miles away, Margaret sighed and discounted the affair of the drawing. Isobel had no talent. All her school reports had said so. It was kinder not to encourage the poor child's delusion. But using her daughter as a uniformed maid . . . That was an outrage. It was difficult to know just what to do. Expenses had exceeded income of late.

"I've just had to pay Simon's last flying school fees . . ."

"*Mummy* . . ." Inside, Isobel felt a sullen viper of suspicion uncurl. Her mother was washing her hands . . . Would this have happened if it had been Simon or Rupert?

"I suppose I could sell Granny's little ruby brooch," Mrs Jefferson said faintly. "You know, the one which should have come to you . . ."

"Then I'll hitchhike," Isobel spurned her mother's too hesitant offer. It was all very well for the boys to come first but didn't they love her at *all*? Poor Mummy, she adjusted her thought automatically, she practically worshipped that brooch. It was the last thing of Granny's she had left. "Lots of other girls do it . . ."

"Oh no, please don't do that, darling," Margaret Jefferson was alarmed. "You mustn't hitchhike. It's too dangerous. Promise me, please. Your father would never forgive me. Give me a day or two . . . There's someone I know . . . used to know."

Hearing Nina's high heeled step approaching outside, Isobel gave her promise hurriedly. There was no time for further negotiations. Two days was a life sentence. But if there was no rescue by then, Isobel vowed, she would walk over the Alps in her duffel coat and those *bloody* brown shoes.

The next day was Sunday again.

In the middle of lunch a woman called the Contessa Lucia di Larizzi telephoned. She wanted to speak to Isobel. Handing her the telephone, Nina maliciously enquired, under her breath, how she could possibly know a fashionable Roman socialite . . . a woman who got her name in American *Vogue*.

Isobel didn't, but she took the telephone receiver from Nina's hand and listened in silence.

"Are you there?" Whatever the name, the voice sounded perfectly English. Bubbling, bright and confident. "Is that Miss Isobel Jefferson? Just say 'yes', if it is."

Isobel did so.

"I was at school with your mother."

There was a pause, while Isobel froze, unable to answer. So Mummy had not let her down. Nina was hovering close.

"Where you are now . . . Could you just pack your bags and leave?"

"No, I don't think so," Isobel replied.

"Are you going to church tonight?" The whole conversation sounded as if it was in some sort of code.

"No. I wasn't."

"When would you leave if you were?" asked the voice.

Isobel told her.

"Do it then. A man called Alessandro Montenaro will be waiting outside your apartment main entrance in a dark blue Mercedes. Go with him. Courage, my dear, everything will be all right."

And with that scant information, the lady rang off.

Isobel announced her wish to go to church, regretting now that she had not established the practice instead of allowing it to go by default.

"You should have told us before," Nina said. "I'm afraid it's out of the question this evening. We've arranged to go out."

Josef was immured with his interminable papers during this exchange and all afternoon Isobel wondered what she should do. Her chance came when Nina, after spending hours playing Frank Sinatra records in the *salotto* with the doors closed, stated her intention of retiring to rest. Estella was enacting some complicated drama with her dolls in the nursery. Soon she would have to be fed.

Alone for a moment in the kitchen, Isobel saw Nina's handbag open on the kitchen table and in it the keys to the lobby doors. They were always double locked. Fetching her coat and shoulder-bag with her passport in it, Isobel purloined the keys and left.

She tried the lift first but it wouldn't come. A light indicated it was stuck in the garage below. Someone with luggage. Painfully slow. Starting for the staircase, Isobel heard the door of the Fischers' apartment open and voices. Estella had raised the alarm. Her mouth dry, Isobel removed her shoes and ran silently upstairs instead of down. There was still some time to go.

She hid among the buckets and mops of the *portinaio*'s third-floor broom cupboard until the hour of the rendezvous came nearer.

Nina's hysterical voice ricocheted all over the building. She banged frantically on neighbouring apartment doors . . . asked the tenants questions. Secrecy, it seemed, was now at an end. But no, none of the politely murmuring neighbours had seen or heard anything of Signora Fischer's maid. They were not even aware that she had one.

She ran up and down the little used staircase, with what Isobel judged to be Josef's step following reluctantly behind her. He pleaded with her to go back to the apartment. To lower her voice. Estella was upset . . . There was nothing they could do but wait . . . Perhaps, in a while, the police might be contacted . . . Poor Miss Jefferson was obviously in some kind of trouble. She would never have stolen the keys otherwise . . .

Isobel heard that part of the conversation all too clearly. They were standing just outside the broom cupboard. Both at once, Isobel felt an overwhelming urge to micturate and to sneeze. If she didn't do one, she feared, she was sure to do the other. Sneeze and she would be discovered. If she peed . . . well, you couldn't meet anyone in wet knickers. And how was it that Nina Fischer had the power to frighten Isobel Jefferson into a *cupboard*?

Doubled over with one hand between her legs, heart thudding and the unreleased sneeze sparkling in her head, Isobel gave in to primitive instinct and stayed where she was. When at last the Fischers moved away, Isobel sidled shamefaced from the broom cupboard and half crept, half stumbled down the stairs into the street. It was five minutes past the agreed time. Supposing he hadn't come . . . or hadn't waited?

Spotting the dark blue Mercedes, Isobel gave a joyous whoop of deliverance. The window on the passenger side of the car was rolled down and a man with a creased, clever monkey face peered at her enquiringly.

"Miss Isobel Jefferson? Do please get in if you are . . ."

"Oh, you don't know how grateful I am . . ."

Something made Isobel glance behind her and upwards before she said any more. At a second floor window, Estella's little face appeared aged and desolate. A look that clawed at the heart. For the first time, she looked like her mother. For an unreasoning split second, Isobel felt she ought to go back. She had no right to escape when others were trapped.

"*Andiamo*," Alessandro's cheerful voice drew her attention back to where it should be. "Let's go. My wife's waiting to interview you for a position with us."

The rescue, after all, was conditional.

THREE

To say that the power of forecasting her immediate future had now reduced to a matter of little more than an hour, Isobel's exterior fortitude was impressive. She had counted up her money in that cupboard and there was nothing like enough of it. Not if she should fail to get this job.

The journey to the Montenaro residence in the Viale Regina Giovanna was short and jet propelled.

"Pah!" Alessandro said wrenching the wheel over violently as he turned in to the underground garage, "Milan is full of very bad drivers." The Mercedes came to rest beside a battle scarred Lancia. "That is my wife's car," Alessandro announced. "I refuse to have it repaired. She will never drive fast enough to keep out of trouble."

Isobel saw nothing to laugh at in that. A sensible point, if ever she'd heard one.

The lift took them to the first floor and decanted them directly into the Montenaros' cavernous lobby. It glimmered with Venetian glass mirrors reflecting murky paintings of corpulent saints posed in attitudes of sacred suffering, gracefully draped.

"The contents," Alessandro explained with palpable irritation, "of the third attic of the second *castello* of my wife's parents. The roof fell in. I am an architect, but they failed to consult me."

"*Papa! Papa!*" A pair of small boys hurtled from behind a door and launched themselves on their father who allowed himself to be wrestled swiftly to the ground. Giacomo and Marzio. The boys' recumbent parent introduced them from within a confusing tangle of limbs. "They are ignorant children," he gasped. "They speak only Italian. *Rosaria!*"

A maid attired in deep violet with lace encrusted cap and apron appeared from without the gloom. Her matte black eyes were bracketed with brows that met over her nose and there was a straggle of dark hair on her long upper lip.

"*Signor?*"

"Take this young lady's coat and show her in to your mistress," Alessandro instructed above the squeals of his offspring. "We will

45

meet later, no doubt," he added, managing some kind of bow from the floor.

Like her sons, the *Principessa* Giulia Montenaro spoke no English. She was confident, however, that intuition would suffice to carry her and Isobel through this interview. What need of words when the heart overflowed?

"Ah," she wrung her hands in an ecstasy of sympathy for the plight of this interesting waif. "Ah," she moaned again invitingly. "What unimaginable torment . . . and how exciting an occurrence. Just like a book . . ."

Giulia had no idea just how exciting Isobel's flight had been.

She went on to recount what little she knew of Isobel's career since the first day of November. No one, she averred, should be unhappy for so long in Italy. It was an insupportable affront to her patriotic feelings.

Isobel understood not a word. "*Mi piace, Signora,*" she stated firmly. "*Buona sera.*"

And once she had delivered the single courteous line of Italian she had painstakingly rehearsed in her head, Isobel felt she had done her utmost towards averting disaster. For the rest, it was purely a matter of standing properly braced at the wicket, as taught by her brothers, to confront whatever balls were bowled at her.

From the first, Giulia found Isobel's deportment almost excessively gallant . . . the child's chin was held so touchingly high. It was not the ideal beginning when Giulia had everything ready for a comfortable cry.

Drawing her guest kindly into the room, the *Principessa* asked herself, were these really clothes? And if so, in whose opinion? It was enough to melt all the snow on the Alps. How pathetically, elegantly thin the child was . . . Such an astounding physique, the profile so patrician, and those eyes like aquamarines . . . Lucia Larizzi's report had lacked colour. But then she was English by birth and had a faulty appreciation of pathos.

"Never mind," she said aloud. All that was now in the past. Here was a happy ending to everything. It remained only to salute the departure of affliction with an appropriate drenching of tears. Isobel must not hold back. It was not good for the health.

Giulia knew nothing of cricket or stiff upper lips.

While she gave vehement expression to her random thoughts, Isobel regarded Giulia steadily, anxious to act on any cue that might be given her. Verbal communication was clearly out of the question. How was she to recommend herself for this job, whatever it entailed? On the way here, Signor Montenaro had been too taken up with the demands of motorised conflict to say what it was.

If she got the job, Isobel decided, she would sleep at the youth hostel ... if there was one and she could find its address. The problem of her luggage and starting date could be addressed tomorrow. If, on the other hand, she should fall short of the Signora's requirements, she had best, in the interests of economy, sleep in the Centrale Station. No. Perhaps some unlocked church would be better. Safer and warmer. Her journey home could start the next day. It looked as though her easel was lost for ever. She would probably never need it again.

"Come. Come over here," Giulia carried on in Italian, shepherding Isobel to a needlepoint sofa. "Sit by me. Now you must drink this all up. It is very medicinal," she said, pressing a goblet of pink fluid on Isobel. "Good for the liver," she insisted, indicating the location of that organ as being somewhere under the navel.

Having no power of speech to reject it, Isobel sipped cautiously at the curious tasting wine. Very herby. Giulia talked and Isobel looked.

In her hostess she saw a woman whose face was piquant rather than beautiful, lit by great liquid brown eyes. Her hair, as a cap formed from feathers, clung close to her skull. The latest style in Milan. Her dress was of blinding white gaberdine, cut like an inverted regal lily from which silken legs descended like stamens into glacé kid slippers. Around her throat and wrists she wore South Sea pearls bigger than wrens' eggs. Isobel could not know they were real. A sartorial witticism she supposed. Odd, because in Mrs Jefferson's canon, costume jewellery belonged in the realms of bad taste. But good taste was boring and Isobel found Giulia's golf balls endearing.

"You will stay with us, won't you my dear? You must never go back to that place ..."

Isobel tried to look intelligent while she thought about bare earth survival. How fragile the membrane between herself and destitution had been. She was a canary let from a cage into the forest ...

"We need someone to speak good English to our sons. That is all you will do here, if you agree. I implore you, do not disappoint us ..."

Isobel nodded in vague acknowledgement of Giulia's pressure on her hand.

"It is all agreed then? I am so happy. You would care for an olive?"

Isobel shook her head, thinking that to eat would be unforgivably insouciant when this lady's eyes were gushing from some mysterious source of grief. It was a shame, though. Olives were sustaining and food was expensive. One simply didn't know ... What had possessed her to take up vagrancy in December? Too late, Isobel's fingers hovered.

Giulia whisked the dish away approvingly. Lack of appetite at a time like this was *simpatica*.

"Alessandro!" Giulia greeted the appearance of her husband's simian features at the edge of the door. "We have arranged everything to our complete satisfaction. Miss Jefferson . . . dear Isobel has consented to bestow herself on us for the benefit of our sons. We shall be so much in her debt."

Alessandro pulled Isobel's pigtail gently in passing, lit a cigar and threw a log on to the strangely makeshift grate with its copper flue rising through the towering height of the ceiling. The weather outside was bitterly cold.

"I see," he remarked easily, seating himself, "that you and my wife have reached a good understanding. Dolour is agreeable to her. Will twenty thousand lire per week be adequate recompense for your nice English vowels . . . and all you can eat? You will stay with us tonight, of course, and later I shall deal with the Fischers . . ."

It was not until then that Isobel realised her reprieve. Alessandro said she must have been deranged to think they would have turned even a wall-eyed stray dog from their door. Much less her. Had she wished to go home, she would have been sent there on the very next plane. That was all. It was his fault, he supposed, for having spoken cryptically in the first place. Isobel, on the other hand, he chided, was painfully literal.

There would be no youth hostel, after all, and no Centrale Station. There would, however, be Asti Spumante to seal this most delightful of contracts. Good heavens, ten pounds every week! It was all nearly too much. Isobel had to work very hard to control the awful, humiliating wobble of her chin.

Giulia engulfed her in a prolonged embrace whilst Alessandro ate all the olives from the dish.

"Ah, Isobel *carissima*, you must learn how to weep. You would get so much pleasure from it," Giulia assured her in Italian. "The best medical opinion recommends it."

At Rosaria's entrance into the room with more glasses on a silver salver, she shot Isobel a look of envious loathing. So this shabby giantess with the proud, pale eyes was to be the *Principessa*'s favourite. One of those foreign maids who, as Serafina the cook had summarised matters, accepted low wages to take the bread from honest Italian mouths and gave themselves airs. *Merda*.

"Tell the cook to throw the pasta in the pot," Giulia ordered her sharply. The Signorina, who was to join the household forthwith, was hungry. So were they all. And whilst the pasta cooked, the second guest room was to be prepared for Isobel's occupation. The Swiss embroidered sheets and plenty of towels for her bath. The flowers were to be taken from the small *salotto* as fresh ones could not now be had.

This was a new, imperious side to the *Principessa*'s character, Isobel noted, though she heard only the tone.

"Aha!" Alessandro chirped. "No more water now. First we eat, then I fetch your things from Majno."

In the Montenaro dining room, gorgeous with gilt and the light of multi-coloured chandeliers, Isobel was packed full of sausage, *fusilli*, loin of pork with prunes, salad and cheesecake. Sending Rosaria away, Alessandro served the food himself, exotically vested in a flowered pinafore over his pin-striped suit. Isobel could not eat everything he set before her, but to please him she tried.

"Oh what have we done?" Giulia wailed, torn between nurturing instincts and care for Isobel's figure.

"She cannot get too fat for me," Alessandro maintained in Italian. "Have you seen her poor little wrists?" To Isobel's astonishment, he seized one of these and kissed it. The Montenaros were like that. They did nothing by halves. Lame ducks were their speciality and Isobel was, in their eyes, a cygnet, whose ragged plumage promised wonders.

Plenty more was said then, which was not translated to Isobel. It was as well.

"I cannot comprehend the heartless folly," Alessandro griped, "of people who would send a child of seventeen across two national borders to live with complete strangers, without having the means to get her back. Without even," he brandished the carving knife ferociously in Isobel's direction, "a letter of introduction to the British Consul. Is this the secret of their national success? Toss out the children and see whether or not they come back?"

"Have I done something wrong?" Isobel asked innocently.

"No, but you have been wronged," Alessandro snapped. Isobel reapplied herself to her plate contentedly, assuming it was the Fischers who had invoked Signor Montenaro's wrath. They were horrible people and Isobel wished them most heartily to hell. She didn't know whether Jewish people believed in it or not but the Fischers were in for a nasty surprise. Christian faith, she observed smugly, had its genuine comforts.

She was put to bed early, as if truly a child, by Giulia herself. All her needs were supplied from the *Principessa*'s abundance. Rosaria scurried resentfully, fetching nightgowns and robes. No, this one did not suit the Signorina. Too tight under the armhole and the colour was unbecoming. Did Isobel prefer a bristle toothbrush or a nylon one? Giulia unplaited her hair and brushed it with a hundred strokes like her mother once used to do. At the end of this *accouchement* Isobel found herself soundly kissed on the mouth like a seven-year-old and advised to have sweet dreams.

It was not as simple as that. The end of a sadistic relationship bears some resemblance to a shattered love affair. The victim sorts through the ashes, searching for reasons, some material for self-repair.

Isobel thought of Nina in her sterile magnificence on the Viale Majno. There had been a demon of absence there. It was a place where one thing had not led to another. Every incident had been an inexplicable, self-contained horror. Angrily, Isobel raked over the details.

*   *   *

At approximately that same moment, around half past ten, Alessandro presented himself at the entrance to the Fischer apartment, having confirmed with the *portineria* that the couple were at home. He rang the bell and waited. After some moments, he rang again, keeping the button depressed with his thumb.

A sliding, clicking and clanking preceded the appearance of Josef, haggardly peering through a crack in the double doors. Sensing that they were about to be closed in his face, Alessandro robustly inserted his toe.

"*Buona sera.* Do I address Signor Fischer? Possibly you expected Miss Isobel Jefferson. I am here on her behalf. My card."

Alessandro handed over a stiff piece of pasteboard engraved with his name and that of his firm. Josef's eyes widened. Alessandro Montenaro was a well known industrial architect. He had projects all over northern Italy, even in France . . . as far afield, in fact, as Holland. A worthwhile contact for Stylo Fischer. Now, thanks to the Jefferson business, that opportunity was lost. Josef computed the implications with the automated section of his brain, reluctantly opening the door wider. He was in his shirtsleeves, rumpled and tieless.

"I'm afraid I cannot invite you in," Josef ran his hand nervously over his wire-wool hair.

A gust of tarry disinfectant assailed Alessandro's nostrils, twitching his nerves. The place stank like a well managed abattoir.

"My wife is unwell . . . Miss Jefferson, you say . . . Do you know where she is?"

"Certainly. She is at my home in the care of my wife. Here is her passport," Alessandro displayed it to the unhappy man before him and then flipped the pages to show the residence permit. "I should be obliged if you would gather her belongings together. I wish to take them away."

Josef stared in confusion at the page held under his nose, making no immediate response. Au pair? In the background a woman's voice sang a few notes and then stopped abruptly. Josef started, hesitating with his hand on the door handle and glancing over his shoulder.

"Tomorrow," he blurted, looking back at Alessandro. "Tomorrow my wife will ... You understand, nothing of hers is packed ..."

"No, now, if you please. I will pack the things myself ..."

"No! Wait, please."

Josef started to shut the door but thought better of it. "If you could take a seat," he indicated a chair in the lobby, "I shall not be a moment."

Alessandro declined the chair but stood just inside the doors, hating the antiseptic stench. There were sounds of muffled conversation some distance away and the sound of a door slamming. A small white figure appeared fleetingly in an ill lit corridor, stared at him and fled.

Josef Fischer came back laden with Isobel's luggage and easel, his face harrowed with lines of anxiety.

"I'm afraid she won't find everything there. You understand, some of Miss Jefferson's clothing is at the laundry. My wife took some things to the cleaners today ..."

Alessandro raised no objection. The place gave him goose flesh and he wanted to leave at once. Refusing Josef's offer to ring for the *portinaio*, he tucked Isobel's holdall under one arm and carried the easel and suitcase, one in each hand.

"Oh, and there's this," Josef Fischer thrust a dog eared, folded square of cartridge paper at him. "It looks quite good. She might want it. I'm afraid my little daughter ..."

Alessandro didn't wait to hear any more but beat a hasty retreat. The woman had started singing again. The sound harried him down the stairs till the rasp of bolts cut it off.

In the car, Alessandro found himself breathing hard. He unfolded the paper Josef had given him. *American Friends*. The impact of the drawing, despite the childish scribbles, was disturbing. A record of durable innocence shone up from the paper. Unsure what to do with it, Alessandro later locked it up in his desk, a nugget of sunshine rescued from Hades. He felt certain that Isobel would wish to see it again, but perhaps not immediately.

Giulia examined the clothing before she retired to bed. What

51

little there was, had been crammed pell-mell into the suitcase and bore signs of an earlier, frenzied attack. At least, that's what it looked like. These few garments, reeking of carbolic and a sickly, gardenia scent, were no doubt the miserable survivors. Giulia personally threw them down the apartment's rubbish chute. A good excuse. Something plausible to tell Isobel could be worked out in the morning. Administrative difficulties, real or invented, were not scarce in Milan.

When morning came, Isobel had breakfast in bed, flanked by Giacomo and Marzio. It was a sticky, affectionate, wriggling affair.

Leaning back against her pillows, her hair jammily replaited by the twins, Isobel wondered what she had accepted here. A job . . . or a life.

* * *

"I'm glad you're more comfortable now . . ." Margaret Jefferson's long distance telephone voice was distrait. "I'm up to my eyes here, darling. Christmas is getting so near . . . Where on earth are you? It sounds like a bar."

It was, as Isobel confirmed. One of those that had a call box for public use on the way back from Giacomo and Marzio's school. Today was the last day of term. They were playing dual roles in the school's nativity play. Cherubim in the first scene and asses in the last. The Montenaro household were all going to see them perform in the afternoon. Alessandro was in a fever of joyous paternal excitement . . . racing back from his architectural practice's branch office in Turin on the lunchtime plane.

The bustle of early morning customers who stood to drink coffee and munch pastries on the way to work, drowned most of what Isobel said.

"How nice for you, darling," Mrs Jefferson replied, as she usually did when any tidings of Isobel's escaped her. "I daresay you'll be able to make yourself useful. I must tell you our news . . ."

Isobel strained to hear it above the '*buon giornos*', the roar of the espresso machine and the grumble of trams.

Something was said about Simon's new job with a small commercial airline in Greece. It was to start in the New Year. Rupert was coming home for Christmas in triumph. His little film was finished. Not a penny over budget, it was going out on restricted release and was entered for some obscure section of the festival at Cannes. Wasn't that wonderful? Fabulous, Isobel agreed sincerely. She had no comparable achievements with which to compete. But then, they were all used to that.

"So we're going to have a lovely family Christmas again, all together . . . except for you, darling," Margaret Jefferson corrected herself just in time. "What adventures you have. I must send a card to the Smallwoods as well as Lucy . . . I expect they've all been terribly kind."

Isobel murmured something vaguely affirmative. She had said nothing against the English chaplain and his wife. There was no need to admit either, in response to her mother's routine enquiries, that she would never again attend services in the Via Solferino. Wherever the Montenaros went, if at all, there also would she go. Mummy would not understand. The Anglican Church was her life.

"How's Daddy?" she changed the subject quickly.

"Well, we really don't know . . . They think it may be arthritis now. He's having some more tests some time soon. For the moment they're trying gold injections in the joints . . ."

Isobel winced. It sounded horrific. And this was the first she'd heard about *tests*.

"Shall I come home? I could . . . Giulia said . . ."

"Oh, no darling, no. There's nothing to worry about really . . . Not that it wouldn't be marvellous to see you, of course. But the Montenaros must want you to help with the twins. You can't let them down after all the trouble Lucy Larizzi went to on your account."

Isobel decoded the message with pain. Her mother wanted her menfolk all to herself. Her relationship with them was different from the one that she had with herself. On its quality, Isobel hardly dared dwell. Somehow she had disappointed her mother. She had grown up too tall and outspoken to fit into that adoring, subordinate role which was reserved for sisters who would one day become wives of men like their brothers.

And of course, she had been a nuisance. Margaret Jefferson disliked arrangements that went wrong. She was in all things a perfectionist, rejecting anything that shivered the mirror-calm village pond of her life. One always paid for that at the Parsonage. Justice did not enter into it.

Leaving the telephone booth, Isobel paid at the cash till. A space widened around her as the milling office workers stood back to observe her in focus. Conscious of their stares, Isobel put it down to the effect of Giulia's spare sable coat and reserved her attention for the cashier. The *Principessa*'s loans and hand-me-downs were apt to give a false impression. People dressed as Isobel was did not generally appear on Milan's sober streets before noon . . . as Isobel was becoming aware. She counted out the notes and received a foil wrapped sweet as change. No small coinage again.

So that's that, Isobel thought, walking back through the narrow, urban alleys to the rear of the Montenaro apartment building, the scent of a Milanese fog in her nose. She was not wanted at home for Christmas. Or at any rate, not much. What were they afraid of, Isobel wondered bitterly. The cost of the airfare? Giulia had offered to pay. It was a good thing that hadn't been mentioned. It left a shifty, face-saving area of doubt. One could pretend.

Isobel decided to tell Giulia that it was her own decision to remain in Milan over Christmas. To say anything else held out only the wounding prospect of Giulia's indignation at her mother's seeming indifference. They must all be protected from that. And Giulia would be possessively delighted to think she and her family were preferred by Isobel to her own flesh and blood. It was a delicate balancing act between those who should want her and didn't – and those who need not, but did.

Before any lump in her throat could thicken, Isobel told herself she was lucky. After all, when you had nothing to lose, you could stake everything you had, heart and soul, on the future. Everyone had to grow up some time. It was just rather sudden . . . but very exhilarating. One had to look on the bright side.

Banishing seasonal nostalgia for her childhood home, Isobel turned into the tiny premises of the ironing woman to collect Alessandro's shirts. Rosaria had called out to her not to forget them when she set out with the boys. An odour of warm linen and brown paper greeted her as she pushed open the door. Nobody, it had turned out, ironed at home in Milan. How would the poor ironing women earn their bread? Giulia was able to calculate to a horrified nicety just how much Isobel had saved Nina Fischer on this domestic outgoing alone. Enough to pay three au pairs.

There was no parcel of shirts waiting for Signor Montenaro. Isobel was perplexed. The woman explained in quick fire Italian that the *Principessa* had already sent Rosaria to fetch them. It was not suitable for the Signorina to carry mundane packages in the street. Ladies of family did not do that. "*Bruta figura*," the wizened proprietress finished knowingly, sucking her teeth.

Completely mystified, Isobel went home to say that either Alessandro's shirts were not ready or they were lost. Her Italian had not stood up to the ironing shop test.

Rosaria sneered. Serafina flexed her muscular forearm, stirred a pot, and gnomically informed the Neapolitan girl that fortune was fortune. It was ill luck to curse the object whereon it had smiled. Rosaria had better watch out. And then, by way of precaution, Serafina made a hideous spitting noise to deflect the evil eye, that being the most that hygiene allowed.

Isobel derived nothing from this exchange but the cook's amiable thump on the back and a freshly candied chestnut to eat. She need not, Serafina contrived to convey, worry her head about Signor Montenaro's shirts. That was for others, she jerked her head in Rosaria's direction.

Then there was a tortured explanation of Giulia's absence from the apartment. She had gone to chair an emergency committee meeting of the orphanage to which she and Alessandro devoted much of their time and funds. From there she was proceeding straight to Elizabeth Arden's salon on the Via Montenapoleone to have her hair done. Isobel was to take a green taxi and join her there at ten. They must both cut a *bella figura* at the nativity play for the sake of the boys. Six-year-old *machismo* called for tender concern. Surely, Serafina urged, that much was clear?

Isobel's hair was shampooed, dried, burnished with silk, cut and curled to frame her ear lobes. The salon's director was in ecstasy. Isobel, whose hair had always been trimmed by her mother before, was in a state of shock. All this pink satin and fuss. The sight of her severed blonde pigtail where it lay, a dismembered limb on the pink marble tiles, made her feel faintly sick. But she did like the look of the arresting stranger who gazed back at her from a kaleidoscope of apricot tinted mirrors. Hardly *belissima*, as they would keep on saying, but certainly much improved. Line, mass and shadow, in Isobel's own opinion, were now seen in better alignment.

"Thank you," she said gravely to the mustachioed stylist, "for giving me my grown-up face."

The speech, made in English, was translated for its picturesque character all over the salon. Isobel found herself surrounded by well-wishers, some of them clients in capes, still in various alarming stages of process. What a striking thing to have said. Who *was* Isobel? The daughter, Giulia let it be known, of a friend of a friend. Acceptable credentials, muttered one blue rinsed dowager to another, as she returned to her place under the dryer.

It was thus that Giulia, with her economical touch, presented her protégé to the otherwise impenetrable world of fashionable Milan. A word from her was enough.

"Do not," she said distinctly, threading Isobel's arm through her own as they stepped into the street, "look where you are going. The nose is worn in the air. It is for others to mark your path. The right of way in this city belongs to those who perceive no obstruction."

Enchanted that she had understood every clear, well separated word, Isobel obeyed. The tops of other people's heads made quite an interesting subject for study.

A gust of gardenia announced Nina's proximity as she emerged from an adjacent shop. Giulia did not know her and Isobel did not see her, experimenting as she was with this new, semi-blind mode of progression.

There was only a qualm in the pit of her stomach, whose source she was unable to trace.

* * *

Giulia, who had given birth to a stillborn daughter some years previously and could have no more children, was prepared to allow Margaret Jefferson what was due to her physical maternity. She took unto herself a yet more powerful motherhood; that of speech. From her, Isobel learned quickly and well.

The classes she attended at first were soon abandoned. Italian, thought by so many to be an easy language because of its imitable rhythms and memorable vocabulary, is not. Laid down in black and white, its classical grammar is daunting.

"It's of no importance," Giulia excused Isobel the classes. "You will learn only bad habits and ugly modernisms. Here we can give you Italian which is a better exchange for the English you are giving my sons. You will learn by ear and by touch."

Any fear of reprisals from Signor Crivelli were scotched with a single phone call from Giulia. A middle ranking civil servant who stood to receive Giulia's call was advised of a change in Isobel's status. She was *not* an au pair in the strict sense but a house-guest. Paid? Of course she was not. What a revolting idea. She received occasional gifts of love from her friends, as was natural. Pah!

None the less, generous sums concealed in an envelope were laid without comment on Isobel's dressing table each week. The amount always exceeded Alessandro's notional remuneration by quite a margin, augmented from the *Principessa*'s own dress allowance. Isobel's embarrassed protests were instantly silenced.

"A girl," Giulia said, "must go shopping. *No?*" Particularly when she had such a figure to dress. To neglect its adornment, she stressed devoutly, would be a cynical rejection of divine favour.

'God's gift', as Isobel took to mentally dubbing her person, was paraded in and out of shops all over the Via Montenapoleone, Via delle Spiga, Borfospresso, Santo Spirito and Gesu until the soles of her feet smarted with the sting of the pink granite setts. Giulia was teaching her shopping technique.

"Display the slightest enthusiasm," the *Principessa* proselytised, eyes glistening with missionary zeal, "and trust me, you will pay the full price."

And so Isobel, who was, after all, a very good mimic, learned to dispose her limbs in a pattern of ladylike debility on all the watered silk sofas in the crucial square mile.

"*No!*" Giulia would say to every garment Isobel liked, with the sharp, open Italian *o* and correctly contemptuous turn of the head. And then, as the deferential saleswomen returned offending jackets or skirts to the storeroom, Giulia would lean over and whisper loudly, "If you want it, *carissima*, ask to see it again as we are leaving, and finger the price ticket with the tiniest frown. Then they know we're prepared to discuss it. We must have a discount of twenty per cent."

"*No!*" Isobel practised the syllable in the Lancia as Giulia drove it home in the wrong traffic lane at a snail's pace, oblivious to the enraged hootings around her.

"Ah," she said, pressing her clenched fist to her heart, "How I have longed for a daughter."

*   *   *

Isobel's other gift was neglected for months. Nor did she struggle against her own impotence. There were too many other things in her life. Making papier-mâché carnival masks for Giacomo and Marzio to be ready in time for that freakish, spiteful week which preceded Ash Wednesday, making voluptuous chocolate cakes with Giulia on Serafina's day off, absorbing the vital statistics of all the jewels in Giulia's collection. No gem, it turned out, could ever be too large. The question of vulgarity here was irrelevant. Australian sapphires were fit for nothing, and when buying emeralds other than those of unimpeachable quality, it was wise to murmur 'beryl' disparagingly. It helped with the price.

"One must know these things," Alessandro mocked cosily in English when enquiring after their daily amusements. He was learning the use of the impersonal pronoun from Isobel, admiring, as he did, its aristocratic modesty. The Montenaros, Isobel found, attached moral value to elegance.

Against this background of ever deepening domestic affection, Giulia planned a dinner party to be held on the last day of carnival. The motives for this entertainment were several.

Attention was due for business reasons to some people named Bonetti, large scale concrete suppliers who were moving into construction. In addition, to be giving a party at home forestalled any need to accept invitations that meant venturing forth on a rowdy night full of water pistols and exploding bladders of paint.

"The risk to one's gown," Alessandro clarified for Isobel's benefit, pirouetting absurdly.

It would also be Isobel's eighteenth birthday. A handful of young people of a suitable kind were to be invited with their parents so that the event would serve in some measure as Isobel's Milanese debut. She was not likely to be given another elsewhere, as Giulia knew. It was all to be as grand and gay as Montenaro resources and talk of pre-stressed concrete would allow.

Giulia sent out her cards endorsed with the handwritten rider, 'To introduce Miss Isobel Jefferson'.

Some of the recipients knew the name already, or were on terms with others who did. Miss Jefferson had been seen about accompanying Giulia. And if Isobel was daughter to her, she became honorary niece to a number of Giulia's friends: chattering, charitable women with contacts and money.

It was through visiting them in their treasure houses that Isobel became intimate with the secretive, wisteria wound courts with their plashing stone fountains, or crystal, rooftop pavilions set in aerial gardens whose greenery lidded the city with jade.

Milan presents a forbidding aspect to the stranger, locking its heart against interlopers. Shoulder to shoulder, *palazzo*, office skyscraper, Roman fragment and bank are formed into ranks, erecting a wall of reserve with no chink through which the outsider may spy. But there is something engaging about a place that so carefully chooses its friends. Milan selected Isobel with fastidious fingers.

What could be more *affascinante* than a half-orphaned Valkyrie with a direct line of chat, both humble and gutsy? Collective opinion translated more or less like that.

"You will amuse yourself much tonight," teased an elderly, stick-thin Contessa on the morning of Giulia's dinner party, when Isobel called at her palazzo apartment with a message from Giulia. (The errand was only a ruse to enable the *Principessa* to collect Isobel's surprise birthday present at leisure.) "All the nice girls in Milan would die for the chance to sit beside Furio Bonetti for an hour . . . he is never normally still."

Furio, the son of the concrete magnate, was a noted jazz musician, lionised by jazz lovers in Italy where his avocation was not well rewarded. He combined it with an executive role in his father's expanding construction empire. On Giulia's placement, Furio had been allocated the seat on Isobel's right. Which ought, Alessandro judged dotingly, to flatter his parents, and afford Isobel some fun.

Furio was an engaging young scamp. He had studied civil engineering at Milan University and Business Studies at Harvard. It was said he found Italian attitudes neolithic. A stimulating notion, when his family's profits were so noticeably modern in scale.

"I do quite like jazz," Isobel answered the old lady matter-of-factly, folding a committee report to take back to Giulia, "but I know nothing about it, Contessa, so he'll find me uninteresting company."

"I doubt that, dearest child. Men adore ignorance. I myself have preserved a seductive lack of information on most topics since tenderest youth . . . and observe, if you will, that I've been most successfully widowed three times. Divorce is more profitable, they say, but alas, in this country, unavailable. We groan, here, under a lack of investment opportunity."

"Has he got a super-fast car? That's all *I* want to know," Isobel laughed, catching the Contessa's mood.

"As to that, I could not say," the Contessa replied, ringing a china bell by her chair to summon up lemonade, "but he does have a rather good face." She rummaged amongst a pile of magazines on a low table and produced one with a photograph of Furio Bonetti. Isobel scanned it with interest.

"You can't really tell with that thing in his mouth . . . What is it, a saxophone?"

"I believe so. Here's another, a close-up. *E bello, no?*"

Isobel studied the grainy blow-up as she drank the refreshment brought by the maid. Furio's beauty now could not be denied. Long, waving, grape dark hair, nostrils that arched in mettlesome curves and wide open eyes which, if the camera didn't deceive, appeared to be somewhere between blue and black. Not common, the Contessa acknowledged, but not altogether rare.

"Not a serious boy, I don't think," she added lightly, taking the magazine from Isobel's hand. "These southern families are unreliable . . . God knows what they amount to . . . half of them are just jumped up bandits. Still, my love, he will do for you to cut your teeth on. Enslave him for practice. I will see you this evening."

Isobel floated down the broad staircase from the *piano nobile* and into the sun dappled court with an unfamiliar sensation of flying things beating gossamer wings behind her breastbone. A beautiful, musical bandit.

On the way home, she decided, she would buy some very, *very* grown-up perfume with one of those zestful names that were as good as the smell. 'Crescendo de Balmain' sounded volcanic.

Furio, Furio, Furio! A name for one of nature's irresistible forces.

* * *

Alighting with practised panache from the rear platform of her tram in the Duomo Square, Isobel was still thinking of the evening and what it might bring when she felt a pluck at her sleeve. Turning in surprise, she found herself looking straight into Josef Fischer's worried brown eyes. A tremor of revulsion snaked down her spine.

"It *is* you. I thought it was . . . in spite of the transformation. Excuse me," he reddened, seeing Isobel's stony expression. "Miss Jefferson, I'm so glad we met," he went on, reaching inside his coat for his wallet. "Look, I'd like you to have this . . ."

He extracted a bundle of notes and pushed them at Isobel.

"Go on," he insisted shaking the money. "Please take it, it's yours."

"I don't know what you mean," Isobel retreated a step.

"You were an au pair . . . I really didn't know. You worked the hours of a maid . . ." Josef grabbed at Isobel's hand, forcing her fingers round the banknotes. "I worked it all out. This is owing to you . . ."

"The *hours*!" Isobel threw back at him in disgust, the cash still clenched in her hand. "Do you think that's all I care about? How *dare* you offer me money . . . Keep the lousy stuff to yourself," Isobel opened her hand, "I never want to see you again!"

The lire notes drifted down between them, wafted by the whirr and flap of pigeons' wings while Josef's gaze locked sadly on to Isobel's, holding it till they were rudely shoved apart by three shrieking women.

In the uproar, Isobel saw that one had an infant slung on her hip. She saw nothing further, blinded by a crumpled newspaper rubbed in her face. It was over in seconds. Not a single note remained. Easy pickings for scavenging gypsies.

"Well," Isobel said unsteadily, "I didn't want it and I suppose you wouldn't have picked it up." Feeling something else wrong, she realised her handbag, the pretty crocodile one with the intricate chain, which Alessandro had given her for Christmas, had been snatched from her shoulder.

"*Oh, no!* I can't bear it . . ."

Josef waved his hands, feebly solicitous.

A nearby pair of *caribinieri* strolled across. In their bicorne hats, tail coats and cherry striped trousers, they looked a picture of princely composure. The Signor and the Signorina should go to the police, they politely advised, as if they themselves were not. Gypsies ran so fast. A *scandalo*. They were so very sorry, they said, before drifting away.

It was impossible not to laugh, if rather shakily. Josef offered Isobel a restorative in a Galleria café. Too shocked to refuse, she accepted thankfully. She needed a breathing space in which to think. The Viale Regina Giovanna was too far to walk. How could

60

she get home without money? And her lovely handbag ... The small incident, common enough in Milan, converted hostility to fellowship between herself and Josef. Brandy would be just the thing.

With the slate wiped clean, they sat down at a pink napped table set on the mosaic, both smiling sheepishly. Ironically, it was the same café in which Isobel had enjoyed the company of the American nuns. It seemed ungracious to draw attention to the fact.

"May I start again?" Josef began as the waiter turned away.

Isobel nodded, not knowing what was coming next. With the adrenalin flowing away, her guard was down.

"You are quite right, of course. Money cannot compensate you for what you endured in my home. Believe me, I didn't know the whole of it ... I chose not to. And for that, I'm to blame."

Isobel's lukewarm denial was interrupted by the waiter's return. She took a mouthful of the spirit and waited.

"You see," Josef leaned towards her, "I'm very fond of my wife ... And I'm afraid she's not well ... in her mind ..."

"Mad, you mean?" enquired Isobel, bluntly.

"Yes, if you like," Josef blenched. "She's receiving treatment now. I found her a psychiatrist and she goes there each week. Estella's gone home to her grandmother in Switzerland."

Josef Fischer's hands trembled as he lifted his glass. "It might help you to forgive us," he went on, "if you understood something of what my wife has been through ... No, I don't in any way mean to belittle your own sufferings," Josef fended off Isobel's sharp riposte with a gesture.

"You see, my wife's mother had her head cut off ..."

"*What!*" Isobel slumped back in her chair as if she had been struck. She put her hands to her face. "*My God!*"

Josef unfolded a story which dimmed all peripheral sound and vision. For half an hour there was nothing left but his voice and a narrow field of focus enclosing his face and his hands. A history predating Isobel's birth by a mere five or six years was projected across the table like a speeded up, flickering black and white newsreel.

"... They found Nina and her mother under the floorboards of their Rotterdam house. They'd had nothing but tulip bulbs to eat for weeks when they took them away. My parents never knew where until later. It was a concentration camp on the Polish border. Nina was too young, but they made her mother dig for coal on the surface ... hard work for a woman ... or anyone not used to physical labour. In the end, when the Germans were losing and the Russian advance came closer, they tried to cover up what they'd

61

done. They shot some, I think. But ammunition must have been getting short . . . they guillotined Nina's mother."

Isobel gagged. She recovered momentarily and took her hands from her face. She must have misheard. They didn't have guillotines in the last war. They were a French Revolution thing.

"No," Josef said flatly, gazing sightlessly into his empty glass. "Not entirely. Some of the smaller, remoter camps were short of . . . technical facilities."

He glanced up then with a terrible smile to see the effect of his joke. Isobel, not knowing this poignant quirk of Jewish self-preservation, looked at him in white faced amazement.

"They say they press-ganged a local blacksmith and carpenter to engineer this machine. It all came out later . . ."

"But did Nina know?" Isobel leaned further back in her chair, as if an inch or two's extra distance from Nina Fischer's husband could push this nightmare away. "At the time, I mean."

"Not immediately, we don't think. Not for certain," Josef said wearily. "But she saw her mother standing in a queue. At the far end of a compound with others, roped together in dirty, sleeveless white shifts. They'd had their hair cut. The women disappeared, one by one into a shed, and never came out. There were sounds which no one would ever want to describe. And later, baskets and pits . . . It's all there in the Jewish Agency records."

Josef paused in his narrative and passed a hand over his brow.

"And there are eyewitness reports. At the last minute, Nina's mother blew her a kiss. She was watching, you see, from the women's barracks. Nina screamed out and stretched her hands through the bars . . . A sudden, childish insight . . . I don't know . . ."

"*Oh my God. Oh my God . . . Why are you telling me this?*" Isobel fought down nausea and the remembrance of Estella's face, glimpsed through a window as she had stood on the pavement outside the Fischer apartment in the Viale Majno so many weeks ago. Not Estella's face, but Nina's face at the same age. At the moment her sanity had been sliced off for ever. Isobel's mind reeled at the image of Nina madly saluting her fridge.

Her animosity against the Fischers shrivelled to nothing, leaving a hole burned out with acid and filled up with blood.

Josef couldn't be stopped. He told the rest of the tale whether Isobel willed it or not. She heard it in snatches. Before the Russians overran the concentration camp, the Germans abandoned it, leaving some prisoners alive. Of these, a few made their way to the Allied lines. One party took ten-year-old Nina with them. She arrived in Switzerland and was adopted by her parents' old friends, the Fischers. They had got out of Holland before the invasion. Nina was erratic and strange throughout the rest of her childhood. It was a question of time, the psychiatrists said. She would get over it, as others had done. A benign prediction which had seemed justified by her late teens when Nina went off to Paris to do a little finishing course, returning a year later to Switzerland, ablaze with vitality. Bewitching. Time had done its healing work, so it appeared. She married her older brother by adoption, despite some stifled misgivings of the senior Fischers. Josef had been deeply in love. It was only after Estella's birth that she had become . . . moody again.

"You can't imagine what she was like before. Full of life, full of plans . . ."

"I met her in London," Isobel interrupted him drearily.

"Ah, yes. Then you know. She was up and down then. The truth is, after you came to Milan, she went down and down. I don't know why."

"It's my fault," Isobel supplied the unspoken conclusion.

"*No!* How could it be that? But perhaps you triggered something. A look of somebody, perhaps. A reminder of something. You're the only person with whom I can share this. In the family, you know, we don't speak of it. Only 'moods' and 'depression'."

"It's my birthday," Isobel said, tangentially.

"Then I must wish you many happy returns, Miss Jefferson, and buy you a present."

"Please don't," Isobel rejected the offer rather too sharply. Softening, she said, "And it's Isobel, please. I feel as if we've lived through some kind of lifetime together."

Josef drove her to the corner of the Viale Regina Giovanna and dropped her there. No, he would not come in and meet the *Principessa*. However, they parted friends.

"Give my love to Nina," Isobel said finally, the words just tumbled out. "If you think it will do any good."

Hearing about the gypsies – the only reason Isobel gave for her lateness – Giulia was horrified. She must spend the afternoon in bed recuperating in time for her party. *Madonna*! That this should happen in Milan. And on Isobel's birthday, too. An outrage. Now what about a really good cry . . . essential treatment for shock.

Isobel played it all down. She had already got over the shock. Giacomo and Marzio were coming home early from school to don their clown outfits and masks ready for the final expedition of carnival to the *Giardini pubblici*, with licence to terrorise adults there, foolish enough to be caught out of doors. Isobel would not disappoint them. The walk would do her good.

FOUR

F urio Bonetti was among the last to bow over Isobel's hand as
she stood at the end of the receiving line in the flower-garlanded
lobby. The swirl of arrival which had filled the apartment for
twenty minutes was beginning to settle: wraps, exclamations, satin
gowns gleaming, reports of teenaged pranks on the streets, crack-
ling dress-shirt fronts, names and introductions. The lift disgorged
group after group.

Isobel, who had wondered earlier in the day how she could ever
be guiltlessly happy again, found she was. As she smiled, shook
hands and kissed strange faces, she enjoyed being officially young.
That part of herself which had been artificially, irreversibly aged
by the encounter with Josef, stepped aside and looked on. To be
the centre of so much undeserved attention was a treat.

Lucy Larizzi had come up from Rome. "Such fun to meet you,
darling . . . Haven't seen your mother for *ages* . . . So glad I could
help . . . Giulia is absolutely the best person I know . . . Let me
introduce you to Max . . . He's an art dealer, darling. Madison
Avenue . . ."

Max was a rolypoly person of indeterminate age with a gash of
a smile and careful eyes. On fingers and thumbs he wore chunky
gold rings.

"Hey," he brayed. "So you're the belle of the ball. Swell to meet
you. Have a great time."

Isobel would have asked him more about his gallery in 'Noo
Yark' and the one he was setting up with 'Loo' in Rome, but
Alessandro was turning towards her to introduce Furio.

"Our young friend, who celebrates her eighteenth birthday
today . . ."

He looked at her as if there was nobody else in the room, a
trick some men acquire along with the other accidents of puberty.
Endowed with a cherubic curve to his cheek and a spurious anticipation of hurt in his navy blue glance, at twenty-six Furio did not
know what it was to fail with a woman, be she laundress or heiress.

His casual preliminary assessment of Isobel was auspicious. Miss
Jefferson lived up to her whispered reputation for Doric perfection.

64

In her slender, corded white silk gown, she glimmered like a pillar in moonlight. There was only the dimple and the sand bar of shadow behind her pacific blue eyes to prove she was human. Quite intriguing.

"*Mi piace, Signorina . . .*" Furio smouldered routinely as he unbent. English girls, however they looked, were in his rich experience all the same. Gigglers and precipitate leapers into the bed that was always prepared in his bachelor lair. Still, Isobel Jefferson was protected by a formidable thicket of home-grown formality, which made things a little more interesting than usual. "And how do you like Milan?"

"I like it as much," said Isobel with a flash of prideful candour, "as it seems to like me." It was her evening, after all.

"I hear it's about to fall down at your feet," Furio admitted generously as Isobel half turned her back, leaving her head to turn more slowly away.

Alessandro, already enmeshed in talk of tensioning cables with Furio's stocky, silver haired father, watched Isobel complacently from the corner of his eye, repressing a chuckle. Their little one knew her own worth.

With the unconscious instinct of their race, Giulia, Alessandro . . . even Giacomo and Marzio, had taught Isobel how to flirt in the fan-snapping, Latin manner. It had come with the language, an inherent part of the package. Thorns to enhance the appeal of the bloom.

Hours later, when dessert was on the table and the candles guttering low, Furio was hardly aware that he was eating morsels of Serafina's surprise birthday cake from Isobel's plate. He was enraptured.

Throughout the meal, Isobel had addressed him unfalteringly with the cool obliquity of the Italian third person feminine singular. Quite a feat for a foreigner.

"Couldn't you call me *ti*?" he pleaded after a while.

"No, I don't think so," Isobel answered consideringly. Giulia was strict in these matters.

"Or we could speak in English," Furio suggested.

"No, that would be rude. Not everyone here understands it." Isobel's reproof was gentle but humourless.

Furio's request and its refusal scarcely broke Isobel's stride as she continued with a brisk exposition of current engine nomenclature and its faults as she saw them. The abbreviation *GT*, was a bad excuse for falling short of motorists' justified expectations of the description *Gran Tourismo*.

Eyes dancing, Furio was happy to agree with whatever she said.

It was all staggeringly apposite, anyway. Did Isobel drive? No, she said, she did not. Her father's car was a decrepit old Riley on which both of her brothers had learned, but she had not, as yet. Would she care, Furio asked, to learn on his Lamborghini? It would be a privilege to teach her if only the vehicle met with Isobel's exacting requirements.

"Oh, I know," Isobel deprecated herself, "I'm disgustingly pompous about cars. But you couldn't take such a risk . . ."

It was Furio who giggled. Isobel's vocabulary was enchanting. She trotted words out delightedly, like a girl flourishing new dresses from her wardrobe.

Their heads confidingly close, the one so pale and the other so dark, attracted mature attention. Cars? This was not about cars. But it was all very *gentile, no*? Sweet.

Seated at Alessandro's right hand, at the head of the table, Furio's mother, a well corseted woman with a helmet of black lacquered hair, smiled her agreement thinly.

"And now," Giulia rose from her place, stilling the hubbub of conversation, "I have another surprise for our *debuttanta*. A birthday present from Alessandro and myself to remind her of the day and where she spent it."

There were a few scattered oohs, aahs, and genial masculine gruntings.

Giulia handed a small, scarlet leather case across the table. It was passed from hand to hand until it reached Isobel amidst an anticipatory hush.

"With all our love, Isobel *carissima*. I hope you will like them. Open it . . ."

The case contained a pair of *pavé*-set diamond carnival masks, one with mouth turned tragically down and a minute cabochon sapphire for a tear, the other with upturned, laughing mouth had particles of ruby to carmine the lips. The tiny masks were mounted as earrings on specially cast yellow-gold blanks. The backs were engraved with the date.

Isobel felt her insides lurch. Her gaze swung between the sparkling little masks and Giulia's encouraging, hopeful face.

"You do like them, *cara* . . . ?"

"Oh, how could I not? Diamonds for *me* . . ." They were real, of course. Isobel could now spot a fake instantly, thanks to Giulia's tuition. "However can I thank you . . ."

There was a ripple of relief up and down the table. The moment had been peculiarly tense. Isobel left her place to hug Giulia and Alessandro, to show the case and its contents to the thirty guests ranged on either side of the long table. She seemed overcome. But that was quite as it should be, one or two nodded. Isobel, dear as she was, was not, after all, a Montenaro relation.

"Try them on . . ."

"*Squisito* . . ."

"What a marvellous idea . . ."

Who had done the work? The little masterpieces would be copied, inevitably. It could not be prevented.

"It can indeed," Giulia challenged, nettled at the suggestion that her gift was incomplete. "I bought the copyright."

Lucy Larizzi helped Isobel adjust the jewels in her ears. Tilted outwards, they should be. Tragedy and comedy. Youthful, charming and witty.

Half the party was on its feet, craning for a closer look, offering advice and admiring comment.

"I'm so *jealous*," enthused a well brought up Italian girl with good humoured frankness.

Giulia's gift was more descriptive of the day than she or anyone else present was ever to know. The jewelled masks represented not only the last day of carnival but the juxtaposition of sorrow and elation which had marked Isobel's birthday. The realisation of Nina's continuing torment in which she herself had shared on the one hand, and this outpouring of goodwill on the other. She had done nothing to earn it. There was Furio too . . .

Amid the noise of congratulation and toasts, Isobel's thoughts rushed in on succeeding waves of contrasting emotion. It was all so completely unexpected . . . and on top of everything else. This time, tears had the victory over self command.

"Ah, you see," Giulia sobbed triumphantly, "she is *completely* Italian!"

It felt wholly natural when Furio encircled Isobel's shoulders with a comforting arm. He smelled of trees. There was a rattle of sentimental applause, a rustle of sighs and a dabbing of mathematical, Milanese eyes, temporarily misted with moisture. What a climax to carnival!

"*Te voglio bene*," Furio whispered, nuzzling Isobel's neck. I wish you well. Isobel was moved to hear it because, in Italian, the phrase meant rather more than it said.

It was the senior Bonettis who broke up the party just a minute or two after midnight. It was now Ash Wednesday, they pointed out with unnecessary ostentation. Lent had begun.

"One would prefer not to be reminded," Alessandro muttered crossly in English, defiantly signalling the hired footman to pour Max Cooper more brandy. Such killjoy *punctilio*. Pah!

Furio stayed as late as he decently could, holding Isobel's hand under the table. The best place to learn to drive, he assured her, was Monza stadium. He would arrange it.

"Certainly you may call on Miss Jefferson the day after tomorrow," Alessandro gave his permission breezily as Furio was taking his leave, "if she welcomes it . . . between six and seven. My wife will be happy to receive you. And if after that she finds herself at leisure, you may escort Isobel to any restaurant of repute in the city."

Isobel circled her thumb and forefinger, vibrating her hand where only Furio could see it. A gesture full of innocent ardour.

* * *

"Your mother is disquieted," Signor Bonetti rose from his monumental desk as the cowed departmental heads straggled out of the tender meeting. "Sit down."

Ignoring his father's instruction, Furio retreated a pace and put his hands in his pockets. Nobody with the bowels to resist sat down within range of the 'altar', as his father's notional work table was irreverently called. All the chairs were so low.

Furio had an idea what was coming. His parents' abrupt departure from the Montenaro party the previous night had not been prompted by religious devotion.

"*Papa* . . ."

"Hear me out. Miss Jefferson is a striking girl. Most unusual," Bonetti walked round the desk to clasp his son's broad shoulders. He was smiling but his brown eyes were hard. "We know nothing of her, of course . . . But she has found herself some powerful protectors. The *Principessa* . . ."

"Come to the point, Papa. What do you mean?" Furio eased his shoulder free of his father's kneading fingers.

"She is not to be taken lightly, my son. Nor yet, you understand . . . seriously. *So*," Bonetti tweaked a lock of Furio's hair painfully, "dinner at Savini's, a nightclub perhaps, and then home, uh? The goods are returned in perfect condition. Miss Jefferson has enjoyed her evening out, the Montenaros have no cause for offence and that is that. Our Furio has larger matters to concern him."

Bonetti kissed his son on the mouth with crushing force. It was both chastisement and caress. Furio's heart convulsed inside him with hatred and love. He wanted to wipe his mouth with the back of his hand but dared not. He turned to go.

"You are not yet dismissed," Bonetti rapped out. Turning his own back, he took up a spouted, silver-gilt vessel his secretary kept full of water and placed on the 'altar' each morning. Signor Bonetti liked to tend his own geraniums. He stepped out on to the loggia

68

overlooking the Corso Mategna. The sound of traffic entered the room. "Your mother expects you to dine with us this evening at the villa. I take it she may count on you . . ."

"No. I'm sorry, Papa. I have an engagement to play tonight . . ."

"Then cancel it," Bonetti turned smiling, back into the room. "You are an artist, my son. Have you no temperament?"

"I have accepted money to appear," Furio said woodenly.

"And what is money to you?" Carlo Bonetti raised his arms high above his head, the palms turned out an angle. His powerful figure was silhouetted darkly against the light from the casement. "Since when does Furio Bonetti need money? My beautiful boy . . ."

"It is not the money, Papa," Furio interrupted, repelled by his father's nitroglycerine endearments. "I am flattered that people think it worth paying me. Also, it is a matter of contract. I must be there."

"Your mother will be disappointed," the older Bonetti reseated himself. He seemed to have lost interest in the immediate contest. "Take these figures and have them re-analysed by an independent firm of quantity surveyors. You are a good boy."

That was an order, Furio realised, not an observation on his filial virtue. He picked up the file his father pushed indifferently across the desk. It was labelled 'Stylo Fischer Estimates – Pirelli Site Redevelopment'. The name of the tendering company held no significance for Furio.

"And you will think of your family," Carlo Bonetti's voice grated again before his son's stride had covered the ten-metre distance between his desk and the ceremonial portals. "Miss Jefferson has nothing to offer. She is a foreigner. An entanglement would be troublesome. Do not oblige me to intervene."

Furio left, having said nothing further. He dealt summarily with the file, pulse racing with an explosive mixture of fear and resentment. The freedom he exercised was an illusion. No more, in fact, than a leash which his father twitched harshly at unpredictable intervals. *La famiglia*. That cage round the heart that was both homestead and prison.

"I shall go out and not return," Furio announced over the intercom to his secretary and her junior in the office adjoining.

"Monza?"

"*Si*." Furio let go of the switch.

Less than half an hour later, he was hurling his car round the deserted track. It cost tens of thousands of lire to scream out his frustration this way. Nothing was ever for nothing. As the speedometer needle crept round the dial, Furio's thoughts became calmer.

The price of his education, his short years of freedom at Harvard, was submission to *la famiglia*. Everything he had learned that was useful to that rapacious deity was to be placed at its feet. But the spirit of ultimate, limitless liberty alive in the smiles of his fraternity brothers was not, said the deity, for Furio Bonetti. The interests of the family must be served.

And one day, a day that could not be too long deferred, that would mean the right girl. A girl of sound Italian stock, whose family had influence where it counted and stood well with the Church. A girl, moreover, who didn't need to be told her duty. It consisted in producing heirs, futurity to those shelves full of boxes containing the cotton wrapped bones of Bonetti forefathers. The skeletons of Calabrian peasants, crying out for appeasement with an endless repetition of the way they had lived. Furio hated those bones.

Most of all he hated the mummified body of *Nonno* Bonetti which the entire black garbed family was forced to look upon once every year. The desiccated husk weighed practically nothing and last *Ognissanti*, the old fellow's arm had come off. It had been like crumbling a piece from a biscuit. Furio shuddered at the memory. He had never told the guys in the fraternity dormitory about those annual scenes.

Mama had been changing *Nonno*'s winding sheet. Papa had wept shamelessly, copiously. He always did. *Nonno* was entitled to special respect. He had been the first Bonetti to abandon the ancestral olive grove to trade in cement. *Nonno* had rescued his posterity from ignominy, obscurity and poverty. They, his successors owed him an incalculable debt. A debt, Furio raged inwardly on his sixth lap of the stadium, he was required to pay with all the obedient years of his life. Why?

Because, Furio told himself, decelerating the engine as the chequered flags waved him down, the family was the source of all honour and manliness. Desert it, and a man was no more than a seed blown on to stony, uncultivated ground. A profitless weed.

Rounding the final bend, Furio tried those thoughts out in his American English. In that language, they lost most of their meaning. But in his native imagination, he saw that it meant the loss of his mother's, his sisters', their children's, and his father's respect. they would never forgive him. freedom, at the end of the day, was only the licence to throw away what you had.

"Bodywork's rattling, Signor," remarked the stadium mechanic who accepted Furio's signature on his running account. The red Lamborghini was not new and hard used. Perhaps the Signor would discuss a price for *la macchina*? Soon, very soon, Signor Furio

70

would be thinking of getting another. The new series was out.

Not yet, Furio parried the opening moves of negotiation, though the mechanic clearly yearned for the car. First he was going to teach an *amica inglese* to drive it. Better in this than a new one.

The mechanic cupped his right elbow in the palm of his left hand, grinning in oily complicity. He oscillated his forearm obscenely.

"*Basta!*" Furio spat the word quietly and spun on his heel.

Isobel was not in that category. She could not be used. Alessandro Montenaro was a man who took things personally. The treatment of Isobel was bound up in *his* honour. And more to the purpose, he had a great many sizeable contracts to award . . . to construction companies like Bonetti's. These were things Carlo Bonetti had not needed to say to his son. No girl would be allowed to blight the crop sown in the order book.

Exorcised by speed, Furio drove back to Milan and his evening engagement at the Locale Ticinese. His mind was not on the programme. Rather, he wondered idly how Isobel Jefferson would react to an afternoon spent stirring the dust of his ancestors . . . watching Mama re-dress them all tenderly as if they were so many broken dolls.

She might laugh, a reaction which Furio realised would hurt him . . . or show freezing contempt for such barbarism. She would probably, he decided, have some devastatingly shrewd observation to make. Even worse. But he would never tell Isobel about those things. He liked her . . . *tanto, tanto!*

Furio beat his clenched fists on the steering wheel. There would be problems.

*   *   *

The problems were not evident to Isobel. As Giulia had prophetically said, the way forward was clear for those who perceived no obstruction.

Every second night for three weeks, Furio called at the Viale Regina Giovanna to collect her. If Alessandro was there, he stayed for a while to talk over matters of purely masculine interest. Juventus's prospects in the World Cup, the boom in construction.

Everywhere in Italy on the fringes of cities, they were building tower-block housing to shelter the tidal wave of peasants who were leaving their land to toil in the factories. The design briefs were mean, the consumption of concrete, enormous. Many a drab, half-built escarpment had the name of Bonetti blazoned on the scaffolding. Alessandro had a retrospective distaste for his involvement in some of them.

How could a family of eight or more live in two rooms in the sky? Such conditions bred violence. The traditional, fowl scratched *cortile* was needed for the overspill of emotion. Didn't Furio, speaking dispassionately, agree?

Dispassionate discourse was not Furio's forte. He was a man of the south before he was a man of his times . . . however fervently he wished the balance reversed.

While Isobel chased Giacomo and Marzio into bed, Carlo Bonetti's son uneasily defended the tower blocks with talk of running water and lavatories. He had to. Bonettis were not in the social harmony business. *La famiglia* had escaped its few earthen floored rooms, stagnant well and yard fouled with goat droppings in *Nonno*'s day, less than three generations ago. Concrete had bought their ticket out.

It was with a sense of release, therefore, that Furio burned away from the Montenaro apartment with Isobel at his side in the greening Lombardy spring.

With her, life was uncomplicated. She was shallowly rooted here. She cared nothing for Italy's socio-economic problems, nothing at all, in fact, for anything but him. With his sure, young male's instinct he read all the signs upon her. Hair, eyes and skin all luminesced with invitation. She couldn't hide it and didn't try to, being unaware of the ways in which she beckoned him. Day by day, what was left of adolescent angularity rounded out in love for him.

With her blood quickened for the first time, Isobel knew no description for her feelings. Only that everything that had gone before him – home and family, Nina, the Viale Majno – had, in his presence, a flat, low quality existence. Furio's light made of everything but himself and her, a dim and dusty history.

The drive to *il centro* was the first joy of their evenings together. Furio pushed the ageing Lamborghini to its limits. No vehicle ahead went unchallenged. No pavement or traffic island was too high to mount, no competitor's chariot was too wide to pass and no light too red to defy.

The *Vigile Urbano* gave chase on several occasions, sounding their klaxons which only added music to action. Disciplinary measures were never seriously contemplated. Police sympathies lay with any young man celebrating his girl's beauty with the worthy tribute of horse power. That was *l'amore*. Furio's bravura in courting disaster only to cheat it, was the admiration of Milan's traffic department.

"Ah, this blonde one," it was said more than once at shift changing time, "she inspires him."

In general, they dined at Savini's immaculate Galleria premises. It was the way in which Furio openly tested his father. Several appearances with the same girl in that forum were bound to stimulate comment at Milan's most senior level. What could the Bonetti heir mean by it? Was this courtship sanctioned, or not?

Isobel was content. Black marble, gilt and white linen formed a perfect backdrop for the faces.

"What faces?" Furio asked.

"Well, that one over there, for example," Isobel actually pointed. "Wonderfully antique and tawdry." It was early, and in the half-empty restaurant Isobel's voice rang out clear as an evening Angelus bell.

Gleeful, Furio shielded his own face with the menu. A few tables away, the owner of the features so roundly condemned, fumed fatly. She was an operatic diva, ingesting a substantial supper before her gargantuan endeavours at La Scala.

"*Ti amo, ti amo,*" Furio avowed, nose pressed to the day's list of *antipasti*. I love you, I love you.

"What?" Isobel said while an attentive waiter snickered softly. He loved her, too.

The world famous songstress snapped to her companion that those azure glaciers of Miss Jefferson's would not last her for ever, nor the damask smooth lips which reported the glaciers' findings so prettily. That young lady should take good care whom she offended. Giulia Montenaro was not entirely omnipotent.

It all helped to build Isobel's little legend.

Later, as on several occasions before, Furio and Isobel drove to the Ticinese, the run down canal port of Milan. It was the heartland of his off duty social and musical life.

It was there, in dark smoky caverns, that he played at Isobel and to her. Whichever band Furio was with, they followed his lead, casting thunderbolts of sound at her feet. Brazen bouquets. Between them, it was a language of passion which he alone spoke but which she understood, returning assent with her eyes.

The dialogue was always accompanied by stamping, hand clapping, whooping calls and flashing blue lights, irradiating for split seconds the people around her at the eye of this electrical storm.

She knew all the people or at least she had met them. Whenever Furio arrived at a club, whole roomfuls of people stood up to greet him, leaning over tables to shake him by the hand or clap him on the back. As for Isobel, his left hand on the nape of her neck was enough to declare her his property. And as they were seen many times together like this, the nocturnal world of young Milan drew the inevitable inference. The uncatchable Furio must be in love.

It mattered little, certain Milanese girls felt in their wisdom of ages. Isobel was English and could not last long. Giulia Montenaro's house-guest or au pair – descriptions varied – would fly away in due season to her own breeding grounds in the north. Someone with a right to Furio would eventually get him. Let Isobel have her fling.

On the night of the diva incident, Furio played a piece in a Ticinese dive which he publicly announced was a composition of his own. It had a title. 'Isobel': When it was over, he threw his instrument aside and leapt down from the little stage to kiss her chin-to-chin and nose-to-nose as professional cameras snapped.

The long lidded Milanese girls clapped the tune heartily enough. If this was art, then art had never had a clearer motive. Blatant foreplay. Furio would now sleep with Isobel as night followed day. And that would end it for her. The brief reign of *La Jefferson* would be done with by dawn. Furio's heart and hand would be empty and free.

*   *   *

Furio's bachelor apartment was close by. The converted loft of a waterside warehouse, it overlooked the shining black pool of the Porta Ticinese where a few wooden hulled freighters lay at anchor. The gantry opening had been replaced with a floorboard-to-rafter plate glass window. They stood before it together in darkness.

"Let me love you, Isobel," Furio murmured with his mouth in her hair. "All of you, darling. I can wait no longer . . . I must have you now. Your skin, every inch of it . . . I will suck all your toes . . ."

Isobel was quite quickly divested of her clothes. Once she knew what he wanted, she stripped them from herself recklessly. Furio led her to his bed, nestling her between the sheets.

"Wait for me, *tesoro*, I shall come back. Then we shall go to heaven together . . ."

Isobel was aroused. It was all new to her. Wavelets of delight shimmered through her, lapping her nerve ends with small slaps of pleasure. An unknown mouth yawned between her legs, stretching, aching, demanding. A groan of tortured ravishment left her.

"What are you doing, Furio? I have this terrible, wonderful pain . . ."

"Wait for me, darling," Furio's thickened voice called from the bathroom. "Don't go without me . . ."

When he came to her, she was rocking herself from side to side on his bed, her eyes already glazed with the cataracts of coitus.

Furio covered her body with his own, moaning at the touch of her flesh.

"Oh, Isobel, oh, *Isabella*!" His erection enlarged and stiffened, ready to pump life from his shrieking loins.

"What is this?" Isobel slurred, her tongue darting over his nipple. She grasped at his shaft with her hands, a long boat to sail into her cave . . .

"*No!*" Furio tore himself from her suddenly, leaving her bereft. "Get dressed, Isobel. I'm taking you home."

"What is it?" Isobel recoiled from his words like a splash of cold water. "What have I done?"

"Nothing. Get dressed. It's what I nearly did. Not you. Get up."

Mortally wounded in her spirit, Isobel did so, slowly. She veiled her breasts from his glance with her hands.

"Don't you like me without my clothes on?" she hissed. "Not as nice as other girls . . . Is *that* it?"

Furio sat on the edge of the bed, his head bowed in his hands.

"Oh, *Isabella* . . . How can you ask that of me?"

"Easily, when you're so bloody rude," she sniped, struggling with her suspender belt. "It's jolly risky, this taking-your-clothes-off business," she stormed, every individual cell scratching and biting its neighbour with the rage of rejection. "I don't think I shall do it again."

"No Isobel, *carissima*." Furio strode across the room and standing naked, submissive before her, cupped her angry face in his hands. "Do *not*. No matter how much I beg you. This is not for you."

Isobel struck him across the cheek and left in a taxi.

* * *

In the morning, Alessandro did not leave at the usual hour for his office. He had a few matters touching Isobel to attend to. He sat closeted with her in the study he so rarely used.

The first thing needed no words. Isobel had overshot her curfew last night. Alessandro's looks spoke everything regarding the breaking of mutual trust.

"I am sorry," she choked gruffly, believing that this was the whole of the trouble between them. For her conscience, it was more than enough.

"We will not speak of that," Alessandro said sombrely. "I had it in mind to tell young Bonetti that he monopolised too much of your time. But he has got ahead of me."

"What do you mean?" Isobel looked up. Surely Furio had not betrayed himself and her. Furiously, Isobel blushed.

"This morning, early, I received a proposal of marriage on your behalf. A note was delivered by hand. It asks," Alessandro lifted a sheet of cream paper wearily, "that I should give my consent."

"What did you say?" Isobel licked her dry lips. She didn't know how she felt. She had never thought of marrying anyone.

"Thus far, I have said nothing. I shall write, however, and say that the power of giving or withholding permission does not rest with me. You are not my daughter," Alessandro met her eyes, "I'm sorry to say."

Isobel didn't know what to say. This was an odd way of going about things. But Alessandro had not finished speaking.

"I must tell you also that late last night we received a telephone call from your mother."

At that news, Isobel stiffened. Her letters home of late had been few. Now she felt the omission. But the gulf between her new world in Milan and her old one in Plymstead Magna had seemed too wide to bridge with a ballpoint pen.

"I must tell you," Alessandro went on with a visible effort, "that your father, Canon Jefferson . . . I have his title right?" Isobel nodded. "Is seriously ill. You must go home at once. They need you there. You know of course, there is always a place for you here, if and when, you wish to return to it."

Isobel paled. So much for rheumatism. The string that joined her to home, which had drawn so fine and thin in recent months, shortened and thickened with a sickening jerk. Even Furio, with whom she was angered, was forgotten.

"And there is this," Alessandro took two newspapers from those on his desk. One, a disreputable rag, showed a front page picture of her kissing and being kissed by Furio at the Locale Ticinese. The other, a journal carrying more weight, had a smaller shot, taken at another angle, on an inside page. Isobel stared at them in silence.

"In Italy," Alessandro said quietly, "such things can be the cause of difficulties."

He did not tell her he had also spoken with Carlo Bonetti on the phone that morning. The things he had said about Isobel were unjust, but far from agreeable.

Alessandro took Isobel to the airport. Before he left her at the barrier, he gave her the drawing which he had kept locked in his desk.

"Whatever happens, *carissima*, whether you come back or not, you should consider this. You have a gift. Cherish it or it will slip through your fingers."

FIVE

"I'm afraid you won't be terribly comfortable as most of the furniture's gone." Margaret Jefferson swung open the door of Isobel's room. Her voice was thready and tight. "But I expect you'll manage for now. Come down when you're ready."

Her mother's footsteps clattered away on the carpetless stairs.

Isobel stared around her in the low ceilinged room at the top of the house. Sun rays slanted in dustily, striking the bare wooden floorboards. Forlorn as a sleeping tramp, a rug was rolled up by the skirting board.

There was nothing left here now but the old, high iron bedstead and mahogany wardrobe. Both had been bought by the new incumbent along with anything else that was too big for the bungalow.

Isobel sat down on the bed and closed her eyes. Where had her safe, dull, protected childhood gone? They had taken it away without warning. Like the time a loved but neglected teddy bear had been scooped up in one of her mother's periodic raids and sent to a jumble sale. Just like that . . . no getting it back.

You're so lucky Isobel . . . You should be grateful . . . There are plenty of other little girls who'd like to be in your place . . . The scolds of her mother, aunts, even the dear old daily who had 'done' for them, came echoing into her ears.

It wasn't fair. She couldn't have known, when she was sulking up here, doing her homework or wistfully drafting poison pen letters she could never send to the nuns . . . that at other times, in other places, there were children like Nina who needed a place like this. Nina should have had this room.

Daddy. It had all depended on him. Daddy in his black cassock, hitched up in his belt to bike round the village or do his bees. He'd always made a major production over wearing clerical dress . . . even going to the lengths of getting one of those spooky cloak things. His Dracula get-up, he called it. Pure theatre.

Daddy with his outrageous, dangerous opinions and rows with evangelical enemies. There had been his famous rebuttal of the Thirty Nine Articles in *The Times*. After that, they'd had to build an ugly annexe to the church with a public address system to accommodate the swell in his congregation. They came from miles away. Incense, Laurence Jefferson said, to the general discomfort in clerical circles, was 'fun'.

"Buttocks on benches," he had trumpeted one night, rumbustious with the parsonage rock-bottom claret, "is simply a matter of competent showmanship. What it comes down to is audience ratings. Give the people what they want and they'll get what they need without noticing."

Isobel could hear his overbearing, richly fruity voice now. She had said something pert in reply, she remembered, and been instantly slapped down by her mother. Attention grabbing was rude. Sent to bed early, she had trailed from the room, conscious of the childlike, skimpy corduroy smock that didn't quite cover her fifteen-year-old knees.

"It's really not nice to hear well brought up girls like you answering back," her mother had said later, sitting on the edge of her bed. "Why are you in such a rush to grow up? Daddy and I want you to enjoy your childhood for just as long as you can."

"I can't make time stand still, Mummy." Isobel had still been at the stage of attempting to reason with her mother.

"Oh but you can, darling. That's the magic of childhood."

Somehow, Isobel had never quite managed to capture the much vaunted magic and now, never would. Daddy was too ill to manage the parish. He was in hospital. Bone cancer. A new man was coming to Plymstead Magna, bringing his wife and family. The chance to review her childhood home through adult eyes was lost. Whilst her back was turned it had vanished.

"Well, I must say you look very smart," Margaret Jefferson greeted her daughter's appearance in the kitchen disapprovingly. "I don't suppose Daddy will recognise you."

That was the kind of remark Mrs Jefferson made. It excluded all discussion of Isobel's clothes and where they had come from. Facts of that sort were irrelevant to Margaret's life and might be unsettling. She herself was authoritatively nondescript in a threadbare tweed skirt, checked cotton shirt and man's cardigan.

"Tea?"

"Yes please," Isobel nodded, glancing round the bare cream painted dressers where the willow pattern plates used to be. Everything inessential had been taken away in a van. This was their last night at the Parsonage and Daddy was not even here. Nor were the boys.

"What will happen when Daddy gets out of hospital?"

Margaret eyed her daughter with dislike. She couldn't help it. Isobel always put questions, the answers to which, she should know without asking. It was a pity she had to be here at all. A disruptive influence at a time that was stressful enough. Now she was back again with her clumsy way of digging out the unpleasant. Someone or something, thought Isobel's mother, as she busied herself with the kettle and Aga, had made a beauty of Isobel. It was somehow unsuitable. But she was just the same. Wanting a statement again . . . like some pushy little low grade detective with his pencil and pad.

"Nothing will happen, Isobel." Margaret reached into a cupboard for cups. "Your father is dying. Is that what you wanted me to say?"

"What's the point of not saying it?" Isobel looked through the open scullery door, watching a parsonage cat stalk a bird. "How long have you known?"

"A few weeks." Margaret poured water from the kettle into Granny's dented silver pot.

"Then why didn't you tell me?" Isobel exploded. "Didn't I have a right to know? I could have come home . . . I could have . . ."

"There was nothing, Isobel, that you could have done."

"But I should *like* to have been here. This was my home . . ."

"That's typical of you, Isobel. You always think of yourself. No thought for *us* . . . It's what *you* want, what *you* have to have . . ."

"Well, I haven't had very much, have I?" Isobel flashed back. "I had to tell you six times when I was twelve that my shoes were too small before you'd take any notice. But Simon and Rupert . . . rugger boots, running shoes . . ."

On Margaret's whitening cheeks, hectic patches of red suddenly bloomed.

Isobel could have torn out her own tongue by the roots. Her father was dying and she could talk only of shoes. But she had been excluded again. Left out.

"I'm sorry, Mummy," Isobel shook with the awfulness of what she had done. "It's all so hard to take in. I just can't pretend . . ."

"Pretend what? Whenever have I asked you to pretend anything?"

"All the time," Isobel responded steadily, "I was to pretend I didn't mind wearing second hand clothes when the boys got new ones for school. I had to pretend that everything was perfect, would go on for ever . . . that this house belonged to us and no one could take it away . . . that my mother loved the three of us equally. I had to pretend to believe all Daddy's claptrap about the validly Catholic Anglican church, when it's so obviously schismatic . . ."

"I don't think you're qualified to have an opinion on matters like that," Margaret broke in on her daughter, coldly. "How many years have you spent at a theological college?"

"Or any kind of college," Isobel snapped.

The row escalated from there. It ended with Isobel apologising, saying she was overwrought before her mother could do so. Discontent was inadmissible here and must always be seen to proceed from some easily disposable cause. Home truths damaged the surface.

"I think we'd better leave now," Margaret brusqued, looking at the old fashioned electric kitchen clock. "If we're to get there in time for the start of visiting hours. You know, Isobel, darling, it might help you if you were to think less of yourself and more of . . ."

"I could hardly think less of myself than you do," Isobel checkmated her mother.

"I haven't the least idea what you mean," was the best that Margaret could do. "The whole world knows how I dote on my children . . . quite silly about you all."

She slammed the door of the Riley more energetically than was good for its fabric. There were times when she suspected, unwillingly, that Isobel was the cleverest of all her children. It was a disorderly circumstance and no good could come of it. Therefore, it could not be true.

*   *   *

It was on the third day since Isobel's return to Devon that she was finally alone with her father.

Margaret was waiting among the packing cases at the semi-detached clergy retirement bungalow on the outskirts of Plymouth for Rupert's hoped for arrival. It was difficult for him to get away in the middle of a shoot. Simon, they knew, had flown into Stansted that morning, piloting a transport. He had got compassionate leave to hire a car and drive down. Their mother was busy with bedding and stocking the larder.

How they were all to fit into that pint sized house, Margaret Jefferson didn't know. She had said so a dozen times since breakfast. Did Isobel think that Rupert would like to take his presentation oars, the ones he got for being skipper of the Cherwell School Eight, back to Los Angeles with him? Isobel said she supposed he might, which scratched Margaret's pride in her eldest son's list of achievements. Isobel, she said, took so little interest in family things. She was totally self-regarding. That was her trouble.

Isobel was glad to get out of the house.

Canon Laurence Jefferson lay in a side ward at the North Devon Infirmary. There was little now that could be done for him. The

80

cancer, whose presence he had intuited many months since, had invaded the whole of his system. It would only be a matter of days.

A nurse withdrew a needle from the Canon's wasted arm as Isobel approached the bedside. Her rose coloured wool velour suit felt all wrong in this place which smelled of faeces and fleshly corruption, bravely combated by Spring Bouquet air freshener. She mustn't notice the smell.

"You look nice in that." Her father's smile was ghastly in his waxen face. Looking down at him, Isobel saw his handsome features destroyed with pain and the eyes more sunken and flat than when last she had seen him, a matter of hours since. They hadn't talked then. They would have had nothing to say because her mother had been there to somehow discourage conversation between them.

"Thank you. Does it help? The injections, I mean."

"No," Laurence rasped. "Call the nurse back. I can't bloody well talk at this angle . . ."

The nurse helped Isobel to adjust her father's backrest and shift him. His body felt both liquid and brittle under the flannel pyjamas. Biting her lip, Isobel fought against any show of revulsion. But he was querulous and cried out at the pressure on his skin. Tears darted into Isobel's eyes. To inflict pain was terrible. Couldn't they do any better than this?

"Only at the cost of deadening my brain," Laurence Jefferson said. His voice rustled drily, autumn leaves swept by a brush. "I can't have that. I must have my mind. We have to go on to the end with whatever is left . . . Don't we?" he demanded after a pause.

Nina Fischer's mother had had no choice but to go on to the end with her mind cruelly intact. That blown kiss to her daughter . . . Isobel deliberately scrambled her detestable thoughts.

"I can't say, Daddy. I haven't got anywhere near the end yet. I'll be able to take a view when I have."

Two rings of fire encircled the shineless pupils of Laurence's eyes. A dull glow of coke rimming iron stove doors.

"You're a clear headed girl, Isobel. I'll give you that." Again, the death's head smile. "You get it from me . . ." There was a gasp and Laurence's lips peeled back from his teeth. Alarmed, Isobel rose to press the bell. Laurence motioned her to be seated again. The spasm had passed.

"Is it hurting?"

"Yes. You're very angry, aren't you Isobel?"

"What about?" Isobel arranged her features into a look of innocent surprise. Whatever it was her father had finally noticed, it

81

was far too late to talk of it now. Her life was no longer here, she realised. It lay in Milan. Everything else had fallen apart months ago.

"Getting the rough end of the stick . . ."

Hurriedly, Isobel began to talk across her father, frantically parroting all the things she had been repeatedly told and tried so hard to believe.

"I had the best childhood anyone could have . . . You didn't make me go away like the boys. The loveliest place . . . all that peace and security . . . The space . . ."

Canon Jefferson shifted slightly, impatiently. He had heard all this before from his wife. To hear the old pot-pourri of lies from Isobel's lips was torment. Death was an unflattering mirror.

It had been sending Rupert to that ruinously expensive film-directing school in Hollywood that had drained them of any resources to provide for Isobel's future. But Margaret had insisted. It was what the boy had wanted to do. He would have been bored to death, his mother said, if he'd had to read English Literature at the perfectly estimable red-brick university where he'd got in. Rupert had a horror of boredom. Simon, bless him, was a plodder. Excellent science A-level results. So good, in fact, that BEA had paid most of his flying-school fees and given him a tenderfoot job with a wholly owned subsidiary at the end of it.

Isobel? Well, she was really still only a little girl, her mother had said. There would be plenty of time to think of her later. It wasn't as though she was more than averagely intelligent. It suited Margaret's book to think that. The money had been hers. Laurence had been left with no alternative but to give in. A sense of shame at having abandoned Isobel had caused her father to look away from her. She was her mother's concern. Meeting his own eyes for the first time in connection with this cowardly sin of omission, Laurence Jefferson was appalled. He had left it too late to hold out a hand to his daughter.

He fell asleep then, as he did with increasing frequency. His head lolled horribly on the pillow and Isobel rang for the nurse. She couldn't sit and look at him like that till her mother came at lunchtime. In twenty minutes or so, Laurence was awake again.

"What will you do?" He looked straight at Isobel.

"Me? I'm going to marry an Italian. Furio Bonetti. He lives in Milan." The decision had been so simply made. She had found in Italy another home, another life. The only one left. Not to take it would be completely perverse.

"Do you love him?" At that moment the ward sister came in with a covered bowl full of broth.

"Would you like to give this to the Canon?" Her voice was reverential.

Isobel screwed her face up and Laurence turned his head away listlessly with a faraway look.

"I'll leave it then, Miss Jefferson," the bowl was deposited on the locker. "Perhaps he'll feel like it later."

"That's another one you've got fooled," Isobel said, cynically.

Turning his head back towards her with surprising energy, Laurence cackled. "She thinks I'm a saint, poor woman. There's a bottle of plonk claret in that cupboard. Let's have some. It all goes straight through me, you know. I don't know why they insist on this nourishment pantomime. I've a better chance of getting drunk than well fed."

Isobel and her father drank and talked. She had never had so much of his attention before. He slept intermittently, resuming their former topic as soon as he woke. His was a disciplined mind.

To Isobel's relief, the question as to whether or not she loved Furio was not raised again. She thought she did. She hadn't seen him since their quarrel. His proposal had soothed maiden pride . . . and there it had rested. Unfinished business. There were still unfathomable depths and far reaching distances to explore. It would be a jump in the dark. An adventure.

"Will they expect you to change your religion?" Laurence asked.

Isobel shrugged. "I don't know. If they do, it won't really matter to you . . . professionally, I mean . . ."

"Because I'll be dead," Laurence finished for her cheerfully. "I must say it's a pleasure to talk to someone with a grasp of realities. You must be prepared for your mother to make a bit of a fuss. She'll say you've betrayed my life's work . . ."

"Do you think so?"

"No, of course not," Laurence's laugh was no more than a rattle of stones in his throat.

"Then why . . . ?"

"Your mother, God bless her, has a mind that can contain only one idea at a time."

There was some more discussion about Furio's wealth. That also was likely to give rise to objections, Canon Jefferson said. Isobel's mother had a suspicion of riches not garnered so long ago that their disreputable source had been muffled by time. Agricultural rents were one thing, profits quite another. Tainted with utilitarian acumen. Rupert, of course, was in *art*, a divine pursuit which excused his superabundance of dollars.

"What about Simon?"

"Ah, our middle one," Canon Jefferson emitted something

approaching a chuckle, "God help him if he ever earns more than Rupert. Your mother's unforgiving about things which undermine her order of preference . . ."

Seeing the look on his daughter's face, Laurence stopped. Isobel, he knew, had followed the logic. Her mother would object if she married into wealth because she ought to have less than the others.

"Sorry, old thing," he said. "You get a bit trigger happy when you're dying, you know."

"It's all right Daddy," she said. "I've always known. It's just that I didn't realise you did. Never mind, Simon and I had each other. There's a big gap between runners up and the winner."

Isobel had to go out of the room then. Something extreme had happened under the bedclothes. Laurence's eyes sharpened with anger and misery. They came and did whatever had to be done while Isobel waited outside in the corridor. At length she was sent back in to him at his own request. Rest, said the ward sister, was meaningless in the face of Death. She actually said it with a capital letter, exaltation written all over her face. Isobel laughed. "Nerves," said the sister.

"She, your mother, will be counting on you to stay with her after the funeral . . ." Laurence carried on, ignoring the interruption.

"All right. But she won't really want me. It'll just be for the look of the thing . . . Because I'm the girl. Why couldn't one of the boys stay? I suppose, because of their careers . . ."

"Any excuse. But your mother won't give them an opportunity to reveal themselves," Laurence said painfully. "You go and do what you have to, darling. There's nothing for you here. Have a good life. Tell you what, I'll take the steam out of your mother for you. Leave it to me."

Isobel was spared from responding to this belated concern for her welfare by the arrival of her mother with Simon. He was dapper in his navy blue, double breasted suit with the brass buttons, a white cap under his arm.

"Blimey, Iz, I wouldn't have known it was you," he said hugging her. "How come you got your hands on a million dollars? Rich wop boyfriend?"

After Isobel was excused to go home and return in the evening, Canon Jefferson used his remaining few ounces of strength to tell his wife that Isobel had indeed got a rich wop boyfriend. One she was going to marry. One whose father, moreover, had made his money putting up slum property in city suburbs all over Italy. Roman Catholic? Of course he was. Did that affect Isobel? Of course it did. Considering her background, he added slyly, his daughter had taken a most original line. It had been quite a shock to what was left of his system.

"I knew she'd make trouble . . ." Margaret said grindingly. "She can never resist drawing attention to herself. How could she do this to you . . . after the upbringing we gave her?"

"Well, well," Laurence bit the inside of his cheeks carefully, to prevent the giveaway smile that was forming. "At least she plans to be present at my forthcoming obsequies. I must say, I'll be flattered if Rupert deigns to adorn that occasion. The expense of his elaborate education appears to have put him outside my reach."

Laurence Jefferson died on that acid-drop utterance, in the irresponsible belief that his daughter would know how to manage the consequences. He had, he felt, in some small degree atoned for his neglect. Redressed the balance. Avenged her. As the sport of trouble-making went, he'd never relished a bout so much.

Margaret howled aloud when she understood that her husband was gone. Her words were whirling and wild. This was not the sanctified death-bed scene she'd imagined. No soft falling tears, no holy oils, no blessed mutterings. No final, priestly benediction of dutiful sons. By what devilish cabal had Isobel stolen the blessings which belonged to Rupert, their firstborn, and Simon?

Numbly, Simon attempted to close his father's eyes. Much easier done in the movies, he discovered, than in the real situation. The dead eyes mocked on, refusing to shut.

There would be a stiffish reckoning to come, Simon foresaw with foreboding. Old Iz had created a hell of a shindig.

*   *   *

The shindig was of seismic proportions.

Rupert arrived in an aura of open air glamour. His Levis were teamed with a lemon suede windcheater which toned with his wheaten, sun bleached, hair. He kept tossing it back from his forehead while he listened to the plaints about Isobel interweaving his mother's tearless, racking lament for her husband.

"Bloody hell," he sighed occasionally, *sotto voce* to Simon. Iz had always been making some kind of rumpus at school, but at home, she'd kept pretty quiet . . . as far as he could remember. So Iz was planning on shacking up with a racketeer and going in for the other kind of jujitsu. It was all pretty hard on Ma.

Teeth gritted, Isobel washed up teacups in the Formica slit called the kitchen. So much for Daddy's idea of reducing the head of steam in her mother. Thank you for nothing.

"You mustn't blame yourself, darling Rupert," Margaret

grizzled. "The only reason Daddy died before you could get here is your sister's obscene revelations. So selfish. He died of the shock, you see . . ."

Dashing a cup to the floor, Isobel burst, blazing, from the kitchen.

"You *wicked*, stupid woman! Daddy died of the cancer . . . which might have been helped if you hadn't pretended it was rheumatism . . . You'd do anything not to admit that the world isn't perfect . . . If you've got to blame anyone, blame yourself . . ."

"Oh, I say, Iz. Steady on . . ."

"Shut up, Simon. I'm talking to Mummy. Let her *listen* for once."

There was much more in that vein. Rupert regarded his sister and mother in turn as if he followed the path of a tennis ball. Simon sat hunched and dejected, wishing his older brother would do something.

Next, Isobel turned on her brother. It was Rupert who was selfish. Selfish and spoiled. He should have left California earlier. Did he expect Daddy to hang on to fit into his blasted shooting schedule? Yes, of course he did. Because the Plymstead Magna Parsonage had always had to fit in with *him*. It was because of Rupert and his arrogant assurance that nothing was too much or too good for him that she had been left to submit to the cruelty of madmen and strangers, had been rescued, thank God, at the whim of yet more strangers and now lived on their charity. That was the truth. One that none of them wanted to face.

"You forget yourself, Isobel," Margaret screeched. "Rupert's talent entitles him to special advantages . . ."

"Rupert's talent? It's of a fairly low order, isn't it? Who couldn't gratify their imagination with a sack of other people's gold to buy actors, writers, musicians . . . everyone, in fact, who does have some measurable talent? Any fool can look through a camera."

"That's about the size of it, Iz," Rupert acknowledged handsomely, pushing his mother's clutching hand from his arm.

"And as for this idea of Mother's that I should sleep on the sofa tonight while Rupert sleeps in the bed I was graciously permitted the use of last night, the answer is bloody well no! You sleep on the sofa, or go to the Royal Hotel which you can afford and I can't. Unto him that hath shall be given . . . Well, not this time. Forget it!"

Hysterical, Margaret hung on her son's neck. He was not to listen, he was not to leave them. She needed him near her. Rupert disengaged himself gently. It took patience. His mother's arms kept coming back, flexing with octopus-like determination to imprison. Eventually, it struck Simon to replace his brother as target for these demonstrations. He held Margaret in a vice like grip until the desert-dry sobs died away and she grew still.

"Pretty hip, this sister of ours," Rupert wound up the scene with a dazzling, toothpasty grin. Iz could have the bed and he would take them all out to dinner. They ought to try and recover their collective cool. Dad's last big show was awaiting direction. Rupert embraced his mother and sister. One to each arm. Both avoided the eyes of the other.

"Get it together, you two. Let's have the old happy family scenario."

"Can't be shouting the odds over Dad's coffin," Simon encouraged with muted humour, earning a smile from Isobel. "Where are we planting him, Ma?"

Order was restored. But within the bereaved group, there occurred a subtle shift of loyalties. Isobel's eldest brother had been surprised and not a little impressed by the fork lightning she'd unleashed. There was something in what she said. Things *had* been unfair. In spite of it all, Isobel had turned into one hell of a firecracker. She'd go down a bomb in L.A. Better still in Athens, Simon supported.

"A high-stepping lady, is my sister," Rupert said as he took her arm to walk through the foyer of the Royal Hotel. "Isn't she, Ma?" he threw over his shoulder.

Margaret Jefferson was afraid. Isobel might or might not have taken her husband from her prematurely. Now she seemed to have the power to deprive her of her sons' undivided attention. Even Rupert's. She had never believed she would ever be jealous of Isobel. This was a new sensation which could not be named.

Isobel spent that night in the room she had occupied on the previous one. She was restless, too much so to sleep. Her thoughts were full of her mother, wakeful too, on the other side of the plasterboard partition.

Had Nina Fischer loved her mother? Or been loved by her? It had all ended when she was too young for complications to have arisen. Isobel's eyes rested on an Edwardian, sentimental religious oleograph which had hung in her room at the Parsonage. It depicted a blond, bearded Jesus with his arms around a group of noble, fair haired children. The boys in suits of shining armour and a girl in a trailing white nightgown. Repulsively smug, they looked now. Isobel had always thought of those children as herself, Rupert and Simon.

There they were, snuggling up to the King of the Jews. She would like to have smashed the glass and torn it to pieces on Nina's behalf. Oh why wouldn't she and her disgusting story go *away*?

Isobel's fingers itched for a thin stick of charcoal. But to redraw her life as a pattern of chaos would take for ever and she didn't have the skill. She would have to find some simpler representative image.

* * *

The late vicar of Plymstead Magna was entombed beneath the aisle of his own parish church, the last incumbent to enjoy the honour. His more orthodox successor, charmingly briefed by Rupert, left his predecessor nothing to wish for in the way of censer-swinging and purple-coped gloom. The *De profundis* swelled and boomed and there was enough Latin about to tax Caesar Augustus.

After a post-interment gathering, held by embittering permission of the new vicar's wife on the parsonage lawns, there was nothing left to detain the Jefferson children.

While their mother received the condolences of the last, tea drinking mourners, they wandered by the willow fringed stream, in orchard, gardens and stables. Remembering the good times and the bad. There was the old mounting block where Isobel had been made to pretend to be Anne Boleyn while Rupert played Henry VIII and Simon was executioner with a toy wooden sword. Her brothers' retrospective enthusiasm for that old bit of play-acting sickened Isobel.

"*Shut up! Shut up, both of you!* I can't bear it. It wasn't funny then and it isn't funny now. I never wanted to do it and I wished I hadn't ... *Vile, horrible, filthy* ..."

Astonished, Simon and Rupert stared at their sister. She stood in the middle of the old cobbled yard, shaking uncontrollably with her hands to her ears. Was this some kind of fit?

"Come on, Iz," Simon put his arms around her. "What's the matter, old thing?"

Rupert joined his brother in attempting to console his sister, to protect her from whatever inner eclipse overwhelmed her. They had never seen her like this before. She had been as happy as they in their distant nursery days, to join in ghoulish tableaux and dramas.

"I'm cold," Isobel went on shivering although the temperature was above normal for the time of year.

"Here, take this," Rupert stripped off his jacket.

"No, just hold me ... Don't let me go ..."

Margaret Jefferson rounded the stableyard corner to find both her sons wrapped tight round her daughter. The sight plunged a spear of envy deep into her heart. Here was more of Isobel's insatiable greed for attention.

The leave-takings were strained, controlled on every side by a fear of further dissension. The events of the last few days had been lascerating. Not one of the Jeffersons had any appetite for more. Margaret nearly brought herself to be gracious to Isobel.

"You will always have a home with me, you know, if you change your mind about this man. How could you, Isobel? How *could* you? After all your father stood for . . ."

Simon intervened before the conversation got out of hand again. They would have to leave at once if Isobel was to catch tonight's direct flight to Milan. Her mother had rejected her offer to delay her departure until the bungalow was set to rights.

"I know you mean well, dear. But you know how clumsy you are . . ."

Waving from the observation lounge at Heathrow as Isobel mounted the companionway, Rupert and Simon regretted seeing her go. She had grown up out of sight. There were gaps to fill in. Rupert in particular had hardly known her except as a very young child.

"It's a pity Ma kept her down so much. Do you think she'll ever make anything of this art job she used to be keen on?"

"Shouldn't think so, poor love," Rupert replied with a shrug. "No training. Never mind, she's got this Italian guy. Who do you reckon will pay for the wedding? Millionaire bash . . . Bit beyond Ma's touch."

*   *   *

Furio was waiting in the Arrivals concourse at Malpensa.

Isobel felt an uncharted space inside her go suddenly hollow at the sight of him. It made walking more difficult but delicious. Every step towards him a repetition of pleasure. There was no question that she loved him. This was the feeling. It could go on and on, now. And with it, a new and longer lasting security.

"*Furio!*"

He came to her running with his arms outstretched, ablaze with relief and desire.

"Every day," he gabbled in Italian too fast for Isobel's less accustomed ear, "I ring the Viale Regina Giovanna for news of you. When do you return to us? Have you answered my question . . . Do your parents give their permission? Ah, your father is dead . . . last night I heard . . . I am so sorry, *carissima* . . . Was it all very bad with your papa? Will you marry me?"

There was a great deal to say. But most of all, Isobel said yes. Permission? She would get it. Nothing should stand in their way. Did Furio's parents know of their plans? When should she meet

89

with them? In a few days. Isobel and Furio were conscious of nothing around them. They noticed Isobel's old suitcase only when it fell, pushed off the conveyor by others crowding behind.

The sight of it reminded Isobel of her first, lonely arrival in this place. Now, she realised, she was one of those miraculously invulnerable women whom she had tried to draw while she waited for Josef. Her life had changed in six months.

"Wait," Isobel said, darting away from Furio's side. "Just wait a moment."

She approached a sandy haired girl sitting in the very seat where she had sat last November, watching the digital clock.

"Excuse me, but are you English?" Isobel knew very well that she was. The girl confirmed it and volunteered her business in Italy. She had come to be an au pair. Her employer was coming to fetch her.

"This is my name," Isobel took out her diary and tore a page from it, "and my telephone number. And this is exactly what you do to use a public call box . . ." Isobel listed the action in pencil. "If anything is not right, you must call me. Please. You must. You will, won't you? Walk out and call me."

"You know this girl?" Furio asked when Isobel returned to his side.

"Sort of," Isobel said quietly.

Furio had a brand-new Lamborghini waiting outside. A conveyance worthy, he said, of his *fidanzata*. It went like a rocket. Isobel's sensations were of shooting forward into a far better future.

90

SIX

The Bonetti family could not envisage a future for Isobel which included their son. Her acceptance of Furio's unauthorised proposal was neither here nor there. Bare mention of her name triggered a visceral, knee-jerk reaction.

Furio declared his intentions formally at the Villa Rondine, his family's recently acquired northern property which lay on a rise to the east of Gorgonzola village, close to Monza and not far from Milan. His rebellious intransigence on that occasion moved his father to threats.

"Do this thing and you are no longer my son. I shall erase your name from my memory. Not even your mother shall speak it to me again. Your presence affronts me."

So saying, Carlo Bonetti marched from the domed atrium of the house where he had received his son in audience, his wife at his side. Hands clasped over her mouth, Beatrice Bonetti stared at her son with frightened eyes as her husband's retreating footsteps echoed doom in the resonant house.

"Why do you wound us, my son? You are your father's heart and liver . . ."

It was the wrong imagery to use with Furio at that juncture. He could not possibly, he asserted, function in that organic role for anyone but himself. It was, he realised, the sort of thing Isobel herself might have said.

"I will be a son to my father, but no one shall choose my wife. If this is what his love is worth, then let him discard it. It is not for my good or his."

Furio turned on his heel and left the house, descending the twenty-five broad stone steps from the high columned loggia in a series of wrathful bounds. The top was off the Lamborghini and he sprang into it without opening the door, hounded by his mother's wails. Wrenching the car into gear, he spun the wheels on the gravel. The car lurched forward, startling the bell collared cattle grazing the park. Horn blaring, Furio swept past the terrified guard who opened the wrought iron gates with not a second to spare. One or both of them could have been killed.

In *la famiglia* Bonetti there was discord, muttered the old man crossly, brushing the dust from his blue denim overalls. And at dusk, when the maids who lived in the village passed the gate lodge, he would know the meaning of it all. There would be something of moment to report in Gorgonzola's rustic *taverna*. Ill tidings made a man popular, especially if they boded no good to the rich.

By nightfall, Gorgonzola curiosity had fed on the tale. It was carried the short distance to Monza by a youth on a motorbike who lived there. In that more worldly arena the story might have evinced little interest were it not that certain autodrome employees, who drank in the town's lowlier bars, knew Furio well.

It was there that the *fidanzata* who was not welcome at the Villa Rondine di Bonetti was clearly identified with the *amica inglese* who was being taught how to drive in Furio Bonetti's old Lamborghini. So Miss Jefferson was an adventuress, was she? *Allora*, good luck to her, said some. How sex appeal made the way straight, frowned the traditionally minded, for greed and impudence to follow unchecked. A very bad thing.

With emotional momentum like that, the essentials of the Bonetti conflict between father and son travelled the few kilometres into Milan by morning. There, it is true, they had to compete with much else of interest during the day. But in a community of Lombard bankers, atavistically ambulant in their manner of conducting business, a word in passing concerning the private affairs of depositor and borrower was part of the everyday conversational currency in café and street.

Alessandro Montenaro heard it on the forecourt outside the Banco Santo Spirito. He paused as a group passed him and then slowed to form one of those businesslike huddles so familiar on Milanese sidewalks. There chanced a temporary lull in the traffic and the voices were intermittently audible.

If he went through with it, one advised his companions, Furio Bonetti would be cut off. A split in the established, approved line of succession, shrugged another, would certainly give rise to unrest . . . As for her, whoever she really was, what price her friendship with Montenaro's wife then? Furio could take his unpopular bride to America, of course, and perhaps start again. But the unscrupulous Jefferson might well ditch him there for a wealthier man . . . these types were well known . . . their only capital, fine, foreign looks . . . battened on kindness . . . knew they must cash in before . . . Remarkable what a nuisance one unimportant English girl could be . . .

The flow of intelligence to Alessandro's scarce believing ears ceased at the rumbling approach of a tram. It stretched credibility that what he had heard concerned the graciously ingenuous Isobel. And yet it was so.

Interpretation was not far to seek. The disturbance in Carlo Bonetti's family might bring many a house of cards tumbling down. Money, emotion and confidence were linked. And whilst Bonettis were not over extended, they were very well borrowed indeed. In an harmonious atmosphere of stability, an excellent thing – amid internecine strife, a potential threat to interest payment schedules. A serious matter, if it were true.

Alessandro went straight to his office and telephoned his wife. It was a quarter to five in the afternoon.

"Where is Isobel? What is she doing?"

"She and the boys are drawing and painting . . . Marzio has done a pterodactyl . . . Isobel is doing such queer things. She keeps tearing them up . . ."

"Good. Is young Bonetti coming tonight? Because if so, he must dine with us. On no account is Isobel to be seen in public with him until I've had time to talk to them both."

Giulia heard with scorn an outline of what Alessandro feared. Such nonsense. Rumour mongering amongst clerks and counter tellers. Pah!

Alessandro overrode his wife's objections. Large forces were ranged against Isobel's romance with Furio Bonetti. There could be no happiness for either of them in cutting across the grain. So far the engagement had been of short duration, unannounced, unofficial. It ought to be reconsidered. Withdrawal was possible with no loss of face. *Madonna!* The pair had only known each other six weeks. Why all the haste?

"What *is* she drawing, exactly?" Alessandro was curious to know, in spite of immediate anxiety.

"Plaits . . . pigtails," Giulia answered distractedly. "Like the one she had herself . . . Do you remember? It seems so long ago. Piles of the things, cut off and . . ."

"Any good?" Alessandro interrupted.

"She doesn't think so."

*   *   *

Furio and Isobel were immovable.

When Rosaria had removed the cloth and closed the dining room doors, Alessandro, cigar in hand, began his representations. He could not care less about a little flurry in the banking dovecotes, he said. That was nothing to him. Mere straws in the wind. But that Isobel, for whom his affection was deep, should be exposed to

93

publicised rejection by the father of a man to whom she had been introduced under his roof, was an insult not to be borne.

"By whom," Giulia interjected pointedly, pouring the coffee, "Isobel or you?"

"By Isobel, of course," Alessandro defended aggressively. "I have a regard for your father," he turned diplomatically to Furio, "but his attitude places us all in an invidious position . . ."

The arguments went round and around with Alessandro doing most of the talking. In this impasse he saw no possibility of dignity, let alone felicity for either Furio or Isobel. They would find themselves isolated, marginalised, at best squabbled over by factions . . .

"And not for long," Alessandro jabbed his cigar at Furio's chest. "In all Italy, your father's seen as a rising man. If he chooses to forget your name and Isobel shares it, then she will be buried with you."

It was all futile. When two young people of uncommon vitality are bound by physical magnetism, reinforced by interlocking personal agendas, their elders have little hope of prising them apart.

"I have offered myself to you," Furio got up and went to stand behind Isobel's chair, his hands resting on her shoulders, so that his words, although addressed to her were directed to Alessandro and Giulia. "I shall not dishonour my promise or be comforted if you withdraw from yours." His voice shook and Isobel put up her hands to cover his, conducting a current of sympathetic accord.

"There it is," Isobel said quietly. "They can't tell us what to do. Milan is not the only city."

"No, but it is *our* city," Giulia said unexpectedly, examining an empty space six inches above her husband's head. For once she seemed disinclined to tears and in her eye was an alien gleam.

An apprehensive silence followed.

Isobel thought she was right to cleave to the man she loved since he stood by her. It was 1966, after all, not 1366. She had no genuine place of retreat. Nor could she remain for ever with the Montenaros. It was necessary to assert her independent existence by changing her name and condition. It must be now.

Furio's own reflections were not dissimilar. Isobel intoxicated his senses. She was passionate and pure . . . kept so by him. He smelled an Atlantic breeze of freedom in her hair. He would have her. Between himself and his father, it was the single great contest he must win. The ultimate manhood of Furio Bonetti was wrought up in this. Isobel Jefferson was the anvil on which his father's love should be tried. She would prove hardily resistant to the blows. For this, he loved her.

Giulia guessed most of it with a subtle intuition. She was on the side of liberty. Had she not married, herself, for love?

Alessandro thought everyone had missed the point. None of them knew, and he would not tell them, how Isobel herself was reviled in the streets. *Punto morto*. Deadlock.

Intractable as the lovers were, Alessandro obtained one valuable concession from them both. Isobel should take the holiday which was due to her and already long overdue. It would be no bad thing if she were to have some undisturbed time to get over her father's harrowing death. Such things took their toll . . . Distorted judgement. A period of two weeks in Florence, say, would afford an opportunity for maturer consideration of all she and Furio had in hand.

"This is sensible, *carissima*," Giulia added her support briefly. She seemed inattentive.

After that, the *sala da pranzo* was quit in favour of the *salotto* and the talk there was more convivial. There were suggestions as to what Isobel should do and see in Florence. What *pensione* as compared with which hotel. Furio said he would drive Isobel down. No, said Alessandro and Giulia with equal emphasis. A deal was a deal. Furio grinned and said it had been worth a try.

Isobel kissed him goodnight in the lobby. She was allowed a moment alone with him there. It was Alessandro who went down in the lift with Furio and unlocked the street door since the *portinaio* had already retired.

"If neither of you will shift, then your father must. Rest quiet, my friend, and let me see what can be done. Some mediation . . . some form of compromise . . ."

"Sir," Furio answered in English, "what compromise? One is either married or not."

More Jefferson phraseology, Alessandro thought to himself, re-entering the lift. The surest sign that Isobel had got under somebody's skin. What next?

The question, rhetorical in origin, recurred in Alessandro's mind when he found his wife, already in bed, wearing a look of guileful content beneath the vast modernistic crucifix which had supervised all the blameless embraces of a thirteen-year marriage.

"So?" he prompted slipping in beside her after disrobing in his dressing room.

Giulia kissed her husband smartly. She was tired and wanted to think. Which was very unlike her, Alessandro mused tolerantly, as he got out of bed again to open the casements and lock the shutters. The first hot nights had begun.

A shine on the pavement below suggested that Isobel's light was

95

still on. She was the only person, Alessandro realised, who had ever reminded him exactly what it was like to be young. To be a powerful, innocent predator, ready to thwart any will but its own. She knew nothing of what she did beyond her absolute right to do it. Would she . . . could she, bring down the house of Bonetti? And to whose benefit if she did?

The subject of these meditations was sitting up in bed, drawing. More plaits and pigtails. So far they looked fatuous in Isobel's opinion. She would go on until they looked sinister. It was something she had to get out of herself.

*   *   *

Isobel had already been some days in Florence and the usual optical biliousness had set in when it was dissolved by the sight of Cellini's Perseus holding the Medusa's severed head aloft. All her perceptions, blunted by a surfeit of artistic excellence, were sharpened again.

She stepped forward to touch the bronze, weathered to a luminous malachite green. How did these people do it? Make something so brutal not only bearable but beautiful . . . Was it the size? Perseus' stature was less than her own . . .

"You got taste," a gravelly voice, male and American, made her jump. "That's my number one favourite, too."

"It oughtn't to be, though, ought it?" Isobel responded, momentarily dazzled as she spun around to face into the sun flooded square.

The owner of the voice proved to be a short, broad shouldered man with battered but regular features, thick dark hair and a pair of intelligent currants for eyes. He had a Panama hat on his head like her father had worn for cricket. Blue blazer, open necked shirt, white trousers and tennis shoes. He was encumbered with cameras and guidebooks. She took this all in at a glance.

"I mean," she continued earnestly, "we ought not to like anything so callous . . . so abominably cruel. That's the worst thing any human being can do to another . . ."

"I guess the Medusa's not human," the man said, taking half a pace back, startled to have his casual remark taken up so completely. Isobel had drawn his eye from the other end of the arcaded piazza wall where he had been on the edge of a group listening to a scholarly guide. He had detached himself and ambled across for the pleasure of looking closer at a specimen of living, breathing sculpture for a change. She was imposing.

"Oh yes she is," Isobel continued. "Perfectly human. You can see quite clearly that someone modelled for that head. The sculptor

96

didn't get it from nowhere. She shouldn't have done it . . ."

It went on from there. Ed Mazzerella, for that was his name walked several times round the Signoria square with Isobel, disputing, explaining, agreeing and laughing.

"You want lunch?" he said finally when most of the knots of tourists seemed to have melted away. "Some place down by the river? Might catch something at the Principe . . ."

"Isn't that frightfully expensive?" Isobel asked. "I thought it was an hotel . . ."

"Dead right. I'm staying there. C'mon, my treat."

They were lucky and got a table outside, overlooking the leisurely, mud-coloured Arno.

"Great," Ed seized the wine list as soon as their menu was decided. "Now, tell me about yourself. From the beginning . . ."

"What, no skipping?"

"Not a damn thing," the American encouraged, giving his order for a bottle of Nippozano with something *frizzante* to keep them busy till it came. He was, Isobel noticed, a generous host. Was this really all right?

None the less Isobel recounted her life history from shortly after birth to the present moment, leaving out the Fischer affair and glossing over her father's death and its aftermath. A person who was paying for such a lunch as this ought not to be distressed or disgusted. She painted an hilarious portrait of English clerical life, to the amusement of nearby English-speaking lunchers. Ed, however, was intent, unable to distinguish between the fanciful and the factual. Meanwhile, the Arno slugged by.

"Your turn," Isobel concluded her narrative laying her knife and fork together beside a well picked rib of wild boar.

"Well, ma'am, you've left me with the *dolce* and cheese to give you the count-down on forty one years. It's kinda rough, don't you think? Say, if you promise to put in the rest of the day with me, I'll try and give value for money."

So toiling up the steep hill on the Oltrarno side, Ed Mazzerella explained his name, the Italian origins of his family who were sailor folk from Genoa, and their subsequent emigration and natural gravitation towards the US Navy. His was the second generation to attain officer rank and he was now Naval Attaché at his country's embassy in Rome. Isobel was impressed.

"Don't be. I got the job because I speak Italian and my big brother kicked some ass in the right department. He's a pretty big noise in the Pentagon. Also, I got contacts in the Vatican . . . My other brother's a career priest. They just made the smarmy son-of-a-bitch a Monsignor. Kinda guy who keeps his nose clean."

From time to time they stopped to examine the life-size Stations of the Cross they were passing, reminded by Ed to do so. Tourism was responsible work for the tourist.

"You spend your dollars, sweetheart . . . you make sure you take a hold of the goods. My God, I'm glad I'm not dragging a cross."

Ed referred here to the heat beating out of the surrounding stones, but Isobel commented on the kindness of Italian artists. How tenderly they protected the human body. The most appalling events were rendered harmless by them. As if they rectified the atrocities of history, made less painful the wounds and anaesthetised the agonies.

"Do you think it's so *we* shouldn't suffer . . . or a sort of way of trying to make it less bad for them . . . even though it's too late?"

Ed didn't know. That was too deep for him. He had majored in maths, not fine art.

At the end of the day, after eating, or rather leaving a mountain of pasta in the rowdy working man's café where Isobel insisted on paying the bill, Ed walked her back to her little hotel near the Ponte alle Grazie.

"Won't you come in for a drink? The bar stays open quite late . . . we could sit outside if you don't think it's too cool now."

"Say, better not," Ed demurred. "We don't know what spies your big-time boyfriend has gotten posted."

Open mouthed for a moment, Isobel quickly recovered herself. Commander Mazzerella was quite presentable in his decayed, middle aged way. But he was roughly the same age as Alessandro . . . and very optimistic if he thought for one single moment that she could think of him in *that* way.

"If anyone's doing some spying," she replied, "it's much more likely to be Furio's father than him . . ."

"Well, if what you tell me is true, that old gangster might have done just that. I don't want to louse anything up for you, sweetheart. That's if you really wanna go through with this thing . . ."

"Why not? I'm marrying Furio not Carlo and Beatrice Bonetti."

"Guess you're right. Well, I'll take myself off. May I call for you tomorrow?"

Isobel could see no reason why not. She felt comfortable in Ed Mazzerella's company.

After that every day began the same way. Isobel was woken by the sun stencilling tiger stripes through the louvred shutters on her room's dark oaken floor. Leaning her elbows on the tiny, wrought iron balcony, she greeted the city's innumerable, upturned terracotta breasts, nippled with crosses and bare to the sky. Outside the room, in the tiled corridor itself, was a cranky iron showerhead, curtained hopefully by a sleazy sheet of plastic. It didn't matter, the other rooms on this top floor contained only lumber.

By the time she returned from the shower, wrapped in the tuftless cotton bathtowel, Ed would be seated on the terrace far below, reading Italian newspapers or the day-old *Washington Post*. At Isobel's signal, the strident, two-finger whistle which the school nuns had deplored, he ordered American coffee, bread and *succo di arancia* for them both. Ed could live without a lot of things, he said, but not orange juice.

There was too much to see in Florence, but Isobel and her new American friend filed past it, through it, over it and under it, taking the occasional thing in. For the most part they were occupied in talking about themselves.

"Passive absorption, sweetheart," Ed consoled when Isobel apologised for wasting the Uffizi Tintorettos on a critique of the new Lamborghini series. Ed was interested in cars. In fact, he was looking round for one of that particular marque to buy second-hand and do up.

"Well, why don't you have Furio's old one? The one he's teaching me on. When I pass my test, you can have it," Isobel's face lighted up. "I'm sure he won't cheat you. He's too rich to need to," she added with matter-of-fact satisfaction.

"Say, do you mean it?"

"Well, let's ask him. We can telephone from your hotel can't we?"

They had taken to lunching at the Principe as a matter of course. That way it went on Ed's bill as breakfast went on Isobel's which satisfied her sense of proportionate fair play.

Furio was telephoned at his office on Ed's behalf by Isobel, which was really against the rules of Alessandro's moratorium. Yes, the old car was up for grabs when Isobel had finished with it. Her friend could have first refusal. Just who was this *tizio* anyway, he sniped jealously.

"You should see him, *caro*," Isobel ended her description gaily. "The nicest chap, but honestly, he's old enough to be your father and mine put together."

Furio was mollified. He loved her and missed her. On enquiry as to how things were with him, he said they were all right, or would be. Was Alessandro making any headway with Carlo, Isobel pressed. The absolute opposite, Furio replied grimly. She was not to worry. He would never let her go.

Isobel was not worried. When she rejoined Ed at their regular table he was idly sketching the *palazzos* on the other side of the Arno. Another mutual interest was discovered. He showed her other pages in the sketchbook. Venetian scenes, taken from camera shots when he had been there on his last local leave.

"Whole place is sinking into the mud. You read the headlines today? Floods. They got turds coming right in by their front doors."

Fascinated, Isobel took the sketchbook from his hand. Ed's work had an exquisite, chocolate box prettiness. It was not her style, but the appeal of the drawings was undeniable. The technique had a sureness of touch which nothing she'd ever done could approach.

About her own work, Isobel was deprecating. The only thing she was proud of, or had been, had met with an accident. Funnily enough, it had been a kind of portrait of some of his country-women.

"More of your pick-ups, honey?"

"Mmm. I seem to do good with Americans," she smiled, mimicking one of Ed's quainter grammatical constructions.

For Isobel, it was the last day but one. She was both glad and sorry. Ed had made her separation from Furio far less irksome than it might have been. But her life's real urgencies lay elsewhere. Until she had a husband, she could not afford friends, not permanent ones.

But in that direction Ed showed some determination. He told her for one thing, that he was tired of the Navy, had no ties, being separated from his wife with no kids, and intended to get some other strings pulled to take early retirement. He'd take his pension and a bit of family money to set up an antique shop somewhere hilly and quiet. A farmhouse in its own juice, a couple of fields and what he could make from rooking the odd tourist would do him just fine.

"So what do you say, sweetheart? Shall you and me keep in touch?"

"Why not?" Isobel responded warmly. "It looks as though Furio and I will need all the friends we can get."

Ed was silent for a moment. Bonetti was a name they couldn't help knowing at the Embassy. It was plastered all over the outskirts of Rome. Isobel was getting in deep with a scary big league. He hoped she could handle it and he very much wished that he had met her before this Furio guy.

"When's all this going to happen?" Isobel queried later that day. "You retiring and buying a farmhouse . . ."

"Not for months, sweetheart. The Navy doesn't let you off the hook that easily. There'll be a whole crock full of administrative chicken shit to trawl through. Meantime, you can get me at the Embassy pretending to advise H.E. about the Italian bumboat outfit. You seen those cute hats they have . . . with the pom poms?

They're the best bit of tackle they got. Charm a Russkie sub right out of the ocean."

They were standing in front of the Ghirlandaio *Way to the Cross*. Ed shone a torch on it, the one he kept, as he said, for beating basilicas at their own gloomy game. Isobel saw a procession of glorious women, sumptuously gowned. The overall impression was of a paradisiacal pink. A glow of well-being.

"Rose madder, I betcher," Ed commented knowledgeably on the pigment. "Can't get the good stuff now . . ."

He turned, expecting Isobel's agreement and found she had left him. Alarmed by her desertion and not a little hurt, he searched the church for her frantically. Eventually, he spotted her through the western doors, standing alone in the piazza, her shadow a black pool at her feet in the noonday sun.

"Hey honey, you should have told me you were bored . . ."

"Where did those women think they were going?" Isobel demanded unreasonably.

"The title says . . ."

"I know what the title says," Isobel snapped. "Oh, Ed. I'm so sorry but it reminded me of something. No," she shrugged off his steadying hand on her arm, "I can't talk about it. But please believe me, I'm not bored and it has nothing to do with you."

"Say, sweetheart," Ed cajoled her. "What say we give art the bum's rush? Let's tuck in and shop for the rest of your trip."

Art, Ed was beginning to think, was far too dangerous. Isobel's response to it was intense and unpredictable. And her friendship was far too important to risk.

They spent the rest of the day admiring jewelled trinkets on the Ponte Vecchio and trying on Ferragamo shoes. Isobel bought a pair for her wedding, reluctantly accepting the American's offer to pay as some kind of cockeyed restitution for her earlier rudeness.

With shoes and jewels, Isobel just about managed to shoulder aside the memory of that other, more recent procession in a Polish concentration camp. There had been no velvets there and no pearls. Nor had the end been in any sense triumphant.

Before dinner, Ed checked up on Isobel's train times. Tomorrow was the very last day and he didn't want to waste any of it on tedious detail.

*   *   *

The last day of Isobel's Florentine sojourn was also the last day of Giulia's campaign. Awaiting the final results she expected at least partial gratification.

It had occurred to her fairly swiftly, that if Carlo's rumoured

101

objection to Isobel could unsettle the financial underwriters of Bonetti Construction, *her* friends' counter-objection could precipitate an even greater crisis in the magnate's affairs. By means of anonymous, decisive action, a change of heart should be forced on the father of Furio.

Blackmail – *ricatto* – Giulia told herself, was not a nice word. Not one that would be used by any gently reared Italian and certainly by none of her friends. It was to them that she went. The *bella figura* of Isobel was at stake, as indeed, was that of herself. They could not be seen to lose any ground to a ruffian like Carlo Bonetti.

At every one of the expensive addresses which Isobel had visited both with Giulia and alone, the widows and ladies of independent substance who lived with their husbands, agreed absolutely. For one thing, it was all so romantic. What could they do to assist the young couple?

Giulia expounded her proposed tactics in detail. They had enormous appeal. Power wielded behind the veil, so to speak, was both feminine and effective.

In *palazzo* and penthouse, precious old decanters containing spirituous fluids were produced. Maids were instructed to close *salotto* doors firmly and repulse every caller with the news that this Contessa or that *egregia* Signora was not at home. Eavesdroppers? A ubiquitous pest. No matter what the heat, let the casements be closed.

To begin with, secondary leverage was to be operated in order to discover every bank and financial institution that supported Bonetti enterprises nationwide. Husbands, brothers, nephews and lovers could easily be tripped into careless admissions. The Contessa who had first shown Isobel Furio's photograph offered her apartment as clearing-house for information. She felt in some degree responsible, she said. She had failed to put dear Isobel sufficiently on her guard.

Within a few days a list was finalised. The ladies foregathered to inspect it. Between them they had significant funds invested in each and every one of these banks. Immediate, wholesale withdrawals were put in hand. The reasons given to discomfited deposit managers were bald and simplistic. Such and such a rival institution was offering a better return by up to 0.05 per cent. On a fixed income, cooed each lady in turn, these trifles made a difference. No, no. A rearrangement would not be necessary. The *eccellenzas* had made up their minds. Some fancied a flutter on the London Stock Exchange . . . it looked exciting at the moment, didn't it?

The conspirators didn't delude themselves or each other that the sums they controlled, although large, were threatening by Milanese standards. What they did was to suggest the start of an investment slide in a market that was already restive.

The credit rein on substantial borrowers, particularly Bonettis, was prudently tightened by lenders. If there was to be a shortage of funds, reasoned the bankers, there must also be a corresponding reduction in facilities. One small independent bank called in its entire loan to Bonettis a month early – a result better than Giulia or any of her cohorts could have hoped for.

Interest rates went up by just short of one per cent. A phenomenal and unjustified rise revealing jitters in high places. There was no real panic, just gloomy talk at Savini's and in Alessandro's club of a probable slowdown. Construction would be the first industry to suffer . . . Perhaps the good times were already over.

It remained only for Giulia to send her card to the Villa Rondine, addressed to Beatrice Bonetti. She was invited to take some light afternoon refreshment at the Montenaro apartment. Giulia couched her invitation in the most flattering and intimate terms. Poor Beatrice Bonetti was lonely, she calculated, stuck out there at that villa. Nor had she yet gained any acceptance among the desirable Milanese circles to which Giulia held the key.

Beatrice came to drink tea. It was then very delicately made plain to her that the continued prosperity of her own husband and Giulia's largely depended on her influence with Carlo over the question of her son's marriage to Isobel. Giulia calmly presented a plate of delectable pastries.

Beatrice's small, plump, red taloned hand was arrested in mid-air. Her black eyebrows shot into the helmet of hair. She did not understand. Carlo never made her privy to any of his business.

Giulia obliged by making Beatrice privy to quite a lot of it, for which the southern bred woman was grateful. It made a change from grandchildren's nappies and novenas.

"You don't mean . . . Oh, *Principessa* . . ."

"Isobel has the soul of a lioness," Giulia drove home her point. "She has a great many friends . . . of considerable influence. Believe me, my dear, this is only the beginning. More tea?"

Beatrice goggled.

"She does love your son so," Giulia kept up the pressure. "So do we all . . . such a tragedy if your family were to be irreparably split . . . and the damage to your business . . . But I suppose there's nothing you can do. If Signor Bonetti were to suspect for a moment that Isobel was in any way behind this . . ."

Carlo's wife flumped to her feet, maternal curves aquiver with purpose.

103

"My Carlo's a faithful husband, *Principessa*. Attentive, you understand. I have my ways."

Before Beatrice went about her mission, however, Giulia had no difficulty in persuading her to join in a ritualistic session of weeping to ratify the treaty. Isobel, they agreed, with that vigorous body and staunch personality, would make a worthy dam for any future Bonettis. Church? Pah! That could be fixed.

That same night Beatrice's voice nearly blew off the dome at the Villa Rondine. Denied the comfort of his wife's luxuriant bosom, the hardest man in the concrete *affare* started to waver.

On the day of Isobel's return to Milan, Carlo gave his qualified, ungracious consent with conditions. The day after that, private funds began to flow inscrutably back into the targeted banks. The Bonetti line of credit was loosened.

Alessandro was mystified for Bonetti had refused any parley with him. The victorious Milanese ladies smiled behind their blue painted shutters and said never a word. This was a charitable exercise which had proved modestly profitable, too.

Thus Isobel got what she wanted without lifting a finger. The wanting itself had been strong enough. She took it as proof that every other thing . . . skill and fame included, would come the same way.

SEVEN

Carlo Bonetti's surly provisos were submitted in more or less civil form thanks to the competent editing of his personal assistant. Five pages of double-spaced typing, addressed to Alessandro as Isobel's ostensible agent in the settling of terms.

"Pah!" Alessandro slapped the pages with the back of his hand. "He postures a good deal for a man with a sword at his throat."

To put an end to speculation, blustered the defeated colossus, the marriage of Furio and Isobel must be notified to the usual newspapers and take place within two months. It must, moreover, be celebrated in a manner becoming the Bonetti position.

"Position?" Giulia yelped. "What position, does he suppose, is that?"

"He supposes," Alessandro replied evenly, "that he's in a position, or soon will be, to buy any position he fancies. He wishes us to invite people to Isobel's wedding reception who have positions to sell. A parade of political whores. This is the dowry he demands with Isobel. You and I are to provide it. Let us be thankful it's no worse than that. For a day we are surrogate parents to the bride and procurer to her new father-in-law. I propose," Alessandro concluded serenely, "to enjoy the whole thing – more especially so since he's paying for it. The budget is open ended. Let us think up some fantasy features."

For the Montenaros, that was the easiest part. Less palatable was Carlo's stipulation that Isobel was not to expect any family recognition or attention beyond what was formally and publicly accorded on the day of her wedding. She would have to, as it was vulgarly put, ease herself in.

"You cannot agree to it," Giulia remonstrated with Isobel. "Believe me, *carissima*, whether you know it or not, you have the power to reject this. Beatrice, for one, will support you. She is not a bad woman. You will be the oldest son's wife, the *only* son's wife. You must have your place."

"No thank you," Isobel replied imperturbably, experimenting with Indian ink. "Any place I want, I'll make for myself."

Giulia recoiled. It was a mistake to talk to Isobel when she was

105

drawing. She ringed herself with spikes then, to keep off intruders. It was the only time she was selfish but those times were ever more frequent.

"Do you wish you still had your pigtail, *carissima*?" Giulia looked sadly at the pen and ink study. Isobel continued to pursue this theme with deadly industriousness.

"No, of course not," Isobel replied in genuine surprise, pulling a lock of her hair. "It's much better like this."

"But it looks so . . . I don't know . . ."

"Not nearly nasty enough," Isobel sighed and tore up the drawing.

"But it was good . . ."

"No it wasn't," Isobel packed up her things. She and Giulia had had a lot of conversations like that lately. There were some things, Isobel was certain, Giulia was better off not understanding. Once she had a place of her own, she would be able to work without constraints.

Carlo Bonetti's next condition, in direct contrast with his others, had an air of grudging benevolence. At any rate, Alessandro couldn't adduce any reasonable argument against it. Isobel was to sign a prenuptial agreement stating that in respect of any children of the marriage, should Furio die or be otherwise unable to act for the good of his offspring, his paternal responsibilities should devolve on Carlo Bonetti, who would exercise those rights and duties in his stead.

Isobel signed it in spite of Alessandro's second, more cautious thoughts. He had wanted to show it to his lawyers.

"We won't waste anyone's time or your money," Isobel said. "Just let's get the whole thing over. I want only one thing out of this, and that's Furio." She took the document from his hand and signed it eccentrically with the Japanese drawing brush she happened to have in her hand.

Flinching at her testiness, Alessandro forgave her. Once, he had entertained fond hopes of becoming a fine artist himself before settling to architecture. He had lacked the necessary amoral ferocity. He saw with envy, that Isobel had it. She would turn on anything and anybody who got in her way. Well, he had encouraged her. She had grown up and grown strong when no one was looking. She was no longer tame. From time to time, Alessandro wondered how Furio Bonetti would fare as her keeper.

Isobel's own feelings mirrored those of her hosts. They had rescued her, nurtured her, adopted her and launched her on a fast-running spring tide. She was straining to go, anxious to search the wilder shores of existence with her mate at her side. And in the

Montenaros she felt a corresponding end-of-term feeling. They had done all they could . . . Much, much more than they should. They were not of her blood. It was time to leave them in peace.

It was further laid down that Furio might expect no gratuitous uplift of his income in recognition of his marriage. Not until the first child was born. He and Isobel must manage with what Furio already drew from the company. As this was a munificent bachelor stipend, it seemed to both Isobel and Furio that it would cover their needs. The small spitefulness was beneath civilised notice.

"Poor Papa," Furio was ashamed for his parent. "Don't blame him too much, *cara*. This is the first time he has lost control. We must let him save his *bella figura* in whatever way he can."

"I don't blame him at all," Isobel countered stoutly. "Why should he pay you more money for marrying me? You must do more saxophoning, darling, and I will give English lessons."

"I doubt it will come to that," said Furio airily, having only a theoretical knowledge of financial stringency. Money, when it got low, was always topped up like a car battery. Somebody in the Accounts Department did it.

And finally, Isobel must accept conversion to the Roman Catholic faith. In this, too, she was remarkably docile. Argument here would occasion needless delay.

"I have been told what to believe since I was little. It makes no difference to what I think."

A neat distinction which eluded Giulia who made the arrangements – a crash course with the *presbiterio* at the enchanting little baroque church of Santa Maria Podone. He was the youngest brother of one of Giulia's friends. Isobel, she was assured, would be perfectly safe in his hands. Clean fingernails and a realistic appreciation of timetables. He was no stranger to weddings in *alta società*.

Padre Stefano lectured Isobel at high speed every other morning in his cluttered bachelor bedsit located in one of the flowery gothic courts of the Palazzo Boromeo, just across from the church. The place, fortress faced on the outside, concealed an almost oriental sensuality within. Columns, arches, shadows and fountains, punctuated with regimented pots of geraniums. Isobel liked going there.

"Pay attention, Signorina," the bespectacled young priest always began. "You have a fitting for your gown at eleven. It is my arrangement with the *Principessa* that you should be at Augustino's in time. We are all busy men."

Then, with stylish soutane swaying rhythmically, he swished to and fro between window and door, ticking off the essentials of faith on his fingers. Padre Stefano had method.

The hour passed with Isobel endorsing his points with "Yes, yes," and "I know," while she made not unlifelike cartoons of Stefano in a notebook. His outline was crisp.

"You know an awful lot, Signorina," Padre Stefano reproved, after the twelfth session. "Fortunately I think it's enough to spare me sitting for my portrait again."

The priest held his hand out for Isobel's notebook with a schoolmasterly, confiscating gesture. Flushing, Isobel handed it over.

"You have a spitefully accurate eye, Signorina," smiled Stefano, riffling the pages. "You accuse me of vanity, I see."

"Not at all," Isobel laughed. "I accuse you of looking good in the gear and, fortunately, having no legs. No trousers. I can't draw them, you see. You are my first masculine subject."

"I am flattered. You must go on with this."

Isobel's smile was a sunburst of gratitude. Feeling its warmth, Stefano proposed a stroll, by way of distraction, in the adjoining warren of courts in the *palazzo*. They had a quarter of an hour yet in hand. Signorina Jefferson was interesting company. She had a fine contempt for dogma, combined with a supple willingness to accept it. In the Anglo-Saxon mind that was unusual. She would, Stefano considered, prosper in Italy.

"Do you know yet, where you will live?"

Isobel didn't. She and Furio had looked at a number of places in various parts of the city. So far, they had all been too large, too dull, too small, too far away from the centre or, if not those, too expensive. They had fallen back on being content with Furio's Ticinese studio until after their honeymoon.

"This, I think may amuse you," Stefano waved a manicured hand upwards to the first floor *piano nobile* of a tiny, yellow washed court.

The building here was extremely old, a medieval survivor of wars without number. Its two storeys were lined with a double colonnade of round headed arches supported on squat little columns, pitted with age. In the corner of the court, a sagging stone staircase gave exterior access to the apartment which occupied the whole of the first floor, on the western side.

"It is to be let," said Stefano. "Shall I get you the key?"

The apartment had only four rooms, with a primitive kitchen and bathroom. Pleasantly umbrageous on the courtyard side, the deep gloom in the rooms overlooking the street was pierced by slivers of light shafting through arrow slits. The walls, four foot thick in places, showed exposed herringbone brickwork and hooks from which tapestries once had hung. A smell of mould pervaded the air.

It seemed to Isobel that the place was alive with a thousand forgotten plots, rejoiced over by myriad, invisible faces wearing wily old smiles. Here was the deep, buried core of Milan.

"Any neighbours?"

"Ah, no," Stefano replied gallantly. "Not in this court. There are too few potential tenants about whom I should care to invite . . . But your *fidanzato* can practise his saxophone here without fear of complaint. I believe I have all his records . . . The rent is most reasonable."

It was no great surprise to Furio that Stefano acted as letting agent for the *palazzo*'s owners and pocketed a fee for his marketing efforts. The apartment was taken, complete with disadvantages and charm. The cracked marble sarcophagus of a bath and stone sink in the dungeon-like kitchen were offset by the limpid light in the courtyard, where Isobel could paint on fine days . . . and the sound absorbing walls all around, which would enable Furio to practise his music.

Their projected home was shown to Alessandro and Giulia on the day Isobel was formally received into the Church of Rome.

"I didn't know you were so wicked," Giacomo confided quietly to Isobel as they explored every corner of the deserted *palazzo* courtyard after Isobel's ritual renunciations were completed.

"Nor did I, darling," Isobel said, still smarting from the new-found knowledge that she had trafficked and trucked with the devil. The boys were the only members of the small witnessing party who had not treated the circumstance with positive jollity.

"This is it," Alessandro popped out from behind the massive Roman well-head with its later fountain accretion. "We shall give your wedding reception here, Isabella. Imagine this place with the balustrades all draped with damasks, the fountain running with chianti . . . We can have a small orchestra up there . . . open some of the other apartments to accommodate long distance guests . . . little salons opening out from the ground floor . . . orange trees in tubs in the court . . . We'll have a score of young waiters got up as pages . . ."

"But it's too small," Giulia wailed. "So is the church . . ."

Alessandro, however, was not to be gainsaid. In and among the temporary works, for which purpose a short term lease would be taken, Isobel and Furio's apartment could be surreptitiously refurbished at Carlo Bonetti's expense. Stands of extra seating built in the piazza and shaded by awnings would supplement the accommodation in the church.

Money changed hands and contractors moved into the Boromeo.

The *caribinieri* were instructed to lay their plans for traffic diversions. A cadre would also be required to inspect invitations and guard the wedding presents.

"I'll give that swine a wedding he'll never forget," Alessandro swore, "and a bill even he may live to regret."

Novelty was piled upon novelty. The ceremonial, the visual, the gastronomic and musical.

A round dozen of Furio's musical chums agreed to dress up in cloth-of-gold tunics and blow fanfares on silver trumpets. They would do it for love as well as the money.

"Roast swan and peacock," Alessandro bounced up and down at dinner one night. "Tell the caterers, Giulia."

"They would be inedible, *caro* . . ."

"Excellent, excellent. Let us have the maximum in luxurious futility."

The cards of invitation were immediately sent out, not a moment too early. A creditable list of the distinguished, opportunist and the downright unsavoury, none of whom would care to miss out on a free meal or a spectacle.

New additions to the Bonetti list were sent by Carlo's secretary each day. Giulia edited these without reference to anyone, deleting the grosser impertinences. The American Ambassador from Rome? Carlo, Giulia decided, would have to make do with the Naval Attaché, whom Isobel knew. Lucy Larizzi must certainly come as must the Reverend and Mrs Smallwood to keep Mrs Jefferson company. The Prefect . . . yes. He was married to one of Giulia's friends. The Fischers . . . most certainly not. The line, however low it was drawn, must be drawn somewhere.

As a routine precaution, Giulia prepared a text which she required Isobel to copy on to a postcard addressed to Furio. It said that she would release him if things did not work out as planned. Furio brought a similar document when he came next evening. Alessandro placed both in his safe in the study.

"This is most modern and prudent," he explained. "In Italy, we have no divorce, as you know. What we do have is ecclesiastical annulment. Advance provision of the documentation assures a rapid, economical process. The practice is now well established in sophisticated families."

"Does this mean I'm not marrying Furio at all?" Isobel was quick to see the implications.

"It means," Giulia answered darkly, "that you keep your own counsel."

In the midst of all this, Isobel continued solemnly with her ordinary duties and drew pigtails assiduously. She never tired of the subject. There were a hundred and one ways of depicting these things, and so far, in her own estimation, each one was a failure.

Furio, who came every evening, respected the effort although he could not understand it.

"But why these things?"

"It was a part of myself I saw falling," was Isobel's only reply. "I shall go on to something else when I've got it right."

Furio shrugged. It seemed a harmless obsession. A handhold for the mind until they were married. After that everything would be different. Isobel's hobby would naturally find more normal and much less frequent expression. She would be obsessed, then, with him.

Isobel, too, was interested in what would happen to this repeated image after she was married. It kept on flowing from her hand with no conscious mental activity. It was connected in some way with crossing a line, and also, in many ways with Nina who inhabited her now like a witch's familiar. Her story had been passed to Isobel like a baton in a relay race and she couldn't catch up with anyone else to whom she could pass it. No exterior diversion, not even Furio, relieved her of the burden. A perpetual scar on the mind.

* * *

Isobel retained but fleeting impressions of her wedding. The most comfortable part was the ceremony. Well rehearsed and perfectly choreographed, it passed in the cool of the church like taking part in a play. Furio was just a dark shape beside her, predicating or shadowing her actions. Responses, choirs, gold rings, trumpet carillons, wine from a jewelled cup, a transparent disc on the tongue, fragrant smoke hanging in drifts, a threefold blessing and an impersonal kiss on the cheek. With that it was finished.

Marzio and Giacomo, careful of their curly-toed, medieval shoes, wheeled into position and carried Isobel's train out of the church. There was polite applause from the less favoured seating in the piazza . . . flashbulbs and scribbling journalists. The gown itself was a scoop. On hearing of the finalised location, Augustino had scrapped the original design.

"You must look like an idol," he had said, savagely ripping the toile, with pins in his mouth. "A daughter of the old Boromeo, bred for exchange. Sacks of gold coins for valleys full of corn. A symbol of self-perpetuating plenty. We will contrive a convex contour over the belly," he added struck by his last, incremental thought. "With your height, Signorina, you can stand it. A suggestion of imminent fecundity."

"But nobody's exchanging anything for me," replied Isobel crossly.

"That is the whisper, Signorina," the dressmaker answered equably, bunching fabric into gathers. "So we must put a good front on it, no? With that dimple you will look like Boticelli's *Primavera* . . ."

To Isobel, in the unprecedented heat, the dress was a trial. The sleeveless, open fronted tunic of stiffened white brocade was seamed under the bosom and laced over it to confine a chemise of diaphanous muslin. From the shoulders, there hung a train three and a half metres long, burdened with the weight of seed pearl embroidery. On her hair she wore a rigid gold wire caul enlivened by white sapphires. Giulia's South Sea pearls supplied the 'something borrowed' of English tradition. They hung like balls of lead round her neck.

She stood two hours in the receiving line whilst an interminable line of guests filed past her. Fewer than one in fifteen knew her personally. And of those, every one had shuffled forward so slowly from the glare of the piazza through the comparative cool of the outer courts until reaching this one already seething with bodies, they were beyond giving the bride more than a cursory glance.

She and her new husband were interesting only because their wills, coinciding, had prevailed. But their part in this political and commercial market place was small. They had functioned as an introductory cabaret act. An attractive excuse for the gathering.

Smiling mechanically, Isobel shook hands with countless middle aged, emperor faced men with their hawk featured wives in hats the size of umbrellas. Amid the roar of voices around her and the reedy noise of the orchestra, she caught very few of their names.

There were young women who kissed her coldly on both cheeks and stood chatting to Furio for ages, glancing back at his bride to take in the details of her appearance at their unblinking leisure. Others simply walked past her as if she were one picture too many in a gallery. All Furio's sisters, aunts, uncles and cousins had come before her.

At the head of the line, nearest the entrance, stood Carlo Bonetti, dealing out greetings commensurate in warmth with the importance of the name announced to him. The Prefect got ten minutes. Everyone else had to wait.

Next to Carlo stood Isobel's mother, minimally smart in navy and white. To Isobel's surprise and gratitude, she had come after all. She looked lost and uncomfortable. Carlo passed his guests on to her with the briefest introduction. An indifferent wave of one hand and a mutter from the side of his mouth.

On Margaret Jefferson's left was Alessandro, who was little more helpful. At the family dinner Giulia had given at the Viale Regina Giovanna last night, attended by the Montenaros, Isobel herself, her mother and Simon, conversation had been stilted, hindered, too, by the necessity for constant translation. The two families had no interest in common but the bride. Their experiences of her and attitudes towards her were, they were all conscious, too divergent to make her a convenient topic.

After all that could safely be said, had already been said about the glamour of the forthcoming wedding, Alessandro had turned to art and Isobel's interest in that.

"Your daughter has some talent, Mrs Jefferson, and extraordinary tenacity. I hope she will study . . ."

"Oh dear," Margaret had trilled on false notes of hilarity, wiping the corners of her mouth with her napkin. "Isobel has always done little pictures . . ."

Sensing his mother was haring off on quite the wrong track, Simon tried to head her off, wishing that Rupert had come. He had sent his regrets and a cheque.

"But she never has the patience to finish anything," Margaret went on relentlessly.

"Because her standards are high, perhaps?" Alessandro murmured. "She refuses to persevere with the inferior . . ."

At that point, Simon excused himself. He was invited to join Furio's bachelor party in the Ticinese. Alessandro summoned a taxi for him.

Today, he was propped up by the red running fountain, drinking champagne. Iz, he thought, had done jolly well for herself. Furio seemed a decent enough chap even though his looks were a spot too luscious for comfort. He'd have been buggered to death at Cherwell. Iz, on the other hand, Simon mused vaguely, looked like death warmed over all of a sudden.

". . . I hoped you would not mind my coming," Josef Fischer was saying to Isobel. "I received an invitation only yesterday . . . by telephone from your father-in-law . . . we had been talking some business . . . I wanted to wish you well . . ."

She didn't hear the rest of what he said. All Isobel could see was Nina's face where her husband's should have been, with Estella's misting over it and clearing again, like a cloud. An impression of falling, a heave in the stomach and a distant procession of women . . . Any moment now, Nina would come.

Then Josef, his multiple face and his body, moved on. He was talking to Furio.

"Are you all right, sweetheart?" Ed Mazzerella said. His face swam before Isobel's eyes.

113

"I'm so glad you could come," Isobel replied automatically before she realised who it was. "Oh, Ed. The Lamborghini's just behind the *palazzo* on the Via . . ."

"Never mind the goddam car, honey. Let's get you a glass of water. You look like a ghost."

She looked exactly, Ed thought, the way she had that day in Florence after the lousy Ghirlandaio females had upset her. Spaced out. The water came in response to a swift order to a waiter.

"This your guy?" Ed enquired needlessly. "Good to meet you, feller . . . you'll find my cheque's cleared your bank. Checked right up on it this morning. I'll take good care of your old girl. Sure do envy you your new one," the American added with a significant smile at the bride.

Restored by Ed's ministrations, Isobel greeted Silvano Crivelli, another of her personal guests, and Lucy Larizzi who had a sinuous, fawn eyed youth on her arm.

"Your son?" Isobel said, stretching out her hand kindly to the boy, who ignored it and rubbed himself against Lucy like a cat.

"Spiros," answered Lucy, tapping Isobel's cheek, "is Greek. My little summer indulgence. What a clever, clever girl you have been. Your dear mother must be so proud of you. What a pity your father didn't come."

"He's dead," Isobel said.

"What a pity," replied Lucy charmingly. Isobel warmed to her. There was no pretence about the Contessa di Larizzi.

In the end, there were no more guests left to greet. Isobel and Furio stood side by side like dummies for minutes together before they realised. Someone led them away. They were separated momentarily in the throng.

"In future, young lady," Carlo Bonetti snarled, "you will show *cortesia* to my guests. Courtesy." Isobel did not know how this had happened. She had never before spoken to her new father-in-law. She had seen him only once since her birthday party. On that occasion he had not addressed her directly. What was he talking about? And where was Furio now? Where was anybody that she knew?

"Fischer is important to me. Now he has left. His presence, he tells me, distresses you. If you intend to please me in future . . ."

"I don't intend to please you," Isobel flashed. "I don't know you and don't wish to. Please go away. I didn't want any of this . . . It's all so . . ." she searched for a word, "*vicious.*"

A trio of Giulia's friends saw or sensed the fracas at the same moment. They converged on Isobel, and dextrously came between her and Carlo Bonetti. She was needed elsewhere. The banquet was about to begin.

Isobel had a vague memory of eating something at a long table set up in the court, of toasts, more trumpets, of Carlo making a speech . . . largely about the resurgent industrial might of Italy . . . Alessandro doing the same, referring properly but irrelevantly to the parallel power of young love . . . and Furio thanking everyone in sight while Giulia cried.

Then there was dancing. Isobel marched stiffly up and down the court twice scowling over Carlo Bonetti's shoulder while he bared his teeth in an approximation of geniality over hers. Furio and Isobel's mother looked no happier together. Later, dancing with her bridegroom at last, Isobel saw her mother respond to the louche importunings of Lucy's Greek boy by quietly and conclusively clubbing him with her handbag. Simon was teaching Beatrice Bonetti the twist.

When night descended, hot and black on the court, Furio and Isobel ascended the stone staircase to change.

Below, men were sitting in clumps, heads close together under the colonnade. They were smoking cigars and fingering fountain pens, exchanging cards. A pooling of influence. Alessandro Montenaro had delivered and Carlo Bonetti was pleased. Isobel Jefferson would come to heel in due course. Her spirit was admirable but ought to be tamed. One day, who could say she would not be the wife of the President of Italy? Carlo had large plans for his son. This was only a beginning.

At the last moment, outside in the piazza where the new Lamborghini was waiting, guarded against pranksters by a phalanx of *caribinieri*, Isobel was subjected to a series of crushing embraces. Giulia . . . Simon, Alessandro, from Ed just a regretful kiss, blown from his fingers on the edge of the crowd . . . Beatrice Bonetti enfolded her briefly . . . she said something about making babies and Carlo not being a bad man. Finally there was her own mother, ravaged and fighting back tears.

"Here, darling. This was always to have been yours." She detached Granny's little ruby brooch from her lapel and thrust it into Isobel's hand. Staring at it for a moment, Isobel realised that its small value, had it been cashed, would have altered her destiny. This day would never have happened. But it had been denied her and now her name, her nationality and entire future were different.

"No, Mummy," Isobel pinned it back on to her mother's collar. "Not yet. It's yours. I don't need it now."

Hugging her mother fiercely, Isobel turned abruptly away and got into the car, not daring to look again at the person whom she most wanted to love and be loved by . . . after Furio, of course.

Someone leaned close to the windscreen and made a peculiar

sign with her fingers. Isobel didn't realise it was Rosaria until she saw Serafina loom up and pull the girl back roughly before boxing her ears.

Furio shivered.

"What was all that about?" Isobel turned to him.

"Nothing. A stupid superstition. How did you like your wedding day, Signora?" he let in the clutch. "I feel as if I haven't seen you for months even though you've been beside me all day."

"I hated it, hated it, *hated* it!" Isobel clenched her fists and screwed her eyes tight shut.

"So did I. But I love you, love you, *adore* you . . ."

Furio's voice was drowned by a cacophony of traffic horns from following cars. Younger guests speeding them on their way. It took minutes to shake them off.

"Where are we going?"

"Monte Carlo. There are some races this week . . . one for production cars . . . I might enter . . . And at other times, we will cruise round our own track. You will be a different kind of beauty every time and I will be the driver. I shall steer you, stroke you, urge you . . ."

"What shall I be tonight?"

"You can choose. We will discuss it . . ."

In a broad balconied chamber, overlooking the Mediterranean Sea, on the edge of the old border town of Ventimiglia, Isobel was a Maserati, crashed by her driver into repeated oblivion.

"No, darling," she said after the first time. "Don't do all that . . . you don't need to. Just finish it, *please*."

"Nought to sixty in how many seconds? *Carissima*, you must learn to go slowly."

When Isobel went to the bathroom next morning, Furio scissored out the patch of sheet stained with drops of her hymenal blood. He deposited it in a ready-stamped envelope, addressed to his father. The chambermaid who brought the breakfast tray took it, promising immediate dispatch in return for a tip.

Discovering the damage, Isobel asked how it had happened. She was undeceived by Furio's excuses about the sheet being damaged in the first place. Finally, Isobel got it out of him. He was profoundly embarrassed.

"It is only a custom, my darling. You must understand, we Bonettis originally came from a very small village."

EIGHT

Despite the odds stacked against them, the young Bonettis were happy. They had wanted each other, after all, with a desire which incorporated their mutual strangeness. Her youth, financial dependence, the times and the country itself predisposed Isobel to adjustment.

Wherever the pieces refused to fit, she threw the blame on Carlo Bonetti. The business with the fragment of blood stained sheet had been dealt with like that.

"What earthly good would it have done him to know I *wasn't* a virgin?" Isobel had raged.

"I don't *know!*" Furio shouted, the fourth time he was asked this. "Does it matter? For God's sake let it drop. I promise you this, I will never expect such a thing of our children."

In fact, they quite enjoyed this row. It was like scratching a recalcitrant pimple that oozed just a little before hardening to an interesting scab. Isobel was woman enough to be roused by the hint of primitive oppression and her overt rebellion lent an edge to Furio's virility. It generally ended in bed.

In time, Furio even confided the facts of his family's funerary customs. Isobel, who was eating spaghetti at the time, listened voraciously before splitting her sides.

"I knew you'd laugh," he said, his harlot's mouth irresistibly petulant. "You're insensitive to my feelings ... How can you eat?"

"But I don't know why you're so shy about it, darling. It's so sweet. The idea that the family are always there to be cared for ... That nobody ever quite dies ..."

"When Mama and Papa are gone, I'm going to seal those tombs up. It's time we were a modern family."

"Yes, I should. The poor old things will be glad of the rest. I'm sure they'll last longer, too. They'll be much more interesting in a hundred years' time."

Furio was never quite certain how seriously Isobel was to be taken. She was intimate, soothing, and at times, either sarcastic or maddeningly elusive. But glowing with the effulgence of early fulfilment, she pulled at his generative instincts every hour of the day.

About his grandfather, *Nonno* Bonetti, whom Furio correctly deducted from family gossip to have been a small-time extortioner, blackmailer and assassin, Furio wisely held his peace. There was no need for his young wife to know how the Bonettis had come by their first quarry on a neighbouring peasant farmer's land. For although she said nothing, by September, Furio suspected Isobel was carrying his child.

The pregnancy, if that's what it was, might be a happier thing, her husband divined, if Isobel remained ignorant of the fact that she was harbouring the great-grandchild of a murderer. Anglo-Saxons took a puritan view of these things.

"*Allora?*" Carlo growled at his son, in a certain tone of voice every few weeks. He had been as good as his word and this monosyllabic enquiry was the only mention he ever made of his daughter-in-law. Otherwise he behaved as if the wedding had not taken place.

Up to September, Furio had shaken his head diffidently. No, there was no child yet, he conveyed.

"What is it you do in the evenings?" Carlo mocked once. "Say the rosary? Make lace? Two sapless novices together . . ."

The languorous satiety in his Furio's eye was Bonetti senior's answer. He saw it and grunted, covering his longing to behold any infant got by this favourite child of his own.

But in the third week of September, Furio neither shook his head nor nodded in response to his father's "*Allora?*"

Carlo, transfigured with joy, emerged from behind his desk, arms opened wide and eyes glistening with tears.

"Get out," he ordered his secretary. "My son, my son. Is it true? She is *incinta* . . . *Isabella*? Your wife?"

"I think so . . . I don't know for certain . . ."

"Not *know*!" Carlo roared. "Not know! How can you say you don't know? What kind of a man doesn't know the state of his wife? Were there napkins on the line this month, or were there not?"

"Oh, shut up, Father. Women don't use those things, these days. And even if they did . . ."

"Go, go! Confront her. End this deceit. And bring me an answer at the villa tonight. Then you must fetch her, we cannot have the mother of my grandson in that rat infested den during the winter . . ."

Furio fled before his father's euphoria became yet more cloyingly sentimental. But he was happy and returned to his own office with a spring in his step. Carlo Bonetti had mentioned Isobel's name.

The barriers were down and the family would be together again. He, Furio, had got everything he wanted. The best of all possible worlds. In the spring, when the child was born, there would be more money. If Isobel wanted the whole Boromeo, he would get it for her. Or a first-rate apartment on the Viale Majno. Meanwhile, it was true, she would be more comfortable at the Villa Rondine in the care of his mother.

Isobel's thoughts were at variance. To her, it was a useful coincidence that Furio should blurt out all his father's assumptions and plans before he put the direct question to her.

"You are, darling, aren't you?"

They were sitting in the court, which they had to themselves, drinking wine in the sunshine whilst the little daily maid laid the table for luncheon. Everyone came home for *collazione* in Milan . . . unless, Isobel thought swiftly, they lived too far away, in a place like Gorgonzola . . . So these precious little *tête à têtes* would be over for one thing.

"No," Isobel lied suavely. "I'm afraid your father's jumped the gun and so, darling, have you. I'm not pregnant. I thought I was for a while. But I was just late. That's all. Are you terribly disappointed?"

It simply would not do, Isobel thought, eating her *gnocchi* half an hour later. She would not be manipulated in this way. Not now she was settled and happy with her life. The disruption would be insupportable. Somehow or other she would have to play for time. She had not even been to the doctor yet. Giulia didn't know. She glanced at Furio where he sat opposite her, smoking a cigarette morosely.

"Cheer up, *caro*. There'll be a baby some time . . ."

"It's my father," Furio said, stubbing out the cigarette. "I don't know how to tell him. He was so happy . . ."

"Tough luck," Isobel smiled. "I am concerned with your happiness, but not his."

Furio flung out of the court without another word. He did that sometimes, after one of their spats. They were usually to do with his family. Knowing that he could not stay long away from her, Isobel was unconcerned. She needed to think.

To move to the Villa Rondine was impossible, from every standpoint disagreeable. Her daily visits to Giulia would be curtailed. Isobel had insisted on collecting the boys from school every afternoon during the term and returning to the Viale Regina Giovanna to play with them. Their English, she promised, shouldn't suffer just because she'd got married. Fee? Of course Isobel would take none. Giulia was delighted to have her friend with her so often.

Nor did Isobel want any separation from her at this crucial point in her life. What was Beatrice Bonetti to her?

And then there were her drawing lessons. Those had been Alessandro's wedding present. A retired master from the Accademia del Arte. He came to her two hours in the morning, three times a week, wearing a beret and dark cotton jacket over a navy blue shirt and canary yellow tie. Stooped and irascible, he and Isobel suited each other well.

"Don't tell me what to do," she said to him often. "Just tell me how to do what I'm doing."

"An artist," wheezed Pietro Arnolfi, packing his cavernous nostrils with snuff, "must know her own mind. But if its content is indecipherable to the common man's eye, then she will stand mute before the bar of public opinion and lie in a grave marked with an unmemorable name."

"Precisely, Signor. So make me decipherable."

At the moment they were addressing the relationship between mass, line and movement. Good technical stuff. Padre Stefano had been persuaded to read his breviary once or twice in Isobel's court, walking round the bottom colonnade.

"It's very distracting," he complained. "Being stared at by a beautiful woman."

"This is interesting," put in Pietro clinically. "Try to identify the body-line which speaks to us of prudery . . ."

Yes, all that was going very well. The work could not be interrupted for some whim of Carlo Bonetti's.

As for her father-in-law's deprecating remarks about the apartment, that was all nonsense. It was really very salubrious. Isobel was proud of it. After the wedding, whilst the contractors had been clearing the court, they had tacked the damask drapes on to batons fixed on the interior walls. The place, enriched with the paintings, porcelain, linen and silver that Isobel and Furio had been given for wedding presents, glittered like a jewel-box. The flues had been cleaned. The kitchen had been refitted with reclaimed oak and bright steel. Spot and tracked lighting had solved the illumination problem throughout. No, she was not going to leave it.

And what of her maid? Gentle, efficient Maria. Was she to be put out of work, dragged to the country or paid to clean uninhabited rooms just when the domestic routines had been established so nicely? No, Isobel decided, definitely not.

Not caring for the country very much herself, having grown up in it, Isobel knew she would miss the quiet old Boromeo quarter with its parochial doings and colourful food shops spilling their wares out on to the pavements. The comings and goings in *piazza* and *palazzo*. The harmony of church bells, distant traffic horns and trams. Isobel even breathed in the occasional foetid exhalation of a drain with secret enjoyment. The aroma of abundant, continuing life.

It was a pity she had obliged Carlo Bonetti so quickly. But there was no occasion for him to know of it just yet and no reason at all to fall in with his officious ideas. He had wanted to keep her at arm's length. Let him be content with his bargain.

Carlo, however, was far from content. His hopes dashed, his reaction was violent. It was also irrational. He had been duped, he raved. Manoeuvred into speaking of that gold digging *inglese* as he would of a daughter . . . It was all a ruse, he claimed, to dislodge him from his settled intention of remaining aloof. The Jefferson female had simply wanted to weasel her way into his favour and into his house. She would rue the day she had trifled with the tenderest feelings of Carlo Bonetti. He beat his clenched fists on his chest, face working with the pain of imagined betrayal.

"But *Papa* . . ."

"Go, go," Furio's father shaded his face with his hand. "Leave me to my grief and disgust."

This time, Furio left his father's office torn between indignation and guilt. How was it, he wondered, that a simple mistake could have been turned into a drama on this scale. Anyone would think that his wife had laid some deep, dark plot to bring chaos into his family . . . that she had deliberately lied . . . whereas, in truth, she had never said anything. But reason apart, Furio was upset just the same.

Several layers below that of surface invective, Carlo Bonetti stifled a regret he could not acknowledge. He was, in spite of himself, drawn to Isobel. Nor was the arrogant splendour of her flesh the single attraction.

During their short, sharp confrontation at the wedding he had been singed by a charge of energy that licked out of her with the random savagery of nature. There was a rigidity of purpose in her, he noticed, that had nothing to do with money. A thirsty blade of determination to dominate whatever mysterious fiefdom it was she planned to carve out for herself. Who better to bear the fourth great Bonetti? And there was a pliancy about Furio for which she could compensate. How dared she not be pregnant? How dared she spit on the hand that he offered? Her place was at the heart of *la famiglia* at the Villa Rondine.

Without any particular consciousness of doing so, Carlo fomented a scheme which would punish Isobel's defiance. If there was to be nothing between them but hatred, then let there be hatred. Of all contacts, the cleanest and closest. Unlike love, distance was powerless to diminish it.

*   *   *

"Look, I'm sorry, *caro*," Isobel said a month later. They were leaving a waterside restaurant in the Ticinese. Furio had just completed a recording of early American jazz themes and she had come to meet him at the studio. "I cannot possibly entertain the Fischers. Not at home or anywhere else. If your father wants to make a fuss of them, why can't your mother have them to dinner . . . or take them out . . . ?"

A few people nudged each other and pointed as Isobel threaded her way between the tables, following Furio closely as he made for the car parked on the quay. They were well known in this district. Any visible friction between them was cause for muttered sympathy, tainted with envious malice. So much in the way of good looks, so much wealth in the family and on Furio's side, so much talent. Why were the gods so bountiful to some and so mean with others? The melancholic disparity between peacocks and sparrows. So why were the golden ones pecking each other?

"I will go over it again," Furio said thinly, opening the door of the car for her. "The Fischer Group are more than subcontractors to us. Josef Fischer's father has Europe-wide contacts . . . Jews always do . . ."

"No, don't." Isobel slammed the door. "I've heard it all till I'm tired of hearing it. Vertical production and all that. If your father wants to become some kind of commercial Czar, let him arrange it for himself. Why should I help him? What has he done for me?"

"He is ready to do everything for you . . . for *us*, if only you will give him a grandchild or even, I suspect, simply do him this favour . . . He wants us to be united . . . The Fischers are nearer to us in age . . ."

"Rubbish," Isobel snapped, automatically placing her hand on her abdomen. It still didn't show. "What does their age matter? I've told you, those people used me like a slave. How could you ever think of going near them?"

At two o'clock in the morning, the argument had lost none of its heat.

The Fischers, due to some oversight of Giulia's, had not received an invitation to the wedding, Furio pointed out. That was a gaffe which needed smoothing over. Giulia, Isobel furiously defended, did not make gaffes, ever. Aware of the background, naturally she had omitted to invite the Fischers. What normal person would have acted otherwise? Oh, it was true that Josef himself was less

122

to blame than his wife. And his wife was not really to blame. She was off her head . . .

Isobel paused for a moment, unhappy with the way the cliché rang in her mind. Horrible. It was so difficult to avoid those repulsive pictures. It had been the same when Ed had blown her a kiss just after the wedding. She never wanted anyone to do that again. But she couldn't tell Furio the whole story. To do so would bring it closer again. Keeping it away was like perpetually blocking rat holes in a cellar. A task without end. Sometimes she lay awake at nights beside Furio, unable to stop watching those women shuffle forward to their hideous deaths. She was always standing where Nina had stood . . . Estella? . . . No, Nina, saying goodbye to her mother.

"Furio," Isobel began more gently, "Nina Fischer is not fit for company. Don't you understand? She's completely potty. A mental patient . . ."

It was no use. Furio would not listen to any kind of argument. Why couldn't Isobel forgive and forget? It was only business. And that's what people did in Milan. Business. No one was suggesting they should be friends with the Fischers. Not really. Just one dinner, that's all that was wanted. A gesture.

"I can't talk about it any more tonight. Let's go to bed."

They made love, very slowly for once and without talking. Furio brought Isobel to a shuddering climax, collapsing on to her breast. He lay there in silence whilst she fingered his damp hair with tears in her eyes. His weight on her body seemed doubled with sadness. He rolled off her after a while to search for a cigarette on the bedside table. Lighting it, his face flared briefly in the matchlight, bitter and distant.

"Darling, what is it?"

"I love him, you see," Furio answered. "And even if this is unreasonable . . . If we could just give one single inch . . ."

"I thought it was me you loved . . ."

"*Isabella*, I do. But a man can't be separate from his roots, from . . ."

"Oh, all right. All right. If it means this much to you . . ."

Isobel went to sleep in her husband's arms believing, that after all, the Fischers would refuse. Josef had that much delicacy. She wondered why she hadn't thought of it before. So simple, really. And when Carlo Bonetti's bullying stupidity had been outfaced by that refusal, she would allow him to know that the presence of his grandchild had now been confirmed. Two months at least! But she wasn't going to leave the Boromeo, not for anyone.

*   *   *

Nothing worked out as Isobel expected.

Her invitation, impersonally worded, wasn't refused. Instead, Josef had rung her at the apartment. He would not ordinarily, he said, have dreamed of disturbing her. He imagined some sort of pressure must have been put on her to issue such an invitation. His first impulse, of course, had been to decline. Nina was not yet well enough to make decisions affecting their social life, he added. But there was marked improvement. The clinical reports were encouraging. Nina's symptoms were acute not chronic. Which meant the condition hadn't atrophied into permanence. A cure was in sight.

"I'm so very, very pleased for you," Isobel murmured, smelling gardenias at the thought of her erstwhile employer. Sickly. She must try not to panic. Silly to be frightened. Of course the Fischers wouldn't come. That's what Josef had rung up to say. But it wasn't the case.

"Miss Jefferson, Signora . . . Isobel. Would you, could you allow me to presume on our . . ."

"Friendship," Isobel supplied at his hesitation. She had to, it was she who had tacitly proposed it. Only she had never expected this friendship to progress.

Josef wanted to accept. He had discussed the matter with his wife's psychiatrist. During the therapeutic sessions that Nina had had with him, the experience with Isobel had been explored. Over weeks and months, little by little and syllable by syllable, Nina had been brought to an admission that she had maltreated her employee. The reasons were not clear either to Nina herself or her doctor. That remaining mystery aside, great strides had been made. Nina appeared normal these days. She saw no company to speak of. But as recovery was well on the way, she would have to begin somewhere. It might be an easier process if a start was made with someone who knew her.

"It would be quite wrong of me not to tell you that her man honestly thinks that a face-to-face contact with you might unblock the problem . . . She needs some mild stimulation as well . . ."

All of this was said with many agonised pauses, retractions and qualifications. Conditioning a patient's environment for recovery from the acute syndrome was a matter of delicate balance, Isobel learned. Resocialising the subject was important . . .

Asked for her help in this way, Isobel could not withhold it. She had been told that she would probably notice nothing unusual about Nina. Only, perhaps, a degree of embarrassment. That much she should be prepared for. It would, in any case, be the most optimistic signpost to improving mental health.

Isobel found herself promising that she would not allow Nina to feel any shame. She would reassure her at once. Anybody could be ill. Putting the telephone down, Isobel wondered what she had done.

That was not immediately apparent on the Fischers' arrival on the evening appointed.

Nina looked like anyone convalescing from a severe malady. The refinement of her skull, nothing could disguise, but her skin had lost its creamy luminosity. Her clothes and hair were untidy. Josef fussed over her, straightening her collar with little motherly cluckings while Maria took her coat.

Isobel was moved to see her tormentor so helpless.

There were drinks first, in the darkening court, still warm from the heat stored in the walls, although autumn was come. The men talked stiltedly about business. Isobel tried to engage Nina in conversation. Was she doing any design work, at all? Nina answered every question and observation with a 'yes' or a 'no', sipping her vermouth with a handkerchief clamped round the bottom of the glass for some reason.

"Have you any plans for Christmas?" Isobel asked desperately. Nina would not look at her, but stared around the court vaguely.

"We shall go home to Switzerland for a few days," Josef answered the question addressed to his wife anxiously. "And then back by way of Comino . . . over the New Year, for the skiing . . ."

"How lovely," said Isobel, chasing Nina's glance with her own, trying to draw her in. "We're hoping to do something like that ourselves. You know our friends the Montenaros? They've gone up there this week to look at a lodge they'd like to buy. Now their children are growing up, they think they could make full use of it . . . If they succeed with the lodge, they've asked us to join them for a few days around Christmas . . ."

Isobel heard herself chattering on hollowly and relapsed into silence. Nina laughed at something, she didn't know what. Her head was bent down on her chest.

Seeking refuge in her own thoughts for a moment, Isobel reflected she would not be able to ski . . . or learn to. Probably not. Her pregnancy would be out in the open and too far advanced. It needn't stop Furio. She must tell him about the child now. Tonight, after the Fischers had gone. Something to look forward to. How thrilled he would be. What would her own mother be doing at Christmas? Would she be alone? Perhaps Rupert would pay for her to go out to California. She would like that.

"Dinner is served, Signora." Maria stepped neatly down from the balustrade, pretty in her dark green evening uniform.

125

Grateful for the reprieve, Isobel got up and led her guests in to dinner. She and Maria had worked hard on the food and the table all afternoon. Perhaps Nina would be more responsive after some food. If only she would say *something*.

"He's a doctor," Nina said, looking straight across the table at Furio. "I've seen him before. He's taken off his white coat to deceive me, hasn't he? Josef? Is this horse meat? I like it so much."

Startled, Maria dropped a plate. The accident created a welcome diversion.

Two courses had been served already and Nina had done nothing but fidget and sigh since her husband had unfolded her napkin and placed it coaxingly on her lap. But the food laid before Nina stayed untouched. She just crumbled the bread beside her place, looking restlessly from face to face apparently listening to the strained conversation around her. Now and again, she opened her mouth and stuck out her tongue, her green eyes popping, devoid of expression as boiled sweets. When she did that, the two men looked away. Now she had said something almost coherent.

"No, Nina," Isobel persuaded softly while Maria picked up the shards of china and Josef waved his hands in apology. "It's not horsemeat. It's shoulder of veal . . . Would you like something else?"

Nina did not appear to hear her, but studied her plate fixedly, chuntering in a language unrecognisable to Isobel beneath her breath. She began to laugh again, a high pitched, excited babble. Not very loud. Furio said something to Josef who was scraping his chair back.

"Nina, Nina . . . Do you know me?" Isobel leaned over and tapped the edge of Nina's plate with her fingernail to get her attention.

"Yes, yes, of course I do." Nina answered in English. Raising her head, she both sounded and looked as Isobel remembered.

"You're Isobel Jefferson. The woman who abused my child."

It was clear then, as it ought to have been earlier, that the dinner party could not continue.

"I'm so sorry, Josef," Isobel rose. "I really do think you'd better take your wife home."

Josef was already on his feet, waving his arms like a windmill. He was so sorry . . . Nina had had a relapse. He had been warned this could happen, but the risk had seemed small and . . .

"I do wish, Josef, that you had warned *me*," said Isobel with perfect sincerity while Maria hastened to collect Nina's belongings.

Josef was close to weeping. He kept on saying how sorry he was, his body jerking with half bows from the waist. The Fischers went and the Bonettis had a row, or started to.

"Please, *please*, keep your voice down," Isobel begged. "Maria's still here. I'll take her home and try to explain . . ."

"Perhaps you can explain to her why you were so offensive."

Timidly, Maria put her head round the door of the dining room and said she would take herself home if the Signora would allow. It was early still and there would be plenty of trams.

A storm of recriminations broke out as the apartment door closed. *Now* did Furio understand why Isobel hadn't wanted the Fischers here? What was all this about abusing the child, Furio asked. He quailed at the look on Isobel's face. She would never, ever harm a child. If he could think that of her they had better part at once. Thank God for those convenient Italian postcards that Alessandro had locked up in his safe.

Furio craved his wife's pardon. The woman must be mad.

"Of course she's mad! I told you. I told you over and over again. And I can't do anything for her. I wish I could but I *can't*. Oh why did you have to insist. It was lunacy . . ."

"Did you have to be so brutally rude to Fischer?" Furio swept a glass off the table. His face, Isobel saw, was engorged with blood and his full, generous mouth was tightly rolled in. "What do you think I'm going to say to my father?"

Losing all restraint then, Isobel picked up another glass and threw it at Furio's face. It looked so childish and spoiled. Luckily, the missile went wide.

"Your bloody father and his stupid little games . . ."

Ashen-faced, Furio got up from his chair, walked out of the room, along the short corridor and out of the apartment.

Isobel sat down and cried. It had been a ridiculous argument. It was her fault and nobody else's. She had known the whole thing would be a terrible mistake. She had been weak to agree to it. Why hadn't she stood up to Carlo Bonetti? Nina was madder and more dangerous than ever.

There was nothing to be done but clear up the mess. Furio would be back in an hour or two once he'd cooled off. Heavily, Isobel began to sweep up the glass. Rather nice crystal ones which her mother had given them. It was much too soon to start smashing up one's wedding presents.

I ought to calm down, Isobel thought later, as she began to prepare for bed. I'm pregnant and must take things more gently. As soon as Furio comes back, I shall tell him.

At three o'clock in the morning, there was no sign of Furio. Seriously alarmed now, Isobel started to consider where he might have gone. The Ticinese, possibly. There would still be cafés and clubs open there . . . To the Montenaros? No, of course not. They were away. There were various bachelor friends . . . and the Villa Rondine. He lunched with his parents at least once a week.

Isobel was frightened. The silence in the court had a glutinous quality. Her ears began to whine with the effort of listening. Padre Stefano was near but not on the telephone. Could Furio have gone there? No. He and Furio hadn't really hit it off. In the end, Isobel swallowed her pride and rang the Villa Rondine. With any luck, a servant would answer and she could find out if her husband was there without having to speak to anyone else.

Carlo Bonetti answered.

"*Pronto?*" his voice was wary and irritable.

Isobel explained as best she could without giving too much away. She hadn't seen Furio for some hours. They had had a difference of opinion . . . To be honest, their first real quarrel. About nothing really . . . He only went out to buy a pack of cigarettes somewhere . . . Was he there?

"*No!*" was all her father-in-law said and put down the telephone.

Just before dawn broke, the *polizia* came to the Boromeo and told Isobel that Furio was dead.

The mangled remains of the Lamborghini had been found on the Via Manzoni. Local residents had heard the impact and alerted the police. There was no other vehicle involved. Signor Bonetti must have been driving at speed, and had bounced a wheel off one of the old rounded stone horse hitching posts and cannonaded into a building sideways.

Unfortunately, it was the left side. They had used cutting equipment to get him out but, with such terrible injuries, it had been touch and go as to whether he would survive the ambulance ride to the hospital. He had been found dead on arrival. Nor, at first, had he been recognised. It was not until his clothing had been searched that his identity was realised. They were apologetic, too, that because a letter found in the inside pocket of his dinner jacket was addressed to him at the Villa Rondine, his parents had been informed of their loss before she had. The number of the old Lamborghini would have been enough but . . .

The police were full of information regarding the required certifications and notifications sudden death made essential. They were disconcerted and grateful when Isobel, her native, English imperturbability rising to meet the emergency, made them all tea.

"When was it you contacted them at the Villa Rondine?" she asked.

The two policemen looked at each other and agreed it must have been around one o'clock in the morning.

So Carlo Bonetti had known when he had spoken that single word to her. "*No!*" What a word that was in Italian.

The police left, assured by Isobel that she could look after herself. She was surrounded by friends, she said. When they had gone she went to sit down before her dressing table and looked in the mirror. Her reflection stopped at the neck. There was a dim sort of mist in place of her head. Obviously madness was a communicable disease. Isobel decided to lie down for a while because of the baby.

* * *

As people do when the unthinkable happens, Isobel began to imagine there had been a mix-up. The police had been tactful but their circumlocutions made it evident that the body in the car was so badly mashed . . . It need not have been him. And there were a lot of red Lamborghinis in Milan. Nobody had mentioned the number. There was still a chance that Furio was alive. The letter? Isobel buried that piece of evidence.

A need to be close to those things closest to Furio, to feel some warm vibration of his existence tugged her to the Villa Rondine. She had never been there before. Isobel got up and dressed. She stayed away from the looking glass, not daring to know if she still had a face. She must have, she decided. Her earrings, Giulia's diamond carnival masks had begun to sting in her ears. She had forgotten to take them out when she went to bed. Of course, she hadn't seen them. Fearfully, Isobel raised her fingers to her lobes . . . Yes, they were still there. So was her mouth, her eyes and her nose. All safe.

She felt almost cheerful, hopeful anyway, when she collected her little Fiat from the nearby Via Brera behind the *palazzo* and with the aid of a road atlas, made her way north through the morning rush hour traffic. With wrong turnings and one-way systems, it took her more than an hour to get to Gorgonzola. The Lombard countryside was crisping with the onset of autumn.

A bent old village woman, dressed head to foot in black, walking with a stick, pointed the way to the Villa Rondine di Bonetti. But, asked the woman, did she really wish to approach the mansion? There had been a tragedy. A fatal accident. The family were in mourning.

The wrought iron gates were closed. Adopting the peremptory manners of the country automatically, Isobel blew her horn. Nothing. She got out of the car and tried to open the gates herself. They were too heavy and stuck on the uneven ground. She stood panting for a moment before a man in blue overalls emerged from the lodge.

The *famiglia* Bonetti, he said, were not at home. And yet, Isobel could see cars drawn up at the foot of the small Palladian palace about a quarter of a mile ahead on the summit of a slope.

"You don't understand," said Isobel sharply. "I am Signora Furio Bonetti. Please open these gates."

The man had orders to admit no one since the gates had been closed after the departure of the *polizei* the previous night. But the widow of the son of the house was surely different. His orders could not include her. Grumbling a little, he opened the gates for the *egregia* Signora. He should have been notified to expect her.

The house stared blindly out over its domain, its shutters, upstairs and downstairs, all closed. Parking the car on the gravel, Isobel walked up the long flight of stone steps. The great double doors, too, were formidably shut. Isobel pulled the iron bell knob embedded in the stone. Nobody came. She pulled it again and held it out to make certain the clanging inside went on till she got some attention.

Eventually, there were heavy steps and a voice. Carlo Bonetti opened the doors. At the sight of him, every last tremulous hope shrivelled in Isobel. Furio's father stood before the entrance to his house like Samson in Gaza, eyeless with grief.

"It is you," he said, gazing unseeingly over her head. "You quarrelled with my son and now he is gone from us. This much you told me yourself. You have brought a curse on my house. Never let me see you again. Your presence insults me."

An arctic emanation accompanied the words, isolating Isobel in a zone of heart slowing coldness. The doors were closed in her face and she was alone, staring at their blankness.

Driving back to Milan, struggling with tears that kept obscuring her vision, she wondered to whom she should turn, what she should do. How could any of this be true?

* * *

Isobel rung Ed Mazzerella in Rome on an impulse. Like her, he was a foreigner and would be easier to talk to. She was lucky to get him, he said, glad to hear her voice. He had only a week left before he took off for the hills and freedom at last. He had to go to a duty cocktail party in a minute . . . A thrash for the outgoing British First Secretary. What could he do for her? There was no chance of her coming to Rome, he supposed.

Relaying the facts of her predicament, Isobel listened to her own voice as if it belonged to someone else telling lies.

"I'm sorry to bother you . . . Giulia left me her telephone number for Comino, but I've lost it. I've looked all over. I never thought . . . I don't seem to have any money. Furio always gives me some when I want it. But . . ."

Isobel had tried ringing the Accounts Department at Bonetti Construction already. The switchboard simply cut off her calls at the sound of her name. When it happened for the fifth time, it dawned on her that it wasn't an accident. Today was Friday. She had to pay Maria.

"Is she there? How much does she know?"

"Yes, yes. She came at nine o'clock whilst I was out. She has a key . . ."

Confusedly, Isobel's mind ran on the trivial. Paying the rent at the end of the month. How was it done? Furio couldn't really have gone and left her . . . He was just unexpectedly absent and there were all these things to attend to. Death seemed to be largely a matter of edges unravelling in the fabric of the life left behind. There was no time to take in the emptiness . . . only to catch at the threads.

Realising, then, the enormity of what she seemed to be asking of Ed Mazzerella, Isobel started to say that there were other people, nearer at hand, whom she could talk to. All of Giulia's friends, her drawing master . . . Padre Stefano . . .

"I'm sorry, Ed. I can't think why I'm dragging you into all this when you're so busy . . . Look, you have to go . . ."

"The hell I do," was his instant reaction. The British stuffed shirt could yell himself goodbye right up his own ass. And a pretty fine echo chamber that was.

Ed Mazzerella took charge of everything. He left Rome on the next available flight to Milan and was with Isobel by the late afternoon. In his charcoal-grey tailored three-piece, London-made suit, he looked a different, more serious man.

If he had fantasised on the plane about Isobel throwing herself, grateful and grief stricken into his arms, Ed was disappointed. She was a model of dignified containment. As she said herself, her brain and her body seemed to be lagging far behind the actual events of her life. Wading through glue to steal up on reality. And what, now, was the reality? She was expecting Furio's baby. It couldn't be, could it, that already it was fatherless? What should she do? Her parents-in-law had made it pretty clear they wanted nothing to do with her.

"And that's nothing new," Isobel said, producing a copy of the prenuptial agreement. "But I have a child . . . Furio's child . . ."

"Which Carlo Bonetti will do his best to take off you," Ed interpreted the clause which dealt with the contingency support of any children of Isobel's marriage. He ached to put his arms round her but she sat bolt upright in the chair next to the spindly bureau which had been Lucy Larizzi's wedding present and in which most of the young Bonettis' domestic papers were kept.

Ed was afflicted with a mixture of awe and compassion. Every inch the *gran Signora*, she looked. But she was a penniless widow, from what he could gather, and incredibly, only eighteen. So much the better for him. The gods may have frowned on Furio Bonetti, but in the same moment, thought Ed, they had smiled down on him.

"Does he know you're pregnant?"

"No. I never got a chance to tell him . . . or Furio . . ."

"Good. Let's get out of here before he finds out . . ."

Ed had everything organised. Isobel was to return that day with him to Rome. His apartment, on which the lease was not to be surrendered for some weeks, had only one bedroom. It would be a privilege, he said, to give it up to Isobel. He would sleep at a colleague's, or on the sofa. The apartment here? Let Bonetti sort that out.

"Oh sure, you can bet your bottom dollar that once he cottons on to the fact you're expecting his grandchild, he'll take care of you. But once it's born, you'll have a fight on your hands . . . and no war chest, honey, if what you tell me is right, to hire yourself lawyers."

"But I can't just *leave* . . . This is my home . . . What about Giulia . . ."

Over the next few hours, Ed went through the possibilities with Isobel. The Montenaros? No doubt they could and would help.

Isobel shook her head. The Montenaros couldn't go on fighting her battles, shouldering her burdens for the rest of their lives. "And I'm used to having my own house now . . . " Ed nodded in agreement at what Isobel, with difficulty, explained. It was marriage and motherhood that made women equal. Not age, so-called 'position' or possessions. And there could not be two Queen bees in a hive without conflict. "I couldn't bear that between Giulia and me."

How about a job? But for what was she trained and how should she work as her pregnancy went on? The Bonettis . . . she had no reason to trust them and if they were going to attempt to separate her from her child . . .

"Sweetheart, you're welcome to everything I have . . . What say you and me make a go of it together? We start house hunting right away . . . I don't want to hustle you and I won't come on to you for any kind of commitment . . ."

It was all going much too fast for Isobel. Ed was kind, good and generous . . . Authoritative, brisk and efficient, which was just what was needed in this situation. And though he liked to think of himself as Italian, the fact that he wasn't, not actually, made him the best possible company at the moment. No tears, hand wringing or breast beating. But he wasn't really a close friend. More of a pleasant, casual acquaintance. And he was old.

Isobel backed away from Ed and his offer of shelter as kindly as she could. No man can show a woman any grander proof of his love than a willingness to protect her while she bears another's child. Ed was ready to do not only that but to spend his substance to support them both. Such chivalry is rare and, when found, difficult to understand or believe in. For Isobel, the thing was too big and came much too soon. The smell of her skin was still mingled with that of her husband's.

"Sweetheart, I wouldn't rush you but . . ."

"I think I should go home," Isobel said. "There's really no other choice."

Ed accepted that he had made a tactical error. He had closed every other gate for her but that. She had her mother in Plymouth. It was the escape route she chose. Of the emergency exits which lay open to her, it seemed to Isobel the least bizarre of the two. Did the Queen bee argument apply here or not? Isobel yawned. A warning to Ed not to ask. Logic was all very well in its place.

The following morning, after sleeping in the apartment's spare room, Ed rang the Villa Rondine on Isobel's behalf. There was nobody there except servants. They told Ed Mazzerella that the house was shut up for the moment. The *famiglia* had decamped for their native village in the south where the family mausoleum was situated. The body of their only son was to be conveyed there by road. The funeral was private, the name of the village unknown to any of the Villa Rondine servants. They were all Lombards. Signor Furio's widow? At the mention of her name, the manservant who did most of the talking to Ed became nervous and abrupt, putting the telephone down with a rattle before he could be asked any more questions.

"That's it, then," said Isobel. "I last saw my husband two days ago and I shall never see him again. Not even the wood of his coffin. So, they will not see their grandchild. I wonder who he will look like?" she added tightly.

Isobel left Milan that night. While she packed, Ed went out and bought her a plane ticket. There was no Bonetti money to pay for it.

"There are lots of things, but you'll be able to turn these into money quickly," Isobel pressed the diamond carnival masks on

Ed. They were the last things she wanted to part with but to be taking money from the American humiliated her. He must be able to repay himself quickly. He had already paid Maria's wages. Now he would pay her two weeks' money in lieu of notice. Ed put the earrings in his pocket, seeing there was no way of dissuading her. He had no intention of selling them but bought Signora Bonetti a first class ticket.

Locking up the apartment and leaving the Boromeo for the last time, Isobel didn't look behind her or linger. The Milanese period of her life was over. It had lasted less than a year.

At the airport, Ed kissed her goodbye on the lips, holding her to him. He knew he had gone too far with her when he felt her body go rigid. She had no feeling for him of that sort. Not yet.

"I can never repay you," she said just before handing her new, Italian passport over at the barrier.

"Yes you can. You can write. Care of the Embassy till I get a place. If you don't, I shall come and find you. We sailor guys don't mess around. You got that, lady?"

He went off, looking over his shoulder till he could see her no more. There were a quantity of short letters in his pocket to be posted to various people of whom Isobel wished to take leave. Her drawing teacher, for one. In fact, as Ed was leaving himself within the hour, the letters would be posted from Rome.

Isobel fastened her seat belt on the aircraft reflecting that everything that had happened to her in Milan, had been entirely precipitated by Nina Fischer. All she was taking away was a child about whom nobody knew but herself and Ed Mazarella, and a little more skill in her fingers.

For the first course of dinner there was *prosciutto*. Isobel, who had always loved it before, felt suddenly nauseated by its white ribbon border of fat. She ate nothing but fell to wondering what kind of reception she would get from her mother. Margaret Jefferson had not been warned of her daughter's impending arrival. There was no point, Isobel had reasoned, in telling her mother anything unpleasant in advance of its happening. She would only reject it.

PART II

NINE

"I really don't see," Margaret Jefferson sighed, "why all this should have happened to me."

She sat opposite her daughter in the bungalow's small living room, eyes closed and head thrown back as if in pain. There were hairs sprouting from the end of her chin, Isobel noticed before glancing away, embarrassed by the discovery. Poor Mummy. Why didn't she pluck them?

Afternoon tea was in progress. A weak infusion of PG Tips in Granny's silver teapot and a plate of biscuits from the Pennywise Supermarket. The meal, prepared at half past three was deemed to last until five thirty when both women would go to their bedrooms, wash and change, returning to the living room to sip a thimbleful of amontillado. Supper followed at seven o'clock. Then there was the ritual of the nine o'clock news which effectively ended the day. Isobel glanced at her watch. Ages to go yet.

Mrs Jefferson's remarks concerning her daughter's circumstances punctuated their routine at frequent intervals. The death of her unwanted son-in-law had rapidly become Margaret's own tragedy in which Isobel had only a small share. There was no room in this house for two women to suffer. Margaret had commandeered the privilege.

Robbed of her right to grieve, Isobel concealed a growing fear of entrapment. She knew something of slavery now. And whilst the metal of the chains might be different, the feeling of rising claustrophobia, followed by denial alternating with ripples of fear, were all too recognisable. And yet, the front door of Number 42 Armada Close was secured with nothing more daunting than a single Yale lock. Isobel had a key.

Outside, the horseshoe of modern bungalows, lined by spindly young rowan trees, held neither charms nor terrors. The West Country burr of passers by and neighbours was as familiar to her ear as the buzzing of her father's hives had been. In the nearby parade of uninspiring, suburban shops, the faces were friendly enough if curious. Isobel knew Plymouth but in it, she had no place except with her mother. There were no rescuers here.

All her old schoolfriends were preparing to go away to colleges in other parts of the country. Some had already gone. Their young lives were just now beginning as Isobel's was ending. Guessing all this, Isobel had contacted no one. Too great a gulf separated the pregnant foreign widow from the virgin English schoolgirl newly promoted to the exciting status of 'student'.

After the first few days, Isobel could see only one route to freedom. Money. A measure of independence, however small, was necessary to balance the relationship between herself and her mother. Dependence on a wealthy young husband is one thing, to sponge on an indigent parent is another. And Mrs Jefferson made no secret of her poverty. On the contrary, she exaggerated it, publicly promoted it, referring to it constantly as if it were a mark of distinction that might be overlooked. Prudently, Margaret contrived to convey that she was in rather worse straits than she was.

Oddly, it made her popular with local tradesmen.

"I have my daughter with me now," Margaret purred across the butcher's counter, wicker basket on her arm. "That puts a *double* burden on my tiny budget, Mr Isles. Have you any ideas for me? Such a great girl she is."

Accompanying her mother that day on her marketing rounds, Isobel writhed as Margaret simpered at the man in the striped apron. Overtopping both of them by some inches, she felt like a twelve year old again, large-footed and stumbling. Mr Isles must think her mentally deficient. A big, brainless dumb cluck.

"Well, Mrs Jefferson, ma'am," the butcher tipped back his straw hat to scratch his head in a show of deep thought. "There's trotters. And there's lights. Lung meat's good if you know how to cook it and there's no sweeter meat than a pig's foot if you can fancy it. There's plenty don't know their offal as they should."

Mrs Jefferson was determined not to be among them. After keen negotiation, a pig's trotter was decided upon.

"That'll be just two shillings, ma'am."

Margaret haggled the butcher down to one and fivepence, much to his delight. Mrs Jefferson was one of the old school and it was a pleasure to serve a real lady, especially round here, he sniffed. This was junior executive country. Very junior, if you asked Mr Isles.

More of the same passed at the greengrocer's with Margaret massaging the woman there with a skilful blend of patronage and confiding intimacy. It was the kind of flattery which had so nearly earned her husband a bishop's palace in the past. The greengrocer's kept a special box of cut price produce from which certain items were always removed and kept aside for Mrs Jefferson. A green pepper, less wrinkled than the others . . . a lettuce, hardly wilted at all, and a punnet of late imported berries with very little mould.

All this deteriorating deliciousness was rewarded with a good ten minutes worth of earnest enquiry about the eczema of someone called Tyrone.

"Isobel had just the same when she was a child," Margaret lied extravagantly with a warning glance at Isobel. "Covered with it, poor little love. One simply has to watch and pray as my husband would have said."

Isobel squirmed. For one thing, Daddy would never have said any such thing. Doubtless these toe curling fibs were intended by her mother to remind everyone of her status as a clergyman's widow. It was really quite pathetic.

"How *could* you Mummy?" she expostulated as they crossed the road to Pennywise to comb the shelves for special offers.

"People *like* you to enter into their little hopes and fears, Isobel. And if you'd ever had to support a family on a pension, you'd know the value of goodwill in the neighbourhood. One can't afford to be hoity-toity with shopkeepers. Not on my income."

These reproaches were never far from Mrs Jefferson's lips. Profoundly humiliated, Isobel submitted whilst she waited for a reply to the letter she had written to Alessandro, asking him if he could obtain some money from the proceeds of the sale of the contents of the Boromeo apartment. They had been wedding presents, after all, and she must be entitled to their value. Even Carlo Bonetti could not deny her that much.

Isobel would gladly work, she wrote, but could not hope to get a job until the baby was born. In the meantime she was without funds of any kind. Already, she had been forced to dispose of Giulia's earrings. She hoped she might be forgiven for preferring to save Furio's engagement ring. It was all she had left of him, something to show the child when he or she should be old enough. A wedding ring was not quite enough. One was much like another . . . Even so, the engagement ring might have to go. The baby would need all sorts of equipment which her mother couldn't be expected to purchase . . .

Alessandro telephoned at once to express his shock at what had happened. A child, too! Why had she not said? How long had she known? He gave his promise that he would do all he could. Giulia would see Beatrice Bonetti. The existence of a Bonetti grandchild should transform the situation. Carlo was committed to supporting his son's children. The pre-nuptial agreement bore his signature as well as his son's and Isobel's. At least its enforceability could be tested.

"No," said Isobel on a sudden presentiment. "Don't say anything about the baby. He's the sort of man who might try kidnapping it."

Alessandro laughed that off. Carlo was far too visible these days to risk indulging in that sort of villagey violence. Pregnancy was making Isobel fanciful. She made him promise just the same.

"But come and stay with us, *cara*. There is no need for you to be lonely . . . We'll think what to do about the baby and money when it arrives . . ."

Irritated past endurance by this long conversation in Italian, taking place in the narrow hallway of her own house and which excluded her from participation, Mrs Jefferson snatched the receiver from Isobel's hand and addressed a tirade to Alessandro.

"I don't know what you want but I can assure you that Isobel wants nothing from you or any of those filthy Bonetti people. These have been the worst weeks of my life, let me tell you and I hold you in large part responsible. *You* were supposed to be looking after my daughter's interests and now see what's happened. It's an impossible situation for me at my time of life. My finances simply do not permit my undertaking responsibility for another family. Certainly not that dreadful dago's spawn . . . I've been to my doctor and he says . . ."

But Alessandro had already hung up. Mother and daughter stripped layers of skin from each other until gone midnight.

The next day, Isobel went to the Social Security people. She took her birth certificate and her passport. It was raining and the bus was full of people in wet wool clothes, smelling like sheep. In the centre of town, she tramped from building to building until she found the right place up five flights of stairs.

The dole office, with its case hardened clerks, counters and booths, was littered with spittle and cigarette ends. Directed to sit on a bench, Isobel waited two hours while the names of the many before her were called out peremptorily. People stared as the minutes ticked by. Eventually, Isobel took refuge in the tired looking pamphlets, flopping despondently from their racks.

"You're entitled to nothing," snapped the woman behind the grille, surveying Isobel's military style tunic. The buttonholes gaped slightly under the pressure of her enlarging breasts. The buttons themselves bore a famous designer's initial. Her gloves struck a false note as well. Nobody who came in here wore gloves. Knitted ones, perhaps in winter. But not glacé kid. The woman computed all this detail automatically and unconsciously. Mrs Bonetti or whatever her name was – done up like one of those

140

snooty cows in *Vogue*, anyway – was on the fiddle. A con merchant. Had to be.

"But I think I must qualify for something," Isobel said stiffly, hating to importune. "I have literally nothing. It says in this pamphlet . . ."

"Never mind the pamphlet. You're not English and you've no stamps . . ."

"I thought if I was really destitute . . ."

"Well, you're not destitute, are you?" the woman countered meanly. "Not with clothes like that. You can't be. Not with the way you speak . . ."

"What does that have to do with it?" Isobel shot back angrily. Shaking her head, the woman compressed her lips. No point in going into all that.

"Look," Isobel began again, "I have dual nationality, but as far as I can see, that doesn't matter. I'm homeless, pregnant and without any means of support. I've had two hours to read all your pamphlets and they say you can help me. Why won't you? Perhaps I could talk to someone else who doesn't mind the way I speak . . ."

"Don't take that tone with me," the woman said defensively. "You've no call. I'm doing all I can to help you . . ."

"No, you're not," Isobel raised her voice so that it could be heard all over the office. "Please get somebody else."

"You can fill in these forms," the woman gave in with a bad grace. "You'll have to get your skates on because we close for lunch."

Looking on in suppressed fury whilst Isobel's ungloved hand raced across the pages, the woman stared at Furio's diamond ring flashing its traffic-light colours.

"You could sell that," the woman said nastily. "Looks as if it'd be worth a year's wages to some people."

Isobel's heart clenched in fear. Could they make her sell it? It didn't say anything like that in the pamphlets. How stupid she had been to wear it. But it was like a talisman. The only thing she had left to remind her of who she was . . . had been.

"It's paste," Isobel said after a pause. "Cut crystal. Italy's full of stuff like this."

The woman gave Isobel a sneering, sideways glance.

At the end of it all, it was agreed that Isobel qualified for some support. As to housing, she could go down on the list but she would be lucky to get anything. There was a shortage of council accommodation in Plymouth and many people needing it. It was a depressed area. The place had been bombed flat in the war. Reconstruction was a slow process.

Isobel listened to the litany of explanation in despair.

"Unless your mother throws you out, it's no good coming to us. You've got a roof over your head. You're one of the lucky ones," the woman ended on a virtuous note. "You come for your Social Security money every other Thursday at two o'clock. Queue at Payments, over there."

Isobel left, consoling herself with the thought that the encounter had been no worse than some of her interviews with Signor Crivelli. But he had not despised her. With the Social Security woman it had been different. A squalid transaction between beggar and petty bureaucrat benefactor. Things were not done like this in Italy. There might be shouting, misunderstanding and tears there, but in all of it there was heat. The institutionalised charity of England tasted stone cold in the spoon.

Mrs Jefferson was not pleased with Isobel's news. No member of her family had ever had to go crawling to strangers before. Isobel bit her tongue and refrained from pointing out that the Montenaros had been strangers.

None the less, Margaret was happy enough with the contribution to household expenses that her daughter was now able to make. Isobel turned over all her money save a pound or two for bus fares and the like. The pre-natal clinic was miles away on the Tavistock Road. It meant two changes and a walk of a quarter of a mile uphill.

The increase of income made little difference to the quality of the table kept at Armada Close. Mrs Jefferson put money aside for purposes unspecified. The larder acquired some luxurious tins, hams, tongues, artichoke hearts and asparagus, not to be broached until the visits of one of her sons. She spoke of them often, dwelling on their successes and their affection evidenced by perfunctory telephone calls and scribbled postcards. Rupert's communications, less frequent than Simon's, came in for a disproportionate amount of discussion. Unlike Simon, Rupert was sparing with news of his doings. Too much about brilliant film scripts that would never get made because the money men were such short-sighted fools.

Simon had a girlfriend now. An air hostess. According to Mrs Jefferson, who had never met her, she was such a nice girl and from quite a good family. She was almost bilingual in French and spoke very good German. And of course, socially and practically, it would be hard to imagine any finer preparation for marriage. Now why hadn't Isobel thought of getting such a job?

"I shouldn't have been accepted, Mother. I'm too tall."

"Ah, yes," Mrs Jefferson conceded. "Your height's always been a disadvantage to you, darling. Let's face it, that's probably why you married the first man who looked at you ... afraid you'd never get another chance. And don't call me 'Mother', it sounds common."

Isobel tried to avoid making mental comparisons between her mother and Nina Fischer. Her own poor mother, she reminded herself, had lost everything too. Her life had narrowed to shopping, the cooking and consuming of meals. She talked of what flowers would be blooming in the Parsonage grounds. The snowdrops would be fading now ... those drifts under the elms that she herself had planted. But the new rector's wife would benefit from the early jonquils just coming into flower ... enough for the house and the church ... The *money* she and Laurence had spent on the gardens there ... all for someone else to enjoy.

In the scrap of garden adjoining the bungalow, nothing had been done.

Whilst Mrs Jefferson nourished herself on the past, Isobel thought of the baby. She was big now, wearing blowsy flowered smocks over rib sweaters, bought in a chain-store. She was glad that Giulia could not see her. Milanese mothers-to-be wore one piece dresses that fell in majestic folds from shoulder to knee. Furio would not know her now. Isobel flinched from his ghostly, horrified glance.

She had never said goodbye to Furio which made her long, one-sided dialogue with his child more intense. Like all expectant mothers, Isobel focused on that entity hovering on the frontier between imagination and reality.

This person whose existence was conditional, who had as yet no name and no known shape, was all that held her in a place where she had no wish to be. Carlo Bonetti, it transpired, would do nothing for her unless she came to Milan and arranged with him personally for the sale of her wedding presents.

Isobel refused. These finger-snapping tactics of Carlo's might work on his minions, but not on her.

Writing to Alessandro, she told him that her connection with the Bonetti family no longer existed. She regretted having asked him to mediate.

Even as she posted the letter she recognised the fallacy. She was called Bonetti herself and so would her child be. Furio's only legacy apart from his ring. The child had a right to its name, she supposed.

Letters came from Ed, illustrated with sketches of the tumble-down farmhouse he had taken in the Tuscan hills. The low pantiled roof was guarded by five sentinel cypress trees, slim black fingers pointing up to a sky whose colour can never be painted from memory. There was one of the Lamborghini parked in the shade

143

of an umbrella pine tree. Postage stamp pictures of paradise.

Ed was full of enthusiasm for his new life. There were plans for renovating the house, a bit at a time . . . the triumphant bargain he struck with a neighbour over an old iron bedstead. It was the star exhibit now in his recently opened curio shop. Encounters with other village personalities, some of whom were sharper than Machiavelli himself and others who were, according to Ed, two sandwiches short of a picnic.

The letters arrived every month, rays of sunshine, dried and packaged for export.

Isobel wrote back cheerfully. She was well and happy, she claimed, but dying to deliver the baby so she could get a job and find a home of her own.

How any of this was to be achieved, Isobel did not know. Only that it must be. It wasn't merely the chafing shoe of her mother's company but the absolute need for solitude. Since leaving Milan she had drawn nothing. Lately she had begun to trace lines in her head, imagining the flow of ink from a brush-tip with sensuous longing as a hungry man thinks of food.

But the power that had quickened in her hand was falling away from lack of exercise. She must be alone to describe the curves of her infant's form . . . unobserved and unmocked.

*   *   *

The baby was born with no more obstetrical fuss than is usual. Fuss of other kinds there had certainly been.

At the critical moment preceding the emergence of the baby's head, Isobel had quite deliberately kicked the midwife and sent her flying. She neither explained nor apologised for her spurt of temper. Isobel Bonetti did not take kindly to orders given by a woman who used her Christian name without invitation. Not when she was lying with her legs open, panting like a distempered dog. Not when they had shaved her pubic hair and taken away her rings. They didn't know, these people, who she was. Who she could be and one day, would be.

When the baby slipped from her, Isobel sat bolt upright and seized him, clasping the child to her breast, all bloodied and slimed before a nurse could prevent her. A boy. Enraged at the fierce handling, the infant bawled but was silenced when Isobel offered her nipple. She glared at the uncertain group surrounding the delivery room bed.

"Get my clothes now. I want to go home."

They tried forbidding her to leave, to which Isobel responded by throwing a blood-pressure gauge across the room. She was rather pleased with the range of facial expressions that produced. Highly comical. Next the clinical team sent for a senior obstetrician to advise on whether or not it would be safe to sedate her.

He thought not. Anyway, he quipped, it would have to be a veterinary dart if he did so. She wouldn't let him near her. Best to leave the young tigress alone with her cub and all would be well.

He persuaded Isobel to stay in the maternity ward for two days at least, for the sake of the baby. Isobel filled her time between feeding the child and sleeping with making things difficult for the nurses. She hated her helplessness, was deeply concerned about getting a job as quickly as possible, and was depressed by the way all the other mothers kept their visiting husbands away from her. As if she would look at any of them twice.

She said a word of apology to the ward sister on the day she left, however.

"I'm sorry, it's the smell of disinfectant. I don't know why but I really can't stand it. It makes me quite cranky."

The ward sister who'd planned to wear a 'good riddance' expression found she felt as if Isobel had given her a present.

*   *   *

In Milan Carlo Bonetti thought of Isobel as often as he thought of his son. Not content with murdering her husband with her intemperance, she defied her father-in-law's plainly expressed wishes. It was her duty to come here and accept a rebuke from him. Bereft of his son, cheated of a grandson, Carlo felt entitled to that. But all she was after was money.

He opened his desk drawer and saw the handgun he kept there out of habit. Cool, blue steel. How soothing it would feel placed against his temples. Slamming the drawer shut, Carlo denied himself what would then have been an indulgence. *La famiglia* depended on him.

He might, he considered, mount a low level watch on Isobel. And there again, he might not. Carlo found it difficult to make decisions these days. Hard to concentrate or find any sense of direction. That bitch had half killed him.

He went home early without watering his geraniums or flinging the usual insult to his personal assistant.

*   *   *

Little Sandro, named for Alessandro Montenaro and registered as a British subject, transformed the mood of his grandmother. There was no more talk of dagos and from her savings, Margaret provided

145

a brand-new layette of baby clothes. A present thriftily purchased, in fact, with her daughter's own money.

Margaret's household account books, so meticulously kept, never reflected her sources of income which enabled a convenient forgetfulness in these matters.

"Oh why didn't we knit?" she wailed, fondling Sandro's wisps of black hair.

"Because I can't and you wouldn't," Isobel pointed out.

"Only because it's bad luck to do too much before the baby's safely arrived."

Giulia sent whisper fine cot and pram linen from the exclusive shops in Milan, embellished with hand embroidered monograms and shell scalloped hems.

Tickled to be an uncle, Rupert came up with a generous cheque for nursery furniture. His promised Christmas visit had not taken place and was indefinitely postponed. However, he would be there for the christening if it brought Hollywood to a standstill. Isobel sniggered at the idea of there being the smallest risk of such a catastrophe. Mrs Jefferson was offended. Isobel must realise that her brothers were important people . . . men. And it was the lot of womenfolk to be flexible and fit in with their plans. That's what real femininity meant.

Revolted, Isobel held her tongue and went out to buy a breast pump. It looked like an instrument of torture and was no more congenial to use. But she had an interview for a job in ten days' time. By then she should be able to squeeze into some of her old clothes.

The advertisement, in the Plymouth *Evening Herald*, was for a 'Girl Friday' to help in a new clothing factory down by the Millbay Docks. The company was called Modex Fashions. Concerning the duties of the successful applicant, the job description was vague. 'Artistic bent helpful', it said.

Isobel was ready to sweep the factory floor. Anything to begin life again. To be allowed to draw would be utter bliss. Would they want to see a portfolio? Quickly, Isobel assembled some of the better sketches she had made at the Boromeo under Pietro Arnolfi's supervision.

*   *   *

Isobel got the job. It was not, as she honestly believed, the sketches which had clinched it, but her appearance.

Motherhood suited her as pregnancy had not done. With the elasticity of youth, she regained her figure almost immediately. Her hair shone again and strokes of cyclamen showed on her cheekbones. Her eyes, so large and eager, were full of the special, once-upon-a-time blue, unconsciously respected in a seagoing city. They denoted an unwritten pedigree of ravening, ravaging men who had once sailed down from the north taking what they desired and burning the rest.

Such looks excite and Martin Morrison was excited. He twirled his handlebar moustache till the wax at the tips crumbled. His motives for recruiting a 'Girl Friday' were as clouded as his job description. What he really wanted was a new factor in his life. A counter irritant to his wife, Maureen. They worked in the business together. There were rubs and resentments . . . contests for the loyalty of the staff. Maureen usually won those but Martin intended to have Isobel all to himself. What she did was unimportant. Her job, he told Isobel, would be to 'fill in'.

"Fill in what?" Isobel asked, literal as usual. Some, Martin Morrison thought, would have said obtuse.

"Wherever . . . whatever. You know. Sweep up, brew up, do some filing, answer the telephone . . . packing . . . model the odd garment for a buyer."

That, Morrison congratulated himself, was an inspiration. What girl would miss a chance like that? Modelling. They all fancied themselves at it. What was she? A size twelve . . . a fourteen? Not many London rag-trade houses had a house model as classy as this.

"You said something about an artistic bent being useful," Isobel gestured diffidently towards her sketches again.

Morrison eased the tie knot from the white collar of his pink denim shirt. Design was a minefield. That was Maureen's baby. One she guarded jealously.

He began to expound the background and policy of the company to Isobel. Modex existed to give the girl in the street – secretaries probably formed the bulk of the market – access to top international fashion at a budget price. Not cheap, Isobel was to understand, but affordable.

"Take the suit you're wearing," Martin stood up and walked up and down the room with his hands in his pockets. "Whether you know it or not, it's based on an Italian design. Valentino. Pound to a pinch of shit . . ."

Fascinated, Isobel kept quiet. Already she knew enough of the world not to say that her suit, the one she had worn on the day of her father's death, was a real Valentino. Anyway, it was a bit tight now, a fact that did her no disservice with Martin Morrison.

"So," Martin wound up his dissertation, "let's not try running before we can walk, eh? Fourteen pounds a week okay?"

Scenting a bargaining position, Isobel hesitated. There wasn't much room for manoeuvre but there was some. By chance, she chose the right lever.

"Well," she demurred, "I was hoping . . . You see, I live with my mother. I want a place of my own . . . nearer here. I was hoping to be able to afford to rent . . ."

"Okay. Sixteen, then. Can't do better than that."

Christ, yes, thought Martin Morrison. It was no good if she lived with her mother.

"Done!" Isobel rose and stretched out her hand from which the engagement ring had been left off. "I'll start house-hunting right away."

"You're married," Martin noticed the wedding ring on Isobel's hand with dismay. To withdraw his offer now would be awkward.

"Divorced," Isobel improvised shrewdly. Widowhood was so depressing.

"Great," said Morrrison, relieved. "What we need here is commitment. See you Monday."

Isobel danced out of the converted customs shed bestowing as she left, a champagne smile on a thickly made-up woman in a short leather miniskirt with a blonde, bouffant hair style, dark at the roots. She was coming through the swing doors into reception and Isobel, taking her for a customer, politely held the door for her. That must be her Porsche in the yard. It hadn't been there before.

Maureen went straight to her husband's office, flinging the door wide.

"Got your hands on your lousy cock already, Martin? Well, just so long as you keep them off Princess Pie-in-the-Sky's cunt! I won't have it. Do you hear me?"

TEN

In a day or two Isobel received written confirmation of her appointment. She saw that the salary agreed had mysteriously reduced to fifteen pounds a week, however, and debated with herself whether or not to raise the point at once or to leave it. Made wary of employers' machinations over remuneration by Nina Fischer, she steeled herself to ring Martin Morrison.

"Oh, did we say sixteen?" he answered Isobel's query innocently. "Very well then. Monthly in arrears. Just drop me a line confirming your acceptance and amending the salary detail. Bye now."

Good. So that was all right . . . or almost. Monthly in arrears meant two months without money. Still, she would have to manage. Isobel addressed herself to the remaining contents of the letter.

She was to work from a quarter to nine until five thirty in the evening. She would have bank holidays and two weeks' annual leave. There was no mention of lunch hours. An hour, probably, Isobel thought. As to her duties, these were made no plainer. Much would depend, the letter said, on her particular talents and day to day company requirements.

As it turned out, what Martin Morrison chiefly wanted of Isobel was to listen. His wife, who knew him too well, had long since ceased to offer any nourishment to his vanity.

"Familiarisation and induction," Martin said on Isobel's first morning. He unwrapped his long, flexible limbs which were snaked around the chair-legs and rose to his feet. It was the start of a long day. Coffee came in at intervals, made by Isobel knew not whom. Actually, it was the credit control clerk who had better things to do.

What did Isobel know about the rag trade? Nothing. That was all to the good, Martin said. She would have no bad habits to unlearn, no prejudices to shed.

From a quarter to nine until well past midday, Martin Morrison enlarged on his theory of executive training. A 'Girl Friday' position such as Isobel's, he told her, would produce rewards relative to what she put in. He despised a grudging worker . . . had no time for clock-watchers. Then he went on at some length about his RAF

149

days on the supply side. Hamburg had been bombed in flying suits approved by him . . .

Never still, Martin got up and down from his desk, leaned on a filing cabinet, sat on the edge of the desk nearest Isobel . . . squatted on the floor beside her to show her some obscure graphs. She found his nearness oppressive.

While he talked, Isobel was careful to keep her gaze fixed on him. Tired as she was becoming, it would be disastrous to be found guilty of inattention on her very first day. And Mr Morrison was being terribly kind to take so much trouble. Whenever she felt her concentration slip, she pulled it back and asked some thoughtful question to create a change of pace.

At one o'clock, he showed no signs of weakening and Isobel, whose stomach was growling, began to glance surreptitiously at her watch. If Martin Morrison noticed her distress he gave no sign of it. A lean, stringy man himself, he never ate lunch. Nor did Isobel that day.

Halfway through the afternoon, Maureen put her head round the door. There was a clipped exchange between husband and wife concerning some invoices before Martin introduced Isobel. She stood, one leg buckling beneath her.

"Oh, I'm sorry. Pins and needles. Didn't we meet?"

Maureen grunted, ignoring Isobel's reference to their earlier encounter.

"You'll get more than pins and needles if you sit here much longer. Blains on the backside and rocks in the head, like him," she wagged her head sideways in her husband's direction. "Stop yarning, Marty," Maureen addressed him directly, "and show this young woman round the factory. Find her something useful to do. We could use a hand in packing . . ."

"I'm very interested in what *you* do, Mrs Morrison," Isobel offered.

"I daresay," was the abrupt response. Maureen left the room, slamming the door behind her. Isobel flushed.

"As I was saying," Martin went on as if there had been no interruption, "there's a correlation between the increasing number of women employed outside the home and the overall growth in the textile industry . . ."

It wasn't until fifteen minutes after a shrill electric buzzer had signalled the end of the shift to the machine room operators that Martin said, "Now tell me about yourself . . ."

With tears of exhaustion not far away, Isobel said again what she had said at her interview. The minimum, spread thin.

Taking the initiative herself then, she gathered handbag and gloves together. It was ten past six. Mummy would be going hairless.

"Fancy a drinky-poo?" Martin said, rising from his perch on the windowsill.

"No. That's so kind of you but I really have to go now."

"Boyfriend?"

"No. Baby-sitting for friends," Isobel answered lamely, wishing she could have thought of a more stimulating fib. For some reason she could detect but not define, Isobel judged it wiser not to mention her baby. The chairman of Modex didn't want a 'Girl Friday' with ties . . . let alone a junior executive. Which of the two she was, Isobel had now ceased to care.

Watching from the studio window, Maureen saw Isobel walk a little unsteadily across the car park, her shoulders sloped with fatigue.

"Poor kid," the older woman muttered grimly. Marty's fluffy new toy looked a touch shop-worn

At Armada Close, Margaret was just finishing with baby Alessandro. She was grim and resentful. The six o'clock feed wasn't part of their arrangement.

"It won't happen again, Mummy," Isobel promised guiltily, wondering what on earth she could do to prevent it. Could she join a union or something?

She became adept at being in the ladies' lavatory around buzzer time. Either that or making some breathless, girlish excuse about meeting friends for a drink and a snack before going to the cinema. Martin didn't like it and would keep her chatting minutes after five thirty, but Isobel tore herself away every time. Her mother's goodwill was vital. *She* went off duty at six o'clock prompt.

* * *

The day Isobel received her first paycheque, Margaret opened the front door to her before Isobel could get her key in the lock.

"I'm sorry, you'll have to go." Margaret Jefferson clasped and unclasped her hands nervously, avoiding her daughter's eye. "I've done my best but it's getting too much for me. You must remember I'm sixty now . . ."

"Well, that's all right, Mummy," Isobel kept her features bland and bright. Her feelings, a blend of hurt, relief and sheer fright, were something she could examine later. "If you throw me out, the Council will have to find me somewhere of my own . . ."

"Throw you out!" Margaret broke in furiously. "Throw you out? I'm not throwing you out. I'm asking you to leave because I'm sick of looking after your damn baby. I'm tired and I'm old. I

151

never get a moment's peace. It's all right for you out at work all day . . . I never get a chance to go to the library or the hairdresser without dragging your son along . . ."

It was all true, of course. Babies, Isobel had discovered, were labour intensive. A round-the-clock job. And they took up so much space. Bottles and the sterilising unit in the kitchen, the pram they had to squeeze past in the hall . . . the rack of drying nappies in the bathroom. Number 42 Armada Close had lost its ladylike neatness. Noise and smells had invaded those small, painfully quiet rooms.

As soon as Isobel got home from Modex she gave Sandro his early-evening feed and put him down whilst her mother lay on her bed with the curtains drawn. The ceremony of sherry drinking had been abandoned without discussion. Once her son was settled, Isobel made the supper before rousing her mother. At ten, Sandro was awake again and clamouring for his bottle. By eleven, Isobel would be in bed, hoping to snatch three hours' sleep before Sandro's cries awoke her and she groped blearily in the dark to warm yet another bottle.

Sitting by the bedroom window, looking out over the unkempt, moonlit lawn at the rear of the house with its privet hedge, Isobel asked herself who else was forcibly awakened at this time of night for weeks on end. Political prisoners, undergoing torture . . . and other mothers. At this hour, the baby played with his feed, bubbling the milk provocatively, looking up at Isobel with dark, speculative eyes. It was the sternest test of any young mother's love.

Eight long weeks had already gone by with no end in sight. At six o'clock, Isobel would have to get up again, feed and bath the child before breakfasting alone and taking a cup of tea into her mother. Her bus left at a quarter past eight.

Just half an hour later, Martin Morrison would start talking again. Earlier, if Isobel was foolish enough to arrive earlier.

Each day before tiptoeing from the house, Isobel deposited a kiss on her sleeping infant's brow. The long, sweeping eyelashes curling on Sandro's cheek sometimes provoked a thickening in his mother's throat. A squirm of physical longing with no valid object. The child's face wore that same look of regal gratification which had adorned his father's after his parents had made love.

At such moments, the half remembered contours of Furio's features came sharply back into focus. And his smell. It was hard to believe that he simply no longer existed. Now there was only this posthumous son of his, knowledge of whose advent she had so selfishly withheld. If she had not done that, perhaps the three of them would now be together somewhere else.

The words 'at home', pushed themselves forward, but Isobel turned them away. This was home now, the natural place to be. Milan fled like a dream remembered only because it had been dreamed in colour.

"But we shall have to move house, chickadee," Isobel whispered to Sandro, the morning after her mother's pronouncement. "Granny's fed up with us both. Suits us, doesn't it? From now on it's just you and me."

The question of who would look after Sandro during the day was vexatious. But other people managed. Poor women had always gone out to work. Factory women.

"And I'm a factory woman myself now," Isobel muttered to herself as she closed the front door softly. "Whatever they do, I'll do it too."

On the way to work, Isobel reminded herself that she was lucky. Sandro was a strong child. The relentless regularity of his habits betokened health. They were pleased with him at the clinic. She'd had to take a day off to attend there and making an excuse had been difficult. If she used up all her credible 'dentist's appointments' on Sandro, when would she ever actually go to the dentist herself?

Picking up her handbag to allow a stout woman who always got on at the second Harwell Street stop to sit down, Isobel thrust Ed's unopened letter further down into the side pocket. Reading it would be a lunchtime treat to go with the sandwich she always took with her. With a bit of luck, Martin would have something to distract him while she ate.

*   *   *

There was a council flat available in a tower block out at King's Tamerton, not far from the Tamar Bridge. Isobel went to look at it and hated it. She'd been told it was all there was. Take it or leave it, said the Housing Department official, or go down to the bottom of the housing list.

Isobel decided she would rather go down to the bottom of hell than live there.

The place was miles away from anywhere she had reason or need to be. In the grey plaster corridors there was scrawling graffiti. Gibberish, most of it, with the odd obscenity writ large. The lifts were out of action and half the flats were empty. Nobody else, it seemed, wanted to live here either. Those who did were hollow eyed, chain smoking mothers with unstockinged, mauvish legs. They stood out on the walkways and stared silently at Isobel as she passed, screaming intermittent threats at the children who played vapidly on the iron swings far below.

It was from such desolation that Carlo Bonetti had made his fortune. Horrible man.

Isobel determined to go the next day to a building society. She knew nothing about this sort of thing ... how people without money bought houses. They did it somehow, Isobel knew. She would find out how. Martin would have to give her the time.

He made no difficulty about it whatsoever. A career girl, he said, needed a pad of her own. Martin used words like 'pad' with a ghastly enthusiasm unbecoming to his greying locks. A place, he continued, where she could let it all hang out.

"Let what hang out?" replied Isobel absently. "The washing?" He would take a degree of sharpness from her now.

Martin was very breezy that morning. Shops within shops ... selling direct to the retailer. According to him, that was Modex's next move. Isobel knew enough about the inner workings of Modex now to realise that if these plans ever came to fruition, it would be Maureen who brought them off. Martin was, as he boasted a dozen times a day, just the ideas man.

The branch manager of Tavistock Building Society took a dim view of Isobel's enquiry. First of all, what kind of thing did she have in mind? Where was her husband? She was married wasn't she? Learning that she was alone, the man in the pin-striped suit pursed his lips and steepled his fingers. This, he said, was not such good news. Single women were a bad risk. If the Tavistock was to lend, she would have to have half the purchase price of a property to put down. Did she have any children? Because if she did, that would make her job less secure in the nature of things. Employers had low commitment to working mothers ... who tended to put their children first ...

"No children, not at the moment," Isobel temporised, smiling. True enough, she excused herself. When she got home at nights, she had a baby. Oh, God yes. During the day, she didn't. "And I'm not pregnant." Absolutely true.

They got down to fine detail then and Isobel emerged into the windy, early summer sunshine knowing she could afford the mortgage repayments on a four-thousand-pound terrace house *if* she could find two thousand pounds. Otherwise, the possibilities reduced to a bedsit. Rent, she had also been advised, was money down the drain. The value of property was rising fast, even in Plymouth. The bricks-and-mortar bandwagon was the one to get on.

"Talk to your family," the manager said, showing her to the door. "Parents often come up trumps in situations like this. The way things are going, you'll be able to pay them the capital back when you sell."

Isobel felt the irony of all this but did not dwell on it. Her wedding presents must have been worth two thousand pounds at least. Damn Carlo Bonetti, his wicked accusations and his swaggering, bully-boy demands. Meet him in Milan? Why should she? She had met him within hours of Furio's death at his own front door and that had been enough. They had nothing left to say to one another. Never again, never.

When she got back to the factory, Maureen was waiting for her in reception.

"Come on, I've got a job for you. Never mind Marty. Let him talk to the walls for once."

The job was working the overlocking machine. The usual operator had gone off sick, and there was a rush order to get out. Maureen explained the machine. Isobel was soon happily neatening seam edges with her mind roaming blessedly free. There were nods and smiles from the other girls but nobody wanted to talk. They were on piece rates.

There was a stoppage, none the less, just before the afternoon tea break. Some problem over a collar on a prototype garment to be shown to an important customer next day. Isobel heard snatches of the conversation over the general noise of the machine room.

"It won't fit, I'm telling you."

"Get Keith in here," another voice suggested. Keith was the pattern cutter.

"Nah," yet another scorned. "Fetch Mrs Morrison to it. It's her design. She knows what's wanted."

Isobel left her task and stole up to the group of confounded women.

"May I look?"

"You can, my handsome, for all the good it'll do you. S'too big for the neckline and that's all there is about it." It was wiry, tough little Rowella Teague who spoke, the charge hand and shop steward.

With the inspiration of ignorance, Isobel fixed it.

"Wouldn't it look much better *without* the collar?" She held the half-stitched jacket up against herself.

Without drawing a line, Isobel had done her first bit of design work for Modex. Maureen, when summoned to the scene of the trouble, swept her with a slit eyed glance.

"Try it then," she said finally, clipping the collar section deftly, to convert it to a facing. "It looks as if Miss Clever Clogs here has solved it . . ."

The collarless jacket became one of Modex's best selling lines. Profitable, too, as it took less cloth to make.

"Not just a pretty face, then," Maureen said a month later, handing Isobel her pay packet. There had been two very substantial orders for the jacket as the whole workforce knew.

Isobel walked on air to her bus stop. Everything was beginning to come right. She must write and tell Ed.

* * *

Things continued to improve, due in large part to Isobel's belief that the time had come to sacrifice Furio's ring. She had seen something she wanted more. It was a humble two-storeyed, stucco-fronted terrace house in Northumberland Terrace, just off Grand Parade . . . a spit from the sea and ten minutes' brisk walk to Millbay Docks and the factory. It had a bay window downstairs and was painted pale, pistachio green.

She saw it one lunchtime when Martin was preoccupied for a change and Maureen told her to get herself out for a breath of fresh air.

"Can't have the *real* ideas person round here getting cabin fever, can we?" Maureen, in her rough and ready way, was kind.

The art of elegant subtraction was now looked on as Isobel's modest speciality. Clean lines meant less thread, less cloth, less labour and, if the order book did not lie, more sales. Isobel's job seemed safe. She had found a comfortable niche.

The little house, Isobel believed, would make everything perfect. A nest for herself and her child, a place to begin painting again . . . a retreat from the stresses of Modex. Being talked at by Martin still absorbed a large part of her day there.

Better still, Rowella, to whom Isobel confided her domestic worries in the strictest confidence, had told her there was a baby minder just six doors away. Her own grandchild was cared for there whilst his mother worked in the fish market over Sutton side.

"Fat Freda . . . She's a messy old moo," opined Rowella, "but she'll not let a child cry. I'd have thought you'd want a proper nanny though, someone like you," she added frankly.

"Can't afford one," Isobel replied with equal frankness.

"Crying shame," said Rowella. "They should be paying you double, the amount you do."

Isobel brought her mother to view the house in Northumberland Terrace one Saturday, carrying Sandro in her arms. The place was empty so the agents had left the key with a neighbour for Isobel to pick up at leisure.

"You can't live here," Margaret said flatly, surveying the peeling paintwork and the dingy net curtains in neighbouring houses. "It's not a suitable area. As for this child minder idea of yours . . ."

Ignoring her, Isobel pushed the front door open, against a wedge of football pool forms and circulars that lay on the tiny vestibule's linoleum floor.

Nothing, the agents had warned, had been done to the house in the last twenty years. The vendor, a frail octogenarian, had been taken away to an old people's home.

As Isobel soon saw, he had possessed neither the energy nor the means to efface the artisan, turn-of-the-century charm of the place. Fireplaces, coving, dado and picture rails, the touchingly grandiose plaster arch in the hall with its scrolled corbels . . . all were still there. No central heating, though, and a cranky old gas fired geyser to heat up the water. But the house was dry and the tasteless wallpapers stuck firm to the interior walls.

"Two up, two down and no nonsense," Isobel smiled. "Don't you like it? I do. *You* do, don't you, Sandro? We could have a fire in that nice little grate in your nursery on cold nights. Let's hope for wonderful storms."

Margaret sniffed. Anxious as she was to be rid of her duties as daily nursemaid, the thought of visiting her daughter in such a place as this did not appeal. What the particulars of sale called a kitchen was a miserable back-extension scullery with a cramped bathroom above. The attic, by which Isobel set so much store, was musty with the smell of the yellowing newspapers piled there. Studio, indeed. It wouldn't do at all.

"Well, I think it will," Isobel insisted. "I love it and I'm going to have it."

"I can't think how," Margaret objected. "They want three and a half thousand pounds for this slum."

It was for this reason that Isobel responded to an advertisement she found in a fashion magazine of Maureen's. Richard Ogden's Ring Rooms in Bond Street, London. They would make offers on any stones submitted to them for appraisal. Isobel rang the Bond Street premises and was assured that if she sent her ring by registered post, it would be covered by their own insurance. She need have no fears. An offer would be telephoned soon after they received the parcel. If she accepted it, a cheque would follow immediately. If not, the ring would be returned by the next post.

"In case you don't come back," Isobel kissed the ring before parcelling it up. She felt foolish and rather weepy. In her mind, she spoke to her dead husband. He would rather, wouldn't he, that their baby had a roof over his head than that his mother should keep a jewel blazing unseen in a drawer? She no longer wore it. It made her too vulnerable to curiosity.

Once the ring was posted, Isobel was tormented by doubt. Would she be robbed? What reason had she to think that people so far away in London were to be trusted? She had carelessly thrown away her child's only patrimony.

The valuer rang three days later. The diamond baguette shoulders were a nice, quality feature of the ring itself he said. There was a lot more technical stuff – which, thanks to Giulia, Isobel understood – about the depth of the main stone's pavilion and the spread of the table. A big stone. Close on three carats. Not first water . . . there were a couple of carbon spots which accounted for the colour it threw. Still, he was able to offer two thousand, two hundred pounds. Would that be all right for her? It was a very pretty thing.

Isobel stammered out her agreement, racked with a combination of sorrow, gratitude and elation. Furio's love token was gone . . . but she had Sandro and a new home.

*　　*　　*

Benefiting from the celerity which attends the simple affairs of those who have capital and no house to sell, Isobel moved into Northumberland Terrace within four weeks. And, because she had not yet attained her majority, Simon acted as guarantor for the small mortgage.

"Oh be careful, darling, *please*," Margaret enjoined caution on her second son. After all, he was thinking of getting engaged and must consider himself.

"Iz won't let me down," Simon was short with her. "She's had a rough ride and this is the least I can do. Flesh and blood, Ma."

Margaret put the telephone down, irritated. She felt obscurely jealous of this new excitement in her daughter's life. Why did everyone always take *her* side?

A short time after this, when Isobel had already left Armada Close, she was contentedly painting the front parlour walls at Northumberland Terrace when there was a knock at the door.

Mummy, possibly, Isobel thought as she climbed down from the steps. Lonely, already? No, more likely the milkman wanting his money. It was too late for Mummy to come all this way on a bus.

It was half past eight on a warm August evening and Sandro was asleep in the back bedroom upstairs. Isobel thought of him as she wiped her brush on a rag. The narrow back yard overlooked by his room would be the next job. White wash and geranium pots . . .

158

"Oh, it's you."

The words, unintentionally rude, were shocked from her by the sight of Martin Morrison standing on the doorstep. In one hand he carried a bottle of wine and in the other, a young rubber plant. Beneath the precisely horizontal moustache, his mouth wore a confident grin.

"House-warming pressies," he said. "Can I come in?"

He was alone.

ELEVEN

The secret of Sandro's existence was soon out.

He slept through that hour and a half of strained civility during Martin Morrison's first visit to his mother's house, but at nearly six months old, he was less predictable in his rhythms than hitherto. On a subsequent occasion, he broadcast his presence lustily.

All Martin said, once he had got over his surprise and disappointment, was that he didn't blame Isobel.

"Quite right," he gawked at her. "Private life is private life. What you get up to at home is nobody else's damn business."

Having a baby was hardly 'getting up' to anything, Isobel thought, vaguely troubled by her employer's choice of words. She read nothing into them, however. Perhaps Martin would be more inclined to respect her privacy now he knew she had interests and responsibilities besides her work for Modex.

Unhappily, Martin seemed determined to become a regular participant in Isobel's private life. She found herself powerless to parry his intrusions, partly because they invariably came without warning. A knock on the door, a quick, smiling apology for disturbing her at home after working hours, and there he would be with a sheaf of papers under his arm, which needed, apparently, Isobel's instant attention. Flattering at first, if tiresome.

"I'd really value your opinion on this," he would say, stepping over the threshold. "I say, any chance of a cup of coffee? You're making a smashing job of this place, if you don't mind me saying so . . ."

Of course Isobel didn't mind. She was easily drawn into showing and discussing her purchases of Edwardian furniture . . . available for a pound or two in any junk shop in those days. Afterwards, she cursed the way she had allowed herself to be seduced into lowering her guard. Wasting her time.

When he finally went after one of these invasions – they happened twice or even three times a week – Isobel would be left, with Sandro yelling for attention, herself drained of energy and her evening project untouched. There seemed no way out.

As autumn dragged itself out into the start of a wild, wet coastal winter, Martin adopted a more intimate stance. Could he go up and check on the baby for her? It was the least he could do. And so on.

"Won't Maureen be worried about you?" she asked him hopefully one night when he seemed more firmly glued to his chair than usual.

"What, Mo?" laughed Martin with awful cosiness. "Doesn't give a shit, dear heart, just as long as I'm not spending any loot on totties. With you and me, it's strictly business, isn't it? You're a very businesslike girl, aren't you, Isobel."

Isobel said she hoped so and wondered when would be the best moment to broach the possibility of a payrise. Surely one wasn't expected to live, eat and dream Modex for sixteen pounds a week indefinitely.

Her salary was not the only aspect of her life that Isobel reviewed. Sandro slept through the night now and she ought to have more time to herself. But upstairs, in the freshly painted attic studio, where she had laid out her materials with so much hope and anticipation, no fresh start had been made.

It seemed bad enough to Isobel that Martin Morrison frequently caught her ironing underclothes or dusting her few possessions, or even, sometimes, eating. If he were to come upon her in the midst of a painting or drawing session, it would, Isobel was sure, have much the same effect on her as a telephone ringing during sexual intercourse. Scarcely bearable.

Having only recently escaped the nursing mother's treadmill of four hours' sleep a night, Isobel decided she would have to get up early to find the time to draw. If she was in the attic by five o' clock in the morning, she would have an hour clear, two at a pinch, before Sandro woke.

It didn't work. An artist needs more time than it physically takes to draw, paint, or mentally compose something. There must be a long period, unthreatened by any other imperative, in which she or he can gather courage for an assault on the weakness which assails the strongest creative will. Cowardice must be outfaced. Fear of failure, overcome. Every artist knows that a confrontation with self calls for a preparation of silence. Deep meditation.

There was time, however, Isobel told herself calmly, for her life to quieten, to sort itself out. Four or five years, in fact. She would then be twenty-three or four and Sandro would be ready to go to school. In the meantime, Isobel planned to collect together a portfolio of finished work of which she could be proud. She would qualify, then, for a mature student's grant. She would take her work to art schools, obtain a place at one of them, sell the house

161

and remove herself and Sandro to the town or city in which her future artistic education lay. That she would get there in the end, Isobel had no doubts at all.

For the present, she must concentrate on holding down her job. Bread and butter, the roof over their heads . . . those were the immediate priorities. If she could just work a little . . . A slow start wouldn't matter. Time, ultimately, was on her side. Buoyed up by this scheme, Isobel wrote of it to Ed. It made it seem more real, nearer to full achievement, to see it all laid down in words.

Life went on in this way. Walking a tightrope between Martin and Maureen . . . snatching an hour to go shopping in the middle of the day, when either Martin's back was turned or Maureen gave her permission.

As for a payrise, the right moment never seemed to come.

At the weekends, there were blustery walks with the pram on Plymouth Hoe, looking out over the Sound, watching gulls soar and dive over the grey, wintry waves. Isobel showed the indifferent, chirping Sandro all the statues of England's maritime heroes.

Out loud, she pictured for him the rich men who had been bold with their money, standing at the tall windows of the handsome cream houses on Grand Parade, with telescopes to their eyes, searching for sight of their white winged ships beating against the wind up the Sound. Adventures, small and great, which had made England's name ring round the world.

Plymouth would never be Milan, but if Isobel kept away from the city's new, grey concrete core, with its chain-stores selling gimcrack goods to an impoverished population . . . of which she herself was a part, she could feel empathy with Plymouth. It conjured some echo in her of an unrecorded ancestry, a print carried forward through countless generations, of a venturing spirit. Scream of gull, roar of breaker, scudding, rain bearing clouds and the clean smell of salt . . . all, with an effort, became dear to her.

A second bonding with a second city. In the one she had been a wife to her husband, in this, she was a mother to her son.

On Sundays, there was usually lunch with her mother. It was an affair of starched napery and tiny joints of meat. The talk, mostly of Rupert or Sandro's accelerating development. Simon's engagement seemed to be off. The air hostess girl wanted no children. Clearly, a tart.

"I went out to Plymstead Magna on Wednesday to put some flowers on Daddy's grave," Margaret Jefferson reported on one such Sunday. "I took a peek at the Rectory, of course. So sad. Those people have no idea. They've taken the shell hood down over the front door . . ."

"It was going to fall down of its own accord, if somebody didn't, Mummy," Isobel reminded her. "You said so yourself. It might have killed someone one day."

"Oh, I know. But the *people* we get taking Holy Orders these days."

Isobel was always glad to get back to her little house near the sea.

No painting, however, got done. The fresh block of cartridge paper gathered dust in the attic at Northumberland Terrace. The virginal canvas board set up on Isobel's easel in readiness, waited vainly. Between Sandro and her job, all of Isobel was spent.

Sometimes, in bed at nights, Isobel cried out her resentment and frustration . . . or was it for Furio? Her life stretched out before her: a long, featureless road to the grave. Leached by her offspring's long dependence, she would shrivel unseen like a seed potato.

She was supposed not to mind about it, which only made it worse. There was nobody Isobel knew who would be ready to hear her say that a single mother's life was an open ended sentence. Certainly not her mother. She was lucky, wasn't she? She had a respectable job, a house of her own and a beautiful baby boy. What more could any decent woman want?

"But I don't have *myself*!" Isobel answered imaginary detractors aloud, kicking the cooling hot water bottle out of bed. It burst and in the morning, drips of water were coming through the parlour ceiling. A punishment, Isobel could not avoid the thought, for having told herself the truth.

"We must see what we can do about giving you a company car . . ." Martin said, leaving Isobel's house one evening. "I look on you as a friend you know, a *personal* friend . . . quite apart from your position with us at Modex." His hand, already annoyingly on her back, slid down to her rump and cupped a buttock. Isobel slapped it away automatically.

"Oh sorry," he bridled. "That was quite inadvertent, I assure you . . ."

It wasn't and Isobel complained to Maureen next day.

"I'm sure he means no harm but . . ."

"You must have led him on," was Mrs Morrison's astonishing reaction. "Rather risky in your position, isn't it? Run along to Packing now and see if you can keep yourself out of trouble there."

Trembling with indignation, Isobel spent the afternoon stacking Moygashel summer skirts on rails while the Morrisons had a row which could be heard all over the factory.

On Friday, Isobel got her cards and one week's wages with them.

Maureen, who usually distributed the wages, was with a

customer, and Martin Morrison was out. Convenient for them both. Neither had given Isobel any warning of her summary dismissal.

With her mind in free fall Isobel protested to the woman who supervised the general office.

"I don't understand. What have I done wrong? Don't I get a month's notice? I'm paid monthly . . . it says so in my letter of appointment . . ."

Regarding her with sympathy, the supervising clerk looked up Isobel's personal file. There was nothing there apart from tax forms and Martin's first letter to Isobel, the content of which she had disputed, and her reply, which was supposed to set the record straight. No written evidence that Martin had agreed the terms revised by telephone all those months ago. None at all.

"I'm sorry, love," the woman said. "You shouldn't have come till you'd got another letter out of him. He's a tricky one, is Martin. Look, he left you this."

Stunned, Isobel took an envelope from the woman's hand and opened it. A few cold lines of type. The company's directors, it said, had been patient with Isobel in the hope she would learn to overcome her 'unfriendly attitude'. Since this now jeopardised Modex's 'relaxed, family atmosphere', so critical to the company's working efficiency, it was with regret that the directors had decided to terminate Isobel's probation. Martin had signed it with best wishes for her future.

"What probation? I was never *on* probation," Isobel stood her ground whilst a queue of machine room women waited inquisitively behind. "And he owes me seven weeks' money. I was paid monthly in *arrears* . . ."

"Sorry, love. I only work here. I do what the bosses say. Tell you what, you might catch Rowella before she gets her bus. I doubt she'll be able to do much . . . you're not a union member, are you?"

Isobel left on wobbly legs, hoping no one noticed. A few of the overalled women touched her in commiseration as she passed them in the cloakroom. Most of them had children. Isobel spoke a word or two. It was all right. She would find something else.

This time at least, she had somewhere of her own to go to. But with the mortgage payment due and thirty two pounds in her handbag, that little home might soon slip through her fingers.

*   *   *

Walking the few steps down the street to collect Sandro that afternoon, Isobel pictured herself in retrospect, standing in the Modex general office at the head of the wages queue. In her memory, the composition of that scene had a gloomily cheering parallel.

Well, I only lost my job, Isobel told herself, not my head. The involuntary juxtaposition of herself with Nina Fischer's mother shocked her, as the smile plucking at her mouth shamed her. The comparison was wicked in its triviality, Isobel knew. But there was something in its half visual structure . . . a proportion, a balance, that left the rictus of discovery on Isobel's face. Better than a down turned grimace with which to greet her son. There was nothing on Isobel's horizon to call forth a genuine smile. Freda must be paid.

The fat woman's front parlour, reeking of nappy sterilant and fried fish, seethed with vociferous, chocolate smeared toddlers disputing the ownership of toys. Mothers in thin plastic macs were groping in their purses for the baby minder's dues which Freda accepted, stuffing coins and notes into her pinafore pocket. Friday picking up time was always a nightmare.

"I hear you've been let go," said Freda, eyeing Isobel keenly, as she handed over her four pound notes. "Will you be wanting to keep the place for Sandro . . . because once it's gone, it's gone. I've a waiting list."

"Thank you, yes," Isobel replied with as much dignity as she could muster. Bad news, it seemed, travelled fast in working communities. "I want Sandro to stay. I'll have to go for interviews."

"You'll have something put by, someone like you, I shouldn't wonder," Freda acknowledged complacently. "It's different when some of them are out of work . . ."

Habits of economy came no more easily to Isobel than they had to her father. Much had been spent on the redecoration and furnishing of her house. Only the previous month she had bought a little Victorian Davenport desk she ached for. Paid more than she really had a right to pay . . . She didn't know how long she could survive without another job. A week or two, perhaps.

The thought of returning to that woman in the Social Security office was distasteful. If she didn't it would mean missing a mortgage payment. Simon's confidence in her could not be betrayed. What would her mother say . . . need she be told?

These thoughts harrowed Isobel's mind as she attended to Sandro's needs. He was more lively now and rarely settled for the night before seven o'clock. That evening he splashed and gurgled in his bath, laughing up at his mother, the source of all strength and security. For his sake she hid her despair, reshaping her face against the gravitational pull of anguish.

Rowella came an hour later, just as Isobel was wondering whether or not she should open the only can of soup in the house.

Mushroom. She had no appetite. The knock on the door made her jump.

"I've brought you your proper wages, my handsome," stated the shop steward with something like belligerence. "'S' nearly all there anyhow," she said, handing Isobel a suspiciously unofficial looking packet as Isobel coaxed her into the parlour. "I told that sneath Maureen if she didn't give you what she owed, I'd bring the whole factory out till she did."

Of course, it wasn't true and Rowella took one glance at Isobel and saw she knew it too. Rowella had no authority for such a strike, nor had she had time or opportunity to threaten Maureen with it. She and the other girls had had a whip round for Isobel at their usual Friday evening pub.

"I can't take it, Rowella," Isobel said. "You know I can't. It's nearly Christmas and all your girls have children of their own. Not just one . . . and some of them have husbands out of work."

"What you need's some tea," Rowella said, prepared to lay a long siege to Isobel's resistance. "Proper tongue furring stuff. That's right now, you have yourself a cry . . ."

There was no chance of that. The colloquy with Rowella was interrupted by the arrival of Isobel's mother.

"I see you're entertaining one of your friends," she said without a glance in the other woman's direction. "Here, I came to give you this. I suppose you'd better have it."

Margaret removed yet another envelope from her worn crocodile handbag and placed it in Isobel's hands. Two postmarks had been superimposed, one on the other. The stamps were Italian and the letter had the aged look of one which had been long in the post.

"More of those frightful Italian people. If you take my advice, you'll forget all about that. Oh, *please* don't get up," she said finally, patronisingly, to Rowella. "You must be one of the work people from Isobel's factory. I expect you've got your heads together to bridge the labour relations divide we hear so much about. Visiting each other's homes . . . How nice."

In that moment, Isobel came face to face with the unpalatable fact that she detested her mother.

"My mother's a lady," Isobel said. "Not a woman."

A captivating distinction, which occupied much of Rowella's thoughts for some years to come.

"You've a tongue like a filleting knife, you," she said admiringly, putting on her coat. "Smart as paint, you be. What you wants is a job with training. You'll not take your wages then? Too much the lady, eh?"

"No," smiled Isobel. "Too much the stubborn fool."

166

Charity, she thought, shutting the door behind Rowella, could get to be a habit. She was left with the Italian letter in her hand. She turned it over once before going upstairs to put it on her dressing table. There had been enough of envelopes today. It was time for mushroom soup.

TWELVE

To those who live alone, and who are, like Isobel, of an intro-spective cast of mind, there is something ominous about any letter, the origin of which is unknown. This particular communication, bearing about it the scars of delay – an obstructed journey between originator and recipient – lay several days on Isobel's dressing table.

There seemed no urgency to open it and little point in doing so. Whatever news the letter contained, it was, according to the first smudged postmark, more than a year out of date. Stale. It had been addressed in the first place to the Boromeo apartment in handwriting that Isobel didn't recognise. She may have seen it before, but couldn't recall. The distinct leftward slope of the characters triggered no memory. Whoever her correspondent was, Isobel deduced, she, or possibly he, had not known her well. The letter was addressed to Signora Bonelli. Maybe it wasn't meant for her at all.

The sense of release which this thought occasioned was soon dispelled by the realisation that the word *'appartamento'* had been spelled *'apparlamento'*. This person didn't cross *t*'s. That omission alone made Isobel uneasy. What sort of person eschewed such a critical stroke?

Perhaps there was something in the violent pencil deletion of this block of eccentric script. A diagonal line, Isobel judged, that had started bottom left of the original, handwritten address and finished just above it to the right, terminating in an exasperated, cat's tail curl. Understandable. Readdressing other people's letters must be a bore. Who had done it? The subsequent direction to her mother's house was correctly typed on a label, margin justified to the left . . . and gave nothing away.

One of the several stamps the envelope bore was beginning to lift at the edge. Isobel ran her thumb along the serrations. She put it down again and started brushing her hair, frowning. Tag-ends and fag-ends of her former life must wait.

Downstairs in the squashed dining room behind the parlour, the week's serious business awaited. The *Evening Herald*'s job vacancies columns must be combed. Isobel sat at the table with the paper before her, red biro poised. She had got a job before, she would get another one now. There's no such word as *can't*, her mother used to say in nursery days. Another of those slippery, adult confidence tricks . . .

Would she, Isobel wondered, be any good at selling double glazing? No qualifications or experience necessary, said Kozyseal's advertisement. Full training given. Successful appointees were rewarded with a Ford Cortina and expectations of up to five thousand pounds in their first year with the company. Representatives worked from home, independently.

That would be something, never mind the money. A low level of contact with employers was the best feature of this job.

Do you enjoy meeting people? Are you confident, smart and able to communicate with people on all levels? Isobel turned Kozyseal's words over in her mind. *Only strongly motivated persons between eighteen and thirty with a burning ambition to succeed need apply. Clean driving licence essential. Photograph appreciated.*

"Well," Isobel murmured to herself drily, "I have a burning ambition to pay the mortgage. My driving licence is Italian . . . but clean. And I have a photograph, so I'm qualified. I'm about to have an unauthorised overdraft as well, which makes me mustard keen."

The application, cannily peppered with the word 'keen', was written. So also was one to a dry cleaning firm wanting a counter hand of 'smart appearance'. There was a dentist who wanted a trainee nurse, an hotel seeking the services of a receptionist . . . knowledge of switchboard preferred. Well, said Isobel to herself of that one, *preferred* means what it says, and I'm sure I'll get used to smiling on a continuous basis. But occasional evening shifts? No, that was no good.

Styletex Ltd, located in Plymouth and Modex Fashions' chief rival, had no vacancies that week. Isobel wrote to them anyway with a full description of her broad experience, emphasising her success with the collarless jacket. Designer, model, overlocker, filing clerk, packer and general management sounding-board . . . How could Styletex resist her?

During her first week of unemployment, in between responding to advertisements, applying in writing for every job she could either do or half-do, Isobel amassed a growing body of negative information about the unopened letter from Italy. A game of grandma's footsteps.

It was not a card of invitation to some party that had taken place without her. Too soft. By the same rule it was not a reminder from a shop that some item or other awaited collection . . . much too thick for that. And wouldn't a shop have typed the address? Not necessarily. A modest catalogue . . . a list of sales goods? Yes, almost certainly that. So open it and throw it away.

Isobel did neither.

Whilst she waited for replies to her job-hunting letters, she began to draw again. During the day, her isolation was complete. With Sandro at Freda's and worries about money gnawing her mind, the attic studio issued its summons. There was now no excuse.

It was difficult to put a mark on paper at first, and certainly not on canvas which was much too precious.

One line, Isobel screamed silently at herself. One line, can't you even do that? It need have no meaning, it needn't be beautiful, no one need ever see it . . . just *one bloody line*!

After the passage of an hour or more, Isobel stabbed angrily at a sheet of cartridge with a soft pencil. She held it in her fist like a dagger, prepared to tear the paper in her impotent rage. It did the trick. Calmer now, she began to draw single lines, one to each sheet of cartridge, discarding the sheets one after another. They floated to the floor, forming an untidy pile. Horizontal, vertical, oblique . . . curved, straight, undulating . . . wiggly like the feel of that stamp on the letter.

From there it was a short step to imitating the cantankerous line which crossed the handwriting on the envelope in the bedroom below. That was satisfying. Up and over. Up and round, lightening the pressure as the pencil travels, flicking it away at the last moment to get that petulant curl. So many slight variations.

The time flew.

Isobel was late collecting Sandro from Freda's. She ran down the street, her face glowing with the pleasure of this old, imperfect faculty recaptured. No, not quite that, perhaps, but she had tweaked it by the tail.

"You've found work, then," Freda observed.

"Yes, no. Well, not really. Not yet." There were no words to tell Freda what she had found.

Sandro was rolling on his back from side to side in a corner of the chaotic room. Chortling with delight, he waved a blue plastic dummy in the air before putting it in his mouth. A new accomplishment.

"Should he have that?" Isobel enquired anxiously. Sandro had never been given a dummy and it was a matter of mild concern to know where this one had come from. Freda's ideas of hygiene were suspect at best. And she didn't take kindly to criticism. Fussy mothers, as she'd said before, knew what they could do.

170

"They pick up all sorts, don't they, at that age," Freda commented placidly, removing the dummy from Sandro's mouth before wiping it on her apron. "Builds up a resistance."

"I'm sure you're right," Isobel said quickly, ingratiatingly, wanting to believe it. Freedom to work, to earn a living and draw . . . Sandro would just have to resist the onslaught of germs as best he could. Whole armies of them, if that's what it took.

When the child had ingested his supper of pulverised lamb and mashed carrot with infuriating, sloppy slowness, Isobel put him to bed. It was no longer the swift, administrative task that it had been. Sandro insisted on a sequence of rites which began with complex waterborne exercises for every one of his rubber ducks and boats. It ended with having all ten of his toes kissed goodnight with accompanying rhyme. To neglect any detail invited grumbling, unappeased wakefulness.

To purchase some more hours of quiet, Isobel pandered to Sandro like a strumpet, hell-bent on giving value for money.

"There, you ridiculous globule, I've kissed everything a respectable woman can, and some she shouldn't. What would Granny say? She'd have us both in a reformatory, wouldn't she? Go to sleep now."

Regaining her studio, Isobel noticed that one of the pages lying on the floor bore a line, which, when seen upside down from the way it had been drawn, suggested the bridge of Rowella's nose. Forthright, practical and kind. Why not? There could be no better subject.

*   *   *

Kozyseal Double Glazing were delighted to advise Isobel that despite an unexpectedly high level of response to their advertisement, she was to be granted an interview. It would take place in the Duke of Cornwall Hotel less than a week from the date of the letter. Mr Leadbetter and Mr Murgatroyd looked forward to meeting her.

The interview, in a private suite, went rather oddly.

Talking to Mr Leadbetter and Mr Murgatroyd, whose names were Roy and Colin respectively as they gratuitously informed Isobel – although they preferred formality at interviews – was akin to interludes Isobel could remember with a pair of Jehovah's Witnesses the parsonage charlady had twice admitted to the kitchen there.

Murgatroyd and Leadbetter were young, good looking and went in for excruciatingly conventional attire. They were pressed, starched, and manicured like dummies in a tailor's window. Above

171

all, their remarkably similar faces radiated spiritual exaltation.

"Double glazing is more than a product to us," said one looking at the other for confirmation. "It's a way of life. It's one we'd like to be able to share with you, Isobel . . ."

"Mrs Bonetti," interjected Isobel, thinking that in the matter of names and titles there ought to be parity.

"Quite, Isobel," insisted the other gently. "May we call you that? We just feel that using applicants' first names helps us to get a *feel* of the person," he went on with a voice that was low and persuasive. "You do understand?"

Isobel didn't but thought she'd better pretend to. A car and five thousand a year hung in the balance.

There followed three-quarters of an hour's recital, one man picking up his cue from the other. At times they spoke in unison . . . soft, sibilant, mellifluous. Classless, regionless, the sound went on and on.

Words and phrases kept cropping up. Customer relations. Ability to close a sale. The 'can do' factor. Willingness to go the extra mile. Dedication. Kozyseal admired dedication. She was capable of dedication, wasn't she?

Unaware that she had been addressed for a moment, Isobel overstated her reply somewhat when she realised. Dedicated? That was the question, was it? Oh, *yes*! Her whole life was dedicated to dedication.

"We thought so," murmured Murgatroyd solemnly while Isobel blushed over the absurdity of what she had said. *Fool*.

"We abhor cynicism among our people," Leadbetter elaborated. "Double glazing calls for simplicity, generosity and . . ."

"Dedication," Isobel finished for him, getting impatient. Then she thought of Sandro and the mortgage. "I couldn't agree more with you. Dedication, every time."

The two Kozyseal zealots were rapturous. They 'loved' her attitude.

They went on to say something about the relationship between Kozyseal representatives. Blush-making, evangelical words like 'fellowship' featured a good deal.

"So important," Isobel enthused mendaciously, wearing what she hoped was a converted look on her face.

The interview concluded with a rushed exposition concerning pay and conditions. Basic and commission. It sounded terribly complicated.

"You should certainly earn five thousand pounds in your first year," the pair chorused soothingly, rising to their feet. They extended not just their right hands but both, in a dreadful 'come to Jesus' gesture. Isobel, having no choice, played along, allowing both her own hands to be enclosed in turn by theirs. The touch of their skin was slow-worm silky and dry. "Welcome aboard. Congratulations on winning a once-in-a-lifetime opportunity."

"Thank you very much," Isobel mumbled, feeling idiotic.

It was taken for granted that she accepted their offer of employment. Details of training would follow in the post. Driving licence? No problem. Head Office would fix it. They made Head Office sound like some subordinate level of heaven.

Walking home, Isobel dragged in huge lungfuls of wonderful, cynical, salt laden air. Wouldn't it have been fun to turn their job down? No use in hankering after luxuries like that. The Kozyseal people liked her and she was going to try and like them in return.

Funny, she'd heard so little about the actual work. But they had said, hadn't they, in double glazing, it all came down to *attitude*. A favourite word with employers, that one. Five thousand a year, Isobel was certain, would make hers friendly enough for anyone. Verging on the passionate. More than five times what she'd earned at Modex! And a *car*. She would be rich. A proper nanny for Sandro . . . They could go for a holiday with Ed . . . She hadn't answered his last letter yet.

Light-hearted, Isobel half ran, half skipped the last few hundred yards into Northumberland Terrace.

Now was the time to deal with that other stupid letter. It would turn out to be from someone like her old drawing master, Pietro Arnolfi. He did have arthritis. Hence the funny writing. She should have thought of that before.

Waiting on the doormat at home were two manilla envelopes which had come in the second post. The dry cleaners were 'suited' . . . with a woman of smart appearance, Isobel supposed with amusement. Styletex's personnel officer was afraid he had no openings for someone with Isobel's experience . . . extraordinarily wide though it had been. The sarcastic swine.

From the dentist, there was nothing. Too bad. She had a job now. She didn't need two. Nor would it have mattered two hoots, Isobel reflected, which of these jobs she had got. Her proper work was upstairs in the attic.

Rowella's picture – too early, yet, to call it a portrait – was coming on quite nicely. At least it showed the Rowella-ishness of Rowella. Stripping off her coat, Isobel felt the magnetic pull of a prospering project. She would make a cup of tea to take up to it and deal with that letter on the way. Just like that.

Ripping the soiled envelope open a few minutes later, Isobel saw there were two enclosures. Five sheets of thin paper, stapled together, were densely typed in English. The first page was headed by the printed name of some sort of medical institute in New York. Below, a series of boxes had been completed in various hands, seemingly at different times and in different inks. Initials, reference numbers, authorisations and counter signatures . . . According to one subdivided box, three translators had commented on and authenticated the work of the others. A transcript of tape recordings . . .

Taking it all in at a glance, Isobel threw the pages down, guessing instinctively that whatever was here, it had never been meant for her eyes. A weird confusion over names, after all. She turned to what appeared to be a covering letter, handwritten on private stationery. Her eye froze on the printed address at the top. Number 62, Viale Majno . . .

With her skeleton melting, Isobel crumpled slowly on to her bed, Nina Fischer's letter still in her hand. She had no idea how long it took her to read it, although it was only a few lines long. It was dated the day following that of Furio's death. A bread and butter letter for dinner the previous evening, it was written in French.

Isobel's smattering of schoolgirl French was sufficient to allow her to make the words out. The back slanting script was crowded, as if each letter was trying to hide behind the one that preceded it. A complete absence of *t*'s made deciphering it no easier. Why French? It was a language, Isobel knew, that Nina could speak but never had done, to her knowledge, not in Milan.

Between each few words, Isobel lay on her back, hearing her breath forced out in jets down her nostrils. The events of that last day of Furio's life unreeled in her mind . . . a hem coming down with one twitch of a thread.

She remembered buying purple and white striped egg plant on the Brera to go with the lamb . . . Nina had called it horsemeat . . . Every glance, every movement . . . all the broken crockery and glassware . . . every word of her quarrel with Furio . . . Nina had killed him. No, she hadn't. She, Isobel, was guilty of that. She hadn't kept Nina at bay . . . stood up to Carlo Bonetti. The Morrisons, Kozyseal, Freda and her mother were the punishments . . . No, no. Just consequences. Good did not come out of evil. Bad begat badness . . . Perhaps with time the black dye diluted until in the end, there was no colour left.

Jerking herself upright, Isobel read the letter again. Nina thanked her for a delicious dinner in interesting surroundings with stimulating company. She had enjoyed herself very much and hoped to see her hostess and Furio in the Viale Majno before too much time had gone by.

Bonkers. Hadn't anybody told her?

There was no reference to the other papers which had been in the envelope. Included by error, doubtless. Nina had no idea what she did or what she was doing. Where was she now?

Sliding from the bed, Isobel recovered the typed pages from beside the cold mug of tea on the dressing table. It was a blotchy mimeograph of an original, she saw. This was copy number three of fifteen made, the top page indicated. Already cold, she grew colder, reading snatches at random.

It was Nina's own story told by herself. Through half closed eyes Isobel recognised the threat of horrible, disgusting, terrifying detail. The translation evidently rendered Nina's actual words . . . simple, repetitive. Frequent unfinished sentences. Like a child talking.

Thickfingered she rolled the transcript and stuffed it in the dressing table's one lockable drawer, turning the key. She would destroy it, but not now. She would try and burn it before she read it. She could withstand the temptation a little while longer. What she knew was already enough. Much too much. Scientists, historians . . . delving into dirt was their business. Artists should stick to what they could see.

It was natural, automatic, having closed the drawer and locked it, to glance in the dressing-table mirror. Isobel saw no sign of her face there. Just the pattern of the paper on the wall behind her bed. No mist like before. To her mortification, Isobel piddled on the floor. Then she cleared up the mess, sickened by the scent of gardenia flowers.

Sitting on a stool later, with her back to the mirror, eyes starting from her nonexistent head, Isobel wondered if anyone would notice when she went to fetch her son from Freda's. How much would Sandro mind?

She watched the hands on the alarm clock beside her bed race round to five fifteen. There was nothing for it, she would have to go. The last time this had happened, Isobel remembered, the condition had proved illusory, temporary anyway. This was different. The appalling blankness in the mirror had an unconditional look.

Isobel got up slowly, fearing her weight might have suffered a redistribution, and tipped the mirror upwards so that it reflected nothing but the ceiling. Most peculiar. She felt the same, or almost. As if she'd been in bed with flu and this was her first day of walking convalescence. Well, wherever her brain was seated now, it seemed to be doing its job. Like a machine which had been relocated and was battling on despite a joggling to its nuts and bolts. Better behave as normal.

Briskly now, Isobel went downstairs carrying the cold cup of tea and Nina's insanely inappropriate thank-you letter. The one to be thrown down the sink, the other to be put in the dustbin. Rubbish from a mind collapsed in on itself. Like a house blown up in the war. Isobel herself, a bystander, injured by the blast. Still alive, however.

Next time she went upstairs, Isobel promised herself as she put on her mac, she would certainly dispose of the transcript, too. She had a new life now, a plan for the future. Nobody, particularly poor, mad Nina, must be allowed to come between herself and that. She must put all those old horrors from her.

Opening the street door, Isobel paused to gather courage for the stares of passers-by. It was raining. She felt no drops upon her face.

Later, after Sandro's bedtime routine was over, Isobel forced herself to go up to the studio again. The child had not reacted to the lopping of his mother. Therefore, reasoned Isobel, nor must she. Carry on as normal.

She worked on Rowella's portrait until the small hours of the morning, distracted and absorbed. But many as were the new lines and shadows with which Isobel tried to solidify the Devonian woman's face, Rowella was slipping away from her. Where the lineaments had been plain and honest, they turned soft, equivocal under Isobel's hand. Like a ghost bowing out of a haunting.

What emerged by three o'clock was Nina Fischer's golden apples smile in place of Rowella's grimly humorous mouth. And where the steady, intelligent beam of the shop steward's eyes had been, flat, insensible pebbles stared back.

Taking the cartridge paper from the easel, Isobel tore the drawing across. No amount of work with breadcrumbs would ever rub Nina out.

*　　*　　*

A few weeks later, in the medieval, fortified Tuscan hill town of Castelchiara, Ed Mazzerella was desponding over Isobel's last letter. It was nearly six weeks old. Ed, who had read it many times already, searched the pages he knew by heart for a clue to explain the delayed arrival of others.

Day by day, he became more pessimistic about ever seeing that boldly rounded, upright, italicised hand of hers again. The last he'd heard of Isobel through that medium was that she was planting spring bulbs in pots, outside, in her backyard 'patio' garden. He and the bulbs, he sighed, were equally in the dark.

Could she be ill? Had she found some loaded guy to marry? She had the boy to think of now. And nothing in nature, Ed reminded himself, is as pragmatic as a mother. He couldn't blame her. But why did she leave him on the rack like this?

Ed would have offered Isobel marriage had he been able. But his wife in Baltimore refused to let him go. He had deserted her, she claimed, and her lawyers were going to make him pay. Free? Of course she was not free. She was married, wasn't she? Bound to her husband by sacred ties, unbreakable till death. The Church's law. He, Ed, his wife continued to insist, would repent his actions some day and return to her. It was what all the family prayed for ... before she was too old to bear a child.

But Ed did not want a wife who looked on sex as a mechanical means to a reproductive end. The temperature charts, the thermometers, the calculations. Those coy candle lit suppers, stiflingly intimate, with the telephone off the hook. Three of them in a row some months.

"Oh honey, do you think," she used to simper every time, "that *this* time God will ..." It gave Ed the creeps. One such evening, she had unbuttoned her blouse at him, right there across the table. Three voluptuous bulges. Two of hers and one belonging to the rapidly deflating soufflé. Ed's loins had shrivelled in sympathy.

Getting up, Ed had gone upstairs, packed a suitcase and left by the back door for the officers' club. The next day he'd written her a note saying he couldn't take any more of her holy harlotry. Let God impregnate her if she was so stuck on Him. As a husband, he felt redundant. Cuckolded by a rival who wouldn't get his fists up.

And for this, he had lost Isobel.

During these confused reflections, Ed was not alone. He rarely was in Castelchiara. His shop, established in two dark narrow rooms of a cramped *palazzo* in the alley known as the Calle Ghibelline, with a walled garden behind, which overlooked the city walls, was a magnet to the citizenry. Ed Mazzerella was their very own American. He needed help, advice of every sort and hints as to the whereabouts of stock. Coming from a place where everything was new, perforce, how could he know anything about *antichitià*? But with them to guide him, he was in luck, was *il capitano*.

And did he not always keep a bottle of good wine to hand, cork hospitably drawn in readiness for callers? Or a nip of *grappa*. It was a pleasure to assist the man. At least he knew how to behave himself.

He was exactly the sort of man the *chiarini* liked. One with plenty of time. Never too busy to confer about the astounding absence of radishes from the market. Didn't set any distressing, aggressively commercial trends like keeping lengthy shop hours. No money-grubbing Florentine habits. That would never do. Yes, he was generally declared to be *simpatico*.

So agreeable, in fact, that Ed had a visitor now. The postman on his official delivery round, taking his ease in the rickety chair that stood before the refectory table that served Ed both as desk and counter.

Fortunatamente, Giorgio began tactfully with the good news, the Signor had no bothersome letter from Baltimore. The sight of those, the postman pointed out, made *il capitano*'s face fall. So the day would be joyous, *no*? True, there was no letter, still, from Plymouth, England. A woman, yes? It was no good trying to hide these things from Giorgio. Was he not the friend and confidant of all, he asked, hands interrogatively aloft. Besides the priest, who could know more of his valued neighbours' inmost secrets? A burden shared was a burden halved.

Pretty soon, said Ed to himself, unable to get a word in edgeways, his so-called burden would be infinitesimal. The whole town would have a piece of it. There was not much going on in sleepy Castelchiara but tittle-tattle. The only thriving industry.

A little wearily, Ed poured the postman wine. There was no point in hurrying the guy. His mail, he realised, was in Giorgio's eyes of superior quality. Deserving of close, personal attention.

Today for example, there was one with the Vatican postmark . . . the Signor's distinguished brother, no doubt . . . a thin, pale blue one from Florida . . . an impressive one from London with the Travellers' Club frank. Subscription overdue again. Had not the Signor cancelled this yet? Ah, here unmistakably, was a garage bill . . . What a rogue that Luigi was, the postman sniffed. Lamborghinis? As if that bodger was fit to lay his hand on anything but a tractor.

Seeing that *il capitano*, was disinclined for chatter . . . quite cast down, in fact, Giorgio made greater efforts. If he left the American sad, it should not be his fault. No, indeed. Ah, women, from this Plymouth place to Pisa, they were fickle. The hardness of their miserable hearts . . . the delectable moistness of their mysterious parts.

Ed didn't care to have Isobel irreverently lumped in like this with inferior members of her sex. But what could he do? Giorgio expanded on his theme. The guy's loquacity was unstoppable.

In paradise there would be no women as such . . . Neither male nor female. The priest had said so. Alas, here on earth, what was a man to do without them? But men like them, the postman ingratiated, with the world's affairs upon their shoulders could not sit idly by all day, mooning over women. Here was a little *trattativa* to take *il capitano's* mind off his disappointment . . . and to squeeze another glassful of that wine from Signor Mazzerella's bottle.

"My wife's sister's husband's second cousin has a most rare *armadio* for sale," said Giorgio, eyes sparkling at the prospect of a deal. Any deal. "Much carving, much painting . . . of great, great preciousness . . . and to you, *Capitano*, much cheapness, too."

"Sure," Ed relented and refilled the postman's glass. "I'll bet it's just great as a chicken coop."

"Ah no," Giorgio clasped his postman's hat to his chest, mortally wounded. "The Signor maligns me. We speak here only of a dog," the Italian shot a venomous glance to where Ed's liver and white spaniel, Messalina, lay sleeping lightly in her 'on duty' basket. One silken ear drooped decorously to the ground, the other, turned inside out, was flipped carelessly over her lovely domed head. Giorgio shuddered. He hated Messalina.

"A very clean dog. A pure dog, like the *capitano's* . . ."

To get rid of him, Ed told the postman he would call in at the homestead of his wife's sister's husband's second cousin on the way home and inspect the wardrobe. It was true that in every peasant poultry yard in the valley there were things of value to be found. Most of them degraded to makeshift, malodorous agricultural use and past any hope of restoration at realistic cost.

"Permit me, Signor," said the postman, rising when he saw with regret that his glass was not to be replenished again, "to give you counsel. I, Giorgio, who am a married man and grapple daily with the tortuous nature of womanhood. Your *ragazza*? You must entice her with your eyes, woo her with your hands upon her body. Letters, they are no good. Who but lawyers and tiresome people write them?"

The postman exited tossing his head, lighter now after the debouchment of so much wisdom. Or possibly the wine.

Messalina, whose approach to guardianship duties was individual, roused herself and yapped. She was just in time to snap at the fork of the postman's trousers as he left.

"Leave Giorgio's balls alone, Lina," her master admonished her mildly. "He's right, you know. There's not been much of the go-getter about me lately. Do you see me as an errant knight in quest of my lady's favour?"

Ed turned the sign around at the door to indicate he was closed and sat down to write to Isobel while Messalina sat close to him, her head resting dolefully on his knee. Surely they'd had enough of shop today?

In brief, Ed wrote that if he had no reponse from Isobel within two weeks of this letter's probable arrival, he was coming to

England himself to find her. He had warned her. What was the matter? Was she married? A stamp, and the letter was ready to go.

Walking to the piazza, Messalina trotting at his heels, Ed greeted several passers-by, the padre who was his landlord at the farmhouse – his parents had lived there – an elderly gentleman who commanded great respect for doing nothing with so much faded elegance, and the pinch faced proprietress of Castelchiara's only gown shop. Frumpy black frocks with small designs in white on them. Suitable for advanced widowhood. What would Isobel think of them?

Picking up the Lamborghini from the square, Ed drove through the town's main, medieval gate, the only one wide enough for motorised traffic, round and round the spiralling road which descended from the citadel into the blue hazed valley below, all ablaze with dying deciduous leaves, clumps like fire ships, floating in and out of mist. How could Isobel not wish to see this? Breathe this champagne air. Bathe in this light, all blue and pink and gold. Who else but she could possibly endorse his own love of it worthily?

Keeping his promise, Ed called at the farm where the supposedly antique wardrobe was currently serving as a kennel. And a wretched place it was. A crone with a black handkerchief knotted round her head came out of her open kitchen door, scrawny chickens pecking at her feet and smiled a toothless smile. Yes, she had heard of *il capitano*. He was an *antiquario* and lived in the neighbouring farm but one. He was making a palace of the old place, so all the neighbourhood reported. Inside sanitation!

Her old *armadio*? Naturally it was for sale, along with any other rubbish lying around the place. Of course, she added craftily, the *armadio* was of considerable utility. New dog kennels cost a deal of money . . . Would the Signor be pleased to follow? She would show him where it was.

The wardrobe leaned drunkenly against the rear wall of the house. Inside a thin dog pulled listlessly at its chain. Messalina, normally indiscriminate in her tastes, turned disdainfully from the cur, busying herself with a wealth of animal ordures, variously matured. Donkey, goat and fowl.

Hurriedly, Ed admired the wardrobe and paid the old woman for it. Much, much more than any possible value it could have. He would send someone to collect it, he said, in a day or two, knowing he would never do it. Overcome at the touch of so many crisp lire notes, the woman tried to kiss Ed's hand. To avoid the homage, he plunged his hands into his pockets and dragged out more money. To give the dog a special feed, he stammered, and made his escape with sleek Messalina gambolling on ahead.

Like most middle class Americans, Ed was appalled by poverty. It got the better of his business sense.

Back in his own neat kitchen quarters, Ed put the substantial remains of last night's rabbit stew on the stove. He and Messalina would share it, the dog's portion carefully separated from bones. Meanwhile, he thought, they might go into the olive grove and do some shooting there. At all events, some thinking.

Whistling to his companion, Ed set off for the rear portion of the property, a fold yard surrounded by decaying animal steadings, feed stores and so forth. He kept his gun and cartridges locked in a cabinet there. Often enough, he had pictured Isobel living here safely with her boy, secluded and serene. A setting for a jewel. Arum lilies bloomed profusely here in summer, striking up through the cobbles and an ancient fig tree stained a wall with its bursting fruit. Why waste the place on ghosts? Ed could not occupy it all.

Forgetting, for the moment, his original intention in venturing amongst the disused buildings, he padded in and out of empty spaces, imagining them converted to her use. He forced open swollen doors and rotten shutters. Clouds of perished plaster fell on to his shoulders, speckling his hair. A cumbrous old olive press stood in one room. Rocking it, to see how easily it would move, Ed didn't notice a roof timber stir overhead. Barking a warning to her master, Messalina skipped nimbly out of danger.

The last thing Ed remembered seeing, before the falling beam knocked him senseless, was Messalina scrambling over the debris to reach him. Who would feed her, he wondered.

THIRTEEN

"Awful weather, don't you think?" Isobel challenged the young housewife who answered the ding-dong chimes of her doorbell. "It's Mrs Drake, isn't it?"

"Yes . . . yes, it is," the young woman agreed, drenched by Isobel's impersonal, floodlight smile. She was about thirty, trim and of average height, whereas Isobel, like all Kozyseal representatives, was noticeably tall.

"This *is* the right time, isn't it?" Isobel said, knowing quite well that she was punctual for the appointment arranged by Kozyseal. But it was important to say nothing that didn't elicit 'yes' as an answer. That way a pattern of acquiescence was established which 'targets' found increasingly difficult to disrupt as the sales pitch proceeded to its desirable climax. Yes for success.

That was the Kozyseal marketing theory, anyway. It was enshrined in their training manual – *The El Paso Sell* – a voluminous, mawkishly worded document about which no breath of criticism was allowed. Everything had to be positive.

To get three 'yeses' before crossing the threshold showed promise. Women, said Roy and Colin during the training course, were better at saying 'yes' than men. They actually preferred it to saying 'no'. Women were programmed by society and nature to please and be pleased. Theirs was a 'yes' culture.

"That's how you got me," Isobel had remarked suddenly in the course of Roy's dissertation on creating favourable conditions for the life embracing 'yes'. Roy Leadbetter reproached her with a martyred expression. Questions were designated a slot at the end of individual training 'modules'. Somehow, there never seemed to be time for them.

Now, out in the field, as Leadbetter and Murgatroyd called the residential areas of Plymouth, it was Isobel who asked all the questions.

"Oh, but don't you have a magnificent view?" she went on as she was ushered into an open-plan living and dining room.

Mrs Drake didn't appear to have noticed that she was headless that morning, Isobel mused. Neither had Sandro. It was an unpre-

182

dictable, periodic absence which seemed to worry no one but herself.

She had even cooked and served Christmas dinner to her mother and Simon in this state. Neither had commented. Simon had asked her a few times if she was all right. That had been all. She had very nearly panicked when his present turned out to be a fox fur hat which he'd bought home from Stockholm. She had tried it on, fearing it would simply . . .

Isobel gathered her wits. She really must concentrate. Basic pay for this job was only ten pounds a week. Her income would be made up from commission on sales.

"You can see the Tamar Bridge from here," she said, craning her imaginary neck – it had been sliced clean off when she checked in the Cortina's rear view mirror – "can't you?"

Mrs Drake said 'yes' again and was now saying something else. It was mere diffuse chatter and ought to be stopped.

"And I imagine that all this beautiful glass radiates cold into your room, doesn't it?"

"Well, yes it does," Mrs Drake fell like a ripe plum into the Kozyseal affirmation trap.

"Do you find you have to keep your heating up fairly high?" Isobel spoke her part of the Kozyseal liturgy with the regulation inflections. Her voice, at least, sounded as if it was coming from somewhere . . . it wasn't always the case.

"Yes, actually, we do find . . ."

"I see. So a minimum thirty per cent saving on fuel bills would be a significant factor if you chose to install double glazing, wouldn't it?"

"Yes," answered Mrs Drake, plainly puzzled by her inability to say anything else.

Isobel felt sorry for her. Wasn't she going to put up a struggle at all? Mrs Drake was a part-time drama teacher. Didn't she realise she had been fed her lines . . . given the role of stooge?

Clinically, Isobel closed the sale. She really couldn't afford to lose it. Mrs Drake was one of the very few women she'd come across so far who had the domestic joint-account chequebook handy. She wanted, or had been brought to say that she wanted, double glazing all over the house. A large detached house, too. All four walls pierced with windows.

To Isobel, it meant sixty pounds' worth of commission. There would be no need to come back and wheedle Mrs Drake's wretched husband in the evening, no need to arrange to drop Sandro in his carrycot at his grandmother's. No need, in fact to make much further effort this month. Selling was a rotten, undignified job. It was Isobel's projected policy to do as little of it as possible. Only enough to eat, pay the mortgage and Freda.

A single decent sale in the month and she could use most of her time for drawing. These occasional loathly vampire expeditions would pay for her leisure. The trouble with most jobs, Isobel realised, was the time they took. Time that couldn't be spared.

Obtaining a cheque for the deposit and signatures on the relevant Kozyseal forms, Isobel sidled out of the house feeling like a fox slinking away from a chicken-run.

"I'm a vixen," she muttered, slamming the Cortina door, "with a very hungry cub. I kill for meat, not for pleasure." She put the car into gear and waved to her victim standing between the reconstituted stone urns on the doorstep. She hoped the poor woman wouldn't get into terrible trouble with her husband.

No one, Isobel thought accelerating down Crownhill Road, ever seems to notice what's wrong with me. A man at a set of traffic lights smiled at her. Leaning to the left to look in her mirror, Isobel greeted her own features with relief. The latest eclipse was over. There was lipstick on her teeth. It was one of the snags – putting make-up on an invisible face. Great discretion was needed.

She went to bed quite early with the intention of working at her easel throughout the daylight hours of the following day. Figures copied from illustrated books on sculpture. Things Nina couldn't hitch a ride on to make herself a nuisance. Bronze or marble, photographed and printed ... three whole processes which armoured Isobel's imagination against penetration by the Nina parasite. A three-line defensive strategy of Isobel's own invention.

Her fingers touched the locked drawer of the dressing table and withdrew. She wouldn't, she decided, sear her eyes that night with one more line of Nina's hideous, hypnotic reminiscence. She had been reading it, a phrase or so at a time, like a dipsomaniac housewife taking nips at a bottle of gin. The transcript must be burnt ... the bottle voluntarily thrown away before it was empty. Proof of an earnest attempt at reform.

Lying awake, Isobel thought of sending the transcript back to Josef with a question as to why he allowed his wife to pursue her. But if she did, the cycle of involvement might escalate still further. And then, of course, she had enough to do without writing unnecessary letters. Sandro, the job, her house ... her head.

Isobel lay awake for some hours listening to the wind driven rain spatter the window panes. Restless, she got up and went on to the landing to strain after the sound of Sandro's respiration. Like many young children, he slept with the stillness of death.

When eventually she slept herself, Isobel reached out in a dream

184

for a cord on the far side of the room which controlled the main light switch. The cord had a miniature fox's mask on the end. It flew towards her, biting her neck.

Woken by her own shriek, she saw that Sandro had pulled himself up beside her bed. He was tickling her face with a soft toy. He had learned how to let the cot side down and had crawled the few feet of corridor into his mother's room. A new thing . . . like the time he'd sunk his one and only tooth into her hand, to show that he'd got it. She would never have known otherwise.

"You clever little thing . . . but you scared me," she said, lifting the child into her bed. There was no more rest for her. While Sandro wriggled, Isobel wondered how she would ever keep the pieces of herself all together. She had to suck so hard from the inside to obtain a magnetic cohesion. There was no other glue.

*　　*　　*

Margaret was spreading honey on her half-slice of wholemeal brown toast when the telephone rang. Most aggravating. People were so inconsiderate. Now she would have to soil her napkin or transfer the stickiness on her fingers to the telephone receiver. She could rinse her fingers, of course, under the kitchen tap . . . But then the caller might ring off.

Telephone calls were not so frequent with Margaret Jefferson these days that she could afford to throw them improvidently away. It might be one of her children. One of her boys.

"Hello, hello? Margaret Jefferson speaking . . ."

"Isobel?" a distant voice said uncertainly. There were clicks, buzzes and the intervention of an operator's voice. All the thrilling preliminaries to an international call. Darling Rupert . . . It must be so late in California . . . Perhaps he'd sat up specially to ring her . . .

"Hello," said a stranger's voice, clearly this time. "Is that Mrs Jefferson?"

Disappointed, Margaret admitted that it was. Who on earth could this be, pestering her at this uncivilised hour? Only family members should ever ring one another before nine in the morning, preferably in emergencies only.

"I'm afraid you don't know me, Mrs Jefferson . . . my name's Edward Mazzerella. Correction, we were introduced briefly at Isobel's wedding . . . Say, I'm sorry, for a moment there, I thought you were Isobel. You sound a lot like her . . ."

Oh. One of Isobel's greasy foreign friends. With an American accent . . .

"Isobel no longer lives here, Mr . . . er . . ."

185

"I know that, ma'am. But you see she's not on the telephone and I can't write to her . . ."

"Then why trouble me, Mr . . . er . . ." Margaret thought anxiously of her tea. She had forgotten to replace the knitted cosy which she used to insulate the pot in private. Without it, the tea remained at a potable temperature for less than eight minutes. She would have to make more . . .

"You see, ma'am, I *did* write to her . . ."

Dear me, how this man did go on. Some long rigmarole about a letter he'd written and a visit. Isobel would have been expecting him . . . which was the first she'd heard of it.

"And I can't call her," Ed reiterated his earlier point, "because she's not on the telephone . . ."

Now that was not quite true. At her new employers' instigation, Isobel had recently installed a telephone for her work. Mrs Jefferson found that she couldn't remember the number so there was no point in mentioning the matter. None at all. Isobel would do much better to avoid contacts with strange men in foreign countries. There had been enough trouble over that kind of thing.

". . . My right leg's in plaster and so's my right arm. A rotten beam crashed down on me in the olive-press room . . ."

Such a catalogue of events, Margaret thought, her attention fragmented. Something about his dog going to get help. Really, people did presume on one's patience so. One was sorry, of course, to hear of anyone sustaining an injury but the details of a compound fracture were surely superfluous . . .

". . . I'm stuck in this lousy hospital in Pisa until at least one of the casts comes off . . ."

"And the purpose of your call, Mr . . . er," Margaret cut across the American sharply, "is what?" It really was too bad of Rupert not to have rung. He was a week overdue.

"Mrs Jefferson, ma'am, is Isobel in good shape?"

"What do you mean? My daughter is safe, healthy and immensely preoccupied with the care of my grandson. I'm afraid it's all I can tell you. I do hope you will soon be feeling better. I fear I must bid you a good morning, now. I have to go out . . ."

"But you'll tell her what's happened, ma'am, won't you? And that I shall be coming as soon as . . ."

"Very well, if you wish," Margaret said coolly, "I shall act as your messenger."

Ed looked at the receiver which emitted nothing further beyond a mechanical drone. He let it fall clumsily on to the mobile apparatus. He was no good with his left arm. Sodding, tight arsed *bitch*!

Too bad. Isobel would soon know what had happened, at least.

She *must* write then. Why the hell hadn't she gotten herself a goddam telephone? The British took a hell of a pride in their barbarism.

"Okay, Signorina," Ed roused himself to speak to the pretty nurse who came in to wheel away the telephone trolley. "What's next on the agenda?"

"Your blanket bath, Signor," Nurse Fiavoli announced flirtily. "We shall have our usual competition, no?"

The contest, on which both Ed and Fiavoli wagered one hundred thousand lire, turned on whether or not Ed would refrain from producing a penile erection. It was played to strict rules to accommodate certain of the American's puritanical prejudices. Handicapped by these as she was, the nurse hadn't yet failed to pocket Ed's banknote. Very good pin money, she thought it . . . and excellent therapy for Signor Mazzerella. He was lonely, frustrated and bored.

Today, Ed had a new weapon in his armoury of resistance. Flaccidity, he discovered, was attainable if he kept his mind fixed on Margaret Jefferson's voice, so fresh in his memory. The clinkety-clank of bone china teacups in a steel kitchen sink.

"You are ill, Signor Mazzerella?" Fiavoli observed, surveying the failure of her efforts.

"No, just more cunning. I thought of my future mother-in-law . . ." a creative explanation which sprang unbidden to Ed's lips. Wishful thinking, he supposed. Bernie, his wife, would never, ever release her grip on him. Isobel, he was convinced now, wasn't married whatever else she was. If she had been, Margaret Jefferson was the kind of woman who would have delighted in telling him so.

"Then you have cheated," the nubile nurse pouted. "For that I claim double."

"No chance. You're a bad loser, Fiavoli. Pay up."

* * *

For her part, Margaret made fresh tea and toast. She felt a momentary twinge of guilt for the way she had deflected that foreign man's attempted approach to her daughter. It lasted no longer than the time it took to boil the kettle. It was all for the best. Isobel was short tempered lately. Barely coping. The last thing she needed was overseas 'phone calls from people who could be of no possible use to her.

And, although the least favoured of her children, Isobel was at any rate available. She was the guardian, moreover, of Margaret's sole grandchild. A grandson. Really, a nice little boy. More than enough, surely, to fill Isobel's life. He deserved his mother's

187

undivided attention. Motherhood absolutely precluded any running about after men.

In the midst of this soliloquy, Margaret contrived to lose any recollection of Ed Mazzerella's message. She couldn't even remember his name. It was quite unimportant. Not the least need to get Isobel stirred up over nothing.

*　　*　　*

A week after that, a letter dictated by Ed to Nurse Fiavoli in Italian – she could not write English – arrived at Northumberland Terrace. Isobel put it aside to be opened later. There was quite a collection of unopened mail lodged behind the chipped Toby jug on the scullery windowsill. Most of it was brown-envelope stuff which could wait.

Isobel had begun to look on all mail as a burdensome demand for attention. As rain soaked week succeeded to week, even letters from identifiably benign sources, like Ed's, joined the sorry looking wad behind the Toby jug. They got spotted with washing-up water. In a fit of domestic organisation, Isobel put an elastic band around them. Which, in her pleased estimation, gave the wearisome assemblage a satisfactory air having been acted upon. Much better.

More urgent things were in progress. Isobel had bought a book on portraiture and was working industriously through the excercises proposed by its author. Because of Nina's spectral trespasses, it was a calculated risk.

Living models, present in the room, were essential to evade the pestilence. For live models she used Sandro . . . Rowella too, when, at the time of her occasional visits, she consented to sit mute and motionless. Not that she was given much alternative.

Her own face would have been useful, were it not for its sheer unreliability. Each morning now, it was a matter of more curiosity than dread to see whether it was visibly present or not. Convinced that a significant part of her reason had left her, Isobel saw no possibility of admitting to symptoms. She had Sandro to care for and their living to earn. She couldn't do that locked up in a loony bin.

Like many a victim of severe nervous stress, Isobel sincerely believed that no one could help her. She must wait for the phenomenon to go away or endure it in silence to the end of her days. It was all Nina's fault, or rather that of the people who had killed her mother. Now they'd got her, Isobel, as well. To keep quiet was the only way to prevent the spread of infection.

It was not all down to Nina, of course. Far from it. In less than two years, Isobel had lost her husband, been hatefully rejected by his family, borne his child with grudging support, gone out to find

188

work only days after the delivery, established a home, been ground in the mill of someone else's bad marriage, and lost her job in consequence. Now she was doing one which corroded her soul. And with all that, her mind functioned, though queerly at times.

Before eating a meal, she would go and look at herself in a mirror. If she saw no face there, she threw her food in the bin.

"I will paint you when I must," Isobel spoke to the blankness, "I'll clean your silly teeth. But if you want feeding, come back when you're hungry."

She lost weight, inevitably.

"You d'be getting thin, my handsome," sighed Rowella, her plain face full of affectionate concern. "You be pining . . ."

"Nonsense, Rowella. Keep still. The lower jaw *clenched*, please."

One good strong line should do it. Just as long as it was the *right* one. No fuzz or covering up with artful smudges.

And Rowella, who despite the increasing warmth of her feelings for Isobel had learned to fear these periods of ice cold detachment, respectfully resumed her very awkward pose.

Between bouts at the easel, Isobel would look at the list of sales appointments she collected each week from Kozyseal's regional offices in the centre of town. Picking two or three at random to be followed up herself, she then rang her colleagues at home, delegating her tasks to them with queenly liberality.

"Here's one that may suit you, Tom," she advised the hungry young father of three. "Mr and Mrs Petty out at Estover, not a stone's throw from you. They get a lot of aeroplanes going over so I daresay they'll give in . . ."

Isobel's largesse was eagerly accepted. Extra appointments meant additional potential sales and more commission. The Kozyseal sales team had quickly given up offering to share their percentage with Isobel.

"Certainly not," she objected. "I'm not doing the work and shan't take the money. There's a limit to the number of times I'm prepared to hear people saying 'yes' in a week. You're welcome to it. I'll send you the forms."

For a while Isobel's anarchic work redistribution system went unnoticed at regional headquarters. There was contentment all round. Isobel made the little she needed and enjoyed ample free time. Her co-representatives picked up commissions that might have been hers and the company reaped the same profits at the end of the day.

So, when the mutually beneficial scheme was uncovered, it was with a sense of injured innocence that Isobel reported for a disciplinary interview in the close carpeted offices over which

Leadbetter and Murgatroyd presided. She was careful to dress for the confrontation without the aid of a mirror. There was only so much irritation one could tolerate in a morning.

Roy and Colin as they permitted themselves to be called by 'accredited' representatives of the company, received Isobel standing with arms open wide. Ignoring the cloying invitation to embrace, Isobel seated herself on a chair which was far too low and gestured her superiors to follow her example. Startled, they obeyed. The unexpected was not catered for in the Kozyseal Management Method. Not even in the Appendix.

"Now, what's all this about?" Isobel opened crisply.

In understanding tones, they explained. It had never occurred to them that Isobel could so have misjudged her responsibilities to the company. They blamed themselves. Forgiveness was freely offered if only Isobel would now keep *all* the appointments allocated to her. It was a matter of trust. And she really must earn her target income of five thousand pounds that year.

"To do that," Isobel deposed, "I should have to work all hours God sends and some he doesn't . . ."

"We both had such high hopes for you," groaned Colin, shooting his dazzling cuffs and searching Roy's features. "Hadn't we Roy? But at the moment, you're just not earning your basic . . ."

What followed was an hour's worth of 'guidance'. All about doing herself justice and the Kozyseal pledge of support to loyal employees. Isobel left in a flurry of self-righteous indignation, having given her reluctant promise to do no more delegating in future. It was going to be extremely difficult to fit everything in. Where did she go from here?

She went, in point of physical fact, to the house of an elderly marine biologist where she concluded a sale with ease and disgust. Her customer, in carpet slippers and pebble-thick spectacles was no match at all for the El Paso Sell. It could not go on.

By the end of the week, so far from selling double glazing to anyone else, she had explained in exact, vivid terms to a number of 'targets' why it was that their pens were now poised over their chequebooks. The Kozyseal ethos and method got reckless exposure in a number of places all over Plymouth. Isobel hadn't felt such exhilaration in ages. Not since creaming round the Monza racetrack with Furio.

It wasn't long, either, before the Ford Cortina became part of an enjoyable fantasy: a mythic steed sent by the gods to convey their chosen agent from one heroic denunciation to the next. Isobel, the whirlwind destroyer of evil.

To the less lyrical eye of a couple of traffic policemen, Isobel's cavalier treatment of speed limits and Highway Code pieties was provoking. There was a fair haired hooligan on the loose, one patrol car radioed another. Female. In a metallic blue Cortina. Out of her skull.

"Bit of a looker," crackled the answering report as she was glimpsed zig zagging at speed down the Western Approach. "Her looks," replied an interlocutor dourly, "are no fucking excuse."

When three police cars, acting in concert, finally ran Isobel to ground, uniformed passengers and drivers piled out in a fury. They would throw the book at her, they roared. Speeding, dangerous driving . . . Good God, was she effing drunk?

Isobel's dimple was much in evidence as she accepted the ticket which was written out for her with trembling hands. She was truly sorry, she said, if she'd alarmed anybody. Perhaps her performance had been a touch frisky . . . What did this thing mean? Oh, court. Oh, her licence would be endorsed . . . At the very least. Oh, well. She thanked them all for their trouble and pulled sedately away leaving no impression of contrition behind her.

Briefly, the farce that was Isobel's life seemed to her to have acquired the authentic flavour of comedy.

Retribution, however, was imminent. More than one grateful citizen wrote to the *Evening Herald* to warn others about Kozyseal salesmen and their methods. Nor did it take Murgatroyd and Leadbetter long to identify Isobel as the traitor. Her glorious rebellion against the 'yes' culture could not go unpunished.

The week's devastation was brought home to Isobel as she sat in her parlour that Friday night, going over the returns which she was bound to make to the company. For every enquiry, there was a form to fill in with details of the appointment and how it had gone. Sitting curled up on the old sofa in her dressing gown with her newly washed hair wrapped up in a towel, Isobel recorded 'no sale' in red biro on form after form.

It was too late to remind herself now, that whilst it was all very well to indulge in a spate of audacity when she alone risked the outcome, Sandro could neither eat nor wear his mother's euphoria. It was all over now. Isobel contemplated the future with trepidation. Perhaps living on the dole was all she was fit for. She was no good at anything.

Maybe, she thought, she would get away with it this time. But Isobel, who never read the local paper if she could help it, didn't realise just how much damage her rampage had wrought.

She was resigning herself to more prudent conduct in the future when there was a knock on the door. Two short raps. Rowella. She'd said she might look in. Friday night was her bingo night. It finished at ten o'clock and it was twenty past now. Should she tell Rowella what she had done?

"Oh, I . . ."

"Good evening, Mrs Bonetti." Roy Leadbetter and Colin Murgatroyd stood outside, shoulder to shoulder, both carrying briefcases. It was always difficult when one of them spoke to decide which one it was whose mouth had actually been open. The thought flitted through Isobel's distracted mind like a bat.

At a disadvantage in her old quilted housecoat and childish tartan slippers, Isobel wondered what the dapper duo on her doorstep could want with her. They hadn't seen the sales figures yet . . . They looked like a couple of undertakers . . .

"How nice to see you," was Isobel's wary response. "What do you . . ."

"We thought the situation called for an immediate meeting. May we come in?"

Isobel didn't answer at once but noticed how their shadows fell, in the light of the street lamp, black slicks of oil, oozing obliquely across the shining wet pavement. The rain had stopped and there was no wind.

"Well, I'm not dressed, as you see . . . my baby's asleep and . . ."

"This really won't take long, Mrs Bonetti. Best to face up to things isn't it?"

"I shan't say 'yes', if that's what you're after," Isobel's voice shook. "Oh look . . . No, I'm sorry . . . You just can't . . ."

Isobel never understood how it was, exactly, that they got into her house. They seemed to flow past her as if their bodies had half liquefied during the crucial moment . . . mollusc-soft and as frightful.

They solidified again, Leadbetter and Murgatroyd, in Isobel's parlour. The electric light there seemed suddenly unbearably bright. Without a discernible movement, they had turned the ceiling light on and a directional lamp Isobel never used herself. They seated themselves side by side on the sofa and busied themselves with the locks on their briefcases. Papers were shuffled.

"You may sit down," one of them said.

Finding herself without the power of speech, Isobel sank into a chair. She would recruit the strength and the words needed to eject these unwanted visitors in a moment. Oh, if only Rowella would come. Murgatroyd reached for the lamp, adjusting it to shine into Isobel's eyes.

"Turn that off," she said, reaching into a four-fifths empty barrel of resolution. She was ignored.

"That's better," one of them said. "Now we have just a few questions and then we'll deal with the termination procedure."

Peculiar language. Isobel looked with longing at the bent poker that was propped in the hearth beside the embers of her dying coke fire. Could she? If she tried, would they harm Sandro? Best keep calm and see what other opportunities offered.

Murgatroyd and Leadbetter proceeded to give full rein to their unctuous vocabulary. Betrayal, disgrace . . . Gross dereliction of duty. Head Office's displeasure could not be averted. Never had the company been so let down by one of its privileged, trusted representatives. Kozyseal, in its never failing, open hearted goodness, had been duped.

"Just a minute," Isobel was stung to defend herself, "I'd like to know who duped who? What about the money you said . . ."

But Murgatroyd and Leadbetter's duet went inexorably on, never rising in volume or deviating in tone. Isobel was mesmerised. She sat stock-still like a mongoose immobilised by a swaying cobra's winkless stare.

She would be taken to court. There would be a civil action in which Head Office would employ the most distinguished QC money could buy . . . Isobel would lose everything she had. What did she think this house was worth? Not that it could begin to compensate for the business she had wickedly stolen from them. But an example had to be made . . . It was only for this that Head Office would stoop to notice the transgressions of one as low as she . . .

The knock on the door came just then. Rowella! Oh, thank God. It wasn't so much what these people threatened as the slime they secreted . . . Isobel tore herself from her chair, ravenous for the everyday, wholesome smell of Rowella. Her cigaretty hair and the fish and chips she usually brought . . .

"Rowella!"

The image of her friend was so strong in Isobel's mind – the way she stood with her legs apart and her toes pigeoned in the shoes that were always too tight – that it seemed for ever before her mind would register that it was not Rowella she saw standing before her. It was somebody quite other. Some one she knew but the texture of whose actuality she had forgotten.

Isobel stood there, looking at the man with the walking stick and the sling. He wore a light coloured mac with the collar turned up. Uncertain of his welcome, his smile was twisted, an S-shape lying on its side. His body sent shock waves of heat into the dimly lit vestibule.

"Is it you?" Isobel leaned for support against the doorjamb.

"It's me. Sorry, no flowers. There's no kiosk at your lousy station . . ."

"Ed. Ed, please, *please* come in. There are some people here . . . some horrible people . . . They're from Kozyseal, the people I work for . . ."

Edward Mazzerella was an officer of the US Navy and knew what to do.

"You . . . cocksuckers," he said pleasantly. "Get out."

Murgatroyd and Leadbetter semi-liquefied again and wordless, slithered out into what was now a fine, starry night. They faced a peculiarly illustrious future.

Shutting the door behind them, Ed saw a stationary car on the other side of the street with someone sitting in the driver's seat. Completely unremarkable.

FOURTEEN

Ed was gentle with Margaret Jefferson. Typically, as a sailor, he accorded women immunities from censure that no member of his own sex dare count on. It left him encumbered with an unapportioned share of blame for Isobel's depleted physical condition. Not only that, but the symptoms of nervous debility he saw in her gestures, heard in her bitten off comments . . . and identified in the spoors of malaise all over her house. He should have come sooner.

Removing coffee cups from the parlour to the kitchen on the night of his arrival, he had seen the neglected bundle of letters which included some of his own. On a trip to the bathroom upstairs, he had passed the open door of her bedroom. It was impossible that he should not glance sidewards and see that the dressing-table mirror was swung round on its hinges to face the wall. A negation so emphatic that his pulse missed a beat.

What it could mean, Ed didn't know. Instinct alone told him that Margaret Jefferson had contributed something to this state of affairs. Neglect, he supposed, rather than active persecution. Nothing, however, could be done or said unless Isobel threw the first stone. Even then, accusations from him would muddy the waters. Every child has a score to settle with one or other of its parents. Outsiders involved themselves at their peril.

None the less, Ed figured, she must be told what had been decided and the sooner the better.

A meeting between himself, Isobel and her mother was arranged on neutral territory at the Duke of Cornwall Hotel where Ed had a room. Apprised of his guest's arrival by a signal from the hall porter to the cocktail lounge bartender, Ed excused himself from Isobel and went to greet Margaret in the foyer. He had seen her only once before in a generalised blur of faces.

He had not asked Isobel for any description and needed none to recognise her. The voice he had heard when lying in that hospital bed, had been a cracked bell denouncing all pleasure with every swing of its clapper. The hair tidily crimped round a smooth crown, the cream, pin-tucked blouse with its modest ruby pin at the collar and the jersey suit which had never been fashionable but had always been good, said it all. The sartorial statement of women the western world over, for whom generalised disapproval and frugality both of purse and of heart, are an habitual reflex.

Margaret stood, lips pursed, with her Burberry half-on, half-off, shifting her old crocodile handbag and umbrella from hand to hand like a derelict queen, perplexed that no page materialised to assist her. Ed pitied her. It must have been hard to lose a husband when what was left of her own life might last as long as her youth. But no new lover would come now to gild the horizon or shorten the days.

"Mrs Jefferson, ma'am," he hailed her, "I wish you'd allowed me to fetch you . . ."

"No need, I assure you. It's Mr . . . er . . ."

"I'd be flattered if you would call me Edward," he said, disengaging his arm from the sling to help her with the coat. "I guess my surname's difficult unless you've got an Italian kink in your tongue . . ."

"There's some awful Yorkshire ice-cream man with a name something like yours, Mr . . . er . . . He has show-jumping horses and calls them puerile names after his products. Very successful."

Isobel's mother, Ed smiled to himself, made successful trading sound like a social misdemeanour.

"I wish I shared his industry and good fortune, Mrs Jefferson. Mr Yorkshireman Mazzerella sounds quite a guy. And please, do call me Edward."

Margaret was suspicious, but could find fault neither with his manners nor his manner. He had actually, she realised, the colour mounting to her cheeks, corrected her own deportment. Foreigners could be so ridiculously stiff.

On closer appraisal she saw that his linen was clean and unfrayed. His shoes, of decent quality, were well polished and in good repair. And his navy blue blazer wasn't an off-the-peg affair. Nor was it new.

If anything, she liked him less for being a man to whom it was difficult to condescend. She knew more about him now. Any navy's upper deck commanded a degree of respect. Four generations, was it? Respectable by American standards. Not an immigrant, no.

After kissing the air beside her daughter's cheek, Margaret was soon settled with a glass of dry sherry and the run of a bowl of stuffed olives. A copy of the luncheon menu was placed in her hands. No prices. It was all very awkward. Egg mayonnaise and steamed plaice shouldn't commit her to anything. She searched in her bag for the packet of ten cigarettes . . . She didn't often smoke but . . .

"Allow me, ma'am," Ed lunged across the low table with a lighter. The flame, maladjusted, nearly singed Margaret's eyebrows. There was a moment or two of general, stage-managed consternation. All three felt the utility of mishaps in breaking the ice. Particularly Ed, who'd turned the flame up deliberately.

"It's nice that you're free to have lunch with your friend, darling. But don't you have appointments or something to go to?"

That whole matter was quickly got over. Ed produced a copy of *Time* magazine which carried an article about Kozyseal and similar franchise operations. American-based, their selling techniques were now the subject of open debate. The US courts couldn't touch them, it seemed, but Isobel had struck a blow for natural morality.

"I've been sacked, Mummy."

Despite the comfort Ed's nearness gave her, Isobel shrank inside. Unlike her brothers, she never seemed to have anything to report to her mother but failure.

"But what on earth do you intend to do for a living? Poor little Sandro. You have responsibilities. It isn't as if you're in a position to pick and choose. Really, Isobel . . ."

It was the opening Ed wanted.

"Isobel won't have to do a damn thing about that. She's coming to live with me in Italy. I would have asked her before if you'd told me she had a telephone number. Why didn't you tell me?"

Margaret's incipient dewlaps wobbled like a turkey's wattles. She stubbed out her cigarette. To mention this oversight of hers on such an occasion was very ill bred.

"Oh, was that you? I think . . . yes. Something about an accident. I seem to remember a rather confused call . . . very early in the morning when I was expecting my son to . . ."

"My brother, Rupert, probably," Isobel put in, anxious that the circling word 'lie' should not be allowed landing permission. "He has a regular time."

Some residual feeling of filial loyalty to her mother made Isobel dislike the prospect of humiliating her. This meeting had not been intended as a trap. It had only one purpose. To put an end to this chapter of grey, truncated existence and announce the title of a new one. Tuscany and Ed.

Their agreement was simply that she and Sandro should go with him, share his life and home. They would take everything else as it came. Isobel would run Ed's house and if she cared to, involve herself in the antique business. Neither were onerous activities.

These plans were unfolded to Margaret over three indifferent courses, consumed in the hotel's cavernous dining room. A troop of underemployed waiters listened to talk of Tuscany's incomparable, crystalline air, the freedom and safety in which Sandro could grow up. There were olives, figs, vines and lemons on Ed's property. Pomegranates, too. The place swarmed with rabbits, partridge and fat pigeons roosting in the trees. It was a garden of casual plenty. A miniature Eden.

"I guess I get carried away," Ed smiled, ending his eulogy. He would have gone on but sensed Margaret's growing restlessness.

"Please, do let me get this clear. Am I to understand you propose to employ my daughter as a housekeeper?" She covered her glass with her hand when the waiter took the wine from the ice-bucket. "No. No more, thank you."

"Why not, Mummy? I've done it before . . ."

Isobel leapt at the rationalisation her mother suggested. It seemed the easiest way to explain things. Nothing in Margaret's temperament or experience could make her understand that a man and a woman might gamble on each other. No promises, no signatures, no lasting obligations. Each day, a short lease on harmony, chancing eviction at short notice. Isobel herself would agree to no securer tenancy than that. What was to happen to them or between them, was open to hazard.

"Let's just say Isobel needs a rest, some sunshine and a guy to depend on."

Ed's eyes sought Isobel's for validation of his summary. He chose light words to clothe the strength of his own commitment to their experiment, lest she otherwise take fright and flee from any pressure she was too fragile to counterbalance.

She had told him little of her own volition other than that Plymouth's interminable rain was depressing. And, after some coaxing, that her two working experiences had given her a terminal distaste for formal employment.

It was one he shared. To sell the brightest hours of the day, submit to bodily imprisonment by some business enterprise which could exploit a mere particle of the human powers they ensnared, was prostitution of the ugliest and commonest kind. Seed that would not come again, spilled on unfertile ground every day. Gone to waste. Squirrels gathering nuts in the forest had a better life than that.

That had been the substance of an intense conversation between them. It was then that Ed suggested that his patch of earth was big enough for both of them. The mighty intellects of classical Greece had fed on a crust of bread and a handful of olives. What did they need that Socrates and Pythagoras had managed without?

A bare sufficiency was enough to enable the cultivation of productive leisure. Painting, books, gardening and music. Education was wasted on work.

Specious arguments, perhaps. But there was much in them to charm Isobel. She badly needed an excuse to step out of the shadows. On this basis, she could surrender herself and Sandro to the geniality of chance in this kind, clever man's private Arcadia. He laid no sexual siege to her. He asked nothing of her but friendship. What could go wrong?

Now these ideas, or as much of them as could be minced into digestible morsels, were to be filtered through the narrow funnel of Margaret Jefferson's mind. From the outset, any such attempt was doomed.

"I see," said Margaret, having listened inattentively to a description of the independent living space that would be available to her daughter in Tuscany. "You and Isobel are engaged to be married. I do wish . . ."

"No, ma'am," Ed exposed his position. "I'm afraid not. I'm married already."

Margaret dropped her knife and fork immediately as if they'd gone red hot in her hands. Her mouth gaped briefly before she shut it with an audible crunch. Isobel lowered her eyes. This would be the difficult bit.

"Yes," Ed admitted quietly. "My wife has been living in Baltimore for the past ten years . . . on maintenance cheques and acrimony. We've no children. That's the trouble with the Catholic Church," he smiled. "It allows an angry woman to call God as her witness. And not even the civil courts can prefer other evidence. It's divorce by mutual consent, or no divorce at all. My wife does not consent."

"She might die," Isobel interjected factually but unhelpfully. "Not that it matters because . . ."

"Not matter!" Margaret pushed her knife and fork together with the tips of her fingers. "I didn't know I'd been invited to share a table with your . . . your gigolo, Isobel."

Ed pushed his chair back from the table. Glancing at him, Isobel saw his mouth had paled. For a moment he did not speak.

"Now look, Mummy . . ."

"If you mean, ma'am," Ed interrupted, speaking through gritted teeth, "that I shall be Isobel's 'protector', then you are right. She seems to need one, since her family have done damn all . . ." The waiter came at that moment. "May I offer you dessert?"

It was all downhill from there. There was some ill informed wrangling about religion, provoked entirely by Margaret. Ed, who had abandoned the exterior practices of his church long ago but accepted both as permanent features of his interior landscape, kept quiet. These things were never spoken of. Except by consenting adults after midnight.

"You seem to forget, Mummy," Isobel protested at one point when her mother's diatribe had already drifted well off course, "I am a Catholic, and so is Sandro."

"That child hasn't even been baptised . . ."

"No, if you remember, we were waiting for Rupert. He's to be godfather, one day, according to you. The man who never comes."

Margaret's expression was murderous.

"I think you've both said more than enough."

Forgetting the English custom, Ed snapped his fingers at a waiter who brought the bill only after some pointed delay.

In the powder room, Margaret glared into the looking glass to meet Isobel's eyes. She opened her compact and darted the puff at her face in feverish pecks. Her complexion was mottled with wine and with temper.

"If you go with that man . . . If you take my grandson from me, I shall never speak to you again."

Isobel made no answer but looked past her mother at the wholeness of her reflection. Hair, head, neck, shoulders and the rest. All there.

"He's a dreamer, don't you see? A loose living adventurer. A hardened adulterer . . . Too old for you, anyway."

"I'm sorry you can't marry Rupert, Mummy." Isobel had no idea why she said it.

Margaret turned slowly from the mirror. "You dirty minded little *sow*!" Her features were drawn up and back, away from her small, regular teeth . . . as if she battled a contrary wind . . . hair bristling erect in its follicles.

Kali, thought Isobel calmly. She had seen a picture once, of the cruel, blue skinned Hindu mother goddess, necklaced with skulls. Whose *were* those skulls? Her children's?

"Filthy, dirty . . . disgusting trollop. I never want to see, or hear of, or speak to you again."

There was some sort of crackle then in the space between Isobel and the mirror. An impression, merely, conveyed from one human spirit, the thick sediment of which had been rudely stirred . . . to another, whose mind had fallen cold, clear and bright. At any rate, Isobel's mother was gone.

The thing about Rupert had come to Isobel's mind like a telegram from some supranormal information repository. The

200

unspeakable, unthinkable desire of widows for their sons. That was why Rupert never came. He knew in his flesh that his mother would eat him.

Unrepentant, Isobel lingered to welcome the whole of herself. There she was, a steady, coherent image. Now she and Ed could take care of each other. She should have allowed it to happen before.

* * *

Carlo Bonetti interviewed the representative of the international surveillance agency he employed in his office.

"*Allora?*"

Not invited to sit, the agency's Northern Italy co-ordinator knew better than to try. Carlo had used his expensive services many times before. He squatted, therefore, on the floor to extract some papers from his briefcase. Carlo's monstrous desk, bare as an empty mortuary slab, was sacrosanct.

The instructions had been imprecise, as was invariably the case with briefs issuing from Bonetti's office. Carlo was a man who preferred that nobody should know which wormhole of ignorance it was, in the whole honeycomb of his affairs, he wished to plug.

On this occasion, the impersonal order form had merely requested that Carlo should be put in possession of all the significant facts surrounding one Signora Isobel Bonetti, an Englishwoman, believed to be living in Plymouth . . . who might there be known as Jefferson. A person, according to the brief, unconnected with *la famiglia*.

A likely story, which no one privy to the particulars of the enquiry requisition believed. Patently absurd. However, when Carlo uttered a lie, it became true for his employees, direct or subcontracted, at the moment of utterance. Overt incredulity could cost livelihoods.

This sniffing after Furio's widow was Carlo's first whim of the sort since his son had died nearly two years ago. Requests for covert information lately, had been confined to routine industrial espionage. What the change might signify, no one could predict.

Carlo's temper, rancid in the good old days, had grown steadily more toxic. The turnover in private secretaries was an indicator of the man's despair. But who can stop to sympathise in the crashing path of a pain maddened carnivore? Not the Bonetti headquarters' staff whose self-preserving instinct was to play dead or run whenever their chief came near.

"*Allora?*" Carlo repeated to the man before him. "Where's your leprous tongue? Let's hear it." He leaned back and laced his fingers across his stomach menacingly. A useful pose which he adopted in the common way of business. Carlo prepared to listen.

The account began with a compression of the usual data, verifications of addresses, names, hours put in, coming quickly to the meat of the enquiry.

"Signora Bonetti has been dismissed from two low grade jobs and is presently unemployed. There is a sale board outside the house."

This, thought Carlo, was quite interesting.

"She is disposing of goods?"

"No, no, signor. *In Vendita*. The house is for sale. Here are the agent's particulars . . ."

Carlo glanced disparagingly at the sheets of paper that were passed to him before letting them fall to the floor.

"She owns this hovel?"

"She is the mortgagor, Signor. There is no indication that the institutional mortgagee is selling over her head, however. Her removal appears to be voluntary." The representative licked his lips. The next item called for tactful presentation.

"Signora Bonetti's infant son," he went on, consulting his file notes, "concerning whom we received no specific instructions, is cared for between the hours of eight thirty in the morning and six in the evening at . . ."

A lifetime's practice enabled Carlo to maintain the opacity of his eyes. The Jefferson girl? A boy? Furio's child or some bastard . . .

"The birth," the other man went on, "was registered at Plymouth on 14 April 1967. Of course, Signor, you doubtless have alternative sources of information concerning these purely administrative details . . ."

The dates, Carlo's rat trap mind computed, tallied. Could it be? Alessandro Bonetti . . . Furio's son. No. Not possible. And yet . . . His grandson! *Isabella* had a child. *Incredibile*!

Still, Carlo showed no emotion. It would be unseemly to let anyone, least of all this bottom-feeder know that he, Carlo Bonetti, had been deceived in such a matter. This matter of indifference . . . And yet, if he could only believe it . . .

"The child," interrupted Carlo. "He is well?"

"He is well, Signor. The outside nurse's care is adequate but her premises are insanitary . . ."

Carlo waved his hand abruptly.

"The Bonetti female . . . has she friends?"

"She is visited daily by an American."

202

"You have particulars?"

"All but his current address. The Embassy in Rome would not release that . . ."

The file was placed in Carlo's outstretched hand.

He read the outline biography of Edward Mazzerella swiftly. It made no reference to his attendance at Furio Bonetti's wedding, or to the fact that the American had purchased his son's car. Where, then, had Isobel met him? Florence . . . it came to him. He hadn't troubled to butter her feet on that occasion either. A miscalculation. Had he known about this Mazzerella then, it would have been easy to ruin Isobel with Furio. Cameras could achieve so much. But *now* . . .

Grunting, Carlo tapped the report with the back of his hand. This American could not marry her. That was good. The shape of an idea was forming in his mind.

"He comes to her bed?"

"Nothing in his demeanour or hers suggests that, Signor. We consider . . ."

"You are not paid to consider. You are paid to look through the window . . . through the keyhole, under the door . . . of the *gabinetto* if need be. You understand? I wish to know how this *inglese* comports herself."

"Impeccably, as far as we are able to judge . . ."

Carlo waved his hand to silence the man. This required more thought. Very possibly what lay behind Isobel's decision to move, was her son's welfare. He must be at least a year old now. Talking, walking. He should be in the country . . . at the Villa Rondine. The home that was his birthright.

What money had Isobel, if any? Was this American her lover? And if so, how could that be used? Used for what purpose, Carlo had not yet decided. It was simply inbuilt in him to manipulate all circumstances for advantage . . . or the satisfaction of the exercise. It was a long time now, since he had felt any inclination for such sport. Inwardly exulting, he felt a rush of the old excitement. A grandson! He must look like Furio. That face, so loved, could not fade in Carlo's memory, nor fail, as he believed, in the transmission of the Bonetti features. The grape dark hair that whitened, alas, so quickly . . .

"I am to know of it, wherever they go." Carlo spoke without looking up from the report. "Get out!"

So, thought Carlo, swinging his revolving chair around to face the window, *Isabella* has done her duty after all. But she had hidden that of which he had a right to know. That which belonged not to her exclusively but to *la famiglia* . . . to *him*. A cruel, immoral woman. Turbulent and destructive. Not content with being instrumental in Furio's death, she deprives his heir of his inheritance. Isobel had not waited submissively for her father-in-law to forgive her, as it was her place to do. Instead she had chosen to avenge herself for a mild rebuke that day when she had intruded upon his grief. Had she only told him then . . .

Before long, Carlo had worked himself up into a good, hot, relishable rage. He felt invigorated. Almost, he thought, his old self again. Positively sprightly.

To turn the tables on Isobel would be an epicurean pleasure. Devious, malignant and implacable as she might be, in those respects, she had a lot to learn from him. He would teach her a lesson she would not forget. The only reliable regulator of Isobel's behaviour would prove to be family discipline. The old ways were always best.

A few days should be enough for her, Carlo considered. A week, perhaps. Maybe two . . . Longer, and the attention of the authorities would place an intolerable constraint on normal business activities. Sanctimonious talk of bribery and corruption from those whom he himself had often bribed. These double binds were unpredictable. So, a limited action. A temporary but effective measure. Quick, quiet and cheap. And then a celebration. Perfect.

Carlo laid provisional, flexible plans. Very soon, he would place her grandson in Beatrice's arms. In his mind's eye, he saw his wife's features, aged and drawn with sorrow soften at the gift. His gift. She, who had turned from him after their son's death, would turn back to him again.

Isobel was moving house . . . a disrupted schedule should provide innumerable opportunities. Which moment of the many would he choose?

Feeling the need for a little constitutional, Carlo went out into the Corso Mategna below and looked in the windows of baby-linen shops. On his way back, he paused in the outer office and told his secretary to take the funereal look off her face or go and work for someone else.

This, for Carlo, was affability.

*   *   *

Furio's old Lamborghini was waiting at Pisa's embryonic airport. It was parked in a locked shed some distance from the rough and ready Arrivals building. Ed went to get it while Isobel stayed with the luggage and Sandro. The child, querulous at the disruption to his routine, claimed all his mother's attention for fifteen minutes or so.

"A wet nappy, undoubtedly," a grandfatherly figure in a beret opined. The entire population of Italy, Isobel reminded herself, took unto itself rights of co-parentage where children were concerned. She had had some experience with Giacomo and Marzio in Milan. So long ago, it seemed now.

"A fine child, if I may say so, Signora," the man persisted. "Why don't you change him?"

Delighted that her ear could still process these sounds into meaning, Isobel shrugged at the queue outside the all-sexes lavatory and the general absence of privacy or facilities. The nappy, she hardly needed to point out, was worse than wet.

"I think we must wait, Signor."

The man in the beret was having none of it. He reached into Isobel's holdall to pull out a fresh napkin and briskly stripped the soiled one from Sandro's squirming body. Relegated to the status of nursery handmaiden, Isobel received a clucking, snorting lecture on the evils of rubber pants.

Amused, grateful, Isobel handed him a cotton ball well moistened with baby oil.

"Ah, in this at least you are sensible. Greatly to be preferred to lotion," he said, making a thorough job of cleaning Sandro's bottom. "Now he will be comfortable."

She was still thanking him for his expert assistance when the Lamborghini drew up. The sight of it unnerved her. Ed got out, wincing with pain. The old man politely moved away.

"Come on, honey. You'll have to do most of the driving. My arm's not up to . . ." He stopped, puzzled at the haunted look on her face. "Oh, honey. Look . . . I'm sorry . . ."

"It doesn't matter, I learned to drive in that car. You've looked after it well." Isobel's voice had risen an octave, her eyes gone suddenly shiny. "Really, Ed," she reassured him, "it's all right."

Stricken, Ed cursed himself silently for a crap headed fool. He'd thought of just about everything but that. At least it wasn't the one Bonetti had died in.

While they loaded the luggage into the back seat and boot, leaving a space for Sandro's special seat, the man in the beret quietly took his place in a bus queue.

Isobel caught sight of him as she was about to get in behind the wheel.

"*Grazie tante . . . tante, Signor,*" she waved to him.

"*Prego, Signora,*" he bowed and smiled, dismissing her thanks. It was nothing. No trouble. He occupied himself with appreciative contemplation of the animated group round the car. The American was still rearranging luggage. His body obscured the registration number but every time he shifted from one leg to the other, one or other of the digits was revealed.

Casually, the old man withdrew a steel spectacle case from an inside pocket. He had a notebook in there somewhere, and a pencil. His fingers, lubricated by the baby oil, let the case slip. It clattered to the ground. The old man stooped stiffly, cursing, to retrieve it. Others in the bus queue came to his assistance. Their efforts were inept, hindering those of the man, who, despite his appearance was both a little younger and a little nimbler than he would want it known . . . although not much.

A fat, bossy woman blocked his line of vision, lamenting over the fracture of the spectacle lenses in the case. He must, she advised, get them replaced with perspex. She recommended an oculist whose manufacturing turnaround was highly expeditious . . . Others had competing suggestions to offer. The old man silently damned his countrymen to hell . . . any excuse to talk.

He heard the Lamborghini engine rev and through a tangle of unwanted arms and legs and bosoms, the start of accelerating motion.

Breaking free of the knot of sympathisers with a violent shove, the old man snatched the spectacle case and ran after the departing Lamborghini. Too late. The number-plate was a blur, the high-resolution lenses useless. Producing a small camera from his pocket, the old man pointed it at the car and pressed the shutter. No good, the car had swerved to avoid another before disappearing round a bend.

Disgusted, the old man hurled the camera into some nearby bushes. His first field assignment for months and he had fluffed it. Too old . . . or lack of practice. The misadventure had cost him a very substantial fee. Not to mention a premium for changing the *pannolino* of Carlo Bonetti's grandson. A red Lamborghini? Hired . . . second-hand . . . or merely old? Still, it was not the commonest model on Italian roads . . .

Apart from that limp assessment, all the local freelance agent had to relay was Isobel's unsatisfactory reply to his disingenuous enquiry as to her business in Italy. On holiday, she said, for an indefinite period. He had not dared press, at that moment, for fuller details. Suspicion, he'd been told, must on no account be aroused. His instructions had been to get the registration number of the car, and if possible, to discover her destination together with a description of the parties. With emphasis on the child.

The child, he mused, was on fighting good form. His mother's lake coloured eyes looked strange set in his good, olive complexion.

And his hair was brown, not black. A detail worth recording, surely?

*   *   *

Isobel's spirits vaulted as she swung the great car round the first few bends in the road. To her, it was an Olympian horse returned from the past to carry her across the deep, sucking marshes which divided the old fair country from the new. She must write to Simon about the house . . . To hell with her mother, with Rupert, Nina Fischer and all the rest. A sweet road lay ahead.

Tuscany proved to be that never-never land glimpsed over the shoulders of oval faced, quattrocento madonnas hanging in city galleries or between the slippery leaves of coffee-table books. Places that Isobel had often strained her eyes to see through layers of murky brown varnish and the trickery of Old Master brushstrokes. Silver ribbons of water snaked between blue hazed hills crowned with fortified towns shimmering in and out of ambiguous mists. Every new prospect drew exclamations from Isobel.

"There, there it is," Ed pointed out the *città*. It soared up, a static eruption on the skyline. "Castelchiara. Lightcastle, I call it. It's where my shop is . . . Kind of pretty, isn't it?"

Pretty was not the word. Castelchiara knocked the breath from Isobel's body. It sat enthroned on the summit of its high, conical hill, tightly hugged by its girdling walls. Twelve slender towers reached up, copper gold in the sun which was already slipping behind them. A thin road ascended from the deep river valley below, peeling a white spiral through the hill's clothing of trees.

Isobel used words that Ed could only grope for. He delighted in her strictures. It was one of the things he loved her for. Her bigger verbal palette and school-teacherly willingness to share it.

"Pretty?" She scorned him. "Oh Ed! What a washed out word."

Why was it that the American vocabulary, so virile . . . so creative when it touched things that were either funny or dire, was so utterly impotent faced with mystery and splendour? She asked him and he could not answer her. He was, he said, just a simple sailor.

"And yet you found this unearthly place and brought me to it."

"It's not as famous as San Gimignano," he deprecated shyly, as Isobel let the car drift slowly to a halt. "Much smaller . . . and nothing like as crowded in summer . . . Say, we could mosey on up there, get a bite to eat and take a look at the shop. It would give Sandro a break . . . Carry on out to the farm later on."

Letting the clutch in, Isobel swooped the car down the road, a nesting eagle that has seen her eyrie.

207

"Hey, honey. Ease up . . . Not too fast. Remember you're out of practice . . ."

"Ed, Ed. You can never go too fast."

Grinning, Ed relaxed, giving himself up to whatever would happen. Isobel was right. Caution belonged to the nine-to-five world which was no longer theirs.

Isobel's eaglet crowed with delight. Fear is a delectable toy to infants, who alone among mankind know that no harm can ever result.

* * *

In that same hour, the man who'd changed Sandro's nappy at Pisa airport was writing his fifth version of the encounter.

His wife answered the suburban flat's second, business telephone twice and said her husband was not at home. No, she wasn't worried, she assured the caller. No more than usual. Yes, yes, her husband would naturally make contact as soon as he came in. Didn't he always do so? In the next room, she heard the sound of paper being ripped from the typewriter. For the last time, the enquiry agent surveyed the sum total of his afternoon's achievements. They were not impressive, no matter how he rearranged the sparse material. Brown hair . . . blue eyes . . . red Lamborghini . . . on holiday. That was not the level of intelligence the Bonetti organisation expected or were prepared to pay for.

Better, mused the agent bitterly, to have no reputation at all than one that was in shreds. At best he would be a laughing stock in the private detection fraternity. At worst, a target for Carlo Bonetti's wrath.

Once it had been rumoured that, as a young man, Carlo had shared his father's reputation for expressing dissatisfaction over shoddy workmanship with bullets. A rumour long since scotched by Carlo's tame image-builders . . . but the savour lingered on.

Tearing up the revised report, the agent took it and his business cards to the communal garbage chute, passing his wife on the way there without a word. Returning to their flat, he informed her, as she took washing in from the balcony, that in future he would revert to the full time use of his family name.

It would be sensible, now, to pack a few necessities immediately and drive to Piombino to catch the next ferry across to Elba. They needed a holiday. They could stay with her sister. Panicking? Of course he was not panicking. He was merely taking a wise precaution as any professional would. Probably unnecessary, but better safe than sorry, eh?

A smear of baby oil had ended his career and, incidentally, Carlo Bonetti's line of scent.

For the moment, Sandro was safe from his grandfather's inbred predilection for vendetta games. And Isobel, it seemed, would go unpunished. The last recorded sighting had been at Malpensa, Milan, at the boarding gate for the Pisa shuttle. After that, nothing.

Hearing that his chance of both revenge on his recalcitrant daughter-in-law and reconciliation with his grandson had been thrown away, Carlo collapsed with a heart attack.

FIFTEEN

"I dleness," said Ed, "is a travesty of leisure," or so he condensed his theory of unemployment in the process of leading Isobel out of bondage in Plymouth into queenship in his promised land. He soon had cause to regret his epigram. Her interpretation of it was far too literal for his comfort.

She did not make the transition from driven toil to spontaneous pottering either immediately or easily. No sooner had she bestowed her own and Sandro's belongings in the pair of communicating rooms which Ed had retained builders to restore whilst he lay in hospital, than she displayed an alarming eagerness to earn her keep.

Meals? Where, Ed wondered, was the theoretical crust of bread and handful of poetic olives? Isobel cooked with the laboriousness of a restaurant chef and fairly often with comparable success. Never, since the days of his marriage, had Ed seen such chopping, larding, mincing, simmering, reducing, marinading, and glazing. Isobel, unfortunately, had brought a cookery book. Elizabeth David's *Italian Food*.

"Say, honey, I sure do appreciate this," said Ed, facing up to a most elaborate pie, "but simple food's what I'm used to . . ."

"This *is* simple food," replied Isobel firmly. "It says so in my book. Pizza Rustica. Eat it up."

She was charming when she had these fits of English nannyishness, so, of course, Ed gorged himself against his better judgement. *He* was not twenty-one with a cast iron digestion. For love, however, a man must take conspicuous risks and a quantity of liver salts in private.

The copper saucepans hanging from the kitchen ceiling on a rack, were burnished with a homemade paste Isobel remembered the Parsonage charlady making. Cupboards were turned out and tidied. Mattresses were turned . . . another Parsonage habit, the practical purpose behind which, eluded Ed entirely.

"Er, honey . . . Why are you doing this?"

"I haven't a clue," Isobel arched her eyebrows beautifully. "It's something proper housewives do."

A misdirected arrow which cut Ed to the heart. Was Isobel going in for all this busyness to synthethise a security she felt she did not have?

"Don't be silly, Ed. I'm just trying to pull my weight."

Deciding to let her settle down in her own way, Ed reflected that every female animal likes to personalise her lair . . . put her smell on it and on her mate.

Of actual mating, there had not yet been any. Untroubled, Ed bided his time. It was essential to him, that when that happened it should be Isobel who came to him and that she should be ready. He'd rushed her once and blown it. In the meantime, he watched and waited, with patient fascination.

Messalina, on the other hand, found Isobel's energy at variance with her congenital indolence. On the days she did not accompany Ed in the pursuance of shop business, she was turfed out of her daytime basket at the farm four or five times to spend pennies she could very well have saved till later. Walks, exercise . . . what were they? A dog went with her master when permitted or slept all day.

Making the best of this adjustment period, Ed applied himself during what would otherwise have been his extensive leisure to work on the remaining courtyard buildings. The builders had made the structure sound, but since there was no urgency for them to be completed, Ed himself was doing the plastering, painting and any tiling needed.

Isobel found herself a job in the courtyard, too. Scraping all the encroaching weeds between the cobbles to a soil depth of four centimetres, to enable the hollows to be filled with mortar. A labour of Hercules.

"It'll look smart," she defended the self-imposed project to Ed, "and it will mean we can see if there are any nasty creepy-crawlies lurking at a glance. We want Sandro to be able to run around in bare feet without stepping on a scorpion, don't we?"

He had to admire her foresight there and Isobel went to work. The task was repetitive but not in any way beyond her strength. An oyster knife from the kitchen drawer proved the most efficient tool. The work had other beneficial offspins.

Normally, she did it in the afternoons when Sandro had his nap and when Ed, who closed the shop at lunchtime during the winter months, was plastering nearby in the cow byre he intended for Isobel's studio. A surprise she didn't know of yet. In the lengthening hours of sunshine which grew warmer every day, they were close but not intimate. Companionable but not talkative.

Messalina idled her time away between the two of them. Licking Isobel's face as she bent over the cobbles, jumping up on the first

211

rung of Ed's stepladder. She would have much preferred to have them cuddled up somewhere together so that she could keep an eye on them with a minimun of effort. That human puppy in its ridiculous high basket had an easier life than she did.

Isobel was equally free to indulge all her passing thoughts and examine some of them more closely. Instead of pushing Nina Fischer away, she now realised, she had actually, actively to call her back to mind. Nina was in full retreat. Perhaps sending the transcript to Josef before leaving Plymouth had hastened her on her way. Why had she not done that months ago, Isobel wondered. Then perhaps, there would never have been that trouble with her head.

That was almost over, too. In fact it *was* over but Isobel was still inclined to mistrust any reflective surface. There weren't many mirrors in Ed's house, but when Isobel encountered one, even the one above her own washbasin, unless she had prepared herself minutes in advance she tended to avert her glance. She must stop that. It was one thing in private, but to an onlooker, it must give her a distinctly shifty look. And Ed was not to know anything at all about all this. What he'd done for her was quite enough without him having to find out he'd taken on a total fruit cake . . .

"How about we stop and have some tea now?" Ed's voice carried from the byre, disturbing Isobel's reverie.

My God! Was that the time? Isobel looked in amazement at her watch. Half past four. Long, long after Sandro's waking up time . . . Her heart began to thud. He must be dead. Obviously, or he'd have started bawling at his usual time. Babies died in their cots quite regularly. Mothers put them down to sleep and then couldn't wake them up. Because they'd choked, or smothered . . . or stopped breathing . . .

"Ed!" Isobel's voice was faint with fear.

"What is it, honey? Do you want me? Shall I make the tea?"

"No . . . please. Come here . . . It's Sandro . . ."

The way she sounded brought him rushing to her side. She was grey faced and shaking as if she'd been bitten by a snake.

"I daren't look at him," she said. "He wakes at three and cries . . . Look at the time now . . . Could you, please? I'm sorry, I don't want to be the one to find him . . . I think he must be . . ."

Recognising her dread without understanding it, Ed put his arm around her shoulders and hugged her quickly. "Sure I will, honey. He probably slept longer because he had a busy morning . . . He ate a whole heap of noodles . . . more than I could . . ." He spoke as he went towards the door which led to Sandro's nursery.

There was a silence whilst Isobel gripped the hair around her

212

temples and tensely held her breath. What was Ed *doing*? Why was he so long . . . ?

"My, my, my," said Ed in passable imitation of a black mammy nursemaid, pushing open the nursery shutters to look out at Isobel. "You sho' better come look at this, Miss Izzy. Seem's like we got one o' dem fresco painters in the family."

Sandro was not only alive but creatively employed in spreading faeces all over his cot and adjacent walls. More from relief than anger, Isobel smacked him. Not understanding what he'd done wrong, Sandro set up an ear-splitting wail. Isobel smacked him again.

"Oh come on, honey! Get a hold on yourself." Ed pushed himself between the cot and Isobel. "They all do it . . ."

"How the hell would you know?" She struck out at him blindly in that spate of tempestuousness which in mothers denotes the rapid drain outfall of terror. "You haven't *got* any children . . . I was so frightened I could kill him . . ."

"That's all right," Ed said easily, catching her wrists. "That's good. Hammer me as much as you like. But not in front of your little boy, eh? Let's get him cleaned up and fed, shall we . . . first? For Pete's sake, calm down!"

He was right, of course.

"But look what he's done to the work you paid for!"

Isobel gestured at the mess on the walls, the old olive press room walls that had been smooth-plastered and painted to make a cool, spacious room for her child along with her own adjoining bedroom and bathroom.

"Aw, come on, honey. Worse things happen at sea. This stuff'll wash off with soap and water and if it doesn't, we'll repaint the walls and skin the artist, won't we, feller?"

Ed seized the odiferous Sandro and set him down on the tiles, soiling his hands in the process. He grimaced good humouredly.

"Oh, Ed, please let me . . ."

"No chance. You get him in the tub and I'll fetch a pail and make a start on young Michelangelo's work. Share everything, remember. Wasn't that the deal? From champagne to shit."

Gallons of water were expended in restoring order and sepsis. Once released from his bath, Sandro toddled out of an open door into the courtyard where the sun warmed the cobbled paving and remaining patches of grass.

Realising that his elders could not get enough of water that afternoon, he loosened the tap attached to the hose pipe there and directed the jet back into the bathroom where his mother crouched to clean out the tub. Her yell of outrage brought Ed running for the second time that day. He too was soaked. Isobel, unthinking, tore the wet clothes from herself, swearing and spitting, blinded by the spray.

In moments the three of them were prancing stark naked in the courtyard, laughing because there was nothing else to be done. They hosed each other and Sandro for minutes together. How long the unselfconscious abandon lasted, neither Ed nor Isobel could measure.

It must have ended when Isobel noticed that men of forty or so do not have withered skins or horrible, wrinkled old bodies. If Ed's was anything to go by, they had gleaming, bronzed flesh, pectorals defined by the upturned curves of an archer's crossbow, and straight, powerful legs. Her inventory might have ended there if Sandro had not drawn attention to Ed's enlarging erection.

The little boy trotted briskly after him, hands outstretched, determined to look closer at this miraculous implement. Ed feinted away absurdly, helpless with laughter. Futilely, blushing from thigh to forehead, Isobel ordered her son to desist, whilst laughing herself. Soon, the thing turned into a game of tag with Sandro chasing after Ed and Isobel chasing Sandro. Messalina joined in, adding her yaps to the shrieks of pretended dismay.

The horseplay reached a crescendo just as Ed's landlord, Padre Pissaro, leaned his motor scooter against the front wall of the farmhouse. The pleasant spring weather had persuaded him to ride out from Castelchiara with the object of inviting his tenant to buy the freehold from him. He had put in so much work, so many lire . . . surely he must wish to buy. Particularly now, if the *chiarini* newsmongers had it right . . . that the American had his family with him.

A sale would suit the padre very well. He would never live again on his family's property. There was no profit in these places any more. Tuscany . . . Italy was changing.

The good father was minded to take a glass of wine with *il capitano*, anyway, and smoke a small cigar or two. A spot of cheerful haggling, and with luck, a yarn about the sea. The padre had not seen that marvel, never having travelled further than Siena. And he'd not been there since leaving the seminary. Signor Mazzerella was wonderfully invigorating company. To think, he had seen what Noah had seen and more! Icebergs and coral atholls. And no one had ever heard a boastful word from him.

Getting no response to his knock, Padre Pissaro presumed on the licence extended to men of his cloth and pushed open the door. Nobody at home, it seemed, although the red Lamborghini stood in the umbrella pine's circle of shade. It was then, in the silence of the main house, that Pissaro heard the commotion coming from the rear.

Knowing the property of old, he made his way round there. Nor was he altogether sorry he'd done so. A hugely improper scene, no question, but delightful for all that. Concealed in a shadowy doorway, the priest enjoyed watching a trio of satyrs at play with their dog before tiptoeing softly away.

Wobbling down the track on his scooter, Pissaro crammed his straw hat down firmly on to his head. Married? Hah! He was not that simple. He supposed that on balance, the wholesome fiction had better be promoted. A man could choose to have a scandal in his parish or he could choose to have diverting neighbours. The padre chose the latter. Mazzerella and his mistress were most amiable additions to the neighbourhood. Like a fresco come to life.

* * *

"Any chance of Aphrodite putting some clothes on?" Ed asked, shivering, when the sun's rays slanted low.

"Why, are you feeling cold?"

"Hell, no. I'm a god, ain't I? Snow, ice and fire are all one to me, ma'am. I just don't want to desecrate my divine hide with soup stains."

They drank a lot of wine that night. Ed talked of his family, principally his father. A man who'd drawn every breath in accordance with naval ordinances, terrorised his wife and regimented his children.

"He had religion all mixed up with American football and keeping your teeth brushed. He gave my brothers and me a pep talk on sex when we got to be around sixteen."

"Wasn't that a bit late?"

"Never would have been too soon for me, honey."

"What did he say?"

"That he'd thought a lot about it but he figured that a regular guy couldn't help enjoying sex. But if you kept thinking that any time now, one of those little wriggle-assed guys was going to touch base and win itself three years' worth of college bills, that took the edge off it."

"And did it?" Isobel was spellbound.

"Dunno, beautiful. Never did give it a try. Me'n the naval-base barber had an arrangement. Whenever I had to get a haircut, I got a handful of rubbers put down on Pa's bill. He beat me senseless when he found out."

"Is he still alive?" Isobel asked, sleepy with the wine.

215

"Sure is. Puts in a lot of time holding my wife's hand and telling her God will justify her in the end."

"Why did you leave her?"

"I realised she was really the woman my father chose for me. Sure, she was attractive . . . Anyway, I bugged out."

It was against Ed's code to criticise his wife to another woman and against Isobel's to press him to do so. Had she known it all, she might have wondered how he had grown up with so few of what he called 'hang-ups'.

"Hey," he said, "I enjoy unbuttoning to you. Rattling all the family skeletons . . ."

Isobel got the giggles then, followed by the hiccups. She couldn't help telling him, when she got her breath back, that her deceased husband had been in a position to rattle his ancestral skeletons quite literally and hadn't liked it one little bit.

"Poor guy," said Ed and took her up to bed. His room.

To be fair, he hardly knew what he was doing any more than she did. They just fell asleep, side by side.

She was woken some time later by a snuffling noise somewhere outside the house. At first she had no idea where she was, with whom or what the noise was, let alone what the time was. Once fully conscious she remembered. Oh, how could she? She had not even gone to check on Sandro and now there was an intruder on the property. Swinging her legs over the edge of the bed she burrowed her way into a sweater of Ed's, the first thing that came to hand, and creaked her way down the rudimentary, ladder-like staircase that led from this room to the short corridor linking the main house with the courtyard buildings.

Ed too, awoke. Finding the place beside him empty, he threw himself back on the pillows groaning. No wonder she'd deserted him. What a dumb thing to do. Fill a young woman full of drink, drag her off like a caveman . . .

"Ed," Isobel's voice whispered up the near vertical stairwell, "do come and look . . . Out of Sandro's window."

He joined her with alacrity, aware now of the sounds she had heard. Christ! They'd got a burglar and his gun was on the far side of the courtyard, inaccessible, by an indoor route, from the house side.

It was an old boar, nosing round the outside tap, licking drops of water trapped in cobble-nicks beneath.

"He can't be thirsty at this time of year, can he?" Isobel wanted to know.

"No, he can't. I suspect," Ed replied softly, "he knows something we don't. He reckons we're in for a long, hot summer and he wants an alternative water supply other boars don't know about. He probably smelt the water when we were . . . erm . . . playing with it this afternoon. Must have been watching. Say," he added, sliding a hand under the welt of the sweater Isobel wore and patting her naked rump, "what would you have done if you'd met a real desperado down here, a thief and not a pig?"

"Ssh! I don't know. I just had to get to Sandro. Doesn't he look . . ." She broke it off, not wanting to sound soppy. "They'll sleep through earthquakes, babies will, once they get off. Why didn't Messalina bark?"

"She'd know there was no danger to us," Ed answered promptly, far from confident. "Dogs have instincts which work even while they're sleeping."

"Dogs," hissed Isobel over her shoulder, as they crept from the room, "are supposed to have *ears*!"

"You shouldn't have gone down on your own. Why didn't you thump me awake . . ."

"I told you. Sandro. I'm used to doing whatever I have to on my own . . ."

"Well, you're not on your own, now, honey, are you?"

Seeing that she had gone back to his room with him, sober as a judge and with no premeditation, Isobel had to agree that she was not alone any longer.

"Look," Ed took her hands before she could get back into bed, "I'm sorry. I had no right . . . I didn't mean to get you drunk and if you'd rather . . ."

"Are you going to stand there jabbering all night," Isobel retorted, "while I get goose pimples on my bottom? By the way, have we done anything yet? I didn't seem to notice . . ."

Ed grabbed her then and threw her on the bed beneath him.

"Lady," he said laughing, "I'm gonna do something you'll notice."

"Oh gosh," Isobel sighed rapturously, "I'm not sure I can remember how to do it."

"Allow me, ma'am, to refresh your memory . . . as to the main movement at least. Can you help me on the overture?"

"I never bother with it," said Isobel, "all that sort of thing gets done in my mind, months before."

He took her at her word and found that she was right. She was ready for him, more than he'd ever dared to hope she would be. This tall, laconic, sometimes rather distant English person was a tunnel of fire inside. She took the lead, as well, conducting Ed's performance as if she'd known how he'd play his instrument all her life.

217

"Wow," he said, when it was all over. "Well, wow!"

"Glad you're pleased," Isobel smugged, grinning from ear to ear in the dark.

"Oh, honey. Pleased! Say, are you somebody who likes to go to the bathroom . . ."

"No, no," Isobel demurred, "I rather like the leaky bit. Anyway, leaping up seems so rude . . ."

"Hold on," he said. "Let me do the leaping." Knock kneed, he staggered away to his own bathroom, pursued by Isobel's laughter, and fetched her a towel to lie on so she shouldn't wake on a sticky sheet.

They slept entwined, his body as familiar to hers now as an old dressing gown.

In the morning, while they were dressing Sandro, he clapped a hand to his forehead.

"Shit! I was so pissed last night I never thought . . ."

"It's all right," Isobel understood at once. "There's very little chance of that. I'm two days off my period. I didn't think to bring some pills, though. In fact, I've never used them. Do you think the pharmacist in Castelchiara will have some?"

"No," Ed hoisted Sandro on his shoulder, "I figure not. Kinda traditional minded round here . . . But he's a great guy, the pharmacist. He'll point us in the right direction over in Florence, I guess."

Isobel noted that word 'us' and liked it. Why had that other woman thrown him away? If she could have given him back, even now, she would. Before it went any further between her and Ed, she would have to make sure of that. One more step and she wouldn't be able to bear it if he left.

"Look, honey," he said over breakfast, "about this pill thing . . . I hope you don't think I just . . ."

"I don't think any such thing," she replied, looking up at him. "I'm not sure I want another baby and in any case, we'd have to weigh one thing against another. You realise, don't you, that by the time it was twenty, you'd be sixty. Sixty-one or two. Do you want tying down like that for years to come? And darling Ed, are you really, really sure about your wife? I had one man die on me . . . Don't . . . I'm sorry, but I have to ask you . . ."

He came and held her close then. "What oath can I swear, honey, that you'll believe in? Sailor's honour?"

"Yes," Isobel tittered. "That will do."

She really did believe him because although they spoke lightly of the thing, she knew that the life saving mutual trust of seamen, be they fishermen or naval officers, was deeply rooted in him. If he gave her this guarantee of faith, then she could count on him till death.

*   *   *

As the scorching summer months advanced, *il capitano* and his lady, as they were ambiguously labelled by the *chiarini*, became rather more preoccupied with the antique business than they had been. There were advantages, too, in spending the hottest hours in the Calle Ghibelline's shadowy ravine, so narrow that the buildings on one side were prevented from collapsing against those opposite by an arcade of flying buttresses.

The garden, deeply shaded too, was ideal for Sandro. The two hundred foot drop from the city wall which bounded the area's eastern side, was made safe by Ed who fixed a wire grille. It was a pity in a way, as it partially obscured the view of the valley panting down below and the other hill towns soaring above the heat shimmer in the distance.

Lovely in its own dishevelled way, the garden was dotted with broken statuary. Armless nymphs and noseless busts ... half a fallen column and an urn, big enough to stand in. Yuccas, palms and old, tumbling roses were left undisturbed. It was only when a gardenia bush came into bloom that Isobel made Ed uproot it. She couldn't stand the smell, she said ... she didn't know why. Ed indulged her in that, as in all things.

Indoors, Isobel saw, the space was crammed with stock. Ed never seemed to have to go out and bid at country sales. Castelchiara neighbours, every one of whom occupied a *palazzo* (because no house in the town admitted to any less noble description even if it consisted of three or four dark rooms stacked one on top of the other) brought items of interest, or descriptions of these, to the shop on a regular basis. It was a great convenience, they said, to have a *negozio d' antichità* right there on the spot.

Isobel watched Ed conduct business with the townspeople on many occasions. More than half were aristocrats, according to themselves. But *nobiltà* or plain folk, the routine, to which Ed was inured, gave Isobel endless hours of fun with its sheer predictability. It was all as it had been with Giorgio, he told her, and he was only the postman.

After a grappa or two and some repetitive chat about the appalling heat – quite unprecedented, the *chiarini* always claimed – Ed would be given a laudatory description of an *antichità* for sale. A chest, a bed, a press or a dresser. A painting, perhaps. Rarely anything smaller.

Doing his best to act shrewdly in his own interests, Ed asked all

219

the right questions. The replies tripped silkily off *chiarini* tongues.

Provenance? Certainly this chest had been in the family for generations. As for quality, any name compounded with that of Guelph or Ghibelline told its own glorious story . . . as the learned Signor Mazzerella well knew.

Approximate date? Nothing, apparently, ever post-dated the Napoleonic wars. Receipts were only occasionally available. What was paperwork, shrugged the would-be vendors. *Il capitano*'s own experienced eye would inform him.

Dimensions? Oh, *piccolo, piccolo*! In olden days, what of any size could be brought up to this town and into such awkward *palazzi* as these?

Inspection? Ah, that would indeed be difficult. The article was situated on the topmost floor of the *palazzo*, only ever accessible by means of a treacherous spiral staircase in the tower. It was the cost of repairs to this dangerous thoroughfare, which alone forced the sale of the treasured heirloom. So sad.

There would be brave work then, with handkerchiefs and wobbling chins. Ed's tentative mention of potential value, *if*, on inspection, all he'd been told was verified by the evidence of his eyes, had a souring effect on aspirant vendors. Well, if he would not trust as a friend would trust . . .

"Godammit," he said to Isobel one day, "I know I'm a soft touch, but what do they think I run here? A soup kitchen for poverty stricken aristos?"

"That's exactly what they do think," Isobel said. "You pay them far too much because you're always worried they haven't enough to eat when all the time they've probably got sacks of loot stashed underneath the floorboards."

Ed doubted that but at the same time wasn't going to be done out of his *bella figura* by tamely lying down and peeling off greenbacks for stuff he hadn't even seen. Did they think he was stupid?

"Wishful thinking, darling," Isobel soothed after a sniffy interview with a transparent wisp of a *contessa*. "Anyway, you mustn't buy her table unless you see it first."

"I never do," wailed Ed truthfully. The fact being that he both saw and bought more than he wanted to out of a misgiving that the money was desperately needed for basic commodities he took for granted, and a feeling too, of social awkwardness. People *would* treat him as a friend instead of as a businessman. Friends, as he saw it, far too frequently in need. Some of these damn *palazzi* were still lit by candles. Candles, godammit, not even paraffin lamps.

The shop filled up with massive furniture. Much of it had never heard Garibaldi named in its presence, let alone Napoleon. Some was painted, the rest, of an oak so black it looked halfway to becoming coal. All of it was heavy. Too heavy for the trickle of casual tourists who happened into the town. Day trips from Florence and Siena usually passed Castelchiara by. The cars and buses made for San Gimignano. The facilities there were better, the works of art more distinguished.

So Ed and Isobel had an awful lot of stock they couldn't hope to shift other than by sending it in job-lot lorryloads to dealers in larger centres. They did it, but trade margins were a fraction of retail profits. Really, as Ed himself admitted, they were in business to convert a hundred cents into a dollar. What the hell? Shipping was a piece of piss and allowed them time for better things.

Drawing was one of those better things. Ed's own exquisitely detailed pen and ink sketches of the town and surrounding country were tacked in profusion all over the shop's interior walls. He meant to get them all framed and take them back to the farm where Isobel's rooms had provided extra hanging space.

Not officially for sale, the sketches formed the bulk of the portable items displayed in the shop. Now and again, Ed reluctantly sold one to a discerning tourist at what he hoped would prove a discouragingly extortionate price. He would console himself and Isobel then, for the loss of the drawing, with the thought that the few thousand lire it fetched would buy them a feast at Castelchiara's best *ristorante*.

"Don't have the pigeon," Ed ordered Isobel sharply one such lunch time in August, when the proprietor was extolling this item on his menu.

"Why not, is there anything wrong with them?" asked Isobel innocently of Ed in English.

"Sure is," he replied crossly. "He's charging more than six times what I sold them to him for this morning. They're the ones I shot last night and brought up in the car. Why is it always me that gets to be the village idiot?"

Isobel stood up, leaned across the table and kissed him on the lips, while Sandro beamed. Other lunchers put down their knives and forks, and, napkins still tucked into their collars, shouted warm encouragement. Ah, *il amore*, what else was life for . . . at breakfast, lunch and dinner? *Il capitano* had all the luck. What a gift to a man was a young and ardent wife. Soon there would be a troop of little brothers and sisters for the *bambino* to play with. Glasses were raised to them. Italians need little excuse to make a fuss of lovers.

The proprietor threw up his hands and came back with cuttlefish in beetroot, the curious speciality of the house. *On* the house, too, with a carafe of his brother's last but one, lethal vintage.

221

"*Now* who's the village idiot?" Isobel enquired of Ed, sopping up the sauce with bread. "Everybody loves you, me especially. So don't sulk about the pigeons."

*   *   *

For the rest, the farm property grew most of their food.

They talked of keeping chickens for the eggs. The idea was dropped. A countrywoman by birth, Isobel knew you couldn't keep played-out broodies for ever, yet wringing their necks was unthinkable. And no, Ed couldn't turn a gun on faithful old friends. But they could have the vet out, couldn't they, Isobel hopefully suggested, to put down hens past happiness or use?

"That would make the eggs very expensive," Ed told her gently.

One day, raking the baking soil between their lettuces, Isobel rested her sandalled foot on a greyish brown tube which she took to be the hose line laid to irrigate the vegetables. The tube objected and sunk its fangs into the soft hollow just above her heel. Isobel had disturbed a viper's siesta and her scream disturbed the slumbering valley.

Advised by the pharmacist, Ed kept snake serum in the house and injected it swiftly, remarking as he examined the twin punctures in Isobel's flesh that without the antidote, she'd have had half an hour to live.

She spent the rest of the summer sweltering in lace up shoes like those favoured by Castelchiara's widowed sisterhood, carrying the increasingly active Sandro on her hip. At the farm, only the enclosed, cobbled courtyard, speared with lilies, seemed safe enough for soft little legs and feet. And in the Calle Ghibelline, the garden there was too cool for serpents but a paradise for midges.

With children, one set of problems and restrictions is immediately succeeded by another. It made Isobel less and less enthusiastic about having another child.

"It's simply untrue," she said to Ed, "that what you can do for one, you can do for two. You don't immediately get a second pair of eyes, hands and ears, let alone your income doubled with a second baby."

"Hey, honey," Ed protested at this lecture. "You're preaching to the converted here. I don't want to share you with any more people . . ."

So that was settled. To Isobel it was a great liberation. She had grown up with a mother who had believed breeding to be the only copper-bottomed proof of feminine worthiness. The Bonetti experience had reinforced the message. She had been treated as an outcast, warned that a child would be her only ticket to acceptance, a ticket she had refused to use. And rightly so, Ed reassured her on that point also. It made her more than ever free to love him unreservedly.

It was shortly after that conversation that Ed presented Isobel with her new studio. He'd become more secretive about the cow byre lately and taken to locking it whenever he left it or was in there, keeping the shutters closed. The odd van rumbled up the farm track with deliveries in plain brown cardboard boxes. The boxes and their contents were swallowed by the cow byre. Tickled, Isobel pretended not to notice, assuming she would soon be expected to admire whatever was the grown-up equivalent of a model aeroplane.

The moment of unveiling came. Ed gave Isobel the key to the courtyard door, at last, and said what lay beyond it was his un-wedding present.

"Sorry, honey. I guess that's kind of clumsy. But you know what I mean . . ."

Shushing him before she should give way to tears, Isobel went in, prepared to gush over whatever skilfully, lovingly constructed . . . and probably useless contraption should meet her eye.

"Ed, this is too good for me," she said slowly, looking round. Then she pulled herself together and said it was the most wonderful studio she'd ever seen or dreamed of.

There had been a ceiling, but the builders had taken it away, piercing a large glazed aperture in the roof so that Isobel should have the maximum, evenly dispersed light. A sacking cover had been removed, and she saw this now for the first time. There was a sink for washing brushes, a cupboard full of solvents, storage units full of materials, pristine in their packaging and racks for finished work.

"Oh, Ed, I just don't know what to say. Why for me? It's your work we sell, when you'll let us . . ."

"Because what I do is cheap and easy. One day, honey, you'll be a serious painter. I could see from your Plymouth stuff, you keep *fighting* the easy options. I never do. I'm just a smartass who knows some tricks."

Drinking the champagne that Ed had kept on ice for this moment, Isobel concealed an apprehension that working here would be like playing chopsticks in the Albert Hall. For Ed's sake, however, she had to make some sort of effort.

*   *   *

Contentment is a hindrance to an artist. It dilutes the will and makes self-expression less urgent.

223

Left with a generous allowance of afternoon hours, Isobel fiddled. She was disabled by guilt, an obligated feeling that she must have something to show for her leisure. Ed had a right to expect it. He'd taken Sandro off her hands and ought to have some tangible proof of her gratitude. But the interest in portraiture and progress she'd made living in Plymouth, had both deserted her.

In the end she started some abstractions of shadows and patterns of light in the courtyard outside. Ed had treated the same subject but with a map-maker's precision of eye. To Isobel then, that seemed to be the way forward. To work in harmony with him. Wherever Ed's own fine pen had probed and delineated, Isobel followed with a broad hogshair brush. She got through an awful lot of lamp black and flake white.

Not really at ease with this project, bored by the work, she broke off from time to time to doodle in the margins or on a nearby scrap of paper. What she did then was free of any kind of conscious discipline. She put the lines where it gave her physical pleasure to do so. They were only doodles, so it didn't matter that they made no sense. Some of them were so silly that she scribbled them out even though nobody would ever see them. Just rubbish.

A talented amateur himself, Ed didn't criticise the work Isobel showed him. On the contrary, he praised and encouraged. Why not include ultramarine in her palette? She did so and the results pleased them both.

"Look how smart your momma is," Ed admonished Sandro who at that moment was curled up with Messalina in her basket.

Smart yes, but not sincere. Smart enough, Ed privately believed, to be covering something up. Isobel's latest canvases were bland, nothing at all like her. The woman with whom he shared his nights had a chilli-pepper quality. Searing, spicy, sharp ... habit-forming. Ed saw none of it here.

One day when Isobel was absorbed in making bread, Ed broke the unwritten rule that governs the relationship between one artist and another. He went into her studio and poked around. There was nothing to find but the doodles. Stylised faces, most of them. Tiny splashes of acid. Here was the answer.

Looking carefully at one minute marginal composition, he saw that the few lines laid down with controlled, practised aggression represented Margaret Jefferson's features. They had been scored out, but were repeated on discarded pieces of paper all over the studio. There were other faces which meant nothing to Ed. None were tender portrayals.

Disturbed, Ed quitted the studio noiselessly. He had been guilty of the worst sort of voyeurism, he knew. What kind of woman was it that lay in his bed and presided over his table? Recording angel or devil, it was way too late to find out.

Their relationship had already been modelled in clay and in recent months, cast in bronze. Whatever lay hidden in the cavity was unlikely, now, to emerge. Isobel's unexplained likes and dislikes, the topics she avoided, shaped the intercourse they had both come to trust.

Locking his gun cabinet in the storeroom next to the studio, Ed turned a key in his mind. The mistress he'd all but abducted was entitled to her privacy. He would forget what he'd seen, if he could.

Later they carried the kitchen table out into the brief Tuscan twilight to enjoy a bean stew and some salad while the sun poured its garnet dye over Castelchiara. They talked desultorily of this and that. When they should harvest their few rows of vines . . . there was a co-operative winery in the valley. Would the olive crop be worth anything? They would seek some advice. Right off the tree, olives tasted foul. People must do something to them.

Glancing at her from time to time, Ed was grateful his face was not among those in the studio. What fallible human being could live with knowledge of such clinical exposure? When Isobel went to work on someone, her eyes were disembodied from gender or humanity. She was too young to realise how in time, as this ability grew in her, it would progressively alienate her from others of her kind.

All Ed could do was to protect her from the knowledge as long as he could. Perhaps if she went on with the abstract things it might save her. Talent is a terrible thing.

These thoughts were nebulous in the American's mind. It occurred to him, however, that in prying into Isobel's studio, it was he, Adam, who had eaten of the fatal apple and, in doing so, qualified his happiness.

By contrast, Isobel basked in hers. Those things which happened in the studio were only a safety valve. An alternative to the tantrums she used to enjoy so much. Ed, unfortunately, left her no margin for bad behaviour. One did need that occasionally, Isobel thought.

"Shall we have some company in the winter?" she said suddenly.

"Sure honey," Ed answered from under the table where he was coaxing a cheeping cricket on to his finger. "Invite who you want. Visiting's great."

Isobel sighed and gave him a lecture on differentiating between receiving visits and paying them. To Ed Mazzerella, it was as provocative as stocking tops.

225

SIXTEEN

"Please, Herr Fischer," the Institute's director placed his hand under Josef's elbow firmly. "Come away now. There is nothing more you can do here. You have already done what is best."

Not yielding at once to the other man's touch, Josef continued to peer through the spy-hole drilled through the door of his wife's prison. A protective sequestration unit, they called it here.

Padded all over in stout white canvas, walls, floor, ceiling, the interior surface of the door – it was a reduction of the undulating snow-covered wastes outside. The converted tuberculosis sanatorium made a tactful refuge for incurable mental patients. An hygienically discreet receptacle for dangerously active human fall-out. The best that money could buy.

Josef took out his folded handkerchief and blotted the beads of perspiration forming on his upper lip. The Institute was kept uncomfortably warm. Uncomfortable, that was, for visitors in ordinary clothes. The staff were lightly clad in cotton uniforms. Many patients wore the minimum covering for their own safety's sake. No buttons, tapes or zips.

Nina, bare-legged and shoeless, was crumpled foetally in a corner of her cell. Her white arms were folded defensively over her head, concealing all but a few wisps of her spark red hair. There was a fleck or two of coloured varnish on her toenails. Everything else was white. As blank, Josef prayed, as his wife's mind.

That prayer defied the clinical probabilities. Nina was ten years old again. A terrified, tortured child condemned to grinding, till death released her, between the jaws of hell. She had escaped once. Now she was back.

The deep hypnotic regression therapy hadn't worked. Or rather, it had worked all too well. They simply hadn't been able to bring her out of the concentration camp. Not the second time.

"Will you do one thing for me, Herr Schmidt?" Josef finally submitted to the director's urgings to walk away.

"But anything, my dear Fischer. Anything."

"Find my wife something else to wear. That . . . er, smock thing. Her mother was wearing . . ." Josef was unable to complete his sentence. "It's all in the transcripts."

"Of course, of course," the director opened the door of his office to allow his patient's husband to precede him. "Some colour. I understand. To her, it will make no difference. But we must also consider you."

The two men talked for a while of fees, visiting schedules and future medication. Sedatives, mainly. The restoration of Nina's sanity was, realistically speaking, beyond the reach of contemporary psychiatry. Numerous types of mental anaesthesia, on the other hand, were freely available.

"So in the end," Josef summarised bleakly, "my wife will have no mind at all."

"That is so, Herr Fischer," the director admitted. "And if you will permit me . . . it is better so."

"Incidentally," Josef rose to leave, extracting a paper from his inside pocket, "I should have let you have this before. The missing copy of the transcript . . . It was sent to me by Isobel Jefferson . . ."

"Aha," the director took the paper and, frowning, unfolded it. "A name, I recall, that your wife mentioned with some frequency in the earlier tapes . . ."

"Yes. Nina sent the copy to Isobel. God only knows why or how she got hold of it in the first place. I'm afraid that Isobel . . . Signora Bonetti, was caused some distress. She makes light of it but . . ."

"Indeed," the director frowned, passing a hand over his bald patch. "Material like this should never fall into innocent hands. For we professionals, it is disquieting. For anyone else, it could be devastating. If you write to Miss Jefferson, please convey my heartfelt regrets. We have been unforgivably remiss."

Shaking hands with Josef, the director said, "Do not look on this as a total loss. Thanks to your wife's testimony under hypnosis, the Jewish Agency has added some significant names to its records. Their owners may yet pay for their crimes . . ."

"Herr Director," Josef withdrew his hand abruptly, "my wife is irretrievably lost."

Negotiating his car along the Institute drive's frost hardened slush, Josef thought it as well that Isobel had included no address in her letter. Deliberate? He couldn't blame her. The Fischer family had done her enough damage . . . as she, innocently, had damaged them.

She had a good man now, and hopes of a good life with him.

227

She had devoted rather more space in her letter to that than anything else.

* * *

The late autumn brought an end to the prolonged tête-à-tête at the farmhouse. Once the olives and grapes were both safely away for pressing, Isobel and Ed were in a position to broaden both their interests and their circle.

From Plymouth, there was good news.

Isobel's house there had finally sold at a clear thirty per cent profit leaving her with a round three thousand pounds sterling and a couple of hundred to spare. Wishing to use it for their mutual benefit, she placed a number of plans before Ed.

Of these, improvements to the erratic water supply at the farm were the first. A cistern of their own would give them a sense of security through the parched summer months. Choosing between the potatoes and baths for themselves was taking peasant cultivation a little too far, wasn't it? Isobel would like to contribute something to the value of the property on which Ed had already spent so much . . . largely for her comfort.

Or, better still, since the farmhouse was only held on a long lease at present, and they'd always said they'd scrape up enough to buy it from Pissaro one day, why not use her money to swell the fund and get a mortgage for the rest? Perhaps it would be better to buy the house sooner rather than later, before more improvements increased its value to the owner.

Ed's reply was uncharacteristically weary. "You seem to forget I'm twenty years older than you, honey. Better hang on to your dough. I don't know what I shall have to leave you."

Nobody in their twenties can contemplate a partner's death or any period of life beyond the next birthday with much seriousness. Isobel pooh-poohed Ed's reserve and pressed her point on him repeatedly. Now she had something to give, it was unfair of him to prevent her. And anyway, it was obvious, wasn't it, that he'd have the house to leave her?

Ed adroitly side-stepped the issue each time it was raised.

Isobel came up with another suggestion. Too much of their antique furniture stock was unloaded from one lorry and straight on to another. It was sent, they had learned, to a port and exported from there to the States by the container load. Fists full of dollars greeted its arrival on the docks. So why not cut out the middlemen and directly export their goods for themselves? It would mean waiting longer for their money, that was all. With some extra capital behind them, they could afford to do it. Why *not*?

That was all more her speed than his, Ed objected. More risk for uncertain returns. Did she realise they'd have to deal with shipbrokers? Endless paperwork. It wasn't what he'd quit the service for.

Isobel tried a few more times – a few more ideas. She gave up when Ed actually turned on her.

"Climb off my back, Isobel. I don't want your money or need it. Is there anything you want you don't have here? Or your boy? Buy yourself some blue-chip stock and *shut up!*"

Never had Isobel seen him hostile before. Not to her, not to anyone. Cowed by his inexplicable surliness, she gave up.

Ignorant of stock-exchange dealings . . . hardly knowing what shares were except something in long, boring columns at the back of newspapers, Isobel left the money in the Tavistock Building Society account, opened on her behalf by the solicitors who had acted in the sale of the house. The interest rate was very low, but one hundred and fifty pounds a year for doing nothing felt like plutocratic riches to her.

No more was said about Isobel's money other than Ed's ready assent to her diffident proposal that they might use the odd couple of hundred over and above the round sum for a trip to Venice. A sketching expedition. Ed had been to Venice already, but Isobel hadn't. She rather missed large expanses of water. She would like to see what she could do with it in her own work. A change of scene . . . a holiday . . . a sort of honeymoon . . .

"Godammit, honey," Ed hugged her to him, "what's with the itsy-bitsy Tinkerbell voice? It doesn't suit you. You want Venice. We'll go to Venice. You wanna spend your money . . . I guess, we'll spend it."

It was a compromise, balm to relieve Isobel's bruised self-esteem. Ed breathed a sigh of relief. His private worries, he could keep to himself. He needed his exclusion zone around him as Isobel needed hers.

Bernie Mazzerella's lawyers wanted a raise for her again. There had been inflation. Feeling the draught from that fiscal wind himself, Ed saw no alternative but to concede the additional figure claimed. It was a matter of pride with him, a question of his standing in his father's eyes. At least they shouldn't say of him, behind his back, that he had not only deserted his wife but left her broke.

"When can we go?" Isobel wanted to know. "To Venice?"

"Some time in the spring. Winter, it pisses down all the time. Right now, we've got to pretty a few things up. Didn't you say we've got company coming?"

*   *   *

Isobel's letters to the Montenaros, Lucy Larizzi, Pietro Arnolfi and others had brought delighted responses.

Visit her? Of course they would visit her. Why did she not visit them? It was wonderful to have her back in Italy again, where surely, she belonged. Not a word should be said to Carlo Bonetti if she didn't wish it. Who on earth saw the old monster anyway? He was pretty much of a recluse nowadays.

* * *

The Montenaros' visit was the only one of several which gave unalloyed pleasure to both Isobel and Ed. He caught his share of the generalised shower of kisses, hugs and tears which both Montenaros spread indiscriminately over all the occupants of the farm. Only Messalina was neglected until her jealous growls assured her inclusion.

"Oh, *cara* Isobel, *carissima Isabella*, let me look at you," Giulia held her at arm's length. "You look," she said after a suspenseful moment's consideration, "very well. Wonderfully relaxed. So healthy. Are you using a moisturiser?"

Isobel ruefully compared her corduroy trousers and the nearly new pullover borrowed from Ed with Giulia's staggering *completo* of Donegal tweeds. Coat, skirt and cloak, cut by a Milanese tailor. A felt tricorne hat adorned with long green feathers and hand-made brogues stacked on four inch heels completed her sporting ensemble.

"Ah," she opened her arms wide, "I adore the countryside. It is so . . . rural. *No?* So pure . . . so, so . . ."

"*Rustica?*" suggested Alessandro, tartly.

"Exactly," Giulia smiled on her husband gratefully.

The view, of flaming deciduous trees drifting in the valley's azure, autumn mist, with the towers of Castelchiara and distant San Gimignano slipped free of their terrestial moorings, made no impression on Giulia. Hopelessly underdeveloped, as Alessandro would say. She presumed Isobel went to Florence to shop.

Nothing, however, could exceed Giulia's admiration of the flushing lavatories indoors. A luxury unheard of in little farmhouses like these when she was a girl.

Eduardo was congratulated over and over again on the plumbing. Sandro was found to be splendidly big, handsome enough already to wring the coldest feminine heart, and quite astonishingly intelligent. Isobel's recipe for white doves in green grape sauce must be written down for Serafina.

Isobel reciprocated with enquiries about her former charges, Marzio and Giacomo. Naturally, at nine years old, their parents reported, both were prodigies of masculinity and intellectual muscle. As for their English, nothing to compare with it was ever heard in Milan thanks to Isobel.

"Do you continue with your drawing?" Alessandro asked, helping Isobel pick oozing, wasp ravished figs from the little tree in the courtyard.

"Yes," Isobel answered him. "Ed made me a marvellous studio. Do you know, I never liked figs before I came here . . ."

So the subject of Isobel's work, and Ed's marriage too, when once it was touched on, were both skilfully smothered by others as soon as the Montenaros grasped that here were corns that gave pain to their hosts.

Alessandro felt unable to question insistently, or give advice to Isobel now, as he had done to the lone foreign teenager under his protection three years ago. Since then she had become in turn a wife, a widow, a mother, a householder and a citizen of both her own country and of theirs. Indisputably adult.

If her position as the mistress of a middle aged American struck both Alessandro and his wife as both aimless and precarious, they were unable to say so. She was as any other friend who had chosen a path. But in the Montenaro car as it crunched down the farm-house track after an exchange of affectionate farewells, there was instant reaction.

"Did you see her hands?" Giulia said. "Like a cook's . . ."

"Her hands are the least of it," Alessandro interrupted. "If this fellow can't marry her, it opens a route straight over the moral high ground to Carlo Bonetti. He may be able to claim legal custody of his grandson."

"He doesn't know he has one," Giulia reminded him, which was, as far as she knew, still the case. "While Isobel rusticates in that place, he's unlikely to get to know. *Dio mio*, how stupid all this is! Why can't they all be friends? They have so much to lose."

"Because," said Alessandro, "*la Signora Isabella* and her father-in-law both have the same tensility as a bar of old fashioned pig iron."

Giulia, who thought pig iron sounded most unpleasant and didn't know or wish to know what tensility meant, changed the subject.

"Did you like him? Mazzerella, I mean," she snapped open her compact to examine the ravages of a weekend in Bohemia.

"Of course I liked him. Who could fail to like him?" Alessandro snorted. "As practical a fellow as ever failed to marry his wife. Immensely romantic. Pah!"

*   *   *

231

Pietro Arnolfi's visit coincided with the new year. That he came at all was a mark of his sincere regard for Isobel. Travelling was not easy for him.

Severely crippled now with arthritis, he was confined much of the time to a wheelchair. Ed went alone to the station in Florence to fetch him. There would not be room for all of them and the chair in the Lamborghini.

"And tell me, Signor," Pietro enquired as they left the city behind, "how does my dear *Isabella*'s work progress? You do not embroil her in too much domesticity I trust. She is an artist . . . or might be."

"You must see what you think," Ed replied guardedly, his eyes on the road. "If she shows you."

"She will show me," Pietro said pacifically, flipping open his snuffbox. "I am her old master. Do not drive so fast."

Innately responsive to the voice of command, Ed decelerated. Catching himself a split second later, he stirred the gearbox elaborately and improved on his original speed. Pietro closed his left nostril with his forefinger, slid his eyes sideways and shrugged. A quick death between Florence and Siena would be as serviceable, he supposed, as a slow one in Milan. More so, perhaps. All his joints ached.

Isobel did show Pietro her work but only after making a clean sweep of the studio. She destroyed all the doodles and scribbles, tidied and cleaned in preparation for her teacher's august inspection.

"This is . . ."

"Don't tell me what things are, my dear. My eyes are not yet arthritic. I see what I see. I expect to be pleased."

After wheeling himself around the studio for some time without comment, he swung the wheelchair around to face Isobel.

"This is work you really wish to do?" There was incredulity in his voice. "It has meaning for you? What has happened to that asperity? That astringency of yours? Where is that willingness to learn your craft? I cherished that in you."

He gave her a long look which Isobel could not meet and propelled himself out of the studio without further ado.

The rest of Pietro's stay was hard going for Isobel. She could hardly help hating him for perceiving her failure. There was some consolation, however. Concerning Ed's work, samples of which Arnolfi spotted about the house, the old man loftily remarked that it was conscientious junk. Pretty, gift-shop stuff. Well above average in quality.

Ed professed himself flattered. He had no higher aspirations than that.

232

"Not like Isobel. What did you think of her output, sir?"

"I think she should burn it," Pietro asserted. "Unless, that is, she wishes to add to the tonnage of fraudulent daubs littering pretentious galleries throughout the known world."

It was a harsh speech and Isobel bore it courageously. It was no good asking someone's opinion if one wasn't prepared to hear it. She was sorry, none the less, that Ed had been forced to share the humiliation with her. It would hurt him more. Her face changed colour.

Restrained by chivalry towards age and enfeeblement, Ed resisted a powerful urge to throw the old man, wheel chair, snuff box and all, out into the pouring January rain.

"Ah," Pietro remarked equably. "You do not like me to tell the truth. That is what gives me hope. You know it when your hear it and it hurts as it should. Thank you, my dear, I will have more *polenta*. It is only slightly overcooked."

When he had gone, conveyed back to Florence in a taxi, there was a heaviness about Isobel which Ed could do little to alleviate. Arnolfi, he snarled, was just a jealous old back number half out of his mind with pain. An asshole.

"No," Isobel rejected the comfort. "He's a master. And he knows me. He was right."

Isobel made a bonfire of her canvases which was foolish as she could have overpainted them. But the act was cathartic for her. She locked the studio and did nothing more there for the rest of the year.

Now and again, Ed was tempted to confess he knew about those doodles of hers. There was a clue there, he suspected, to what Pietro Arnolfi had meant. But Isobel erected a forbidding wall around the whole matter.

*   *   *

Venice was put off yet again. The spring was dry and the new vegetable seedlings in the garden would need thrice daily watering to survive. Or that is what Ed, who could very well have rigged a crudely automated irrigation system, decided.

May was enlivened by a fleeting call from Lucy Larizzi. An early afternoon stop on her way to a party in Paris. She was accompanied by a glowering stripling from Seville.

"He wants to be a bullfighter," she introduced her companion. "I doubt he will make it. He has style but lamentably little attack . . . Darling, are those beans? None for Miguel. He's the *most* frightful farter."

"What languages does he speak?" Isobel kept a wary eye on the boy while tossing the salad.

"Nothing intelligible, darling. One doesn't want them answering one back. How's your sweet mother, angel?"

"I wouldn't know," said Isobel.

"What a pity," Lucy replied, popping an olive between Miguel's parted lips. "I wonder, Isobel darling, if you could arrange for us to have a teensy-weensy lie-down after luncheon? Miguel is so easily tired."

He certainly looked it when Lucy finally installed him in the back of her Rolls-Royce Corniche before saying her goodbyes.

"I'm surprised you don't put him in the trunk," Ed muttered.

"Oh, I would, darling. But one tries to set an example over animal welfare, doesn't one?

"I say," she added, turning to Isobel, "Giulia says you used to draw rather well. Paint a bit? 'Cos you can always send Max and me . . . you remember Max Cooper? He was at your little coming-out thrash . . . Anyway, we'll sort out your stuff and flog it off in the gallery. Rome or New York, wherever we're short. Doesn't much matter what it looks like, darling, as long as it's modern and fits in with people's décor . . . Here's our card. Now get yourself a copy of *Casa Bella* and check on the colours. Black and white's big at the moment. A range of sizes . . ."

"Lucy, Lucy . . ." Isobel stopped her. "I can't do that sort of thing . . . I burned some stuff like that. It was awful."

"Nonsense, darling. Just do some more. You're a very promotable artist. You'll look good in the gallery once we tidy you up . . ."

"I'm not an artist, Lucy . . ."

"When Max prints your name on a catalogue, believe me, darling, you're an artist. A reception or two . . . an interview for *Vogue* and you're made. Make her see sense, Edward, won't you, darling?"

"Now her, I like," Ed waved the limousine out of sight, grinning broadly. "Satan has shown you the kingdom, honey. Are you going back to work now? Turn a few stones into bread . . ."

"It's no good, Ed. I can't cheat. I tried."

*   *   *

The hot months saw no change. Isobel's surface placidity covered an undertow of boredom which she could not entirely conceal from Ed. Worried, he refrained, on the whole, from suggesting she open up her studio again. Any reference to the work she'd abandoned – for which she may have a market – gusted her temper into nervy squalls, promoting unease in the house.

234

Requests from Isobel that they might soon go to Venice had a similar effect on Ed. The CIT offices in Florence had advised him, he told her, that half the canals had been drained for dredging after the floods. The stench was abominable and the press of tourists at this season hardly less overwhelming than usual. If they went now, they would have to pay someone to water the garden, so vital to their subsistence.

"We shall never go," Isobel said flatly.

"Sure we will, honey."

The truth was that Ed, who spent much time juggling with papers locked away in the rolltop desk he kept in his gun room, did not want to spend the money. Neither his own nor Isobel's. The shop books were finely balanced. The outgoings of the business were too often underwritten by Ed's own private resources. The cash crops they grew on the farm's few hectares might be expanded in volume but not without additional investment. The price of olive oil was falling. Larger cultivators were turning to maize.

Spirits, however, were lifted along with retail turnover thanks to a series of morning visits to Lucca. The old town, where few tourists ever went, boasted an outdoor antiques market. A straggle of stalls, vans and cloths laid out on the ground under makeshift awnings, offered traders from all over the region, the chance to do leisurely business, one with another, encouraged by frequent libations of wine.

There were small ceramics to be had, clutches of artistically distressed Roman coins, thick greenish glassware, also Roman, silver boxes covered in Florentine mosaic and ancient jewellery. Fakes? Some were, some weren't.

Ed carried Sandro on his shoulders, and their money in a belt strapped under the boy's T-shirt. Even amongst the most notorious den of thieves, a child's person was definitely offside.

The traders, always delighted to see Signor *Eduardo* and his so *simpatica* companion, cheated them as the reasonable demands of *bella figura* dictated. Smiling rascality was the agreed order of business.

"No, no, Signora. This piece is quite genuine. From the reign of Tiberius. *Si, si!* Look, the museum has authenticated it, I have here the paper . . . I give to your husband with the artefact. Inclusive."

The museum was always unspecified, the signature on the creased scrap of paper, indecipherable. But Ed could not bear to call any fellow man a liar, especially not one so ingenuous. So the piece, whatever it was, was 'given' in exchange for more money than it was worth and its accompanying document received outwardly, at least, with reverence.

235

After filling the car boot with small scale antiquities of recent manufacture, Ed, Isobel and Sandro ate the midday meal in one of the many vine-shaded gardens before making for home. These were good days which they turned to account. The traders, satisfied with their dishonest bargains were not to know that their complaisant victims enjoyed the last laugh.

Isobel prepared painstakingly handwritten labels for every object they bought. Glamorous biographies in English and Italian, evidenced with bogus cross-references to historic numbers of learned antiquarian journals, available for perusal in imaginary libraries.

Laid out on a trestle table outside the shop, priced to stimulate an exciting tension between hesitation and temptation in the cultured tourist's breast, the doubtful treasures realised a scandalous profit.

Doing all the selling herself, Isobel would enjoin on Ed the sole duty of staying out of sight when a likely mark hove into view. *Furberia* – slyness, almost – was a positive virtue of her new countrymen, which Isobel, not Ed, understood. His forebears, after all, had gone to a new, clean place – whilst hers had stuck fast in civilisation's accumulated dung. Active, with amoral bacteria.

For customer interactions Isobel wore a pair of gold rimmed spectacles found in a wardrobe drawer and sucked her teeth in a pantomime of bluestocking cerebration. She was disarmingly plausible.

"Do, *do* feel free to handle it," she said of whatever item appeared to attract interest. "I must be quite frank with you. My husband stands behind the attribution, but I," she confided, "personally feel it was probably stolen . . ."

Thus withdrawing her false claims, and replacing them with a seductive whiff of illegitimacy, Isobel rarely failed to make a sale. The stock needed regular replacement. It wasn't an enormous trade but it was mostly cash and verging on honest. By the end of August, Ed felt this positive trend justified a treat. They had worked very hard, particularly Isobel.

Venice, smelly or not, had been earned and deserved. The business could pay for their trip. And perhaps, next year, Isobel's idea of shipping direct to the States could be considered again. The future looked suddenly more inviting.

In this sanguine frame of mind, Ed made an excuse to drive into Florence alone one day. A wall clock movement had been repaired and was ready for collection.

Isobel was happy to mind the shop on her own. Ed said he'd be back by siesta-time. They'd close up then and go out to the farm for a couple of hours unless the town looked promisingly busy.

"You want to keep Lina with you, honey? Or shall I take her?"

"You take her," Isobel replied, struggling to understand some request of her son's. "She frets whenever you go out."

"You stay with your momma, big boy, and look after her, okay?"

Ruffling Sandro's hair and dropping a kiss on Isobel's brow Ed left the shop wondering if he had anything left in his wardrobe which would pass muster at the Gritti. Isobel always looked the goods whatever she wore. She wouldn't forgive him, though, if he let her arrive without evening clothes.

Surprises, the set pieces of both love and war, tend to backfire on their initiators, unless flawlessly arranged. All the way to Florence, Ed laid careful, loving plans.

SEVENTEEN

The American Express office in Florence was packed. A rail strike had immobilised Italy for a period of twenty-four hours. Women sat in disconsolate, quacking clumps while their menfolk waved tickets at the clerks, braying disaffection with medieval Europe. Uproar. With so many frantic countrymen to calm and advise, Ed lost track of the time and his place in the queue.

He didn't start back to Castelchiara till gone half past two. Rejecting the old Empoli road, he chose the faster route to Siena. Every few seconds, dazzling mirage pools splashed the road. The traffic was heavier than usual. For a man punctual by nature and training, it was frustrating. Ed had never left Isobel alone so long before. Dumb of him not to have called her before leaving Florence. She might worry.

Dropping a gear, he put his foot down to take a wide swing round a slow-moving wagon. A flat bed carrying scaffolding pipes. The wagon was longer than he calculated. The Lamborghini was on the crown of the road at the start of a bend by the time it was clear of the other vehicle. Directly ahead with fifteen metres to spare was a Mercedes-Benz olive oil tanker. It loomed like a cliff. Ed stamped on the brakes. They bit, melting the tyres.

There was no collision. The man driving the scaffolding wagon pulled hard over to avoid the back of the Lamborghini. His nearside wheels spun silently in the void above a deep ditch. The tanker stopped nose to nose with the sports coupé. Close.

After an eerie pause, the men driving the commercial vehicles pumped their horns. It wasn't until their anger and terror subsided that they noticed that from the Lamborghini there was silence. Only the dry maize stalks, ripe in the fields rattled and sighed. Then a dog was heard yapping. That noise was drowned in the cacophony of klaxons from the vehicles building up behind on either side of the road. Slowly, the man in the tanker slid down from his cab. He walked up to the Lamborghini and instantly turned away. He was seen to lean over the ditch and spew uncontrollably.

Warned, nobody else moved until a police patrol car from

238

Staggia arrived some minutes later. It was they who, green faced and sagging at the knees, released Messalina. They had to pull her out. She wouldn't stop licking her master's face. Blue and surprised, it stared up from the back seat of the car where his head had landed. Like a football. Blood pumped from the trunk.

*   *   *

Isobel was located without difficulty. The pair of policemen, who found her chatting with customers outside the shop in Castelchiara, needed to tell her very little. The fact of their appearance and the state of the whimpering spaniel said most of it. Messalina's coat was filthy and matted because a bystander at the scene of the accident had tried to wash off most of the blood. A bottle of mineral water and some thick mud from the ditch.

"Is he alive or dead?" Isobel watched her customers vanish. Two pleasant Englishwomen. Too nice to cheat. Teachers probably. In that moment before full realisation, they seemed more important than what the policemen were saying to her.

"Are you Signora Mazzerella?"

"Yes. No. We're not married . . ."

The policemen exchanged a glance of relief.

"We're partners . . . Please, just wait a moment . . . I must attend to my son. We live together. My name's Bonetti, actually . . ."

Isobel threw out confused information. Her teeth clacked together. Funny. She felt her face start to stretch in a humourless smile.

The policemen followed her into the shop and out into the garden. Had Signor Mazzerella any male relatives who could identify the body?

"No. Give me the dog. Yes. There is someone. A brother. He's a priest. I don't know his name. I suppose I could do it." Her teeth chattered again. "In the Vatican. A monsignor. Is that right?"

It was enough. The police waited while Isobel locked up the shop. They took her back to the farm. The car was being kept for mechanical investigation. It would be returned later.

Alone, Isobel built a huge fire in the stone hearth. A black scorpion crawled out of the logs and she crushed it with her heel. An unpleasant sensation. Ed had done all the killing.

Sandro was whining for food. The fire took a long time to catch. Ed usually did it. Had all this really happened? Things like this *didn't* happen twice. She was raging with Ed. So bloody, bloody careless. She boiled an egg for Sandro and mashed it. Messalina howled piteously. Isobel warmed some milk for her. She wouldn't touch it.

At eleven o'clock, Isobel was still feeding the fire. Sandro slept curled up on the floor to one side of her. His hair was tawny blond now. Darker than his mother's and his Uncle Rupert's. Stroking it, Isobel's mind rested for a moment on this trivial circumstance. Proper hair. All the dark brown infant down had fallen.

Messalina, silent now, with her muzzle on Isobel's knee, looked up into her face, pleading for some sort of explanation. Isobel brushed her coat for hours. Neither she nor the dog slept all night long.

In the morning she was jerked from semi-consciousness by the sound of tyres outside the house. Thinking it was the Lamborghini, Isobel rose to open the door. There was a white Fiat outside and a youngish man in a Roman collar. He looked so much like Ed. Leaner, paler and younger.

Walking out of the house to greet him, it flashed across Isobel's mind that he had not the least idea who she was.

*　　*　　*

She was wrong there. John Mazzerella had some idea of Isobel's identity. They had thanked him at the Staggia mortuary, for coming so far and at such short notice to save a young woman a traumatic experience. Apparently, the victim and she . . . Well, these were family matters. No doubt the Monsignor knew of the relationship.

He had not known. But it would explain some enquiries Ed had made lately, concerning the effect on his sister-in-law's attitude to divorce if he could show that an ecclesiastical annulment was feasible. Ed chasing rainbows again. How could a tribunal look at his case while he lived with this woman?

Here she was now. John studied her apprehensively. Impressive. Would she cause any trouble?

"You must be Ed's little brother," Isobel took his arm. "I'm Isobel Bonetti. I don't know if you knew . . . You must be very tired. Can I make you some coffee . . ."

She looked a mess, of course. But there was no point in directing attention to the obvious. There were things to be done, to get through. People would be coming to see her all through the day. This time, she wouldn't run away. Couldn't. There was nowhere to go.

"Look . . . uh, Mrs Bonetti, I don't . . ."

"I'm glad to see you, really. There's the funeral and I haven't spoken to anyone . . . I'll make the spare room bed up. Where's your case?"

Grateful to have something to do, some distraction, Isobel had put the coffee percolator on the stove and lifted the grubby Sandro on to her lap before she understood that she was not, in fact, entertaining a guest.

"Mrs Bonetti, believe me I am sorry for you. But your position here is not as you think."

"Isn't it? It's cold in here. Shall we go outside and sit in the sun . . ."

"No," he answered her curtly. "I want you to listen to me, now, without interrupting. There isn't much time. I need to speak to my father and make arrangements for the repatriation of the body."

"What are you talking about?" Isobel's hackles rose.

He told her. Edward Mazzerella was a United States citizen with a family and a widow living there. They would almost certainly wish to hold the funeral on the Annapolis naval base and inter the body in a nearby cemetery close to the Mazzerella home. The whole of Mazzerella family life centred round the base. Whether here or there, his father, Captain Joe Mazzerella, would wish to see his son's remains. It was natural. It was too late to heal the rift but . . .

"I'm not stopping him," Isobel cut in. "He can come. I'll even put him up . . ."

"You are missing the point," the young priest thumped the table softly with his fist. "My father will not wish to see *you*. And I don't want him to see the body. Not yet. So he will come here in a couple of days' time . . . to help me clean up here. And my brother will be flown out to a shit hot embalmer."

"What's wrong with the body?" It wasn't the first question Isobel had meant to ask, but she did, because beside others, it seemed least important. A detail to be got out of the way.

"That's none of your business, Mrs Bonetti."

"Are you mad?" Isobel rose, letting Sandro slip squealing from her knee. "Ed was my . . ."

"No, Mrs Bonetti. No. And if this child is my brother's . . ."

"How dare you? How dare you? Sandro is my son by my first husband . . ."

"Your only husband, Mrs Bonetti, I think. Perhaps you have had others, but my brother was not among them. Forgive me if I sound . . ."

"Get out. Get out of my house!" Isobel's intestines coiled and uncoiled with loathing. Mazzerella didn't move.

"You're telling me this house was bought with your money?"

"No. Ed leased it. But it's our home. We lived here together . . .

241

We were going to buy the freehold soon. And I can pay the rent with . . ."

"That makes no difference, I'm afraid, Mrs Bonetti. This house, or the remainder of the lease, I think we shall discover, belongs to my sister-in-law. Now, if you would be kind enough to show me where my brother kept his papers . . ."

"Follow!" Isobel stalked to the gun room and showed John Mazzerella Ed's rolltop desk. "Help yourself. I must feed my son. My dog is sick." She left him.

He was back in a moment. The desk was locked. Where was the key? Isobel shrugged rudely and handed him a kitchen knife without turning to look at him. "Use your initiative."

He was gone for the better part of two hours. In the kitchen, Sandro talked scribble talk about Ed. The little boy was missing his surrogate father. Isobel wondered how you explained death to a child not yet three. Would he realise eventually?

"Sandro, leave Lina alone. She doesn't feel like playing."

The spaniel had scarcely moved since the previous night. Isobel tried to spoon feed her. The milk softened biscuits fell in sodden crumbs to the tiles.

By noon, John Mazzerella let Isobel know how things stood. The house was held on a quarterly rental from one Padre Paulo Pissaro. Not much security there for anyone. Ed had started negotiations for the freehold but the parties were far apart on price.

No wonder, Isobel brooded, the *chiarini* were never in any hurry to see reason. Discussion, valued for itself, must always be dragged out. She attended once again to what John Mazzerella had to tell her.

The substantial maintenance payments to Ed's wife in Baltimore had been kept up and recently increased. So much was evident from the spent chequebooks found in the desk. If the bank statements were anything to go by, Ed had a few thousand dollars in a US bank. Less in the Banco di Roma. In any case, such as it was, the capital all belonged to his wife. No document showed the existence of a formal business partnership between Isobel and Ed, so those assets too, whatever they consisted of, devolved in similar fashion. Ed's naval pension or a proportion of it, would, in future, be paid directly to his widow. There was a copy of the will, remaindering Ed's estate to his brothers who were executors of all the bequeathals.

"But . . ."

"If it's any comfort to you, Mrs Bonetti, my brother was trying to change his will . . ."

"Why didn't he? You can just . . ."

"Changing a will is easy. But making it stick . . . making it

242

unassailable by a legal wife is another matter. She has the right . . ."

"Tell me. She has God on her side," Isobel snapped.

"I'm glad you see it so clearly. There's something of yours here, by the way."

He handed her a sealed envelope inscribed 'Isobel's earrings' in Ed's hand. The surprise of seeing the little jewelled masks brought the first tears to her eyes. Oh *Ed*! He had been living on the edge, and yet he had kept these for her.

"I'll leave you now, for the moment. I'll need the keys to my brother's business premises. Could you arrange to leave here in thirty-six hours?"

Isobel regarded him narrowly.

"What's Ed's wife's name?"

"Bernadette. Why do you ask?" He turned at the door.

"So I can hate her better. I hope she rots in hell. No, not rotting. Too peaceful. I hope she gets eaten by something disgusting over and over again. That's what you people believe in, isn't it? The worm that never dies . . . Another thing. What *is* wrong with my husband's body?"

He told her, more out of shock than revenge.

"I'm so sorry." Isobel went to him and again placed her hand on his arm. "I'm sorry," she repeated. "How could I? I'm sorry, I think I'm going to be sick . . ."

He brushed her hand from his arm, white about the mouth.

"Mrs Bonetti, the state of my brother's corpse worries me less than that of his soul. He died in mortal sin. You have a share of the blame for that . . ."

Reeling back, Isobel stared at him. She swallowed the vomit surging up in her throat with an effort.

"Your brother was the best man who ever lived. You must be the worst. What kind of a man is your father?"

"That is not for you . . . or me, to judge."

"Fuck off!" Isobel hadn't known the words were in her vocabulary. It was good to know they were.

Slamming the door, she went to see what more could be done for Ed's dog. He had loved her so. The spaniel was dead. Isobel gathered up the warm, limp body and sobbed into her coat. Oh Lina, Lina. We love you. Please, don't go. But Messalina had followed her master. Animals can die when they want to.

Sandro clung to his mother's skirt, understanding nothing, trying to restore everything with the force of his need for it.

* * *

Isobel buried Messalina in the very best thing that she had. The white corded silk gown that she wore for her eighteenth birthday party in Milan. She slit it with the kitchen scissors to make a shroud for the dog. It didn't quite wrap her fully and Isobel made a secondary covering from the plaid travel rug which covered Ed's unused, bachelor bed. After that first night, they had always slept in hers.

She dug a grave in a corner of the olive grove. The soil was dry and kept falling back into the hole. The spade was blunt. Eventually, sweating profusely, Isobel decided the hole was deep enough. It was hard to commit Messalina to oblivion and she nursed the body for some while before laying it down. The first layer of earth, she spread with her hands. And the next.

Demented, Sandro kept trying to reverse the process. "*Lina, Lina. . .?*" Isobel had to smack him in the end.

When she walked back to the house, with Sandro crying in her arms, the shadows were beginning to lengthen. The Lamborghini was back. Against it leaned two policemen. Different ones from before. They sprang upright to salute her.

Apologies for the intrusion followed. The car had been found free of mechanical fault. It had been one of those things. The interior of the car was a mess . . . but they had done their best. Approaching it, Isobel could see that, in pity, they had. Nothing could eradicate the extensive brownish red stains on the car's upholstery, however. But something had been done. It was bad but bearable.

Putting her hands to her temples, Isobel tried to shake the image of Nina loose. She had nothing to do with this. Nothing. Why did she have to come back now? Scrambling the hot wires of memory in her brain, Isobel made her own thoughts unthinkable. Chop everything into confetti . . . mix the colours up and make it go safely grey.

"*Scusi* . . . Signora?" One of the officers touched her shoulder.

They were sorry to have brought her this fresh stimulus to grief but they had received no other instructions. Here were the car's documents, all in order. And other papers found in the glove compartment.

Dully, Isobel leafed through them. What was Ed's passport doing here? She saw in a moment. There were lire traveller's cheques, hotel reservations . . . room charge already paid and receipted, some cash, a docket for a long stay car-park, rail tickets . . . destination, *Venezia*.

Isobel must have said something to the policemen. They must have said something more to her. What, precisely, she didn't remember. When she came to herself they had gone. There was only the car and Sandro. He was poking a regiment of ants with a stick on the gravel.

Rooted to the ground, letting her eyes refocus on the ordinary things, Isobel found the traces of what she had just seen disappearing fast from her brain. Only the few words she had to describe them remained.

It hadn't been a vision. She had seen nothing with her eyes. It hadn't been a dream. She hadn't been asleep. Imagination had played no part. It had been more like a few frames of film, slipped over the forefront of her mind. There had been a soundtrack. She had heard it distinctly without aid of her ears.

Ed had been there, younger than she had ever known him. Wearing long white shorts and knee socks . . . No grey in his hair. No lines on his face. He had been smiling and laughing, calling to Lina. "Come on girl. Here, girl. Come on." That was all. And then, nothing. No message for her.

But there was a message, just the same. A sensation of release spread through her veins. Ed was all right. Messalina had run to him. Safe.

That mess in the car . . . the accident. What John Mazzerella had told her . . . none of it mattered. Ed had spun away into a vortex bathed in white light, his dog scampering after him. She must go on without him, with Sandro, to Venice. Here, there was nothing left for them.

Isobel packed. Clothes for herself and her son. As many as would cram into suitcases which in turn, could be squeezed into the Lamborghini's small luggage space. She took all of Ed's sketches off the walls . . . most of them were here now. She went through his desk. There was a little more cash and some more sketches in a portfolio. Some letters, too . . . drafts he had never sent to her. Isobel took them.

Doing all this, she had no awareness of effort. No conscious decisions troubled her mind. She did everything as if under orders. Someone else was working her brain, moving her limbs. Even opening the studio to pack up her easel, she did without knowing why. She covered the car seats with sheets. Then she dressed herself and Sandro and made up her face.

At the last moment, her fingers already on the Lamborghini's ignition key, she stopped and went back to the house. She took a key from the rack in the kitchen and went to unlock Ed's gun cabinet. A rifle with blue steel side-by-side barrels, a walnut stock and chased silver mounts . . . Ed's twenty-first birthday present from his father. Useful or valuable, Isobel felt entitled to the tool with which her man had so often fed her.

245

Driving away from the farm, it felt perfectly right to be carrying Furio's son in his own father's car. The one that had also been Ed's. It belonged now to a stranger called Bernadette Mazzerella. If they found it in Florence, she could have it. Why ever not? Isobel knew for certain, she would never drive again. This was the last time.

Padre Pissaro was at the bottom of the track, ready to wheel up his scooter. Isobel rolled the window down to speak to him.

"Father, don't bother. Ed's not at home." He had been a kind friend. An unintrusive, unjudging landlord, as well.

All Pissaro could tell anyone later was that Isobel had turned right on to the road. It was a minor one – no signpost to her ultimate direction.

*   *   *

It was twenty-four hours before Carlo Bonetti could make up his mind to act upon the information given him by the Staggia police. Convalescence from his heart attack had left him cautious of exposing himself to emotional switchback rides. No troughs, no heights. His health condemned him to a milk-and-water life.

He arrived at the farmhouse, however, after a day and a night spent turning over the quality of the data he had received. Listed as missing persons with the police at Carlo's instigation, Isobel and Sandro were a low priority case despite the reward offered for clues regarding their whereabouts. Isobel and her son had not been kidnapped. They may well have left the country long since.

Isobel, *Isabella* Bonetti ... Jefferson ... Mazzerella, mother of a child called Alessandro, might be anywhere and live there too, without eliciting any police interest in her past or present identity.

Carlo himself reposed little confidence in the photograph of his daughter-in-law as a fashionable bride, nor the one alleged to be of his grandson, an over-exposed snapshot of an infant in a pushchair, propelled by an anonymous woman in a mackintosh with head and shoulders obscured by an umbrella. And whilst he clung to a certainty that he would find them one day, the expectation was founded on nothing more substantial than a blind belief in the self-fulfilling power of his own desires.

As his chauffeur turned the wide bodied Mercedes into the narrow entrance of the farm track, Carlo quieted his fears. It had to be them. Who else could it be? An Isobel Bonetti who co-habited with an American called Mazzerella and had a son she nicknamed Sandro. Bonetti was a common name ... but all the other, associated details were unique to them alone.

246

"Is this the place?" Carlo grunted at the back of the chauffeur's neck.

"*Si*, Signor. Fifth homestead on the left after the railway line . . ."

"*Basta!*" Carlo did not wish to hear a commentary from his chauffeur when any moment now he might be holding his grandson in his arms. His hands began to tremble. Quickly now, he must take a pill. Calm. No weakness before *Isabella*. This American's death was in some ways unfortunate. It left her in virtuous possession of a respectable little property . . . modest provision for any ordinary peasant boy. But for Alessandro Bonetti, beggarly. An insult to his father's memory.

Had this tumultuous woman no conception of her duty to her son? No, she had none. How could she have? A woman like her who had consorted indecently with another woman's husband . . . and, being promiscuous, might do the same again . . . She should be brought to her senses, however. Furio's child had a destiny for which he should be prepared . . . She could not deprive him. What court in Italy would allow her . . . especially not a court paid by *him*. This time, Isobel should not get away with kidnapping her own child. *Uno scandalo!*

The chauffeur brought the Mercedes to rest under the umbrella pine and got out to open the rear passenger door for his master.

"Wait," said Carlo, surveying the front elevation of the house. An ordinary, pantiled, terracotta place, quite well maintained he saw. Better than its neighbours. The blue painted front door was closed. Rapping it smartly with the silver knob of his malacca cane, Carlo listened to the silence within, a sinking feeling in his heart. No one here.

The door, unlocked, yielded to pressure from the flat of Carlo's hand, and swung open on well-oiled hinges. He stepped inside. The kitchen, he saw, was like those in every peasant house. A jumble of furniture acquired in different places at different times . . . A ham, herbs and sausages hanging from the ceiling. There were ashes in the great stone canopied hearth, an empty dog basket in the corner and a highchair, placed at an angle to the oilcloth covered table. A child's terry towelling bib lay over the back of a chair, smeared with egg.

Carlo touched the steel coffee percolator which stood upon the table with two unused cups. Stone cold. A fly buzzed on the windowsill.

Outside, the chauffeur waited in the car with the window rolled down, out of which he smoked a cigarette. He palmed it hastily at his employer's emergence from the house.

"Get up to the town," Carlo instructed. "You will find my daughter-in-law and my grandson, Alessandro, at the premises of an antique dealer named Mazzerella in the Calle Ghibelline. If not, try the priest's house. Find them and bring them here."

Yes, in the town. That is where they must be. Isobel was attending to her business. Or arranging for the funeral.

Carlo was in the courtyard, peering through the studio window there when he heard a step behind him. *Isabella*, so soon? Spinning on his heel, he saw a man a little taller than himself, looser limbed and as much as ten years older. The physiognomy was unquestionably Italian.

To Carlo, suave in a lightweight, cream aipaca suit, the other man looked like some retired factory worker dressed for an afternoon on the football terraces. Zip-up blouson and ill-fitting, synthetic fabric slacks. The shoes, crude as building skips, were inexplicable as was the quality of the man's regard.

Carlo was not accustomed to be looked at like this by anyone. No more than he was in the habit of introducing himself. It was the business of other people to know who he was. Innumerable human filters at the Corso Mategna offices ensured that this was so. Socially, of course, he had never, as far as his memory would stretch, allowed himself to mingle with the ignorant.

And now, this gardener, this plumber . . . this person of no account was staring at him as if at one of equal status. Carlo regretted sending the chauffeur away. A bad mistake. In his old age, he was becoming careless. Waiting for the crisis of dominance to pass, Carlo did not allow the movement of a single muscle to betray his discomfiture. Speak? He would not utter. Every word was a unit of status spent. Let this *tizio* state his business.

"Yeah?" said the man. "Something I can do for you, pal?"

American, thought Carlo. A friend of Mazzerella's. Was he aware of Mazzerella's death?

Carlo, who heard English with reasonable accuracy, never spoke it or allowed anyone to know how much he understood.

"*Parla Italiano?*" the American snapped, seeing he got no response. He took an empty pipe from his trouser pocket and placed it between his teeth aggressively.

"See here, pal, whatever godamned language you speak, say what's on your mind or clear out. I'm kinda busy round here right now. My son just died. You wanna pick up on the lease, you'd better go see the landlord. Guy goes by the name of Pissaro. Parish priest in the town up there. You got that? Pissaro. *Proprietario di casa*. Pissaro. Stupid bastard."

Hiding a sense of foreboding, Carlo advanced a step or two.

"Where," he spat in Italian, "is my daughter-in-law? Isobel Bonetti. And my grandson . . ."

"That hooker? My other son ran her off the property. Yeah, the bitch damned my boy to hell . . ."

"*Di che cosa parli?*" Of what did this fool speak?

Joe Mazzerella spelled it out for Carlo Bonetti in a combination of broken Italian and American English. Carlo would not concede the language point. What he heard encased his heart in a film of cold white ice and misted his eyes with blood.

This turd, this pile of vomit . . . this gobbet of bronchial puss, with his repellent talk of souls and purity and God alone knew what . . . had turned his *Isabella* and her son, his grandson, the wife and child of Furio Bonetti, out of their home. How depraved were the acts of moral men. How deeply grateful was he, Carlo Bonetti, to be a bad and wicked man.

In spite of every warning, Carlo let that good, wholesome anger claim him. Onyx hard, his eyes glittered with hatred of this man. What a *bruta figura* he cut, strutting like some risible caricature of a recording angel. Who was this jumble of badly upholstered bones to stand uncowed before the anger of Carlo Bonetti? This redundant matelot. This superannuated boatman.

"You say your son's miserable leavings . . . his so-called property . . . his hair combings, the scurf from his scalp, his nail-parings, the wax of his ears . . . are left to this woman, this wife he has not seen for twelve years . . ."

Catching only the general drift of this, Joe Mazzerella confirmed that it was true.

"Then tell her this from me," Carlo slipped without warning into heavily accented English. He walked forward, jabbing his stick horizontally until its ferrule contacted the American's chest. "She has less honour than a prostitute. She takes that for which she has not given value. She has served one purpose. To spare my daughter-in-law from stooping to share a name with her or with you. For this let her be paid with the sweepings of her unwilling husband's life . . ."

It was fortunate that the chauffeur returned then and interrupted the scene in the courtyard. Too taken up with despair at his own failure to find either Carlo's daughter-in-law or his grandson, he didn't notice the escalating threat of violence between the two old men. Joe Mazzerella grasped Carlo's stick and thrust it away. Carlo promptly raised it and pointed it at the other man's chest again.

"Signor, Signor," wailed the chauffeur, "it is not my fault. The priest, he says . . ."

"*Fare silenzio!*" snarled Carlo, lowering the stick. "Search, search the house. Find out where they have gone."

The search, which the American was wise enough not to make any attempt at preventing on account of the youthful chauffeur's athletic physique which suggested a double usefulness to his employer, revealed nothing.

There were signs of a rapid but fairly orderly departure. Some clothes taken, others left swinging on coat hangers. The beds were roughly made and in the bathroom Carlo guessed was Isobel's, there was a brassière and a half-empty bottle of deodorant left.

While the chauffeur continued ransacking drawers and cupboards, Carlo sat beside his grandson's empty cot. A small soft toy, a rabbit with a bell inside, caught his eye. He picked it up and put it in his pocket.

Had she returned to Plymouth, to her mother's house? Surely, she had done that.

There was someone else in the house now. The American's younger son. Carlo could hear him moving through rooms and passages talking to his father. He came into the nursery and spoke to Carlo in good Italian, pale with controlled indignation.

"Mrs Bonetti has removed things, not her own, of sentimental and monetary value, from this house."

"There were things of value in this house?" Carlo sneered, raising an eyebrow contemptuously. "You surprise me, Monsignor. And these trifles . . . Of what do they consist?"

"A series of drawings my sister-in-law would wish to keep," the young priest wasted no time on bandying insults with Carlo, "a sports saloon . . ."

"Of what marque and colour?" Carlo was alert. "You have the number?"

John Mazzerella, a conscientious executor, had the information at his fingertips. Carlo memorised the number. It was somehow familiar to him. A red Lamborghini . . . An unpleasant coincidence.

"You intended to set my daughter-in-law and my grandson adrift without transport? You are a credit to the priesthood. And what other losses have you and your estimable father sustained? A dog, you say . . . a spaniel, liver and white?"

"She claimed it was hers. But I doubt it. My brother favoured spaniels as retrievers and paid to have them trained."

"Doubtless your sister-in-law will miss the services of this motley coloured animal . . ."

"That doesn't matter but Mrs Bonetti has stolen something which means a great deal to us. A custom built sporting rifle my father commissioned for my brother's coming-of-age . . ."

"Ah, yes. This I can understand. A significant memento. It causes your father distress . . ."

"This theft is deeply repugnant to . . ."

"*Eccellente*," said Carlo rising. "*Isabella* delights my heart. What presence of mind. She has inflicted a small but effective blow on her own behalf. Were I a younger man, Monsignor," he added, "it is not one but two corpses you would have escorted back to the United States. Or perhaps three corpses and no escort. I will say good day. Move aside. I find you smell."

Ensconced in his car, Carlo took another pill. It was good that he had said nothing of this affair to his wife. A disappointment such as this might kill her. Still, it would not be long now before *Isabella* and her son were discovered. A red Lamborghini and a liver and white spaniel would greatly assist identification. Had she crossed the border? It mattered little. She would be found in a day or two at her mother's house. Perhaps she was already at the Villa Rondine. That too was possible. She could have very few resources.

Indomitable, Carlo passed the hours of travel in considering what manner of establishment would suit his brave and clever daughter-in-law. She had become so in Carlo's mind only because others, without the right, had presumed to judge her. It was for him alone, patriarch, protector and provider of the Bonetti clan, to criticise its members. And *Isabella*, mother of his only son's only son, was prominent amongst them. That being the case, he would break the habit of a lifetime and sue for peace with her.

PART III

EIGHTEEN

"**B**ut these are really charming! Don't you think so, Tolly? Darling?"

The woman with the diet taut face unhooked a framed print of one of Ed's drawings from Isobel's stall casually, without asking leave. Isobel turned her head away to hide a flash of resentment. Sensitivity was expensive when there was a potential sale in the offing. This one looked too good to lose.

"Nice little frames .. in quite good taste . . ." grated the dry martini voice, as its owner inspected the reverse of the picture. "Not the sort of tat you usually get . . ." Pseudo-knowledgeable, she tapped the mitres with the knuckle of her forefinger.

A professional divorcee, by the look of her, Isobel categorised her customer sagely. On her third or fourth honeymoon. At either side of her mouth, the sickle-shaped scars of a lifetime's remorseless vivacity showed. Good. The value of what such women bought was immaterial to them, as long as the price was high.

That suited Isobel. She never put prices on anything. People paid what Isobel believed they wanted to pay. And just outside the Hotel Danieli's Riva degli Schiavoni entrance, that was usually plenty. An excellent pitch.

"Are they your own work?" the woman asked, producing her Knightsbridge vowels with imperious clarity. "Did you do them yourself? *Parla inglese?*" After a pause she repeated her questions with less self-assurance.

Isobel's studied indifference was intimidating. A factor which enhanced the perceived value of her goods. She was not unaware of it. Or possibly, she thought, watching the half-dozen gondolas moored nearby undulate sensuously on the swell of the tide, she was simply infected by the entrenched offensiveness with which Venice greeted its visitors. Nothing was ever for nothing here. Least of all deference.

"No," Isobel replied at length. "My husband. He was a prolific water-colourist in his lifetime. Unfortunately he would never part with his work and was therefore unknown."

Enough, Isobel thought, for the moment. People couldn't cope with too much information. She hadn't been asked directly whether or not the drawings were original. The extraordinary skill of her printers, which reproduced the exact texture of pencil smudge and nib scratch, fooled the majority. Printing was a Venetian trade, luckily.

As for the colour, she applied it herself on print after print. For that reason alone, no one example was exactly the same as another. The same set of scenes, at dawn, dusk and high noon. Rain or shine, winter and summer. So the work was sufficiently original for its purpose – to provide Isobel with a frugal living and tourists with a bargain souvenir that they fondly imagined was worth more than they paid for it.

An illusion. Nothing in Venice was ever worth the consideration demanded. The city's own resident bacilli of avarice and cupidity saw to that. Lively as flies buzzing on a richly fleshed corpse.

"Look, Tolly darling, do look. Don't you think it's good?"

The case hardened bride caught her groom by the elbow. He was a heavy jowled, trapped looking man with black rimmed spectacles. His suit was mohair and he wore a watch with a diamond bezel. Greek, Isobel guessed.

"The artist's widow is selling her husband's work, to live, poor thing . . ."

The inference, more or less correct but unpleasing, inflated the figure in Isobel's mind by a multiple of three. Experience, as much as emotion. A rule-of-thumb calculation. The thicker the skin, the fatter the bankroll.

No more questions were asked. The couple bought three framed drawings at the impudent figure which Isobel shrewdly named in dollars. In lire, it sounded too much. And all that dividing and crossing off noughts blunted the edge of a foreigner's appetite. Isobel had evolved her methods in the hard school of hunger.

She parcelled up a view of the island of San Giorgio Maggiore, one of cruise ships at anchor off the Zattere, and a third of the farmhouse near Castelchiara. She was particularly pleased about that one. The Tuscan scenes, more numerous than the limited number of Venetian studies, were harder to move. Good old San Giorgio, on the other hand, was a bestseller.

Thank God Ed had once been to Venice. Did he know, where he was now, that he'd provided her with a pension on that trip, taken before he'd ever met her?

Isobel concealed her jubilation until the chattering woman and her husband had passed safely through the Danieli's plate-glass doors into the privileged, deep carpeted hush beyond. As soon as their silhouettes merged into the gloom she unleashed a piercing two finger whistle. Her rare but instantly recognisable signal for immediate attention.

Overtly impatient while tourists pawed over Columbine masks with sequins, or thin plastic Plague Doctors, the other stallholders were agog to know what the *inglese* wanted. She wasn't like the rest of them, a jumble of European flotsam and jetsam. More like a real *Veneziana*, haughty and distant. Never shouted for a handful of change or needed anyone to mind her stall while she went for a piss. Her fellow hawkers were in awe of her.

"*Scusi* . . . Excuse me," a gangling Scandinavian youth with a rucksack approached Isobel. "Is there a possibility to voyage to the Murano island from here?"

"Back over the bridge," Isobel responded in a monotone. "Landing stage opposite the Savoia. You want a Line Five *vaporetto*."

Giving out tourist information was exhausting and unprofitable. The year before last, before she started colouring the drawings, she had done little else. Where was Dragan? Surely he'd heard her whistled summons.

He came towards her, planting his great sandalled feet in slow motion to avoid gossiping pigeons and seagulls. He had always been good to her. It was he who'd suggested colour washing Ed's drawings in the first place. Before that, sales had been terrifyingly slow. Too slow to cover the frame-maker's accounts or the printer's.

"Make sure you get on a *circolare sinistra*," Isobel called after the retreating Scandinavian, regretting her truculence. "Otherwise you'll go all round the houses . . ."

"You finish now?" Dragan, the sad eyed Yugoslav, addressed Isobel morosely, screwing a spindly, homemade cigarette into the centre of his beard.

"Yes," Isobel replied. Communication with Dragan was best achieved in monosyllables. "Have you a client? Because . . ."

Dragan shook his shaggy head and began pulling tarpaulins from behind Isobel's stall.

"Twenty minutes. A man comes back with his daughter. Free now. We do this. I have time."

His nicotine stained fingers were dusty with the pastels he used to execute slick, flattering portraits of tourists in the season. Every day in the summer, he transported his easel and materials in a flat bottomed skiff across the Giudecca Canal from the dreary Isola Sacca. It was there he had his summer quarters, a dank room in a modern tenement building.

Isobel had lived briefly on the same landing. Ugly but convenient and cheap. Cheaper still when Isobel got a lift in the skiff instead of having to pay the *vaporetto* fare. But since then she and Sandro had moved.

Together, Isobel and her friend covered the crude, packing-case stall with the tarpaulins, lashing the whole round with cords, secured by Dragan's impenetrable nautical knots. It was heavy work which Isobel couldn't manage on her own. Dragan would never accept any recompense for his help.

"You do not come back," he stated eventually.

"Not today, no. I can't sell another San Giorgio . . . not the sunset version anyway . . ."

A momentary whiffling of whiskers which served Dragan as a smile indicated both his approval and his sympathy. A bold splash of crimson lake did wonders for San Giorgio.

It was last winter he'd shown her how to do it on a production line basis. A nice streaky wash . . . leave it to dry, then add a watery blodge of cadmium yellow and some turquoise or violet according to mood.

She could do twenty in an evening if she went the right way about it. Subtlety had nothing whatever to do with this stuff. Venetian sunsets were obstinately garish, by nature. It wasn't possible to overstate them. And tourists liked maximum impact for their money. It was prudent, Dragan mournfully instructed, if painful, to cater to their coarse grained addiction to pink. Dragan had a low opinion of public taste.

"Tomorrow," he mumbled, finishing with the last of the knots, "you sell San Marco in moonlight."

"This week's people have seen that one," Isobel said, standing back. "I daren't bring out another till I'm sure they've gone."

"Use the templates," the Yugoslav advised, referring to the cardboard stencils he'd given Isobel last year as his shy Christmas gift. They helped her insert extra figures and water craft to vary Ed's restricted range of Venetian subjects.

"The domino, uh? Very disgustingly romantic. Fairytale shit."

Isobel smiled at him. Why he liked her, she couldn't imagine. She was only grateful that he did. They knew nothing of each other except the most fundamental things. Nationality and gender. That Isobel was a mother and would like to be an artist . . . that Dragan was already an artist.

During the winter months he retired to his wattle and lime daubed cottage on desolate Torcello in the lagoon's northern wastes to pursue his own work. Post modernist he called it. The canvases Isobel had been invited to view appeared to her to be uniformly brown. It had been difficult to know what to say about them which didn't sound either rude or appallingly ignorant. She needn't have worried, Dragan, normally so taciturn, was garrulous when it came to his work.

"Everything is brown," he told her, eyes burning with passion and home-distilled liquor. "All comes from the earth. I do not care what it is. Plastic, steel, silk, stone, grass . . . it is all of the earth," he smashed the balled fist of his right hand into the open palm of his left for emphasis, "and must participate in its essential brownness. There are variations, yes. Shades, tints . . . but believe me, my friend, brown is the origin and destiny of all things."

Dragan's English became very fluent under the influence of raw alcohol. Isobel thought better, on that occasion, of advancing any theory of light and its mitigating effect on brownness. Too dangerous. And it would be immodest of her to take issue with a man whose artistic beliefs were to be tested in the *Aperto* section of the *Biennale* exhibition next June. It put him several classes above her.

"You go now," Dragan said glumly, without removing the cigarette. He was never curious to know her business, the whys and wherefores of Isobel's comings and goings. She would like to have told him more of herself as a mark of friendship but he repulsed confidences as a monk renounces material possessions. They got in the way.

"Thank you, Dragan," Isobel said. "I'm going home early to take Sandro for a huge *gelato* . . . to celebrate."

"Yes?" the Yugoslav questioned with weary politeness, unwilling to know any more.

"I've made enough money to paint this winter," Isobel wilfully inflicted the news on him. "Already. Everything from now on will be a bonus. Extra. And it's all thanks to you."

"I have happiness for you and your son," Dragan shufflingly acknowledged. "I do portrait now. I see the girl coming with her father. Her face is like a bag full of buns." A sufflation of deep regret wafted his beard. "Now I make her beautiful for the first and last time. Not like you."

The last sentence was barely audible. Isobel flushed and touched him lightly on the arm before running away.

*　　　*　　　*

The beggar boy arranged his equipment with steely concentration at the eastern end of the Rialto Bridge just where it fanned into an arc of flashy tourist boutiques. Crocodile notecases, hand printed silks and coral ropes twisted with pearls made a poignant frame for the child's artfully composed tableau of destitution.

Isobel's eye trapped the image as she mounted the stone steps, threading her way through the milling crowds. Thinner, now that the end of October was here. Soon they would be gone, taking their noise and their money with them. In a week or two, grey chiffon mists would shroud the city's tarnished glitter, leaving its secretive population to exult in private over the summer's spoils. Isobel among them.

Like every other Venetian, the beggar boy was intent on shaking loose the last few crumbs of currency from outsiders' pockets. What else?

Busy with her own thoughts, Isobel tightened her grip on the zipped bag under her arm. Its contents represented fuel, warm clothes and food through the coming dark months. Materials for painting could be cadged, constructed or stolen, as Dragan had shown her. But not, unhappily, paint.

Isobel could bring herself to filch flour sacks from a restaurant's verminous back yard or timber from an unattended refuse barge. Together they made perfectly serviceable canvases. But tubes of paint from a shop in the Mercerie, no. For that act of villainy she had neither the sleight of hand nor the will. Of course, she was a clergyman's daughter, Isobel had more than once reflected bitterly. A congenital disability, that.

Bourgeois, Dragan jeeringly called her. She would never be an artist, he'd said once, until she realised that all property was theft. It disappointed Isobel that she could not agree with him. Having next to nothing herself it would have been a convenient philosophy.

As it was, she sailed close to the wind.

So far, the stall on the Riva degli Schiavoni had escaped municipal vigilance as it had in other locations. And she had additional undeclared dealings on which, as yet, she had paid no dues. A grace, no doubt, of La Serenissima's lofty administration, a body which waited patiently in its immemorial shadows for some sign of prosperity worth sharing.

The bureaucrats of Venice, Isobel had realised by degrees, were not as bureaucrats elsewhere. Too grand to dip their disdainful fingers into a miserable tin of chickenfeed. It was but the languor of lions . . . They had chosen to look away from her, as from unworthy prey. How long could it last?

Isobel could not avoid a growing sense that although no official notice was taken of her presence, in Venice she enjoyed a degree of quixotic toleration. Arbitrary, equivocal, and unfriendly, Venice chooses its favourites as it once chose its historic merchandise. Oddities and exceptions . . . elephant tusks and crow black odalisques, webs woven from worms' spit. Deformations of the norm. Coming to the tentative conclusion that she was one of these herself, Isobel had found a low, but protected, place in Venice.

Like this mendicant boy. She was almost level with him now.

Looking at him as she passed, Isobel took him for a native of the working class district of the Cannareggio *siestre* where she lived herself. Blond, blue eyed urchins were common there. Remote progeny of Baltic seamen, or true sons of Greece, perhaps, golden exiles from a golden age. Nobody really knew. Handsome mudlarks, anyway.

This child differed from his irrepressibly cheerful kind only in his demeanour. Intently mercantile and somehow familiar, he was, Isobel considered, older than Sandro who at six, was tall for his age. This boy, on the other hand, must be fully eight years old yet ancient in the way he settled himself to business, adjusting the card which told of his woes and realigning his collecting box with orderly, economic movements.

Some day, those gestures seemed to indicate, he would upgrade his trade to usury. Preside over a lordly banking house with coroneted mooring posts in the Grand Canal. What he did now was an apprenticeship in which there was cause for pride not shame.

Her attention caught, Isobel slackened her stride to watch the mannikin compose himself. Straight backed and stately he sat, cross legged with his hands folded demurely before him. His eyes raked the passers-by, assessing and appraising. A coin from a corpulent, fuzz headed American man was received with a dignified inclination of the head. Small denomination banknotes followed and each time, the measured response was the same.

Intrigued to see what was written on the piece of cardboard, Isobel veered her steps towards the child. No eye contact, however. That would be fatal. She had nothing to spare for charity.

The boy's message, in green chalked, misspelled Italian with an equally inept English translation beneath, was arresting.

My mother is dead and I have two little brothers to food.

Laughable. As if such a thing would be allowed to happen to a child in Venice. In Italy. Amused, Isobel met the child's gaze in spite of herself. Sandro looked back at her, deadpan. No guilt, no shame . . . no fear. How *dared* he humiliate her so!

Seized by a cocktail of combustible emotions, Isobel lunged at him. Too quick for her, Sandro dodged the blow, attempting at the same time to scoop up his ill-gotten gains. Isobel tipped the collecting box over with her foot so that the coins and notes spilled across her shoes, repulsive to her in that moment as a pool of sewage. She made another grab at Sandro, catching the waistband of his shorts as he scrambled to his feet. Already, a murmuring crowd, curious or concerned, was gathering.

"What do you mean by this?" Isobel shook her son as best she could, restricted by the need to hold on firmly to her bag. "You lying little toad! When did I ever let you starve? When? Just tell me *when*?"

Setting up a roar, Sandro struggled to free himself. Whilst his mother berated, he cast agonised, imploring looks into the crowd. The voluble sympathies of Italian elements within it were all with him.

"Shame," they remonstrated, to beat a child. Outrageous cruelty. Disgusting. Were there no *caribinieri* here?

Isobel disregarded the condemnation along with the panicky sweat and hot flush of embarrassment that afflicts every mother disciplining a child in public. Chastising Sandro was not easy. He was strong and agile, a natural athlete. Even when his mother managed to manoeuvre her bag in such a way as to use it as a paddle for his bottom, it was empty air she thwacked.

Exhausted by her futile efforts in the end, for Sandro, despite his histrionic appeals, had felt no pain at all, Isobel stopped, very close to tears. It was so unjust . . . as if she had not worked for him . . .

"You must give all this money back . . ." she panted, gesturing towards the scattered currency she could not bring herself to look at.

Of course, that was impossible. The anonymous donors had long since passed out of sight. Mother and son stared at each other in the dawning comprehension that neither could now stoop to touch their alms. *Bella figura.*

"It's for charity," Isobel flung at the remaining spectators, and yanking Sandro by his elbow marched away with him.

They walked in silence, side by side. Sandro sullen, and Isobel scowling fearsomely to retain every shred of maternal wrath. Begging! What would his English grandmother make of this? Sternly, Isobel dismissed the thought. It was just too funny to be indulged. She was by no means ready to forgive Sandro yet.

That she had neglected him, she knew. A thing not of choice but grinding necessity. Between his attendance at school in the morning and his transfer to Angelina's keeping till the evening, she had no choice but to trust to the elderly washerwoman's robust good sense and kindliness.

She had her own work to do, of course. The few lire Isobel was able to pay her would not defray the rent or keep her in groceries. How many of these escapes had there already been? Was Angelina afraid to tell her, fearing the loss of her small weekly fee? Possibly she was too old to manage Sandro.

` "Where's Angelina?" she said to him, still seething with indignation as they turned into the Terrà Santo Leonardo.

"At home," Sandro shrugged, half running to keep up with his furiously striding mother.

"She must be out of her mind with worry. You wicked, wicked boy. How did you get away from her?"

"She goes up to the *alta* to hang out washing . . . Anyway, she doesn't mind . . ." Sandro's voice dropped sulkily. His mother just did not understand. Other boys of his age were allowed some freedom. Angelina's own grandson, who was only five, was allowed to swim in the canals with his cousins, unless the tide was low. Why must he be different?

The begging . . . well, that had been an experiment. Very successful too, had he not been caught. Better than guarding a bargee's boat for a coin or two while he went ashore to carouse with cronies. Most of them kept big black dogs, in any case, so the work was scarce.

Catching his hand now, Isobel felt more hurt than angry. Though she herself had sometimes gone hungry during their early days in Venice, Sandro had not. And never once had they slept in the open. At first, it was true, they had only coats for blankets. On raw nights when the *Bora* blew, every one had been tucked around Sandro. Isobel had once made do with a scrofulous mat from the floor, left by a previous occupant of the tenement room. But you could not explain these things to children . . . and should not.

Things in those first few months had been badly planned. How could they have been otherwise?

Isobel had arrived bereft, to take advantage of a brief holiday in comfort inappropriate to her real circumstances. No help for that. It had been paid for and the hotel management had refused to refund the money. So she had stayed there, preparing to make an everyday life which took longer to accomplish than the four days she'd spent ghost walking in and out of the Gritti Palace.

Overwhelmed and disorientated by Ed's death and the shimmering unreality of the place in which she found herself, she had not known what to do or where to go.

Later she regretted not grasping those first opportunities. A merino blanket or two could have been smuggled out of the Gritti for a start. Stealing, even stealing was better than begging.

It was ironic that Sandro had taken it up professionally on the day his mother was finally solvent. A celebration typical of Venice. Everything here was upside down, a reverse image thrown back by the water.

"Do you want an ice cream?" Isobel said suddenly.

"Aren't you cross with me any more?" Sandro looked up at her, surprised.

"Very," replied Isobel frankly, crouching down beside him, "but I want you to know that you need never, ever ask strangers for money. What made you do it, darling? I have enough for us."

"You haven't enough for that blue paint you want," Sandro objected. "The ground up stone stuff . . ."

Isobel rocked back on her heels. How did he know about that?

"Because you talk about it sometimes," Sandro said. "To yourself."

In all probability she did, Isobel reflected, allowing Sandro to order the most elaborate confection on a nearby café's menu. Virtually her only companion, her son had always seemed as harmlessly receptive of her thoughts as an arm or leg attached. As little likely, too, to act independently of her. Now, stirring a small black coffee distractedly, she saw he had become a person, capable of distinguishing between their separate needs.

What were his, that she could not fulfil, she dared not ask. To satisfy the least of them, she must work. And what working woman's child, no matter how dearly loved, is ever cared for as he ought to be? It was only in Tuscany that Isobel had enjoyed the luxury of full-time motherhood.

Angelina had been recommended by Sandro's school when he was first enrolled there. In her time, she had looked after many children. She was the best child minder in the district. Never took more than one or two at most. And living, as she did, in the same apartment building as Isobel and her son, there had seemed no better arrangement possible.

Angelina in person, corded arms akimbo, was awaiting them on the quayside outside the crumbling *palazzo* where they lived.

"If you make a *riunione* with your son, Signora," she said, inhaling hugely, "I expect to hear of it. He knows he must return here every two hours or I summon the police. Those are my rules. Lucky for you, Signorino Sandro, that I had deliveries to make . . ."

As she spoke, a slab of stucco on the building opposite swooned quietly from the wall, committing itself to the *rio*'s snot thick water. It took a line of Angelina's washing with it.

Amid the ensuing chorus of advice and lament emitted from every balcony or opening shutter, it was Sandro who sprang down from the quay into a minute *sandolino* moored alongside and deftly poled the craft amidstream to recover his baby minder's ruined handiwork. Manoeuvring in the shallow channel, boat and boy seemed one.

Benumbed, bemused, Isobel watched the scene in which she had no part to play. The children of the very poor, like most round here, shook off childhood quickly. For them, unprotected by the artificial safety nets provided by richer parents, the precocious development of practical survival skills was urgent. Without realising it, Isobel had seen the phenomenon many times. It had not occurred to her previously, however, that it would affect herself or Sandro.

Preoccupied now with the crisis in her primary career, Angelina was in no mood for talk about her child rearing methods. Isobel decided to leave the matter in abeyance until the following day, when Sandro would be at school and her own business with the municipal pawnshop finished.

Single parents, who must both provide and nurture, Isobel had discovered, cannot permit any one anxiety priority over another. Love and money have equal precedence.

Buying a lettuce from a passing vendor's craft, she went indoors to prepare yet another dish of pasta. Sandro would come for it, no doubt, when he'd wrung the last drop of approval from the local busybodies.

Playing to the gallery? Smiling, Isobel remembered, whilst tearing the lettuce leaves, she'd done the same thing often enough during that childhood of her own which had been forcibly extended.

*   *   *

The municipal pawnshop, right on the Grand Canal and housed incredibly in a magnificent *palazzo*, had from the moment of its chance discovery supplied Isobel both with some domestic deficiencies and some much needed ideas. The venerable establishment had become her emporium and financier.

Threading her way through a maze of narrow *calle* and *terrà*, Isobel walked there with buoyant step in the fresher morning air. Sandro, safely deposited in his school, two floors up a winding staircase, would be closely supervised till an hour past noon.

On the *piano nobile* of the Palazzo Corner della Regina, Isobel was greeted by her usual clerk with reserved cordiality.

Pawn brokerage here was conducted in an atmosphere of mutual respect. Businesslike, brisk and discreet, there was no breath of condescension on one side of the counter or need for cringing on the other. In Venice, there was no such thing as a dishonourable transaction.

"*Va bene, Signora?*" the dark suited man enquired with melancholy kindness. "How may we accommodate you today?"

Silently, Isobel rejoiced in his manner, his long, pale Venetian face and the glint in his eye, betokening his keen interest in what she might produce. A gem, a fur . . . an old evening dress. Whatever she had, she knew it would be treated with the same low-voiced seriousness. Was his name not Dandolo? Written in the Golden Book of patricians. Most of them sunk now into white-collar employment as their city sank gracefully into the mud.

"For once, Signor," Isobel smiled as she unzipped her bag, "it is I who have come to accommodate you. To relieve you of the weary custodianship of my earrings. Here is the ticket."

Dandolo's face split in a smile of congratulation. The redemption date on those earrings had been deferred several times already. He had begun to fear that they would soon be permanently lost to his client.

"Ah, this gives me much pleasure," he took the ticket from Isobel's hand. "Your venture has returned you a profit, then?"

"It has. And I'm grateful for your patience, Signor."

"You pay for our patience," Dandolo reminded her gravely. "There is no occasion for gratitude. But for satisfaction, there is reason."

While a messenger fetched the carnival mask earrings from a safe, Isobel counted out her notes and related in outline the success of the project which the loan raised on her jewellery had enabled.

A manufacturing costume jewellery company, established as an extension to a glass foundry business on Murano, had agreed to copy the earrings in base, gold plated metal and faceted crystal. The cost of initial tooling, however, was breathtaking. The company offered to underwrite the cost and distribute the earrings if Isobel would accept a small royalty on sales in exchange for their exclusive use of the copyright design. Its commercial potential as an elegant keepsake of Venice, whose unofficial emblem was the mask, was strikingly obvious.

Keeping her nerve, Isobel demanded to see studio designs and a lost wax prototype before signing any agreement. She was playing for time at that stage, groping for some way of retaining a higher percentage of her asset.

"But that technology is appropriate only to gold itself," the glass-blowing partners argued smoothly. "It will make the prototype unnecessarily costly."

Isobel was adamant and paid for the first cast by pawning Ed's gun. She still wasn't sure how and when she would get that back.

As soon as the prototype cast was shown her, the answer came clear in her mind. Now the manufactory had a substitute pattern to work from, she could take the original earrings to the pawnshop and raise the capital to produce however many copies the money would buy, with something over to redeem the gun.

Outmanoeuvred, the Murano firm's partners remained calm. Their respect for Isobel's acumen deepened. An opponent of some calibre, this one, they agreed. Very strange that she wasn't Venetian . . . and a man. What androgynous creatures they bred north of the Alps. "*Allora*", to business.

They came up with a counter proposal. In the matter of distribution they had experience, and, of course, generations' worth of contacts which Isobel couldn't match. They would oblige her by selling her earrings into a selected number of superior outlets in exchange for a commission to be calculated on each unit placed.

"Each dozen placed," Isobel haggled. "A fee on every twelve."

Twelve? What outlandish, barbarian arithmetic was this?

"All right," Isobel climbed down. "Every ten placed."

The precise amount of commission was disputed for the minimum length of time which did honour to the tenacity of both parties. Isobel travelled across on the lumbering *vaporetto* several times before agreement was reached.

At one moment she threatened to take the whole project away and appoint another manufacturer. This gave her would-be contractors furiously to think. To their bafflement, they found their commercial sinews had been tried to the limit by this compelling giantess in her contemptibly down-at-heel shoes.

A deal was struck. After some weeks, Isobel began to receive regular accountings. Every fourth Wednesday, the manufactory's waterman handed in a note at her bank.

The sums which accompanied the statement, derisory at first, had grown till they all but covered the extortionate rent on two rooms in the water logged *palazzo* she now inhabited and which stood with its green, weedy feet in the *rio* that oozed its viscous way around the Ghetto Nuovo.

Isobel had coveted those two lofty rooms. For all the mould which grew on the walls, they were more beautiful and vastly more spacious than the humid, plain plaster boxes she and Sandro had inhabited on Sacca Fisola and Giudecca. It had been cold water only, there, and paraffin contraptions for heating and cooking. For bathing, there were uncurtained showers which rained heavily on lavatory, washbasin and towels.

Like her neighbours, Isobel had soon learned to regard washing anything much, except the bits that showed, as a warm weather activity. Pointless to fuss about smells. You got inured to them or they went away. Something to do with the chemistry of the thing. It righted itself. Clean teeth and clean pants became Isobel's pared down totems of decency.

With her move to the main Venetian archipelago, she got a half-share in a deep cast iron bath. It reared up on griffins' claws and was filled by a clanking copper geyser fired by a ring of purple gas flames underneath. Angelina did the neighbourhood's laundry in it on Mondays, Wednesdays and Saturday mornings. On Tuesdays and Sundays, Isobel and Sandro immersed themselves up to the chin and stayed there till their skins were unhealthily macerated, crêpey and white.

But Dandolo was not told any of that. Isobel used her bank's address. A facility she had gained with a draft for somewhat over three and a half thousand pounds sterling from the Tavistock Building Society's branch in Plymouth. Money, small in substance but with an unexceptionable pedigree.

It entitled Isobel to a seat in the assistant manager's sugar frosted, frescoed office while the reflection of bright wavelets outside dappled the ceiling as he issued her a chequebook there with muffled warnings concerning the fate of those who overdrew their accounts without permission or collateral.

It was an empty threat designed to add an aromatic puff of sulphur to the interview. An essential ornament to any civilised exchange in Venice, plain speech being fit only for outer island rustics and farmers in the marginal swamps. New to the place and its ways, Isobel never overdrew her account at the bank, preferring instead to incur punitive interest charges on debts to her tradesmen. From today she was out of their clutches.

"I regret your other pledges are gone," Dandolo said, handing over the earrings with a bow.

"Well I don't," Isobel returned. "Old clothes don't leave much of a gap. I'm going to get something new."

By new, Isobel meant something old from among the unredeemed pledges of others, piled in the overflowing wicker-work skeps in the pawnshop's waterline storerooms. Competition was fierce there, between second-hand clothes dealers in homburgs and bow-legged old women with head scarves pulled low over their foreheads.

After a vicious tug of war, Isobel came away with an emerald green evening gown which would be worth both alteration and cleaning. Wild silk, backless with a trained, swishing skirt. Practically no irrecoverable damage at all. The label was Dior. Quite suitable for the Casino.

A woman with two rooms, half a bath and no debts was entitled to some nightlife.

* * *

"If you want your son brought up like a *borghese*, Signora," Angelina turned to face Isobel who filled the door of the bathroom, "you must pay a *bambinaia* to take him to the *giardini pubblici* or to the Lido for his excercise . . ."

"There is a garden here," responded Isobel as Angelina continued the business of wringing out wet garments kneeling beside the bath.

"The garden?" Angelina scorned. "You expect your son to be content with a space six metres square when his friends roam free?"

"He's only *six*," Isobel pleaded. "How can I allow him . . ."

"How can you prevent him?" enquired Angelina, creaking up from her knees. She placed a hand on Isobel's shoulder and shook her slightly. "I tell you, I cannot. I will not be his gaoler. If that is what you pay me for our arrangement is at an end. Believe me," she added, not unkindly, "I have raised my own in Venice. *Certamente*, there is danger. In what city is there not? But for those who speak the language and have friends to learn from, there is less."

"But the water . . ."

"As you saw yesterday, Signora, Sandro is learning to use it and respect it. For a *Veneziano*, that is essential, *no*?"

"I suppose," said Isobel beaten by the washerwoman's logic. "If you don't drown in the first twelve years, your chances of doing so diminish at an ever-increasing rate."

Angelina beamed. The Signora, despite her frequently abstracted air, was really quite intelligent.

"So, we will keep to our arrangement, no? This is Sandro's home. When you are not here, Signora, then I am here. When Sandro is not here, I know of it when you do not. When he has been gone too long, in your place, I act."

Really, it was not at all satisfactory. Too convoluted, vague and altogether Venetian for Isobel's taste. Letting herself into her own apartment she thought longingly of a real nursemaid for Sandro. But cheap as servants were in Italy, they were less so in Venice. By no stretch of the imagination could she afford to pay, feed, or house one. Not in two rooms. Anyway, it was too late. Like it or not, Sandro was growing up his own way. Where was he now?

Mice shot in every direction at the sound of Isobel's footfall. She didn't mind them. Sandro, however, found it difficult to get to sleep when they scurried all night in the wainscots. He would get used to it, Isobel thought. Just as she had accustomed herself to finding mice in her drawers. The droppings were a nuisance. That was all.

Flinging down the green dress, she unlocked the casements and pushed open the shutters to admit the homely gust of salt, fish and faeces. A perfume to arouse all the senses. The soft rattle of a rowlock and a flicker in the angled mirror fixed to the sill announced the stealthy approach of a boat directly below. Isobel missed seeing who was in it.

Sandro propelled his *sandolino* past the *palazzo*'s main, disused gondola entrance, and on to the garden watergate further along. After looping the painter through an iron ring attached to the wall, he threw a parcel over the railings. In a moment he followed it, landing amid the cat infested jungle of untended shrubs.

His mother, he felt sure, fielding the parcel, would be pleased. Hadn't he insisted on taking the advice of the shop's senior assistant? No amateur's rubbish.

"Sandro, where have you been? Does Angelina know?" Isobel rapped questions at him, the moment he came into the apartment's main room, embracing the parcel. "What's that?"

"It's for you," he mumbled, aghast at his mother's vulturine stance. He hadn't known she'd be back so soon. Starting to explain himself in the hissing, bubbling dialect of Venice, Sandro forgot his mother didn't understand it. He had been to the Mercerie. Yes, Angelina knew and what time she could expect him back . . .

"Don't!" she stamped. "Talk to me in English . . ."

Resentful of this treatment, Sandro dropped his parcel at his mother's feet. The brown-paper wrapping burst asunder spilling tubes of paint all over the woodblock floor.

Staring at her son, Isobel stooped down to pick them up, one by one. Good paint. Artists' quality oils. Pure pigments. Things she would have chosen . . .

"And if you hadn't interfered with me yesterday, I'd have got you the lapis . . . stone stuff, as well."

Sandro stamped his own foot violently, to scare away the tears forming in his eyes.

Gathering him to her, Isobel explained that because of his wonderful present, she could buy her own cobalt powder now.

"But darling, how . . . I mean, where . . . You didn't steal any of this did you?"

"No," Sandro began to sob now with relief that, after all, his gift had been accepted. "I earned the money to buy them . . ."

"But Sandro, *how*?"

"I do lots of things," the little boy told her proudly. "Run errands to . . . Oh, far away. Peel vegetables," he shrugged. "Clean fish. Pick up rubbish from the beaches on the Lido. It's good money. I go with my friend's father. He has a barge . . ."

Isobel stopped listening. She had never even been to the Lido. Her tracks across the lagoon were few and well worn.

"And Angelina," she prompted when Sandro began to run out of steam. "What about her two-hour rule?"

"The bargeman is her nephew, so it's all right to go with him."

"And school? Do you stay there when I take you there in the morning?"

"Sure," Sandro shrugged again, a strange reverberation of Ed in his manner. A man of whom he had small recollection. "I read . . . and I do sums. You want to eat?"

He sounded like a man of forty, suddenly bored with women's nagging. "Did you buy anything, or is it spaghetti again?"

"Yes," Isobel replied honestly. "I forgot to shop. Let's go out for a treat."

"We had one yesterday," Sandro said astutely. "So we can't afford it."

"We can," Isobel retorted. "I have to make up to you somehow for not having a proper Mummy."

"No. *No!* You're not to say that," Sandro rained blows upon her wildly. "I have a mother. Just not like anybody else's. I have to help you get famous one day, like you said."

Unaware of ever having said such a thing aloud, Isobel refrained from argument. God only knew what she said during the long hours she had spent alone with Sandro. Where should they go?

"I know a place," Sandro puffed out his chest. "For me they will give a good price."

To please him, Isobel wore her new dress. All creased as it was, too short and with the bodice torn loose from the waist seam. She brushed her hair, not that anyone would notice. When it began to annoy Isobel she cut it herself with the kitchen scissors. The effect was original. To be simultaneously comfortable and smart, she wore her usual thonged sandals and the diamond mask earrings.

"This is my mother," announced Sandro to the startled proprietor of a surprisingly respectable establishment. A small hotel's restaurant overlooking the Cannaregio Canal. "She is famous."

To look as she did, mad but magnificent, the restaurateur concluded, she must be. He had, he thought distractedly, seen her somewhere before. In a newspaper? On the prow of a sailing galley in the maritime museum? No, no. Little Sandro's mother? The boy who had nagged incessantly for unopposed rights to their potato peelings. Hardly. Never mind. As a sample of resident Venetian eccentricity she was a choice item. A conversation piece for his foreign patrons. They would linger over their *dolce* and order profitable brandies.

Rubbing his hands, the proprietor told all his neck-craning guests that the strange lady in green was a celebrity who preferred to

271

remain incognito. Would they be kind enough to ignore her presence?

Isobel left with her son sublimely content with the stir they had caused. No more so than their host whose till had jingled with such pleasant regularity all evening. Some people possessed the knack of creating atmosphere.

The bill? Signorino Sandro would attend to it later, Isobel was gallantly assured. A complex affair of adjustments to the pigswill concession. Not a matter for ladies.

NINETEEN

Less and less astonished by her son's premature practicality, Isobel allowed him to assume the role of watersprite adjutant. He had made of himself a separate entity, no longer a dependent colony of cells. The thick membrane of blind obligation which locks most mothers out of full experience, thinned to a translucent connection. Embarking so early on this riskier phase of mother love, Isobel shrank without consciousness of doing so, from the near-sexual smothering with which her own mother had disgusted her brother, Rupert.

Nor did Sandro's intellectual precocity strike Isobel as in the least unusual. Observant and articulate herself at his age, she had been written off as disruptive, immature or impudent. This was a form of adult abuse his mother was determined that Sandro would never have to suffer. Conversing on a broad platform of equality with her child, came naturally to Isobel. Enlightenment was a rewarding, mutual thing.

The children of artists, moreover, very soon learn that their progenitors see them as incidental creations. Wild suckers which have escaped early pruning from a cultivated main stem. Poverty, for these youngsters, is not the sole motive for accelerated development. There is only so much sap to be drawn free of charge from an artist. They need it for other things.

Something in Sandro's bloodstream told him that he had already had his ration. He knew it months before Isobel did. His love for her became detached, observant and critical. It was also full of pain. His mother, alarming and eccentric in many ways, defied explanation but needed his protection.

A man now, in his own eyes, he was shrill in defence of her slender resources. It was he who supervised the provisioning for the oncoming winter. Isobel was preoccupied with concerns in which her son had no share.

She was stirring hide glue in a pan on a gas ring when she heard Sandro screeching invective at the *palazzo*'s regular coal merchant. An energetic spitting of *x*'s and *z*'s, as lucid to Isobel as the feline vendettas fought out in the garden. The meaning was made plain

273

to her later, after the disgruntled bargee had chugged his protesting engines into reverse.

She refused to pay for her share of the load, Isobel learned of herself, as she added sieved chalk dust in accurately measured amounts to her mixture. Primer. Vitally important not to let it boil. What was all this about the coal?

She rejected the custom adhered to by a countless succession of dim witted tenants. Or so Sandro had told the bargee. She was not such a fool. Others might submit to extortion for the sake of convenience but not Sandro's mother. She was an intelligent person.

Shovelling a part load was not worth the trouble, the bargee had countered. Thanks to the Signora *Isabella*'s craziness, her neighbours in the other eight apartments would lose a signal advantage. Let them fall into the unscrupulous hands of a man less honest than he was. They would pay double for their fuel and know whom to blame.

"Oh *God*, Sandro," Isobel moaned, grasping the implications of his rattling narration at last. "How do *you* know what the cost of coal is . . ." But when she turned towards him, Sandro had beat a swift, soft footed retreat.

He returned a little later accompanied by a sly featured youth, owner of a small steamer coaling concern just behind the station. He replenished the communal coal cellar at a favourable charge. A friend, Sandro said, who was keen to pick up the business.

It was the same friend, it turned out, who allowed Sandro personal use of the *sandolino* in exchange for his effective, freelance disruption of established domestic fuel trading contracts all over Cannaregio. Isobel chose not to probe deeper into her son's widespread activities. A sincere attempt, however, was made at the maintenance of certain rock bottom conformities.

Sandro was not allowed to venture afloat into the Grand Canal, and never on any pretext into the San Marco Basin, nor the Giudecca Canal, the docks or Tronchetto areas. He must not cross the Cannaregio Canal except in daylight or be found on the seaward side of his own *siestre*.

Sandro's parole, in fact, extended to the local network of six or seven *rios*. A sufficiently spacious playground. If, Isobel told him sternly, he was ever spotted out of water bounds, she'd put him in dry dock permanently.

"You don't beg any more," Isobel asked now, hoping not to be told any exact, disquieting truths. "Do you, Sandro?"

"No," he replied. "It's quite quick but it's boring. I only did it once."

"Or steal, I hope, because . . ."

"What am I having for my supper?" Sandro evaded his mother's catechising neatly. Everybody stole things once in a while. Anything left in a boat was fair game. How else was a boy to get started in business? Somebody in this family of two had to make some real money.

"Oh dear," muttered Isobel vaguely. "Are you hungry, darling? You could have scrambled eggs . . ."

"No, I couldn't," Sandro pointed out peevishly. "You're using the pan."

So she was. Fried eggs, perhaps? No. Was there anything else in the fridge which suggested itself?

Sandro inspected the contents of the whirring cabinet which served both as foodstore and Isobel's bedside table. There were a few stalks of cabbage, he reported, and a fragment of *pecorino* cheese.

Removing her glue mixture from the stove, Isobel came to look. She had forgotten to go shopping again. She quite often did. It was partly because she hated spending money on ephemerals like food until physical craving compelled her . . . and had a pathological hatred of standing in queues. Not things she could readily explain to Sandro. He, of course, had a right to be fed and must be.

"Soup? There's some bread," Isobel put her arm round her son's waist persuasively.

"No," he said pulling away. "*Ugh*! Your soup's horrible. And it takes ages. I'll go and get pizza."

He went, formally admonished not to stray out of the immediate district on foot or by water and to attend to his navigation lights. The November night was foggy.

With a sense of superior forethought, Isobel removed two drying canvases from the oven and put plates to warm there instead. She was ready to add the next coat of primer to those canvases now.

Stroking their crisp white skins with the brush was intensely pleasurable. They responded, these virginal rectangles, inviting consummation in a way that sullen, shop bought supports never did . . . pulled shapes and shadows out of her head. Mad, demonic creatures which she always strained back on a leash.

She turned away from the canvases and their seductive, pulsating blankness. Was there such a thing as a mindscape? Lately, Isobel had begun to wonder, teetering on the edge of a narrow-mouthed cavern which entombed a score of cadavers.

"Pornography," Isobel denounced the monsters which importuned in her mind. "You must stay inside till you die. No one's ever going to see what you look like. They'd lock me up for letting you lot go."

She began banging down cutlery on the marble-topped table with huffy, housewifely gestures.

When Sandro came back with the pizza, he found her silent but bristling, as in the presence of unwanted company. It quite often happened. At least she wasn't talking to herself. It was a habit which made her son increasingly uneasy, although fortunately, as far as he knew, she didn't do such things in public.

"Mummy," he asked her in the midst of the meal which they ate more or less in silence. "Are you quite well?"

"I think so," she said, filling his glass absent-mindedly with the wine she was drinking herself. "Don't I seem so?"

Sandro let it pass. Once or twice he had overheard adults in the neighbourhood describe his mother as *emarginata*. He didn't know the word in English but in Italian it had various meanings. Taken together, they had disturbing vibrations. His mother, he found, was a heavy responsibility to which he tried hard to be equal.

Soon after eating, he said he was tired. Isobel helped him get ready for bed in their other, adjoining room. She stayed with him till he slept on account of the scuttles and squeaks in the wainscot. Sweet, glossy black people with thin, whippy tails. Isobel cajoled Sandro into laughter with tales of their quarrels and family histories.

Afterwards she lay down on her own bed and gazed up at the ceiling where ribald ladies were bursting out of their corsets and riding on cows to the applause of adipose cherubs. Everyone, including the cows, seemed swept up on a crest of lecherous, light flooded excitement. The work of the sixteenth century artist, Veronese. Catalogued, so her landlady insisted, in a list of the artist's work held in the Accademia archives. Exclusive rights to the treasure went with the tenancy.

Oblivious to the blare of television sets all around, Isobel congratulated herself once again on her luck in finding this place with its lancet head windows and comfortable odours. The walls had reeded marble pilasters at intervals, terminating exuberantly in acanthus profusions over which the libidinous revellers floated. Heedlessly rollicking through decades of fat laden cooking steam, dropping flakes of paint like flower petals to the ground. Real palaces, Isobel reflected, refuse to adapt.

She would have liked some people to know about it . . . Simon, Giulia and others, perhaps. They must be hurt, angry even, not to have heard from her. They might wish to know she was safe . . . alive.

But she had worked very hard to buy herself the next four months and couldn't afford to waste them on friends . . . if, indeed, she had any left. Better not to have, really. And certainly not sex. A clean empty space inside yourself was the only viable working area.

Of all the artists' materials Isobel had ever purchased, the right to be alone had come dearest of all.

* * *

The second year Fine Art Faculty students of Padua University were, for the moment, employed to the qualified satisfaction of their professor. Copying, as far as their wretched abilities allowed, the work of a master. Each student had been assigned some element of the composition before them, to be reproduced faithfully before the end of the year. A course requirement, this, which some more progressive educators in the field might consider old fashioned. Not so, the professor.

For him, the exercise incorporated two major advantages. It spared his voice in the first place . . . he was prone to laryngitis . . . and it pricked the bombast of those with highly graded essays to their credit. Writing about art was a trivial accomplishment compared with its practice. The professor took a grim pleasure in watching his students grapple with the contradictions of anatomical traction. Their invariable failure here knocked the glibness, for a while at least, out of their richly adverbial blabberings. A salutary lesson.

"Less conversation, ladies and gentlemen, if you please." The professor coughed with delicate malice. "Words will not mitigate the minor difficulties you confront. The eyes direct the hand, not the tongue."

Isobel, who stood at an angle to the professor's direct line of vision, raised the canvas on her easel another notch. From the makeshift podium at the far end of the Accademia storeroom, she was invisible. The less attention she attracted, the better. Infiltrating the faculty classes was unlikely to be as simple a matter this time as it had been last year.

The students themselves presented no problem. A fresh crop, they would almost certainly rely on the same set of conveniently mistaken suppositions as their predecessors. Those registered with Padua University itself presumed Isobel to be attached to the Venetian annexe. The rest imagined the reverse to be true.

Actually, the students had other reasons for leaving their elusive colleague unmolested. A little older than most, outlandish in appearance and forbidding in manner, she stood at the centre of an invisible, inviolate pentacle. Any intrusion into her electrified space was certain to trip a dangerous switch. The unexpressed conviction was general.

277

She must be, the legitimate, fee paying undergraduates dismissed her, a foreign exchange student. That would account for her unsociability. It was unnecessary to include her in anything. Hadn't somebody seen her hawking prints from a stall? *No!* But yes . . . a girl in the first year whose parents had stayed in Venice all summer . . . Surely not! A twitter of commiseration followed. The family's estate on the mainland had been sold . . .

A world that was blind to Isobel's own.

The majority of the fledgling fine artists were girls. Spike-heeled and superbly clothed, their families had known each others' for generations and had small use for outsiders. Their collective ambition was to secure untaxing positions as newspaper art critics when once they held degrees in their manicured hands. An agreeable status-giving occupation which might be pursued without prejudice to their marital prospects. They were not an inquisitive crowd.

The directing staff, on the other hand, Isobel brooded, were not so readily hoodwinked. This particular lecturer had seen her before. Should he recognise her, he might ask himself why a third year student was repeating the second year course. A search of his registers would reveal no explanation in the shape of unsatisfactory marks. Or any marks at all. He would find he had an all too solid phantom on his hands to which no name, receipt of fees or record of performance was attached. How did universities react to stowaway students?

The viewing frame in Isobel's hand wobbled a little as she thought of the possible consequences. Ignominious ejection was probably the worst that could happen.

"Signorina Capello," the professor's thready voice at the other end of the room fragmented Isobel's thoughts, "your beautiful smock has been arranged to elegant perfection. Your tireless pursuit of the ideal impresses me. I advise you, however, to have no more anxiety over your personal draperies. Address yourself please, to those of Bellini's madonna, without further delay . . ."

Oh, bloody hell, Isobel swore under her breath, amid the predictable breeze of suppressed giggles rippling the room. He's coming this way. If he failed to ignore her, she decided, she would tell him she missed this block of instruction last year through illness.

True enough. She had found a few weeks' temporary, unskilled work at the press which printed Ed's drawings. Collating tourist pamphlets while the firm's regular employee recovered from a virulent influenza virus. A mind numbing job which had helped reduce some of the mounting interest on her debt to the printer with a few lire in hand for food.

Then Sandro had caught the same virus and much of the money went on drugs from the pharmacist. Isobel had stayed at home in their Giudecca room to nurse him. Huddled in an overcoat, she had drawn, while her son alternately shook or slept in his bed.

The enforced isolation had allowed Isobel the time to practise what this professor had already taught her in earlier weeks. The structure of the skull and its musculature. What had been intended as mere background information to enrich the descriptive vocabulary of would-be art critics, unlocked a toolbox for Isobel. She had made herself master of Lange's eyelid classification . . .

"*Stupendo!*" the professor paused in his perambulation among donkeys and easels. Isobel looked up covertly from what she was doing to see him rocking back and forth on his toes beside an anguished young gentleman. "As fine an unshelled crab as I ever saw dug from the sand. Our Lady's ear is honoured by the comparison . . . mouthwateringly formless. I said copy, boy. *Copy!* Do not fantasise."

Hands locked behind his back, he continued on his portentous way, offering each student some biting sarcasm by way of encouragement. The subdued laughter of the students at their fellows' discomfiture soon dwindled to silent misery as each contemplated his or her turn. Nobody's *bella figura*, it seemed, was to be spared that day.

Flight, it occurred to Isobel, would be the best thing. A headache? Or just go and say nothing at all? There again, she could brazen it out. Criticism she could withstand . . . welcome, in fact. But along with that luxury might go exposure of her deception and an end to her larcenous studentship. Already caught up in the Bellini icon's underlying secrets, Isobel was reluctant to leave. She would decide what to do in a minute.

Was the Virgin's smile of resignation predicated on a contraction of the *risorius* or the *buccinator* muscle? A moment longer wouldn't matter . . . It may be, may it not, that this wasn't a real smile at all, whatever the artist's intention? It could be that the model's lips were repressed into the automatic, uncommunicative ellipse that gated most faces in Venice . . . in which case . . .

She left it too late. In the midst of these absorbing conjectures, Isobel became aware of a shadow falling over her canvas. The voice, however, was silent. How long had he been standing there? Isobel froze, impaled on his stare.

Taking the fine filbert brush from her hand wordlessly, the professor selected another from her collection. Bigger and broader.

"You would appear," he said to her quietly, "to have identified

279

the central enigma of this work. Who and what, you ask yourself, was the model? You speak Italian?"

Nodding, Isobel took the brush he placed in her hand.

"Your speculations are valid," he tapped the unreconciled hatchings in thinned raw sienna on her canvas. "But you are attempting to draw, Signorina . . . That is wrong. Paint. Start with the mass and work forward till you meet the change in the light . . . or the tone. Don't be afraid to feel with the brush. Discipline you have . . . give a little rein to emotion. Before you leave, come and see me."

* * *

"You have your student identity card?" he challenged her when she presented herself at the end of the class. Isobel shook her head. "I . . ."

"Permit me, Signorina," the professor raised his hand peremptorily, "to do most of the talking for both of us. It will be more constructive. Is this you?"

He took a faded, black and white handbill from a folder on the lectern. Isobel had seen it many times before but not recently. Eighteen months or two years ago, they had been all over Venice, posted on church and landing stage noticeboards. Isobel had removed them systematically, uncertain whether Carlo Bonetti sought his grandson in this city alone or throughout Italy and beyond. How he knew about Sandro at all, she had no means of knowing.

The thought that he did, so chilling in itself, was enough to close Isobel's mind against any rapprochement with that family. When and where had they spied on her? She had been right about Carlo Bonetti all along. Neither she nor Sandro would be his playthings.

"This is your face?" the professor reiterated his question. "My interest, I assure you, is purely academic. Such a pretty puppy princess . . ."

"No, 'fraid not," Isobel said, surveying the grainy photograph of herself on the day of her marriage to Furio. A strange, forgotten face that was no longer hers. She was accompanied, said the legend, by a small, dark haired boy and a liver and white cocker spaniel. Recognition of the group was worth money to somebody. Except, of course, the trio as described did not exist. Too many imprecisions.

The description of herself was accurate as to height, eye- and hair colour. There the similarity between her old and present selves ended. Only an educated eye, accustomed to measuring the space between feature and feature, to isolating the bone from the flesh, could spot the resemblance.

"No," Isobel spoke again. "It's not me."

"Of course it is not," replied the professor easily. "We have neither of us seen this oval cheeked teenager before. To us, she is nothing. Bonetti? It is a common name. We are in agreement."

He tore the handbill across and gave the two halves to Isobel. "You know, an old aquaintance of mine, Pietro Arnolfi, once had a private pupil by the name of Isobel Bonetti . . . of whom he spoke with some esteem. English, I seem to remember he said."

Isobel's pupils dilated, which confirmed the professor's suspicion.

"Well," he sighed, "he is bedridden and she is gone . . ."

"What a pity," Isobel curtly condoled. She had done it, she thought, almost as well as Lucy Larizzi. But to be remembered by Pietro Arnolfi gave her a bittersweet pleasure.

Some leisurely business with a throat spray occupied the next few moments, during which Isobel studied the bisected handbill with a compassionate shudder. How defenceless she had been and how young.

"About my identity card," Isobel started again, "I'm afraid I . . ."

"Allow me to make good the deficiency, Signorina . . . Signora. Please, no more words of yours. Be quiet while I write some of mine. Be seated."

Subsiding on to the stool of a nearby donkey, Isobel waited, mind spinning, while the professor rapidly covered a sheet of headed writing paper with many lines of a looping, forward-leaning script.

The document, as explained by its author, conferred on Isobel a *borsa di studio*. A scholarship which admitted her as of right to any class she cared to attend and acted as a letter of introduction to the owners of private apartments in Venice where future lectures were scheduled. In these places, caretakers and major-domos had instructions to check identity cards for security reasons.

"I regret my little *fiat* does not entitle you to sit the university examinations. It is, you see, unofficial . . ."

"That doesn't matter . . ." Isobel made several attempts at expressing her thanks to the professor's amusement. Grateful she undoubtedly was, but it was refreshing to see how her own priorities kept racing past the castrated phrases of conventional indebtedness.

What, he wondered, was her story. And where had she developed this intently surgical eye? It was all up with the Bellini madonna. She was found out. Neither sanctified nor gentle. Solicitous, merely, for her hourly rate. *Orbicularis oris.*

A sudden squall of wind slapped waves in the canal and rain

slashed at the windows. Isobel admitted she had no umbrella.

"I may give you a lift?" The professor stuffed his notes in a briefcase. "I have the faculty launch at my disposal. Where do you live?"

"Near the New Ghetto but I can go on the Number One from the landing stage here to San Marcuola . . ."

"An interesting quarter. Let us go there at once."

Isobel had never previously boarded one of the shiny hulled vessels which in Venice replaced limousines. The saloon of this one was furnished like her father's rectory study had been, only everything was much grander and newer. She didn't trouble to conceal her enthusiasm.

"How fast does it go?"

"We shall experiment." The professor drew back the bulkhead door which separated the saloon from the cockpit. He was reminded by the waterman that the speed limit within the city was five miles an hour. Already they were doing six and a half, the permissible degree of defiance.

"Then we shall exceed the permissible. My guest is indifferent to limits."

The roar of the throttle and rush of the bow wave prevented Isobel from asking why he had said such a thing. Speed, the long-lost ecstasy, overtook everything, spuming the blood in her veins.

"Look!" She moved from side to side in the cabin, pointing out the famous old houses lining the Grand Canal just as if her companion had never seen them before. "There's the Salviati place . . . my favourite . . ."

"We Venetians," the professor said primly, "find it to be in very bad taste. Like a fairground carousel with all that gold and colour . . ."

"You Venetians," Isobel objected, "are wrong. You don't like the Salviati *palazzo* because it sums you all up. Greedy and gleeful. Of course," she supplemented, "I don't mean to offend you."

"But naturally not," was the urbane response. "It is simply that you would not like to deceive me. Isn't that so?"

Isobel smiled blindingly, admiring the skill with which she had been put in her place. It was perhaps not very safe to be known by people like this. She was not ready yet to show the world anything. Still, she had done very well out of what had promised to be an embarrassing meeting. He would keep his unspoken bond, she was sure. Venetians were addicted to secrets.

Leaving her on the narrow *fondamente* to the side of Isobel's insalubrious building, the professor concealed his dismay.

Ragged washing flapped on lines overhead, strung between

window and balcony. A woman with a sweeping brush pushed a pile of garbage into the side canal. The tide was low, so the detritus landed on mud where a large crab contended with a rat for the prize.

So this was the residence of Carlo Bonetti's daughter-in-law. She, who might have had anything.

"Your lodgings are comfortable?"

"I have a Veronese ceiling," Isobel boasted. "And in summer, there is a fig tree which reflects in the *rio*."

"Ah! Overriding considerations," he handed her gravely out of the boat. "Where the eye drinks," he added archly, "the body feels no privation."

"None," said Isobel humourlessly. The prolonged exchange had wearied her. Stiffly decorous, she bowed to her benefactor as the launch swung away. He waved only once, bruised by his contact with a personality by turns so rebarbative and vivid. She took what she needed and left the rest where it lay.

Above, the *palazzo* shutters were creaking open. An inch . . . two inches, a little further still. So the Signora *Isabella* had found a *ragazzo*, had she? A protector, more like. He looked shockingly old and married. But rich . . .

Isobel didn't need to hear what was said. Angelina came skittering down the stone staircase to ask if the Signora would find it convenient to undergo a fitting for her refurbished frock. What she really wanted to know was the name, address and occupation of the *uomo nobile*. Her enquiries, craftily oblique, irritated Isobel. "I'll ask him," she replied, "if he has a vacancy for a private laundress. You have your references handy, Angelina?"

Which dry response, the backstairs coven decided, offered nothing sustaining to chew on. Typical, they agreed, of the Signora's erratic temperament. Nobody knew where they were with her. Overweeningly arrogant, some found her. Hadn't everyone tried to get on intimate terms? You'd think she'd welcome the company, her being alone as she was. It wasn't as though she did any work these days. But no, she went on in her own senseless, supercilious way, walking up and down her room till four o'clock in the morning, keeping the tenant below tossing and turning. What were her worries? Why didn't she seek the wise counsel they were dying to offer?

And in that ridiculous dress of hers, so Angelina reported, she looked absolutely unreasonable.

TWENTY

During the weeks leading up to Christmas, the city's music changed. All Venice was sunk in her usual seasonal torpor beneath a moisture laden mist. A muted percussion of coughs and sneezes carried through the gloom, answered by bassoon notes of vessels snuffling out deep water channels through the treacherous lagoon. Cafés furled their awnings and there was an end to aimless outdoor sauntering on quay, *campo* and *piazza*. Pedestrian excursions were a dogged, plashing business.

Twice a day the water rose to cover the Riva degli Schiavoni and half the Piazzetta knee deep in water. Isobel went down there to check on her stall and found it gone. An idler skimming about the inundated quay told her that the Yugoslav portrait maker had dismantled it, post and plank, and taken it away on his skiff to Torcello. He had, of course, an outboard motor.

Calling out to the unknown oarsman, Isobel asked him to thank Dragan for her and say she would come out and see him later, guessing she would not. They both had too much to do. Her news about the university's magnanimity would have to wait till the summer came again.

Isobel established a working routine, eschewing all classes that did not add to her technical dexterity. Appreciation of this work or that was not in her line. It was doing not looking, emulating not marvelling that took up her time.

Armed with the professor's letter, however, she went out two or three times a week, to visit some locked *scuola* or temporarily deserted residence. She was admitted by doddering retainers to wander at will among sheeted furniture. At her word, blinds were thrown up, and refreshments, unasked for, brought.

The terms of her introduction were broad in scope and authoritative in tone. In the miniature metropolis of Venice, the professor's signature carried weight.

Would this little table, placed at such an angle to the light, meet the *egregia studentessa*'s needs? When she had done with making her notes and sketches in this chamber, the elderly, knee-breeched parties without exception promised, they would be honoured to show her the remainder of the suite.

Coughing, these attendants slid respectfully away, remarking only that the *egregia studentessa* was fortunate not to suffer with her chest.

In echoing halls and mouldering chapels she seized upon ingredients for the dishes she planned to cook at home. Brand-new Titians, Tiepolos, and Tintorettos ... Veroneses and Vivarinis. Similar models, similarly dressed and posed, engaged in appropriately heroic or sensual activity. Simple copying, Isobel found, was restrictive compared with pastiche which offered a limitless cornucopia of fun.

After a sleep of centuries, these long dead masters' subjects could be woken up again and made to change their clothes ... seen in new perspectives doing different things.

By the first week in December, Isobel had two imaginary noblewomen and a nude picnic party well on the go. Ed's face had crept into that one. It was a shock to Isobel to see how spontaneously her hand conjured his features from clouded regions, distant in her memory. The necromancer's art.

Others, with the lean groundwork laid in, were coming along. Scaled on to small canvases which would fit into a suitcase, they should go very well in summer. With continual use of the gas oven to dry and age successive layers of paint, she could turn them out completed at the rate of three a week. Not fast enough. Dietetically limiting, too.

Sandro was dispatched to locate additional facilities. With the best will in the world and the silveriest tongue, he could not persuade a single restaurant to bake his mother's paintings overnight in the catering ovens.

"What? Not even for money?" Isobel frowned.

"They don't want the taste of turpentine getting into the food ..."

"It's never bothered *us* before, has it?"

Rolling his eyes heavenward, Sandro refrained from pointing out to his mother that for many weeks past, they had eaten nothing but fried food and stews. And most of the latter boiled dry in the pan and had to be hacked out with knives. His mother could not divide her concentration.

In the end he proposed an exploration of the dockside rubbish tips to Isobel. There were often discarded cookers and so forth there. How did he know this? Isobel pounced on him. Ready for her, Sandro told her that bigger boys had so informed him. Salvaging sheet metal for scrap merchants was the prestige trade for teenaged youths. Virtuously, Sandro reckoned he wasn't old enough to join them yet. Maybe when he was ten ...

Inveigled into a scavenging foray by her desire for ovens, Isobel went with Sandro in his slender, curl toed Turkish slipper barque to interview the father of a friend of his who owned a boatyard. The *sandolino*, in land transport terms a mere bicycle, was far too small for carrying heavy loads. They would need something sturdier, broader in the beam, possibly with an engine. Sandro had it planned. His mother, who was too ignorant to fulfil the duties of skipper, could swing the engine while he took the tiller.

Diverted at the prospect of this waterborne rag and bone collecting jaunt, Isobel set out with Sandro merrily. When hailed, the boatbuilder clambered over his hugger mugger pile of filleted hulks and a half-built gondola to greet them, tousling Sandro's hair. What a boy he was! Top of his form by all accounts and the smartest little errand runner in the district. He shook Isobel's hand in the friendliest manner.

Yes, he would gladly let them borrow a small commercial barge he had tied up alongside on his *fondamente*. She would do their job. Sandro could be trusted, he said, to observe the traffic rules and keep them out of trouble. But as for competing on the tips ... he had better send his own son with them. And a bottle of mineral water, one of wine, a hunk of bread, some cheese, a cross-bred Alsatian dog called Sarpi and two very large umbrellas. The picnic party atmosphere reconciled Sandro to his loss of leadership.

The four of them chugged about the scummy margins of the docks, happy in each others' company. Sarpi rode shotgun on the forepeak, quivering with animosity at rival canine mariners. Sandro and the older boy tried to teach Isobel dialect. She could not begin to get it, which pleased them, naturally.

In three or four hours they saw plenty of cookers but Isobel was choosy. She didn't want the top bit with the burners. She knew there was a type without. Couldn't they search a little further? It turned out she had misremembered what she thought she wanted. However, they did find a couple of old Belling table-top cookers with good oven space and minimum superstructure. Would they work, Isobel asked, slogging up a shifting scree of rusty cans and bottles. They looked as if they would, sprouting with wires and things. A shouted conversation with some boys carting a fridge away, suggested that the cookers had only arrived the previous day. Should be all right. Getting them home and trying them was the only way to tell.

On the way back to the boatbuilder's yard, the rain came down in lances, digging deep holes in the water's surface and steaming

Sarpi's coat. Sitting astern with Sandro, sheltering under one of the umbrellas, the day lodged itself in Isobel's memory as one of pellucid amity with herself, her son and the life they were making together.

How many such days in a lifetime does any mother enjoy?

* * *

The arrival of the ovens on the *fondamente* side of the *palazzo*, kindly delivered by the boatbuilder's son and touchingly provided with plugs, occasioned another bout of surreptitious shutter creaking. Venetians, always so childishly keen to cloak their own smallest affairs in mystery, are correspondingly avid to know those of others.

So it caused a deal of ire but no surprise when the fuses blew that evening, plunging half the building into darkness. Worse, the television sets of Isobel's nearest neighbours went inscrutably dark and silent. A catastrophe for which, after a baleful pause, Isobel was roundly cursed. Her and her ovens. What was she about?

There were shouts of vexation, banging doors and thudding feet on the stairs and in the corridors. Within minutes a deputation was hammering on Isobel's door. She let them in although she couldn't understand what the power cut had to do with her.

She was very soon enlightened. The circuit was overloaded. Scuffling in drawers to find a candle, she heard voices, old and young, male and female, name a dozen different electricians who lived nearby. In time, one nominee was settled upon. He was a wizard at bodging old wiring systems. He would certainly come and restore the current even on a wet winter's night like this . . . at a special, emergency rate. There was no question but that the Signora *Isabella* would pay it, since it was her rank stupidity alone which had precipitated the outrage.

While the electrician was fetched Isobel found herself playing hostess to a mob in no hurry to withdraw. At a loose end since the surcease of televisual entertainment, they poked about in the rooms they had not had the pleasure of inspecting since she took up the tenancy. Two of the best, they said. Pleasant to have one with a garden outlook, especially so when the wisteria bloomed . . . What rent did she pay?

Ah, this table with the porpoise pedestal was the landlady's property, was it not? The Signora had no lock on her shutters . . . She must have that attended to . . . They thought only of her welfare. Yes, she had kept things quite bare . . . which, someone sniffed, was thought very good style by *some* . . . The stove, to be sure, was the finest in the house. Almost, you would think, a cast iron replica of San Marco . . .

"It gives off very little heat," Isobel muttered. "It's these funny trumpet flues . . ."

Venetian chimneys were the best in the world, came back a reproving chorus. Built to an exclusive, fire-defensive design . . . never bettered since the fourteenth century . . .

"Oh, please be careful in that corner," Isobel cut across the by now familiar litany of Venetian supremacies, "I've got some things spread out on the floor . . ."

At that moment the lights came on and Isobel's visitors saw what she'd been doing.

For a moment nothing was said while they leaned, craned and jostled each other. Approbation rumbled from the men. They twanged their braces and scratched their heads. A descant of feminine exclamation took over. At first, Isobel was touched and patted, a queer creature to be propitiated. And then she was warmly hugged on every side.

It was not long before bottles of wine appeared from nowhere and Isobel found herself giving a party, amazed at herself for having rather damp eyes.

Her guests, she knew, didn't at all understand the work they saw. She honestly tried to make plain the difference between copyist, *pasticheur* and original artist. She had borrowed style and method, she protested, filched subject matter and recomposed . . . It was a kind of cheating. She wasted her breath.

What Isobel's neighbours recognised, small traders, dockers, simple widows and spinsters, was a reaffirmation of their notion of art, inherited from all they daily saw around them. What was the point of all these other self-styled artists coming here, huffing and puffing on roofs in the summer, daubing their dismal daubs? Making utter fools of themselves and Venice. Couldn't draw a straight line to save their lives, most of them. Such stupid words they used to give themselves excuses. *Post* this and *neo* that. Pah!

Here was someone, on the other hand, who knew an artist's proper business. To make sumptuous, the world. To show living, breathing beings majestically at leisure or nobly misbehaving themselves in the way that art alone could justify . . . and respectable folk unblushingly enjoy. Who was this naughty lady busy pleasuring her servant?

Glancing at the half-finished painting mentioned, Isobel was about to say that the female in question was an amalgam of other people's ideas of Venus. And sure enough, the well fed flesh reclined supine on the painted grass without a hint of muscle tone. Quite in the approved manner. But the face, she noticed for the first time, had a decided look of Lucy Larizzi. Isobel repressed a snort of laughter. Fatter cheeks would fix it.

"Oh, no one in particular," she answered aloud. "Just a general sort of Jezebelly type . . ."

More wine was brought.

Pronounced a genius, in spite of everything she could do to disown the title, Isobel was obliged, in the end, to wear her undeserved laurels. There were some benefits. Her oddities, tempers and excesses were excused. Artists were always barmy. Unfitted, poor things, for everyday existence.

As for Signorino Sandro, the fatherless *poverino*, he too was seen in a new and benignant light. A loner, a leader, a bit of a philosopher, too. His mother's son, of course. A credit to her. How old was he now? Eight, nine . . . only six! My, how he grew. Well, the Signora herself was exceptionally tall . . .

After this impromptu exhibition of her work, Isobel went to bed moderately content. Years of stop-go effort, frustration and failure had culminated in this qualified success. The individual skills, so long and ardently pursued, were now assembled in her hand, making it at last a supple, reliable engine. All she need do to keep it so, was to oil it with continual practice.

Stimulated by the unusual amount of company, warmed, too, by its unstinting praise, she lay awake some time. It was possible, even probable, that this was the only kind of work she might ever do. And as long as she never pretended to herself or anyone else that it was other than it was, revisionist . . . frankly unoriginal, why should she expect to be better than any glass-blower, shipwright or chef?

She was a craftswoman. That was what it was. This was the stopping place. These paintings would pay the rent. People liked them and she liked doing them. Not many could earn a crust so pleasantly. Perhaps, if she could build up a stock, she might give up the stall and lease a tiny shop. A kind of poor man's gallery. Only she would sell her own work and take all the money. No percentages. Isobel squiggled her toes in triumph.

Grateful to have reached this milestone, she let go of all thoughts of fame or status. There was none of that these days for representational, figurative artists. Unless they were into bean cans. To make a name, a serious modern artist, like Dragan, had to depict an inner vision sparely and be prepared to talk about it . . . lots.

Isobel's inner visions were not for publication. Most of the time now, they grumbled submissively like mangy circus lions, cowering down before their ring master's psychic force.

In the room next door, Sandro too, was wide awake. For once

he wasn't lying rigid, ears twitching for the sound of mice. He had graver matters on his mind.

Who had his father been? This evening, when everything happened about the lights and *Mamma*'s paintings, people had started asking him. In the past, he'd shrugged off the same question from other children and adults by saying simply, that he didn't know. Now he found he wished for information. After all, his mother clearly was somebody important. He had always thought so.

Padding into Isobel's room, he prodded her awake just minutes after she had fallen into sleep.

"Yes. What is it? Do you feel sick?"

"No. Who was my father?"

"Oh darling," Isobel groaned, "I'll tell you in the morning."

"No. Now. I want to know."

Sitting up, Isobel looked at him and said, "He was a Milanese businessman."

"Businessmen are rich. Why are we so poor?"

"Well, he was very young, you see . . ."

"As young as me?"

"Oh no, darling. Not quite as young as you . . ."

"Was he *going* to be rich?" Sandro demanded.

"Yes, darling. Very. Do you want to get into my bed?"

"I see," replied Sandro, scrambling in beside her. "He was just like me. I shall be very, very rich when I grow up. You won't have to paint any more and you can live in a whole *palazzo*."

That was an eerie echo of Furio's ambitions for her. He had said something like it that time he guessed Sandro was on the way. Except, of course, that his hopes had been falsely disappointed. Never mind . . .

"Hmm. I like your cuddly smell," Sandro's cheek felt smooth, rubbed against her shoulder.

Turning her back carefully on her son's snuggling body, Isobel made stagy yawning noises. Innocent as he was, Sandro possessed a disturbing magnetism.

*   *   *

"You cannot go alone," Angelina removed the last basting thread from the hem of Isobel's green evening gown. Ten and a half centimetres of black velvet had been added and the garment now looked splendid. "It is not for decent women . . ."

"Nonsense, Angelina." Isobel twitched the hem away from the wittering washerwoman's fingers, disliking her strictures as they might be near the truth. She looked over her shoulder to admire the train's effect. "The Casino Invernale is a respectable municipal institution, not a knocking shop. I need a change of scene. I shall go, look about me, drink an orange juice perhaps, and come home as soon as I feel bored. When that will be, I can't predict. Sandro can stay up as long as you do. He'll be fine in your camp-bed."

"But if you are approached, Signora . . ."

"Approached?" Isobel twirled her skirts delightedly, scattering the pins that Angelina had been crawling round the parquetry floor to gather. "What do you mean by that? Oh get up. I'll look for the pins tomorrow. Where's my cloak?"

Isobel arrived before the Casino's winter headquarters at the Palazzo Vendramin in a hired motorboat. It was a hideous expense because the place could be easily reached on foot through a few narrow, twisting *calles*, no great distance from her home. Still, that would have been infra dig and a poor beginning to the outing. Pedestrians could expect scant respect in Venice.

"*Buona sera, Signora*," the liveried footman who helped her disembark at the private, lamplit landing stage addressed her. "You are to join which party?" he added, seeing she had no escort.

He was curious to know. Isobel's appearance was, to say the least, romantic. Her hair, newly washed, radiated round her head in starry points. The collared, black velvet cloak (another pawnshop find) swung open to disclose a handsome gown. She had no necklace but a matching velvet bow tied with bravura below her right ear in which was fixed a pretty jewel of quality. A mask, maybe, the footman noticed, but not a tourist gewgaw.

Like all those accustomed to attend upon the rich, the footman had a nose for authenticity. The hand that touched his lightly, conducted a prickling, hyper-vitalised reality. A palpable enchantment, evoking the lamented era when all Venice went masked about its winter pleasures . . . Intrigues and assignations . . .

The footman shook himself. What was he thinking of? Here was just another patron's guest to be installed among her friends.

"Your party, Signora?" he said again.

"I'm my own party," Isobel smilingly replied in English, passing through the doors. She surmised the footman's knowledge of that language did not encompass double meanings.

Her pun was overheard, however, by someone with a more sophisticated grasp. Discarding her cloak with a superbly careless gesture into another footman's extended arms, Isobel turned to find herself face to face with a personable man in evening dress standing just behind her. His deportment was erect, his stature, small.

"I too am forced to make my own amusement this evening," he said. "May I introduce myself?" He took her hand and bowed over it, clicking his heels. He straightened to reveal a gap toothed grin, widening between bluish lips, glinting from lashy, treacle coloured eyes.

"I suppose you may," Isobel jokingly coquetted, "'though I'm not sure you should . . . My laundress warned me against speaking to strange men. But then, she is a prude."

The lupine smile lit up again, a flash of gold among the ivory. "My name is Mahmoud al Hamid bin Sur. I am Egyptian, as in modern times all my family have been. None the less, in former days, we were hereditary Deys of Algiers."

"Ah, pirates," said Isobel, who knew about the Barbary Coast.

"You wound me, madam," he steered her to a group of plush upholstered chairs framed in gilt rococo arabesques. "That is not work for gentlemen. I can assure you, my forefathers confined themselves to taking ten per cent. And you? You will confide in me, your name . . . ?"

"Isobel," she announced promptly.

That was a serious mistake. To the Egyptian, the absence of a surname implied that the forename was a *nom de guerre*. And a young woman without companions necessarily invited predators. By claiming one name only, Mahmoud was certain, she deliberately advertised her status. Surprising. Conveniences of this sort were notoriously sparse in Venice and when found, were never more than dog's meat. This was something of an entirely different calibre.

"I've come to look at the rooms and watch people gambling," Isobel revealed her purpose. "Are you going to gamble?"

"I may," the Egyptian answered, watching her closely. "It is fortunate that the game which will claim my attention does not begin in earnest till tomorrow. There is to be a big baccarat table for international punters. It will last a week. The directors are giving a dinner tonight to welcome the invited participants, of whom I chance to be one."

"Then I'm keeping you," she rose in her chair. "Please don't . . ."

"It is of no consequence. The dinner does not begin until eleven o'clock, then there will be a warm up game until half past four or so. I assure you, I shall not be missed. You will drink champagne?"

"Well, if you're sure . . ."

Mahmoud snapped his fingers at a passing waiter who hurried to his side. Isobel couldn't think of any good reason why she should refuse. Money was hardly a point at issue . . . This man was very rich and perfectly polite. In a public place like this, it must be all right . . . He was fascinating too, with his uniform, helix curls so precisely arranged above his brow. And he could tell her all about the Casino and the games played there. A piece of unexpected luck. This was experience . . . a valuable investment.

"Tell me . . . Isobel," he asked her after a silver bucket had been placed beside them, "what is *your* game?" He looked deep, too deep, into her eyes.

"I don't have one," Isobel disconcertedly replied, thinking she had already made that clear. "I only want to look at the people. Their clothes, you know. And to see if they look different when they lose a lot of money. Things like that . . . they interest me."

An hour later, Mahmoud had walked Isobel round the attractions in the glittering Long Room. She had seen *vingt-et-un*, faro, roulette and craps. And not a few of the players and spectators assembled there had seen Isobel. Her costume, for the place, was no more than averagely extravagant. Stylish, none the less. But it was her bearing, unaffected and *réclame*, which drew so many second glances. Who was she? And what could she be doing with a shit like Mahmoud? He didn't bother much with women. His tastes were more specialised than that.

"Low stakes for amateurs," he remarked, skirting the rising springs of interest as they moved among the tables. They looked high enough to Isobel. The least valuable plaques were marked ten thousand lire. "You would like to play?"

Isobel said no, but he sent for some plaques anyway, signing the cashier's chit when the messenger returned with them.

"Come, you shall help me place my bets. Roulette."

Isobel helped to the extent of covering the zero with a fifty-thousand-lire plaque. The rest of the table seemed to be already tiled with Mahmoud's money.

"You'll lose overall," she whispered to him as the croupier set the wheel in motion. "Won't you? Unless zero comes up. Why ever do you do it?"

"Let us wait," he said, intent on the rattling metal ball.

It came to rest in the zero slot to moans and gasps of wonder. The croupier's face was slate-blank as he pushed a clacking pile of plaques in Isobel's direction. A mountain.

"You wish to cash your winnings, or will you play some more?"

Isobel protested vigorously. This was not her money. Had she ever thought she would be subjected to this embarrassment she would never have touched the plaques. Might her cloak be sent for?

Mahmoud was all remorse. He had no wish to offend her, but equally, she must not hurt him either. She had misunderstood his gesture. It was customary among professional gamblers . . .

especially in the East . . . to sacrifice the fruits of preliminary play to appease the jealous gods.

He had never, he claimed with beseeching eyes, supposed for a single moment, that Isobel would keep the money for herself. But naturally not. She would distribute it among the poor for him and thus bring luck to his baccarat game. He was so sorry. He had forgotten, amid all the understandable astonishment, that she could not know the custom. A superstitious sentiment, no doubt, but not to be disdained.

Beguiled by this mythology, Isobel simmered down. She had been wrong-footed, somehow, and felt under an obligation to show she bore no grudge. After some questions concerning the details of the alleged custom, all of which the Egyptian answered imaginatively, Isobel forgave him. So fortune was a goddess, was she, who expected presents? An interesting idea.

Presently, the money which had caused their dispute was brought to her in an envelope. Isobel put it in her evening bag, saying it should be given the following day to the administrator of an old people's home about to open in the Ghetto. Not that any amount could compensate the poor old things for having lived to remember what they did. They had numbers, some of them, tattooed on their wrists. It was impossible to meet their eyes. So saying, she missed the flicker behind Mahmoud's.

When he bade her follow so he could show her the private rooms, she did so. It was early yet and their quarrel was all over. There was bound to be a certain, special atmosphere in places where whole Aegean islands were staked against a card. Just to watch the drama cost fifty thousand lire.

The room they entered was empty. It was the usual Venetian thing. Etched mirror glass and tapestries, chandeliers, brocade and gilt. There was a brass rail to cordon off spectators. A sound of men's voices came from down the corridor. A cocktail party.

Isobel started to ask a few questions about the arrangement of the horseshoe table. She stopped when Mahmoud caught her forearm. He swung her bodily round to face him.

"What are you . . . ?"

"You've made your point. I haven't got all night . . . How much do you want, you clever Jewish bitch?"

Isobel knew she'd been led into a trap but her mind recoiled from determining its nature. Jewish? Mahmoud had her pinned against the table. He plucked at the neckline of her dress, nipping painfully at her breasts. His head only came up to her chin, Isobel noted. She would rather not shout, she thought, if it could only be avoided. This was a humiliating scene. And partly her fault. They had got their signals mixed. She pushed him away with considerable force, managing to dislodge his hold upon her briefly.

"Now look, Mahmoud . . ."

"What's your price?" His breath smelled of cardamon and toothpaste. "Double what I gave you? I expect to pay . . . Women can't come cheap in Venice. But I haven't time to pussy foot around too long . . . Don't overrate your charms, madam. For the week, how much? My launch will take you to the Cipriani . . . I have to go in to dinner shortly. Hurry up. How much?"

She assessed the room, the door's position and the few shallow steps ascending from the table which led past the brass rail. A straighforward exit looked nearly feasible.

"Would you please stand aside?" she said with dignity.

Maddened, the Egyptian gripped her by the shoulders. Isobel opened her mouth to shout but found the side of his hand jammed between her teeth.

"I need hardly remind one of your profession that prostitution is illegal in Venice. Make a noise and I will call the directors. They will certainly deliver you into the hands of the magistrates. Now, I have been patient . . ."

Isobel bit him until she tasted blood. It was the Egyptian who screamed. Her jaws clamped together in a spasm of rage, Isobel was unable to release him. She would have liked the noise to stop but couldn't at that minute think how to end it. It must all look very funny. A deerhound with a rabbit. She was chiefly anxious for her dress.

It was only when the door opened to reveal Josef Fischer's disbelieving features, that Isobel let the Egyptian go. He staggered before tripping on the steps.

Isobel and Josef stared at each other across his fallen body. Eventually she said:

"This man thinks I'm a streetwalker . . ."

"Then he has made an error," Josef flapped his arms in the plaintive way that Isobel remembered. His black, crinkly hair was speckled liberally with white and his cheeks, once plump, sagged about his mouth like empty purses. To Isobel, he seemed to have aged a generation since she had seen him last.

Six years had done the work of twenty.

*　　*　　*

Isobel recovered quickly from the farcical incident which had brought her together, once again, with Josef. After repeatedly assuring him that she was quite uninjured, he explained his presence.

The big baccarat game had been arranged by a syndicate in

co-operation with the Casino's directors. They would charge the usual house commission of five per cent on the syndicate's winnings with a further five per cent to be donated to the Save Venice Fund.

That's what the week's play was all in aid of. Fischer Industries, along with other major European companies had been invited to support the worthy cause. A refusal, Josef added drily, would provoke destabilising rumours. Saving Venice was the latest fashion in corporate charity. The game had received wide publicity . . . the Casino's altruistic contribution.

"But they can't lose," Isobel objected, peering at a blood spot on her skirt.

"What Venetian ever does?" Josef countered mildly.

Mahmoud represented the syndicate and would play as banker until Tuesday. Or at least he would have done, but Isobel would now, of course, press charges against him. The directors, jealous for their casino's reputation, might feel obliged to cancel the game. A scandal involving Carlo Bonetti's daughter-in-law would taint the atmosphere. A misdemeanour of such magnitude could hardly be hushed up.

Isobel differed with him there. A meeting with the directors themselves, however, was unavoidable. Too many people passing in the corridors were aware that an altercation had taken place in the *salle de baccarat*. It was officially barred until after the inaugural dinner . . . Who exactly had been tampering with the shoe? Who was this woman?

Telling her story to the line of long, closed faces ranged before her in a private anteroom, Isobel was not surprised that Venetians had abandoned the mask as regulation social dress. They didn't need it. Nor she hoped, did she.

"We got our wires crossed," she told them. "He thought I was a tart and I thought he was a gentleman. We were both wrong. He is hurt and I am not. And nobody touched the shoe or whatever it's called, if that's what's bothering you. There's no need for me to do anything or you to change anything."

"You are most generous . . . we are grateful for your attitude . . ." Scarcely parted lips uttered their approval. But where, they asked themselves, was the contractual nub? Isobel saw their minds ticking. What had Josef told them?

"My name is to be kept out of this," she said.

A reflective pause ensued.

"Sadly, we have had no time for introductions," was the eventual, grave response.

"And you'd better have this," Isobel extracted Mahmoud's roulette winnings from her bag. "The Dey of Algiers' deposit on my favours. Zero came up downstairs. He told me some cock and bull story about gamblers' charitable donations. Very pretty. I must say, I enjoyed it."

This produced some twitching lips and lifted eyebrows. Mahmoud was a great romancer. But he did not bribe croupiers on low stake tables. Zero had arisen like a star to greet another exception to the ordinary rules of chaos. Isobel herself. Even these things could be calculated.

"I'm obliged to you, Signores," Isobel smiled, seduced by the compliment. "And the money?" She held the envelope up.

Isobel was urged to apply it as she had first intended. She swished from the room with six pairs of considering eyes tracking after her. So that was the mother of the missing Bonetti heir. Nothing, however, could be said, bargains being sacred.

The Directors sent word that their unnamed guest was to be accommodated in the downstairs dining room where Herr Fischer had volunteered to join her.

"How's Estella?" Isobel asked when a lull in the formal observations about coincidence occurred.

"At school in Switzerland. She lives . . . we live in Geneva with my mother. And your son?"

"How do you know I have a son?" Isobel said sharply. "I never said so. I might have a daughter . . ."

Josef shrugged and Isobel abandoned that tack. Carlo Bonetti knew so many things although his intelligence was out of date. She felt aggrieved with him, suddenly, for giving up the chase. A perverse side effect of loneliness. Disappearance had meant obliteration. A twilight life. She made balls of wax from the candle drippings.

"Shall I tell you about my wife?" Josef said finally to break the silence. "I'm sorry, no . . ."

"Please do," Isobel replied. "We can't pretend she isn't the main thing we have in common. Is she any better?"

For the rest of the meal, Josef unburdened himself, telling it all from Nina's first residential enrolment at the clinic. She wore normal clothes now and had normally furnished rooms.

"So there's some improvement . . ."

"Not at all. She's cataleptic. She just sits there in the same position for hours and hours on end. When she's like that, you can pick up her limbs and move them anywhere. Like wax . . ."

"Like a living corpse . . ." Isobel bit her lip. "I'm sorry. I must sound callous. It shows you how desocialised I've become . . ."

"Where do you live, Isobel? And how? In Venice . . ."

Isobel resumed her manipulation of the candle wax, and shook

297

her head. She was not, she mused, a fugitive, exactly. More like a hibernating animal. And that was a posture that couldn't be altered on a thoughtless whim. An inviting vista, though, change.

But what kind of change and on what terms? How much, she wondered, would she lose by it, and what would Sandro gain? Wealth, education, family . . . position. His birthright. But to claim it for him would send shock waves through both their lives. Would they try to take him away from her?

"I don't know, Josef," she answered him obliquely. "How long will you be here?"

He would be here a few days. They talked some more of Nina. She spoke occasionally, in desultory mutters. Or keened noiselessly, rocking to and fro, day into night and night into day . . . Could be fed, slowly, from a spouted cup. Sometimes she would feed herself. Her other functions were erratic. Often, tears rolled down her immobile face. Then they would sedate her. Nobody knew her thoughts.

But there were brain scans and printouts. Long stuttering lines of ink on graph paper punctuated with jagged peaks and valleys.

"What do they mean?" Isobel leaned forward across the table.

She could guess. Intermittent, inescapable embraces with scaly, clawing things. Isobel too, had lived through them. Still did, from time to time. Only her struggles were with the shadows of Nina's memories. Nina had the real thing, trapped for ever in her mind.

"The peaks and valleys . . . ?"

"They call them indications of stress . . ."

"In other words," Isobel said tersely, "she thinks."

"They told me she would have no thoughts." Without warning, Josef began to weep. "A better man than me would kill her . . ."

Isobel simply sat and looked at him, unable to shield him from the stares of others. He did nothing to conceal his facial contortion. Isobel glanced down at the plate of black *tagliatelle* with mussels. A delicacy she loved. It might as well have been ribbons of aluminium with sandstone pebbles. The Fischer factor. From the start, it had made her life harder to live.

"What do you do, Isobel?" Josef said, his tears drying with the same abruptness that they had gushed.

"I paint," Isobel replied wintrily, gazing at the plate of calves' liver which followed the pasta. Another costly dish gone to waste. How Sandro would have relished it.

"You were quite good at that, weren't you?"

"Ah, the Signor, he is cheered now," the waiter interposed with sickly solicitude.

"Don't be impertinent," Isobel flashed.

It was half past two in the morning. And although the evening had been productive of both interest and excitement, Isobel was tired. She had been mistaken by turns for a prostitute and a cardsharp's hireling . . . and extricated herself with reasonable aplomb. It had been fun, in a way, that part. But Josef's despair had killed her appetite for more than food. She asked him to have them call a water taxi.

It was not to be. The directorate insisted that Isobel be conveyed home in the Casino's launch. She would have preferred it otherwise. Too much entanglement with these people could be compromising. There would be more information about her in circulation.

"It's the least they can do," Josef commented, placing her cloak about her shoulders. "You've just saved them a week's worth of unprecedented profits." He seemed apathetic at Isobel's going. "Don't worry about the waterman. In Venice they know what to pay for silence. You'll come again tomorrow? Or later . . . We can talk . . ."

"Yes, yes," Isobel kissed him firmly on both cheeks, desperate now, to get away.

On the landing stage, a stiff Adriatic breeze whipped her clothes and she felt better. From the watermen and footmen, there were ingratiating smiles and bows. The *eccelenza* who had arrived unknown was departing incognito.

Isobel brooded on that minute but significant transformation while the choppy canal waters bucked beneath her. It had been a classically Venetian interlude.

Identities had been mistaken, masks had been torn away and reassumed. There had been pacts and treaties. Infinities of mirror glass and multiplying images. A phosphorescent glitter of corruption. An antique comedy, aptly staged. Amusing. Except for Josef. They said everyone who was anyone came to Venice some time . . . to tip their hats to a world class memory. Even Nina had found a way. Josef lugged her everywhere, like a dead thing, stinking in a sack.

Alighting on her quay, Isobel smiled to see the rims of light appear round palace shutters here and there in the darkened building. How gratified they must all be that she hadn't slipped alongside in a stealthy gondola. The homely Venetian mice were cheeping.

Stirred by her collision with the whirling vortex of great affairs, Isobel paced up and down her apartment for many hours. Her mind was spinning, leaping with colours, shapes and creatures. When her legs would carry her no longer, she sank down at the table and drew a cartridge block towards her.

Her pencil scurried, darting after dreams and wraiths. There were far too many. Make them small and do them fast. Too late, too slow. That one had escaped, gone hurtling down its hole. Make notes . . . lists. Isobel did, encircling groups of words with circles. Formulas for pictures.

In the morning, Sandro came in from Angelina's to find his mother slumped across the table. She was fully clothed and the shutters were still closed. The stove was out and the room was freezing cold. There were sheaves of paper at her feet.

"Oh darling. I was very late . . ." Isobel passed a hand across her face, tight and smooth with sleep. "I had a wonderful time. Did you . . ."

"She's pretty," Sandro pulled the corner of a sheet that had been caught beneath his mother's elbow.

Confused for a moment, Isobel looked down.

"She was pretty. She may still be . . . I don't know."

It was Nina Fischer's face, beckoning with that aberrant, golden apples smile. In all, five pencil lines. Isobel's eye translated it into tone and texture. She could give it volume, weight and temperature. Body heat. She would have to do it.

TWENTY-ONE

I sobel did not return to the Casino the following night or on any other. She had three distinct reasons, each conspiring to keep her shut indoors.

In the first place, she had no stomach for another serving of leaden reminiscences from Josef. His despondency was claustrophobic. A dark, airless dungeon, the interior of which Isobel knew too well. Neither courtesy nor kindness would ever tempt her back there to bear a fellow prisoner company. He must feel the walls as she had, until he found the trap door's edge.

To add to that were the other hazards the week's baccarat game presented. Bonetti Construction would be sure to delegate a player. A nephew, a cousin . . . a senior executive. Perhaps Carlo himself would come. Isobel's half-acknowledged impulse to disclose herself, dispelled. Sandro would be asked to choose between his mother and his father's clan. How could a little boy do that? It would be cruel.

Sandro, Isobel persuaded herself, was better off as a happy water rat . . . pursuing small ambitions in the sea-city's tidal streets. At any rate, an upheaval now, for whatever reason would be highly inconvenient.

Along with the clinker choked stove, the unwashed dishes in the sink and the soft sausages of fluff fattening unchecked beneath the beds and cupboards, further consideration of Sandro's future would have to wait. Minor matters.

Isobel contemplated the signs of her own domestic ineptitude with wilful nonchalance. To her, it was a discipline. In order to get any worthwhile work done, one had to have a mind well above dust. Only amateurs believe that inspiration comes to a head stuck in the oven . . . or the creative twitch to hands desensitised by rubber gloves.

She was working, painting in a way she had never done before. Abducted, mentally and physically by forms to which she had previously denied concrete expression. Apart, that was, from those vitriolic scribbles made in the Tuscan farmhouse studio, which she had rigorously suppressed.

301

Quite right, too, she told herself. She hadn't been up to it then. Neither technically nor emotionally strong enough to grapple with the demon people. She was ready for them now.

Nina in her many guises . . . her mother, Rupert . . . Rosaria, Giulia Montenaro's maid . . . all queuing, obedient yet impatient for release in whatever shape Isobel chose to give them. They came, dual or multi bodied from her memory and imagination, bringing favoured objects and familiars with them. Symbolic luggage.

From time to time, Isobel consulted her notes, in the drily organisational spirit of a prison warder ticking off an exercise list. That person accounted for, this one requiring especial vigilance, others excused or waited for. All the spectres that had once controlled her were at her service now.

Better, they were at her mercy. In the first, savage frenzy of realisation, Isobel spared them nothing in the way of retaliation. She flayed, dismembered, distorted, reassembled and ridiculed them. Brush and charcoal were her weapons. Knives had rarely cut more keenly.

The Casino? Isobel had no time to spare away from her easel. She wasn't hungry . . . forgot to sort the laundry . . . had little cash and could not bear to drag herself to the bank. Too far, too long . . . a toilsome interruption.

Meals appeared sporadically and seldom. Isobel prepared them in a somnambulant daze, asking her son whether he wanted this or that and not listening to the answers. Then she watched him eat, riven by an agony of ruptured creative tension. She ate almost nothing herself and in such comfortless conditions, Sandro ate little more. He could not wait to leave the table. How many more times were they going to have dried pasta with canned tomatoes?

Sandro, who had suffered from his mother's absorptions in the past, took to foraging quietly for himself. It was no good talking to *Mamma* in this mood. It was worse, of course, far worse than usual.

At a loose end, sometimes, he groped beneath his bed and withdrew a cardboard box. In it, he kept a growing stock of banknotes. Tips, fees, commissions, the proceeds of outright sales. More than sufficient to see him through his mother's trance. Squatting over his exchequer, Sandro took comfort in his money.

Occasionally, he had dreamy moments when he felt lost. Mislaid. When would his mother return to him? Be really, properly present. Was there really no one else in the world who belonged to him? If they got a dog . . . But whenever Sandro thought of dogs an inexplicable lump of misery would stifle him momentarily. He smelled earth, dry, crumbly stuff . . . not the Veneto's slopping bog. It was something about separation that his memory could not reach. Like the time before he was born. As far as Sandro knew, he had only ever lived in Venice.

For the next ten days, Sandro kept his mother supplied with snacks. He placed a square of cold *polenta* or hunks of bread and cheese down beside her on the table. Food, he found, worked better this way. No glares or sighs.

"Um . . . Could I have some wine . . . Is there some?"

She never took her eyes away from canvas, board or sketching block.

"When will you have finished?" Sandro asked, pouring Tuscan wine which he had bought himself, knowing his mother preferred its richness to the Veneto's insipid product.

"Soon, darling, soon. Maybe tomorrow. Are you busy?"

Irritable, Sandro shrugged.

"Because, if not, I've got a job for you. There's an envelope in my handbag. Will you get it and take it across the bridge into the Ghetto? Take it to the old people's home. I don't know where it is. You probably do. Ask if you don't. Just leave it . . . post it through the letterbox. There's no need to say where it came from. I don't want people coming here or talking to me . . . Would you, darling?"

It was an order, not a question. Sullenly, Sandro took the envelope and opened its unsealed flap. Inside there was an awful lot of money in fragrant, brand-new banknotes. Sandro pressed the envelope to his face, inhaling deeply.

"It's money," he breathed ecstatically.

"I know," Isobel said. "Just take it, darling. As I said."

"Where did you get it?"

"Is that your business? Actually, I won it."

Sandro started to protest. Why give away so much? Why give any? Didn't they always have a use for money? Isobel, exasperated at all this unwanted conversation, snatched at the envelope. She supposed, as Sandro was being so stupidly obstructive, she'd have to go herself and waste a lot of precious time. Didn't Sandro realise that paint with mastic in it hardened quickly?

They wrangled for a space, more like malcontented spouses than a mother with her son. In the end, Sandro reluctantly did as he was told. Isobel gave herself a moment to look out on the *rio* side of the building and watch him trot, grumpily across the little, humping bridge. An appealing child, she thought, well made and manly. A dearly loved damn nuisance.

Isobel felt badly. It was true about the mastic and Sandro often went to the Ghetto on his own. It was no distance. But perhaps they should have gone together. Sandro was at the end of his tether with her, she knew. But she couldn't cut herself down the middle, could she? And it was difficult to remember, that despite his height and companionable maturity, Sandro was really only very small.

Small or not, Sandro knew his way around. The Ghetto *campo* was one of the few big enough to play football in. Up and down the staircases of the grim, encircling towers, Sandro had friends. Not intimates, because these solemn, sloe eyed boys wore silly looking skullcaps, fixed to their hair with women's hair grips and spent too much time at school.

Their mothers nagged incessantly from plain, square windows high above the *campo*, in complaining, singsong voices. It was time for Talmud school, time for Hebrew or music lessons . . . or Shabat had started . . . they were to be careful of their shoes. What was that? A bag of crisps . . . Where had it come from? Was it kosher? They led tedious lives, circumscribed by rules. No good, Sandro told himself, for business.

But oh, how their mothers cooked! Sandro had come in for quite a few stray bowls of chicken soup and was partial to honey smothered pastries. With this degree of familiarity he lost no time in locating the old people's home. Just behind the *campo*'s only tree.

The administrator, a kindly woman in her fifties questioned Sandro closely. This was a great sum for a little boy to carry. Yes, he said, the gambling profits of a *contessa* great and good who lived far away in Dorsaduro. Three-quarters of a mile *was* far by Venetian standards. It fully justified the two notes Sandro peeled from the wedge with moistened thumb before regretfully delivering up the rest. Transportation costs.

"What costs?" asked the woman smiling, pinching Sandro's cheek. Sandro, she knew. That he should have no family . . .

"Just costs," he replied airily, before vanishing on twinkling feet. His quicksilver mind was already busy with another project. Something interesting to do.

How much produce would he need to buy, and what sort, to load on to his *sandolino* and offer at the Casino's kitchen doors? He badly needed to talk to someone in the know there. To make some useful contacts. What was gambling exactly? How did people do it? It couldn't be too difficult if *Mamma* could manage it. He, Sandro, would look into things.

*   *   *

"Sorry, pal," Max Cooper cradled the telephone between his shoulder and jaw, staring fixedly at the unframed canvases the gallery's

304

black porter was holding up before him, "I gotta problem selling the junk I got here already."

Indignant squawkings on the other line greeted this remark. Max glanced towards where his partner, Lucy Larizzi, was filing her nails, felicitously perched on the edge of a boule and ormolu secretaire. This joker was one of her so-called finds . . . He did wish she wouldn't sit on the furniture . . . That secretaire had cost a heap of dough . . .

"Okay, okay. I'm sorry I said that. They're great works . . . seminal, like you say, pal." More squawkings. Max grimaced. "We gotta go softly . . . I don't wanna flood the market. Three canvases a year. I can't take more. Yeah, yeah baby. Okay now. You keep in touch."

The receiver rattled back on to its cradle.

"Why do you always say that, Max, when you mean drop dead?" Lucy shifted her weight gorgeously from one buttock to the other.

Great ass, Max thought for the millionth time. Kinda made up for her brain. Spoke a heap of languages, too. Almost as many as he did. You had to have that, dealing on the international art market.

"Aw c'mon, Loo. You gotta give these guys something to hang on to. Starving in a trailer park some place ain't a load of laughs."

"Fine words butter no parsnips," Lucy said righteously, putting away her nail file.

"No shit?" Max retorted. Larizzi was full of snotty English nursery garbage. What did goddamned parsnips have to do with anything? But she had class. And her title . . . and her fanny. She could charm big zeros out of Iowa hayseed billionaires. Hadn't shucked a lot of corn lately, though. Fact was, the paintings in the gallery right now were a load of unadulterated, unmitigated, cotton picking crap.

"What do you think of them?" Lucy jerked her head at the parade of paintings that Jep, the porter, was taking on and off the display easel. "I think they have a kind of explosive quality . . . full of Andalusian fire . . ."

"You do? Shit," said Max bitterly. "You gotta realise, Loo. Chucking all this industrial paint ain't art any more. It's history. We haven't sold one of these multicoloured vomit jobs in months."

Lucy sighed. "So what do I tell the guy?"

"Tell him to get some drawing lessons. What does he look like?" Lucy pouted. "Sweet."

"Okay," Max grunted. "You got it. We'll give him an exhibition. Maybe the Manhattan mommas will wanna smooch him up. Buy the painting, shag the painter. Take the fucking things away, Jep, and gemme a pastrami sandwich from the deli. No, ham."

Max really hated ham but he didn't like to overdo the Jewish thing. Or do it at all, in fact. It was limiting. Long since, he'd started telling everyone he came from down Wyoming way. They could believe it or not as they chose. As Max saw it, misfortune was like a bad cold. Private property. Decent guys kept it to themselves.

This Spanish dude . . . maybe they could push a couple of his paintings on his sexual potential. Loo would have checked that out. She always did. She had an unerring instinct for the all important peripheral aspects of selling art. Real taste.

"We'll need head shots," he continued. "Then I want them blown up . . . big and moody. I wanna see suffering . . . Or is he mean?"

"Mean," Lucy advised. "I'd sell him on mean."

"Yeah," Max observed. "One day, just one day, before I die, I'd sure like to sell a guy on talent . . . or even a goddam dame."

Which brought them, by means of a roundabout conversational route, on to Isobel Jefferson.

"Bonetti, now, or was," Lucy reminded Max. "I went to the wedding. He died, her husband. Then she shacked up with an American . . . nice chap. I saw them. Had a cottage in Tuscany . . . Isobel had a studio. I said we'd take a look at her stuff but she went all coy about it. Then she disappeared."

"Great," said Max indifferently. "Nice work, Loo. At least you lost a hobby painter . . ."

"No, not that exactly. A few people I know said she was a cut above. Pretty serious about it, too."

Max, deeply depressed, admired his new gold bracelet. He liked these heavy curb chain links. Looked real good with his Rolex oyster. Covered up his skin graft, too. Gold . . . you could never have too much. A comfort to a poor sodding art dealer with nothing to look forward to but some lousy spic sexual athlete and a ham sandwich. Talent? Forget it. Did Salvador Dali's agent get all this grief, he wondered.

Globular, over fond of personal garniture, Max's unprepossessing exterior hid a romantic soul. The thing about art was that it offered scope. Not just dollars but hope. The lousy world was full of lousy corners. Round one of them there must be a world class talent just waiting for discovery, encouragement, and yeah, love. Max was lonely.

"Right, I'm off," Lucy hunched herself into a sable coat. "Lunch. I'll drum up some advance publicity for Pedro's exhibition. Cheer up, Maxie darling."

"Pedro? You gotta be joking. Sounds like some jerk on a goddam donkey. He just better look good this boy. Yeah, and another thing Loo, try and teach your editor pals that Krug isn't the only goddam drink on sale . . ."

But Lucy was already half way through the smoked glass doors, satirically held open for her by Jep who'd returned with the ham sandwich in a greasy paper bag. A blast of New York's foul wet breath swept through the gallery.

"Shut the goddam doors, can't you," Max snarled at his factotum. "I got highly sensitive works of art in here."

"Thought you said they was no good, boss," Jep taunted, slapping down the sandwich.

"They ain't, which is why you and me's gotta pretend all the harder, boy," Max began to munch the sandwich bravely.

"That slice of little piggy sure going to make a Jew boy I know sick," Jep needled.

"Get out of here, nigger," Max said matily. "I gotta look at the goddam mail yet."

Routine for the most part, the mail contained the usual clutch of invitations to professional, semi-professional and art school exhibitions. Max sorted through them. The *Biennale*, held only once every two years in Venice, would open again next June. Lucy was invited to the private viewing . . . as she would be to the Royal Academy's the month before. The usual milk round.

What about Peru? Ethnics were puking up cash quicker than a one armed bandit, these days. Max tittered softly at the thought of Lucy, hacking her way through the jungle in hot pursuit of Indian boys.

Toddling into his pink porphyry washroom, he thought fleetingly of Isobel. So she pissed off some place, did she? So fucking *what*? Why the hell had they been wasting time talking about some pampered Anglo-Saxon baby? Max was surprised he could remember her. Paint? How could she? She'd been brought up in the wishy washy English watercolour world of happily ending fairy tales, woolly mittens and early nights.

Max's lip curled in a mixture of contempt and envy, after which he heaved into the lavatory pan. Jesus, how he hated ham.

* * *

The day before Christmas Eve, Isobel made an expedition to Torcello. An act, as she perceived it, of pure self-sacrifice.

At the back of her mind, she knew the airing would do her good. She needed it. But what was that when there was work at home which needed *her*? To be exiled from its very presence was an acute privation.

307

The fact that she could make no progress with any of the paintings she had in hand was neither here nor there. In each case, paint, fat with oil, would take several days or even weeks to dry. Anything added before that happened would merely sink and murk, dulling the impact of what was already there. The ovens were all right for ageing imitations. For authentic, new work, they were inappropriate.

Of course, she could get on with her little Venetian revival paintings as she called them. They had been abandoned lately. As much as Isobel felt guilty about anything, she felt some remorse at this. These paintings for the tourist trade were bread and butter. The others, well, they were self-indulgence. Wonderful only to herself. Things she had to do to make peace within herself.

Eager to complete the series, much of which consisted, still, only of notes to reconstitute her imagination, Isobel also dreaded finishing. What would she do then . . . *really* do? Life would be stale, flat and empty. Could she go back to regurgitating other people's work and not feel second rate?

Biting her flannel in the bath, Isobel asked herself these questions. It was, she admitted silently, nice to have a bath. Had Sandro had one lately? She hadn't . . . not for ages . . .

And so, to Torcello, in clean corduroys and socks. Gun, in its canvas carrying bag . . . cartridges and gumboots. They would have to have something splendiferous to eat over the Christmas festival. Isobel was not paying fancy prices in the market for some sad creature that had approached its sordid end in an agony of fear. And definitely not a stringy, fishy seagull hanging forlornly from a string. No, she could do better than that and must make the effort for Sandro's sake.

He was at the boatyard today. They'd had a quarrel that morning followed by a crying fit on both sides and lots of cuddles. A good thing to clear the atmosphere.

Christmas was Christmas, after all. A clean white page, bound in for respite between all the chapters of messy, mortal life. Her father had said that.

The journey involved two separate *vaporetto* lines and took the better part of an hour and a quarter. Visibility wasn't bad. There was the usual traffic. A bright red Fire department launch . . . and a funeral, lush with wind chilled flowers, billowing with women's veils, sootily intense against the lagoon's lazy, platinum sheen. A good day to be buried . . . a better one to shoot.

Not that Isobel was much of a shot. She spent more than three chilly hours among the whispering reed beds, crouching in a punt, hired from and propelled by some toothless ancient. After the fruitless expenditure of many shells, she got two duck and some sort of moorhen. Gummily, the punt man grinned. Isobel gave him the moorhen.

Before returning home, she sploshed through Torcello's muddy, unpaved *campo*. There was a low roofed *cantina* there with steamed up windows. Isobel pushed open the door, whereupon all conversation died abruptly. Visitors in winter were not expected, especially unaccompanied females. Gnarled, suspicious faces stared at Isobel. Dragan's was not amongst them. The barman, however, gave grudging directions to the Yugoslav's cottage, pointing out that he didn't welcome callers.

Scraping open his planked door, a few moments later, Dragan gazed out blearily. Oh, it was her, was it? He supposed she'd better come in. He wore striped pyjamas underneath his sweater and they showed below his trouser bottoms. Isobel gave him one of her ducks, and made as if to leave. She had disturbed him.

But no, he wanted to talk about his work, suddenly. So Isobel was urged into the low raftered room where Dragan hurriedly covered a greyish, unmade bed and bade her be seated on it. There was nowhere else. All the rest of the available space was thickly cluttered with studio impedimenta.

"You want a drink?"

Isobel nodded. She might as well. It was cold in here. The stove, untended by the look of it for hours, was nearly out. On it stood a crock of cooked rice from which Dragan clearly helped himself by the handful whenever hunger took him. Disgusting.

She was grateful for the rice-mash spirit when it came, drawn from a carboy in the loft where the still was kept. Progressively less grateful as the sky darkened outside the clockless room, Isobel listened to a seamless dissertation on Dragan's work. Finally, he showed her an enormous canvas on which the only mark was a horizontal stroke of burnt umber swept over a pale urine coloured background.

"It looks like a skid mark on someone's underpants," Isobel chortled, reckless with the spirit.

Dragan came and cronked down before her, gazing tenderly into her eyes. Isobel felt shifty.

"You are the most intelligent woman I have ever known. From my work, you have read the meaning of human life."

Immediately he clamped his furry face on hers and forced open her lips, searching her mouth with his large, flappy tongue. Isobel put up with it for friendship's sake until he took her hand and made her feel his private parts. That was quite enough, Isobel thought, shooting to her feet. She conducted the leaving ceremonies briskly.

Stamping her feet on the landing stage she inveighed against the utter selfishness of artists. Dirty, disorganised and self-obsessed. With no conception of other people's needs. Imagine, Dragan had never once asked her about *her* work . . .

Once home, Isobel found Sandro frying up cold spaghetti. Expostulating on the danger, she stripped off her outer clothing and took over from him zestfully. He was to sit down beside the stove and tell her all about his day. After supper he was made to get all his school exercise books out so his mother could inspect his marks. An average of nine and a half out of ten, she conceded, was not bad at all. But was he really trying?

"Well, I don't have to," Sandro said reasonably. "It's all so easy."

"Good," said Isobel, as bored with Sandro's school work as she had been with her own.

Then she told him all about the selfish slobbiness of Dragan. Her son eyed her with cynical affection. So wherein lay the big difference between these two grown-ups? Except, of course, his mother, whatever else she was, was never dull.

The following day, Christmas Eve, was devoted to a manic round of domestic cleaning. Where had all this washing come from? Then Isobel plucked the duck. The down feathers flew everywhere, sticking to the oil paintings' half-dry surfaces. Sandro calmly picked them off with his mother's eyebrow tweezers while she stormed and wept.

Christmas Day itself dawned clear as crystal, cold and dry. A powdering of snow sparkled on the city's domes. All the *campanile* bells sang ice pure arias, throwing their voices across the wide lagoon.

For the first time, Isobel took Sandro to church. Something new to do together. Beyond San Marcuola's leathern curtain, a jewel encrusted cavern, swelling with music and scented smoke, lay hidden. Sandro had many questions. Abandoning any attempt to follow the Mass, Isobel sat down in the pew and told her son the nativity story. It was one with which he was quick to identify.

"So this boy hadn't any father?" he probed.

"Well, yes and no . . . he was in heaven, sort of . . ."

"Like mine," agreed Sandro. "And he was a prince, too, really . . . all the time. And only the three Kings knew about it . . ."

"Yes, until he grew up . . ."

"I expect," he said confidently later, tucking into a not altogether unsuccessful dish of roast duck and apple sauce, "That somebody, somewhere knows about me too."

"Oh Sandro, darling," Isobel kissed him wearily. "Do, *do* shut up. I love you very much. Isn't that enough?"

*　　*　　*

At carnival-time, the first painting in Isobel's series was nearing completion. It was finished actually but Isobel, who had started it again from scratch after Christmas was unwilling to find it so. Whilst it still needed her, it was harmless. Nina's many faces, fanned either side from a central image, were under her control.

If she turned her back on the easel for an hour or two, the thing acquired an independent life. The coruscating kaleidoscope of visages, emanating from a common, mist scarved neck, followed her about the room.

The green eyes accused, pleaded, invited. Nina young. Nina old. Nina laughing. Nina with her mouth turned down in the terrible black boomerang of tragedy. Nina cruel. Nina crazy, with her skin dry and flaking. And underneath the faces, a zinc pail, positioned so that its fluid contents should not show. Only a shine of red reflecting on the farther rim hinted at the horror. Isobel could smell it.

The pail stood solidly on a floating platform of black and white hexagonal tiles outlined with steel. Where those had come from, Isobel didn't know. They looked right, anyhow. So did the severed pigtail lying just beside the bucket with the squishy toad's cold, spiky wet fingers on it. A Plymstead Magna toad . . . from the willow stream which ran through the parsonage grounds. Isobel knew that much.

She had never cared for toads. Rupert had put one in her bed . . . It was Isobel who'd been smacked. For making a silly fuss and trying to get her brother into trouble. For years she had slept in two pairs of bedsocks. And mittens too, if her mother had but known it . . .

For the rest, there were only the faint shapes of things. The dim shadow of crude machinery, muffled under patiently applied glazes. The stark underpainting could only be seen when the canvas was twisted at certain angles to the light. Like a holograph. There was no need to see it. An optional feature.

Graphic and mysterious, Isobel found the painting beautiful. It had a clean, photographic sharpness . . . a piercing brilliance of colour. Green and black and white and silver-grey with the hot blaze of Nina's hair. And knowledge of the unseen blood. The objects were tangible . . . the rivets on the pail . . . the slightly coarse texture of the plaited hair . . . the taut rubberiness of the elastic band twisted three times around.

Approaching the easel yet again, Isobel took a magnifying glass and a 000 brush. Two or three split ends would look good . . . and rather fun. The air around this painting seemed very chill. Imagination. Sandro hated it. He made her turn the easel to the wall whilst he was eating.

At the finish, Isobel left it there, as if in permanent disgrace. Her macabre infatuation with her work was over. It would have to go, although where, and to whom it was impossible to say. Her living space was too small to accommodate spots of refrigerated dis-ease. She would start on something new.

Before she could, another kind of anxiety intruded. The incident brought home to Isobel the risks her way of life entailed, with a sickening jolt.

It chanced to be the last day of Carnival, the last opportunity to mingle with the crowd of wealthy foreigners drifting in groups or in ones and twos about the city enveloped in black, concealing cloaks. Neither male nor female, they wore tricorne hats and blank, white masks. Loitering on the bridges, nebulous in February's opalescent daylight, or flitting like pale faced bats through the night-time *calles* . . . What other place but Venice could entice a host of famous faces to pay hugely to be anonymous amid a marshland haze? The price of hotel rooms touched an all time high.

Resident *borghese* Venetians honoured the tradition with customary sobriety. Donning the regulation obfusc after close of business, they promenaded with their small fry identically attired. Giggles, scuffles and admonitions to behave.

Sandro, Isobel thought, was old enough to enjoy the masquerade. At a similar age to his, nearly eight years since in Milan, she had taken the Montenaro children out to fulfil the saturnalian rituals of their native city. For her own son, surely, she could do no less.

Isobel looked forward to the Venetian revels, at once more subdued and more exciting than Milan's. A small boy's domino outfit was not hard to borrow.

There was, perhaps, a little more to it than frivolity. The last day of Carnival, that time in Milan, was the day on which Nina's story had touched her own. A filthy fungus which had sprouted glistening filaments to feed upon her brain. But now, at last, there had been some kind of resolution. All the evil, all the sadness, all the might-have-beens and points of brightness were quarantined on the painting. Deliverance.

And on this day, Isobel had met Furio's father. A fact she wished not to acknowledge to her son, but to celebrate beside him. It was her whim and it was thwarted.

There was a holiday from school and Sandro had spent the morning at home in the apartment. At noon he went out, saying he had arranged a meeting with a friend. Isobel instructed him to be back by half past three so that their companionable contribution to Carnival could commence when scheduled as the daylight dimmed. As to refreshments, they would play it by ear. Could one eat ice cream in a mask? Would one want to?

Sandro did not come. Isobel allowed him half an hour without giving way to worry. He didn't own a watch but depended for the hour on *campanile* bells, passers-by or the position of the sun. Teaching him to tell the time accurately had been part of Isobel's treaty with her son when giving him so much freedom. He had adhered strictly, so far, to their rendezvous. Another half hour went by and still he did not come.

Restive, Isobel paced the *palazzo* corridors. Knocked upon her neighbours' doors. No, they hadn't seen the *mascalzone*. The naughty boy, to keep his mother waiting. He would turn up. Didn't he always? How was the painting going?

She ran outside on to the *fondamente* side and searched the quayside. Nothing. She went back indoors and looked from her window as far as she could lean. There was a boat moored directly below in the *rio* but it was not Sandro's *sandolino*. Isobel made a cup of tea and waited. Later she went and stood on the Ghetto bridge. From there she could see the whole length of their minor waterway to where it joined the broader Rio del Bartello. Her eyes willed the slender, silhouetted figure of her son, poised astern to wield his single oar, to come gliding through the falling dusk.

Wavelets licked the buildings' verdant waterlines. The tide was coming in. Many nightmare thoughts occurred. Supposing Sandro had disobeyed her and crossed the limits of his territory? Sandro out in the wide San Marco Basin, turned turtle in a *vaporetto*'s backwash . . . not seen, not heard . . . drowned. Such things had happened.

She crossed the bridge into the Ghetto. There was no one much around. Just the woman to whom Sandro had given the gambling money, crossing the *campo* from her place of duty to her home. Isobel caught up with her.

A fair-haired little boy? Young but tallish? Rather forthcoming and confident? By the description, it must be Sandro. No, the Jewish lady had not seen him. Not for days. So this was Sandro's mother. Her community would be rejoiced to know he had one, she added sternly. But, she relented, Isobel should not tear herself

313

apart. Was not her boy known for his prodigious navigational skills and seamanship? That he should be so young . . .

Isobel's stomach churned. Seamanship? Surely the woman couldn't mean that word. Flagrant disobedience, her mind screamed, as she ran from the Ghetto. When she found him she would beat him to a pulp.

She ran and ran, twisting and turning through the darkening alleyways stopping short and tearful where *fondamenti* abruptly ended, turning her back from the frisking water.

Eventually, at seven o'clock, she did the rational thing. She went into a waterside café and begged a token from the barman. She had no money with her. Once it was known what the token was wanted for, several were pressed upon her. Isobel telephoned the civic police from there, managing to speak calmly of her fears.

"Where are you now, Signora?"

Isobel told the police switchboard operator.

"A launch will come for you. Then we shall look together, eh?"

Isobel stood waiting in a fever of impatience on the cafe's *terrazza* which abutted immediately on to the Grand Canal. She noticed nothing and no one. A white-gloved hand touched her arm. Isobel turned to see a tall figure, masked and cloaked. She was frightened.

"Do not distress yourself, Signora," the darkling shape addressed her in golden syrup tones. "Your son will be found. This is Italy."

"No it's not," said Isobel starkly. "It's Venice. A port. A . . ."

Isobel broke off, sighting the launch, heeling dashingly to starboard as it curved across the water.

Her unknown friend helped her scramble down into the cockpit and swirled away into the night.

A uniformed policeman emerged from the cabin and invited her to enter. But *state* police in grey. They dealt with crime . . . Isobel felt the saliva evaporate in her mouth. This was how it felt when the worst thing in the world that could happen to you did, actually happen. She had trouble forcing her jaws apart.

"What . . . Is he . . . ?"

They reassured her.

"Your son has been located, Signora. He appears to be engaged in some discussion with a friend of his who occupies a suite in the Hotel Danieli."

"What friend?"

"We shall see, presently," the policeman said while his companion smiled complicitly.

Isobel regarded them with a mixture of understanding and exasperation. All they asked was to manufacture a little secret and keep it for a minute. Venetian born, of course. Out of sheer relief she

314

indulged them. Sandro was alive. A pity she was not quite dressed for the Danieli. But she was wearing exactly the right clothes for spanking Sandro's bottom. What had he done? Did they send children to prison in Italy? Why was he so far away from home?

Watching the red and green navigation lights twinkling in the dark, Isobel felt her temper cool. That was the trouble with La Serenissima, she mused. It could rock all the furies off to sleep in its gently heaving highways. In reality, it was the adrenalin of terror draining from her system. She had some spit now, she noticed, and felt peculiarly sleepy.

They came alongside in a moment.

When she first saw Sandro, Isobel's reactions were not as she had supposed they would be. Here was Sandro tricked out in new clothes, sitting close beside Mahmoud al Hamid bin Sur on a sofa. There were notes of some sort spread out on a table with an abacus. Mahmoud's hand rested on Sandro's shoulder. Her son was smiling. A fawning, lascivious smile. It was like what Isobel had always thought of as Nina Fischer's golden apples smile. Now she understood it. The purchased leer of someone who must please to live.

"Sandro," Isobel spoke frigidly from the door, the police behind her, "come here. Leave that man."

Scenting his mother's warning, the boy eased himself from the sofa and came towards her as if there were land mines buried in the carpet.

"We meet again, Isobel," Mahmoud rose easily. "You will take a glass of wine . . ." His hand moved towards the bell. "Your son? A brilliant child, if I may say so. We have been investigating the rules of probability and chance . . ."

"How dare you? I don't think you realise who I am. You may find yourself in trouble."

Hustling Sandro away, Isobel threw a significant glare over her shoulder at the policemen. They stayed to interview the Egyptian. His varied predilections were not a secret. Nor was Sandro's beauty. *La libellula*, they called him round the boatyards. Dragonfly.

The police boat took them home. In the cabin there was silence between Isobel and Sandro. She could not trust herself to speak. Only a few words to discover that at least Sandro had not traversed the San Marco Basin in his frail little boat. He had gone by *vaporetto* . . . by invitation of the man . . . transmitted by the Casino's kitchen porter who had it from one of the Long Room footmen.

A procurer, Isobel realised at once. Well, *he* should appear before the magistrates if it brought a thousand Carlo Bonettis stampeding into Venice.

Bundling Sandro up the *palazzo* staircase after disembarking at their quay, she gave him what, in interrogation circles, has been known as the third degree.

Lateness ... untrustworthiness ... accepting presents from strangers ... selfish disregard for her feelings.

What exactly had happened? From the very beginning, what had been said and done? What had that man wanted with her son? Where had he been touched ... ?

The answers, given many times over, were hardly satisfactory. The knee, the neck ... But things had not gone as far as they might have done. It had been mostly cream cakes and arithmetic. Sandro persistently returned to the actuarial content of his conversations with Mahmoud.

Roulette was a fool's game. At *vingt-et-un*, a discreet, knowledgeable person could always win. The secret lay in the number of hours available for play. And:

"What did you mean, *Mamma*, when you said you didn't think Signor Mahmoud knew who you were? You told him your name."

"Nothing much. It is just one of the sort of things one says."

The upshot of the incident was that Isobel saw clearly that Sandro's mind needed larger employment ... and his body protection from hedonistic sodomites, if not the sea. She must either surrender him to Carlo Bonetti or move away to a sensible place in which she could learn to lead a sensible life. Which meant a job, regular hours and other distasteful adjustments. No kind of life for a painter. But this was a dangerous life for a painter's child.

"From now on, I must know *exactly* where you are at every hour of the day," Isobel informed Sandro.

"That will not be possible," he replied. "You don't pay enough attention. I must go and make some notes."

"You are an extremely insolent little boy," Isobel stamped her foot. "Do you know how you could have been hurt?"

"Yes," Sandro said contritely. "You showed me. About a rolling pin. I'm glad it didn't happen. I thought he was just going to cuddle me."

"Oh God, Sandro. You're so clever I keep forgetting what you don't know." She took him in her arms and kissed him. "When I have made some decent money, we will go away from Venice and find you a first class school. Go and make your notes, darling. Don't smile at me like that," she shuddered. "Never. Do you hear?"

Isobel had made no money that winter and never planned to. But neither had she done as much as she first hoped to increase her income in the spring. She would have to go to the printer's tomorrow and order new prints of Ed's sketches. The copper plates would probably need replacing. She must start colour-washing and arranging with the framer. Soon the season would begin. The last, for her, in Venice. Another exile.

Re-examining her painting in the light of what she now knew, Isobel looked to see if Nina's smile must be changed. No. It was the same prismatic smile she had seen on Sandro's face. He, it seemed, had been ready to prostitute himself for knowledge. Nina had done it for food . . . or to save her life. She must once have had a normal, open, joyous smile. Her husband, Isobel realised, had never seen it. Nor had she.

Possibly it could be constructed . . . She would have to go back to the anatomy books. They had some good ones in the *Biblioteca*. Repulsively instructive. Thanks to the professor, Isobel had a reading permit. Leaving Venice would not be easy.

TWENTY-TWO

When the summer season came again, Isobel still shrank from her decision to uproot herself and Sandro. She could neither find the finance nor summon up the will. There were dangers, physical and moral, everywhere. And no schools either here in Venice or elsewhere, other than municipal ones, that she could possibly afford. It was back to the makeshift stall and low level commercial drudgery. One such day began as all the others had, and as far as Isobel could foresee, would continue like all the rest. She was out of sorts.

"*E inglese*," the girl with the long dark hair muttered offhandedly to her equally nubile companion as they pawed items on Isobel's stall.

"*Si, sono inglese*," Isobel flashed. "*E voi? Siete marziani?*" They might as well be from Mars, for all the good they were. Time wasters.

Hissing imprecations, the girls moved away, clearing a view of an alert figure standing a few yards off. An elderly man in an expensive pearl grey suit leaning on a barley twist walking stick with a silver handle. He had very thick white hair. A square, jowly face looked intently in Isobel's direction. Her eyes snagged on his for an instant only.

He was no use. All the money in the world but no energy left to buy. The Nina painting would not find a home with him.

There had been some interest shown . . . questions, which Isobel had not cared to answer. It was just a picture, she had said about four times in a 'take it or leave it' tone. Once the price was mentioned, enquiring parties had sheered off pretty fast. Good riddance.

It had been a bad morning. Boring. Trade was slow. All Isobel wanted to do was to sell another couple of framed prints and get home to carry on with her mother's portrait. The Plymstead Magna Kali.

"So. It is you."

Turning her head sharply, Isobel found herself looking straight into the eyes of the man she had summarily dismissed a moment since. Carlo Bonetti. It had been bound to happen. She could be wrong. Must be wrong. This man was older, thinner. His skin,

318

blue grey and looser. The chords of his voice unravelling and tinnier. The eyes were the same. And the mouth. That was all.

"Yes," she found herself saying flatly. "It's me. What are you going to do about it?"

She saw him sway and fumble at his pocket. Darting from behind the stall, she tried to prevent him falling. He recovered his footing for himself.

"A little heart trouble," he grunted. "Pills. You have water?"

She gave him some from a thermos behind the stall. All her thoughts and actions were lubricious with a slipping, sliding unreality. It was like a dull rehearsal ... a passionless read-through for some play that might never be produced. She wasn't ready. There had been no warning. Where were all the feelings she was meant to have? All the lines she should have spoken. The scene had fallen flat.

He studied her and the stall over the rim of the thick, cheap tumbler.

"*Allora!* Now we talk," he said, handing back the glass. "Leave this."

She began to say that this was easier said than done, astonished to hear herself talk to him at all. Hateful, sneaky snooper that he was. There was a man, she said, who usually helped her. But for various reasons she didn't want to impose on him so early in the day and ...

Carlo Bonetti appeared to pay little attention. Before Isobel had finished speaking, he signalled to the commissionaire, just then standing outside the Danieli's doorway. Two hotel porters were subsequently brought to do all that had to be done, under Isobel's own directions, to make her stall secure.

"This?" Carlo seized the Nina painting.

Isobel winced. The varnish would not be properly hardened for nine months yet. The work should be handled circumspectly. But indeed, she couldn't leave it to the flimsy guardianship of tarpaulin and rope. Nor the three little Venetian revival paintings she had left. Carlo sent for a dark suited man who wore a carnation in his buttonhole.

But of course, the paintings would be kept safe in the Danieli's strongroom. Nobody sneered or looked surprised. The uniformed staff held out their palms, which Carlo covered generously. Backing three steps, they bowed before returning to their duties.

"They think you are to be my mistress," Carlo remarked more factually than gallantly. "Take my arm. We shall go to Florian's. It is reliable and it is near. I do not care to walk far."

Bristling, Isobel pointed out that her clothes were unsuitable for such a place. What she really disliked was the way Carlo was establishing an independent pattern of decision. He was bullying her already and she had allowed it. Was any of it really happening?

Pivoting on his stick, Carlo surveyed her at his leisure. Up and down. From head to scraggily sandalled toe.

"You are my daughter-in-law," he pronounced at length. "This will be enough.

"It was your voice, you know," he said, as they were fussily ensconced in one of Florian's private rococo nests. "I should not have recognised you. The eyes ... perhaps. Yes, the eyes ... Where is my grandson?"

That is when the hard bargaining started, or at least, when Isobel imagined that it would. She sat up very straight against the cut velvet backrest of her chair, adopting a combative mien. They had a lot of ground to cover before Sandro's whereabouts could be spoken of. There, she had carelessly given him a hand-hold right away. The name, the sex ... his very existence.

"Anyway, how do you know I have a child? Suppose I'm lying or talking about someone I adopted ..."

"*Isabella, Isabella,*" Carlo waved his hand contemptuously. "You are too intelligent for this. When Carlo Bonetti turns his thoughts to any place in the world ... there his eyes soon follow. Many, many eyes ... This is natural, eh?"

"Well, your eyes conked out on you, didn't they?" Isobel grunted. "Hmm. A boy. Would you have hunted me up for a girl?"

"Who can say?" Carlo shrugged, spreading his hands. "It is a son I lost."

"And you blame me. Perhaps you are right ..."

"I was wrong. I was an angry old man in torment. I wished for vengeance. A male child for a male child. That is in my blood. Then it boiled ... Now it cools and clots. I have to have these pills ... *Isabella*, you see before you a sad, impotent old fool ..."

"Don't say that!" Isobel was startled by the sharpness in her own voice. She leaned across the table and struck a bell close by Carlo's hand. Her father-in-law must have wine and food immediately. He looked frail. She ordered rapidly from the waiter, things she believed would do him good.

It was the beginning of understanding between them.

"Sandro does not need an impotent old man for a grandfather. I shall not give him up for that."

Give him up? It was years since Carlo had envisaged such a thing. And even then, he had only intended to give her a fright ... teach her a little modesty and patience. No more than that.

Now as then, his protection was open to them both equally. But Isobel's mind and tongue were racing on.

Schools . . . special tutoring . . . firm but skilful handling . . . arrangements for holidays . . . companionship of the right age and type . . . her rights to visit him . . .

"Enough!" Carlo's clenched fist thumped the table, causing glass and cutlery to jingle. "You make my heart sore."

"Italians are always talking about their hearts," Isobel sniped, refusing to be cowed.

"Then, Signora," he growled, leaning forward and jabbing crudely at his mouth, "listen to my words."

Mother and son, he said, should never be separated unless temporarily by their own wish and for their good. They should never, except thus, be separated from him. Whatever their present and future needs they should be supplied.

"And the need is great, eh?" Carlo added grossly. "Furio's wife goes dressed in rags. How is it with my grandson?"

Ignoring the insult, Isobel told Carlo about Sandro. Everything except the Mahmoud episode.

Abashed by memories of her own mother gushing over Rupert, she trimmed superlatives from her account in the interests of . . . yes, good taste. It had its place.

Sandro was passably intelligent, not bad looking, independent, undisciplined, uncivilised and generally out of hand. He was old, too, for his years. Which his mother found convenient as she must scrape a living for them both. Oh by the way, Sandro was fair. Blond, to be precise. And there had never been a spaniel, not since the Tuscan period. Certainly they were poor and had been poorer. She let him have the whole of it from Plymouth to this April day in Venice.

Carlo listened with all his soul panting in his eyes.

"So what are you doing here?" she asked him finally.

That was quickly told. Combined international interest was expanding the industrial complex at Mestre, the Venetian satellite across the causeway, on the mainland. Accommodation blocks for workers were needed there, to be cheaply built with maximum expedition.

The municipality had put a large contract out to tender. La Serenissima in her arrogance had declined the usual inducements. Carlo Bonetti had come in person to smooth some fusty Venetian feathers. They were like the British these people, Carlo huffed. Still thought their empire was intact. Too puffed up with pride to take an honest bribe from lesser breeds. Supercilious swine.

"I should have thought you would have retired," said Isobel, laughing at the unintended compliment to her native place.

"I shall never do that until my grandson is of age."

"But you gave up looking for us, didn't you?"

"I was advised by experts," Carlo stated calmly, "that an innocent person who is determined on concealment cannot be found. It fell to me to wait until my grandson came to me . . . as one day he would certainly have done."

Isobel chose not to dispute this. Too much of Sandro's chatter over past months tended to confirm it. He would have found out, eventually.

"Suppose you hadn't lived that long . . ."

"I should have lived," Carlo announced emphatically. "Take me to him now."

As ever, such a procedure was out of the question. God alone knew where Sandro was to be found once school was out. Only Angelina's two-hour reporting rule was moderately reliable. Isobel explained this to her father-in-law, adjusting her pace to his as they strolled back to the Riva degli Schiavoni through the Piazza and Piazzetta. He listened to her, his lower lip jutting with displeasure.

"Oh, look!" Isobel broke off. "That's him! There he is now." She pointed out into the stretch of water which lay between St Giorgio's island and where they stood. "I think it is . . ."

Sandro was poised on the snub nosed forrard deck of the boat builder's runabout barge. This, as long as the man himself was there, or his teenage son, was actually allowed, Isobel told her father-in-law.

Carlo wasn't listening. His gaze was fastened on the fast approaching figure of a half naked boy, stencilled in violet against the whiteness of the sky. A sudden shaft of sunlight edged him all in gold.

Isobel felt a stab of annoyance with her son. This was all so florid. Most unsuitable. It was an occasion, obviously, but distinctly overdressed.

There was worse to come.

As he drew nearer, Sandro emitted some of those strange, staccato, seabird cries. Exchanges with the group of gondoliers who lounged about the quay lying in wait for fares. Its significance – the seeking and granting of temporary accommodation for the workaday barge among the gondoliers' exclusive mooring poles – was lost on Isobel.

Beside her, Carlo stood immobile. Without seeing, Isobel knew his hard old eyes were brimming. She retired a few steps from him, behind and to the side, afraid of what was brewing. She watched, face half averted, out of the corner of her eye. As the vessel bumped the quay, and Sandro made fast, Carlo sank slowly to one knee, letting go his stick. His arms were opened wide. A one man Magi doing homage to his prince. Isobel turned away, unable to bear more of it.

How many moments passed, she never knew. When she looked back towards the quay, Carlo Bonetti and his grandson were standing side by side, hand in hand. They walked towards her solemnly.

"This is my *Nonno*," Sandro said to her, "I am his *nipote* because he is the father of my father. I knew that one day, somebody would come."

It was very hard for Isobel. She was unaccustomed, now, to be swept by strong emotion without a brush to cling to. Her Italian family, however, approved the tears which burned painfully down her whitened cheeks. It was fitting.

*   *   *

None are so shocked by poverty and its incidents as those who are but one generation distant from the memory of it. Carlo remained in Venice two whole weeks to eradicate every trace of penury from his loved ones' lives.

For they were loved, if not quite equally. Isobel was the semi-precious matrix of the Bonetti jewel. The jewel himself showed an impressive loyalty to his parent.

In private conversations with his grandfather, Sandro described the texture of his attachment to her. Because, he said, *Mamma* was both mother and father to him, she was not like either.

The blend of these two functions, Carlo understood, did not make an easily separable mixture. More a kind of compound, a parenting alloy with its own distinctive properties. As a mothery mother, *Mamma*, said Sandro loftily, was 'good enough'. Just fussy enough to make him feel safe . . . And, of course, he was luckier than other children with brothers and sisters who had to share their parents. *Mamma*, when she was, Sandro qualified, *all there*, was completely his . . . But in a way, he did have to share his mother. With herself. It was difficult to explain. Sandro had thought about it often when she was in one of her 'not there' moods.

"What *Mamma* wants is to be left alone to do her painting."

And if Isobel had sold Sandro short when describing him to Carlo, she got her comeuppance here.

Carlo learned that in her son's opinion, Isobel was a businesswoman of below average competence, a slipshod housekeeper and a wretched saleswoman. She could collect as many friends as a boat bottom had barnacles, but she scraped them off fastidiously.

323

Painting, painting and yet more painting, Sandro yawned. Was she good at this? How should he know? Some people thought so. But lately, she had been doing shivery things. Who, in their right mind, could begin to understand such queerness? Sandro put the question man to man.

"We shall enquire," Carlo said on that occasion, signing his grandson to give the gondolier instructions to take them back to the Danieli. "You will want your chocolate cake and I must have my nap. Later, we shall send a water taxi for your mother. Perhaps," he added drily, "she will choose to dine with us. She may find herself disposed."

"Perhaps," said Sandro unenthusiastically, knowing that his mother's presence would dilute the attention devoted to himself. "If not, we can talk more about your business, *Nonno*, can't we? That is not good for women."

They saw eye to eye on that.

Beatrice Bonetti learned of her husband's reunion with their grandson when Carlo telephoned her at the Villa Rondine. When the inevitable outpouring was over, she was heard shouting to a maid, to shout in turn for a chauffeur. She would be on the next fast train to Venice. Or should she come by plane? To think, all this time, they had been so near! Oh, oh, and again oh. She could hardly breathe for joy. She would bring the trunks full of little garments bought in hope . . . and for *Isabella*, mother of Furio's son . . . She would spread the news far and wide . . .

"You will do no such thing," Carlo forbade her. Beatrice was an obedient wife by habit and need not be given any reason for the prohibition. "You will see them soon enough. I have affairs to manage here. No one is to come just now. When I am ready, an announcement will be prepared."

Indeed, thought Carlo, dialling his office next, the world should never know in what abject circumstances his flesh and blood had been living. *Bella figura*. There must, first of all, be an alteration to their residence. Intolerable that *paparazzi* should photograph the dilapidated exterior of that scuttling, scurrying mousy warren. Carlo's inspection, inside and out, had been enough to confirm his grandson's unsentimental description. Sandro's beauteous head was replete with wisdom . . . As for *Isabella*'s, hers was full of air. But her spirit? That was of a steel to match his own. Why had she not come to him? Did she think him such a bad man?

She must be taught to bend a little. To take what she was offered.

The Milan headquarters received directions. Carlo's personal assistant's personal assistant was to be immediately entrained for Venice. So was an accountant of the middling rank, and an executive from the land valuation department. They would report to the Danieli and dine together out of Carlo's sight, awaiting Carlo's pleasure.

In addition, a list of the premier modern art dealers in both Milan and Rome was to be telexed within two hours to the Danieli. Bonetti expertise did not stretch to art except as judicious portfolio investments in Old Masters, dead artists being the safest bet. And the longer dead, the less subject to fashionable fluctuations. New stuff? Well, the best counsel should be sought and paid for.

Having seen only two canvases of Isobel's, her father-in-law was, to his surprise, wrenched out of his usual confidence that under the sun there was nothing new. That portrait of her mother. An insignificant sort of woman whom Carlo had met only once. And yet Isobel's depiction of her sucked the memory of that face . . . the antiseptic touch and smell of her . . . whizzing back down all the intervening years. Shocking as a rook falling down a chimney.

Carlo could not forget it. Moreover, the parable of the talents was his favourite. Did he not tell it to every boy-child that had ever sat upon his knee? Now here was *Isabella* with her unwomanly obsession. Let it be of profit to *la famiglia*. The Bonettis had not yet branched out into culture. It gave a certain bloom to money that material things could not.

If *Isabella* had talent, then she should be given freedom to exercise it without restraint. A market should be made for her. A name, that was also his. Theirs. Sandro's. *Alessandro*'s. The syllables of the conqueror's name sat well in Carlo's mouth.

Tightening the sash of his silk robe, he trod softly to the door which divided his bedroom from the adjoining *salotto*. He opened it a crack, once more to feast his eyes upon the child. His heir, engrossed with his new calculator was eating chocolate cake. Fairly covered with it . . . and the carpet. It mattered not. The boy promised to have a head for business. Better than his father's.

Of course, Furio had been brought up soft. Whereas, by misadventure, Sandro, mused his grandfather, had shared the true, aboriginal Bonetti experience. How painfully logical were the ways of Fate.

Isobel came to dinner, resplendent in her pawnshop gown. Artists in general, have no objection to food whatsoever as long as it is cooked by someone else.

She was shown the teletext list of art dealers in Rome and Milan. No, she recognised none of them . . . except, she hesitated, this one. Larizzi Cooper. She remembered now. Lucy Larizzi she knew, and had met her partner once. On the same night as she met Furio, as it happened. There was a silence which Carlo ended.

"*Allora*," he said at length. "We shall see them. The omen is favourable. They have a claim. So be it. I like your . . ."

He pinched the stuff of Isobel's skirts.

"Yes," she said in a ringing tone. "I didn't want to disgrace you again. I got it at the pawnshop . . ."

Carlo cringed and Sandro rolled his eyeballs in sycophantic sympathy. He had warned his grandfather. *Mamma* did not give a damn about her *figura*. *Bella* or *bruta*, it was all the same to her. She was a man-sized burden they must share.

*   *   *

Carlo found surprisingly little difficulty in persuading Isobel to take everything he wished to give her. Her entitlement as a Bonetti widow and Sandro's mother were superfluous excuses. Her dignity, as she saw it, rested solely in her art. Anything that promoted its continued development, she was ready to accept.

The stall was entirely given up. Isobel was glad to see the back of it. Trestles, planks and so forth were taken away in a refuse barge. Feeling she owed Dragan some sort of explanation, Isobel procrastinated. She'd had what her brother Rupert called a 'break'. Rather a big one. Dragan, after longer years of toil, had not. But there was still the *Biennale* to come. Perhaps that would do something for him. Isobel sincerely hoped so. Every artist needs a patron.

After some token mulishness over her old apartment, Isobel inspected three others Carlo's land valuer recommended. Her choice, approved by Carlo, was the whole *piano nobile* of an eighteenth-century palace in the exclusive San Marco *siestre*.

Three great reception rooms opened on to a stately balcony and boasted painted ceilings in a better state of preservation than that in her old place. No one had ever cooked beneath them. The reflected lights of the broad *rio* outside flickered over them unceasingly. There were, in addition, three good bedrooms, two lavish bathrooms, a proper kitchen and accommodation for staff. They were to have access to the rear *calle* and a useful market close at hand by means of a small electric lift which Carlo had installed as a condition of the tenancy.

Ingress and egress for *la famiglia* – that was Isobel, Sandro and their guests – was to be over the water washed front threshold.

Together, Carlo and his grandson viewed many second-hand launches then on sale in Venice. A small one of superior marque was purchased. It had been the property of a lady so its chintzy cabin appointments were, apart from cleaning, left unaltered. The previous owner's device was removed and the Bonetti *B* emblazoned on the re-varnished hull. So also was the Eye of Horus. A local superstition that, which Carlo endorsed. Let all the gods have their due.

It was the launch that prompted Isobel to call a halt. She and Sandro were more than happy with the excellent *vaporetto* service. She was overruled. Bonetti family members were never to be seen dead on public transport.

A waterman was hired who was to double as handyman. Carlo's personal assistant's personal assistant interviewed the shortlist, reinforced by Sandro.

"My grandson will set you right," Carlo said dotingly. "Pay close attention to his judgement."

Naturally, the fuming executive resigned on his return to Milan. Since when were seven-year-old boys considered to be judges of men? Even if this one did know the depth of every stinking creek and channel in the whole rotten Veneto. Or so the little show-off claimed. A ludicrosity.

Beatrice was then allowed to come. Her help was needed in the selection of a housekeeper. There were indispensable preliminaries, of course.

Huggings, weepings, scoldings. The squirming Sandro was cuddled as often as he could be caught. Heaven was blessed and called to witness this truth and that. Carlo was operatically abused for having ever turned Isobel from his door. A dozen times an hour, Beatrice turned her soulful gaze on Isobel and sighed. Ah, *la poverina*! How they had all been punished for one man's fault. Only the Virgin's limitless compassion had given them surcease. On and on.

Carlo and Isobel eyed each other covertly and put up with it all as best they could. These grandmotherly effusions were only to be expected. Nobody mentioned Sandro's other surviving grandparent. Or his maternal uncles.

The second day after her arrival Beatrice pulled herself together and got to work. She saw what was wanted. A good woman in the kitchen who would combine the roles of nursemaid and wardress to both Isobel and Sandro. There was to be no more stirring of gluey messes in the saucepans. No more missed meals . . . She took her line from Sandro. And clothes. Surely, she expostulated, even the poorest person could mend them?

"They could if they had time," Isobel replied serenely.

Beatrice took Sandro off to the Mercerie in Isobel's launch to augment the emergency wardrobe that Carlo had bought him.

327

Settling her vastly increased bulk amidships, she made the vessel heave. Sandro met the waterman's conspiratorial wink with a steady, unforgiving stare. This was his *Nonna*, fat and excessively kissy though she be.

Sandro did not have it all his own way. Far reaching amendments were made to his fluid daily programme. Carlo put it about that he was seeking an educator of especial calibre for his unusually numerate grandson.

Among the contenders for the post was a young monk of the Servite order, a Venetian foundation. About thirty, open faced and smiling, he wore nothing more alarming than slacks and sweater. He had been a prize-winning mathematician at his university, was a man of culture and a spare time yachtsman. He spoke good Italian and tolerable English. He and Sandro spoke to each other in a language, however, that neither Isobel nor the admiring grand-parents could follow. Venetian. Brother Paulo would not have it called a dialect.

So that was fixed. Sandro would attend a respectable private convent school in the morning and in the afternoons, he and Brother Paulo would discuss more elevated matters. Not necessarily indoors. History, nature study, for example, was as well considered in a *sandolino* as in a *salotto*. Good God, thought Isobel, at the same time grateful and envious. Sandro was going to enjoy twice the education she'd had.

At least there would be no more unsupervised roamings . . . well, not many. She thought it tactful to allow the older Bonettis to imagine that Brother Paulo's custodianship would be complete.

Official family visits would take place twice monthly. Every second weekend, Isobel was to travel with her son to render an account of her own and Sandro's progress at the Villa Rondine. For the rest, the Bonettis would come to Venice and check up on them . . . in the most affectionate spirit.

Bills and accounts of every kind were to be settled direct from Bonetti headquarters in Milan. Isobel would be given pocket money. She was not fit to have charge of anything else. Not to be bothered with things outside her narrow scope. She didn't tell them about her little costume jewellery business. It would have been unkind. If Carlo Bonetti wanted her to be, in English parlance, 'hopeless', then she would be so. To please a patron, an artist must make compromises.

She pleaded against any press announcement in the near future, however discreet. Reacquainting herself with the world she had lost would take time. For the moment, her work, neglected for many days, reproached her.

Seeing he had met the impermeable substratum of his daughter-in-law's will, Carlo agreed. She should be left in peace. Sandro was to spend the Pentecostal holidays at the Villa Rondine, meet his cousins and be generally adored. Fully reassured on every side that his mother would be safe and happy in his absence and still there when he returned, Sandro was not unwilling. He was an adventurous child.

An hour before their departure, Carlo was barking on the telephone to Milan. Lucy Larizzi, who was known to be normally resident in Rome, must be tracked down over mountain range and desert. When found, she was to report by telephone direct to Carlo for her orders. Priority.

Rewording of Carlo's messages was always done behind his back. Waving the launch on its way, Isobel saw Beatrice frantically blowing kisses. With an effort, she did the same. The Nina picture was done with. Finished. And all the baggage that went with it.

Too wide of mind, or perhaps too blinkered, to be unduly disturbed or much impressed by the enlargement to her comforts, Isobel went straight back to her easel.

She worked with unvarying concentration on the graduated pearl necklace her mother always wore until the light failed. Nudging the milky surface of each sphere so that to the close observer, it might seem to reflect a skull. An accidental trick, no more, of light playing on the microscopic, nacreous plates. The same treatment on the four or five largest pearls would produce minute, iridescent portraits. Recognisable, but not instantly visible.

To be of durable interest, a painting, in Isobel's view, should reveal its secrets one by one.

TWENTY-THREE

"I don't know how you do it, darling," Lucy unscrewed a bottle of linseed oil and sniffed it luxuriously. "Hmm . . . Cricket bats . . . white flannels and lovely, luscious sixth-form limbs . . . I mean, I should just have to have a man."

Isobel withdrew the mahlstick from the canvas and stood back from the easel, her head on one side, to study the effect of what she'd done. It pleased her that the added detail, so small as to be invisible from normal viewing distance, contributed to the richness of the whole. A ladybird on a blade of grass . . .

"Take that toothsome monk of Sandro's . . . I shouldn't be able to concentrate," Lucy persisted. "I thought artists were supposed to have appetites."

"Yes," Isobel said absently. "I suppose they have. For their work, mostly. It isn't that one doesn't notice men, it's just that if one were to have one, there'd be no room left. Involvement of that sort is so very filling." Isobel paused, anticipating the mistaken construction which Lucy would place upon her words. "By that, you realise, I mean too *psychologically* nourishing . . ."

"But naturally, darling," Lucy smiled laconically. "No one would ever accuse you of meaning something you didn't say or saying something you didn't mean."

"I do try," said Isobel earnestly, taking up her magnifying glass. "Has Dragan sold anything yet?"

Lucy groaned. "Not a damn thing. I peeked in at the Zattere this morning before coming on to you. Thirty big, brown canvases. No more, no less. Your professor chum was there staring at them, poor fellow, as if they spelled the end of the civilised world. You were mad to think Max would take that feculent collection on."

"I don't see why," Isobel turned to her wide-eyed. "He told me he mainly dealt in crap. I was only trying to help."

"Do you have to be so literal, darling?" Lucy spoke before she counted up the layers of meaning in Isobel's apparently simple thought.

Her ingenuousness, the Larizzi Cooper partners had discovered on their alternating monthly visits, proceeded not from any simplicity of mind, nor even from a fondness for less obvious puns. On the contrary, it sheathed a determination to serve her own interests. Or those of her art, from which she revealed no signs of independent existence. She was it and it was her.

Her grasp of the document drawn up by Carlo Bonetti's lawyers had taken everyone aback, including her father-in-law. Prepared initially to give formal effect to Larizzi Cooper's agency in respect of Isobel's artistic output, Isobel herself had sent the draft back repeatedly with pencilled amendments, refinements, additions and deletions. Her demands, audacious in the extreme, had been acceded to. She knew now, her powers and the value of her work.

After his first visit to Venice, made at Lucy's urgent insistence, Max had raved over the quality of the four paintings Isobel then had ready. He had offered her a one man show on the spot. The venue of her choice. Rome or New York. All he asked was that she should complete a minimum total of twenty canvases. Size and subject matter immaterial. She had eighteen months to do it in.

At that stage, Isobel had merely pursed her lips and said she would give the proposal her consideration. Would Mr Cooper be kind enough to put his suggestions in writing for clarity's sake?

No very great detail, Isobel assured him, was necessary.

Just the dimensions of his galleries, their locations and an honest appraisal of their relative prestige. Relative, that was, not only to each other but to rivals. A list of artists currently and previously promoted . . . the price range of their works in the first year of public exposure . . . and subsequent escalation. It should be sufficient, said Isobel, to enable her to form an opinon regarding the likely success of any future association between herself and Larizzi Cooper.

Max had supposed that to be in the bag.

Reeling, he had returned to New York, with Lucy at his side. This kid was something else, he babbled. Sure, you expected a big name to get picky . . . but a complete unknown? Wasn't he doing her a favour? Didn't Loo think she was out of her goddam tree?

Lucy didn't. Not unless a one track mind was evidence of mental instability . . . which it might be. Isobel's mother had been much the same. Her sons. Particularly her eldest. She had become such a bore about him . . . Rupert, Rupert, Rupert. Frankly, said Lucy, that's why she'd let that old schoolgirl friendship slide. One could take just so much of somebody else's bloody hormones.

Not interested in this except in so far as it helped to solidify the portrait of Margaret Jefferson, at once so unnervingly competent and so full of unspeakable ambiguities, Max brooded. The kid was too good to lose. Even if she did bug him.

Okay, so she was a goddam genius, but did she have to tell him his job? Up-lighters, down-lighters, two angled spots to illumine at successive thirty second intervals . . . for *each* canvas? Damn right. Max would have chosen the same lighting scheme if he'd thought of it which didn't improve his temper. Of self-confidence in artists, you could have too much. Of *Isobel* you could have way too much. But of her work . . . could there ever be enough?

She communicated an intensity of experience direct from paint surface to eye in a single high impact explosion. Titles were redundant. No explanation needed. Pure, white-hot sensation. Her paintings hit like hand grenades. Then the bonus features. Deadly, slicing detail. Uncannily playful, grimly witty.

The critics, Max foresaw, would wear the type right off their keys with hype. Loo wouldn't need to persuade them. She wouldn't be able to stop them. *Searing use of colour, underlying geometricity, academic, scientific, abstract concepts, figurative expression, heightened detail, atmospheric, awesome technique. . .*

And the one word they would never come up with was the one that really counted. The one that didn't exist in any language known to the human tongue. A soundless vibration received only by the central nervous system . . . which took shape and meaning only in the soul. Yeah. Whatever that word was, the lousy kid had got it.

Touching down at John F. Kennedy, Max knew he was a man marked out for a mission. To show Isobel Bonetti to the world. He felt, as he said to Lucy, like John the fucking Baptist. It was gonna be tough. Real tough.

It got tougher. Isobel decided she wanted her exhibition to be held not in Rome, still less New York, but in Milan. It was, she said, the nearest thing she had to a home town. She had been married there, conceived her son there . . . and also the ideas behind the first painting in her series. The Nina painting. This point was not negotiable. So sorry. Perhaps Max would find it more convenient if Isobel approached a dealer with premises already established in Milan? There was one in the Galleria . . .

Over Max's dead body. Vowing unspecified vengeance on artists as a species and on Isobel in particular, Max got on to a realtor in Milan. There was a shop in the Galleria that he could have on a one-year lease with option to renew. It had been a cramped antiquarian bookshop. Gutted, rewired and refitted, there would be adequate space to hang twenty canvases.

Then came Isobel's next bombshell. Her series would not run to twenty. She could produce only twelve paintings. She had never planned to do more with this particular seam of inspiration. After much thought, fourteen months' worth to be exact, she had concluded that her available subject matter was not capable of expansion, repetition or division. She was sure Max would see at once that any dilution would involve a corresponding loss of dynamism.

Devastated, Max rang Isobel in Venice. It took four attempts to get past her dragon of a housekeeper.

When he succeeded, Isobel passed smoothly over the matter of her twelve paintings. She had a suggestion. She could share her exhibition with a very prolific artist working right here in Venice. He deserved a chance. His work, now displayed as part of the *Biennale* exhibition, was profound. Executed in a style which contrasted with her own and employed a muted palette . . . Everyone's problem would be solved. A new appendix to the agreement could be drawn up . . .

"Now you listen to me, young lady," yapped Max. "I don't want to hear any sob stories about some no-hoper friend of yours. I'm not signing any more goddamned clauses. You got that? You got my hands tied fast enough. We're talking big bucks here. And I'm gonna spend them how I like. You gimme twelve canvases. No more, no less. Don't give me any more shit like this or the deal's off. You got that?"

"Yes I have, Mr Cooper," replied Isobel demurely. "And thank you."

"Aw come on, Isobel. Call me Max."

"All right, Max," Isobel said sunnily. "So nice of you to call me."

The difficulty about the extent of her *oeuvre* overcome, Isobel was jubilant. Twelve was perfect. Her intended generosity to Dragan was stillborn. She had tried her best for him which was all anyone could do. With her conscience almost clear, she returned to the contemplation of her work. This must override all other real or imagined obligations. Anything else was against nature.

"Well," Lucy said finally, after many moments without conversation had passed, Isobel being preoccupied with her thoughts, "I suppose you're dying to get rid of me."

Isobel did not deny it. "I have to get this thing finished by the end of next week, you see."

"Darling, it looks perfectly finished to me," Lucy stepped up to the easel, shaking out her coat with resignation. "What a handsome family you were. The parsonage family. That's how your mother liked to refer to herself and you."

"I know," said Isobel drearily. She wished Lucy would go. The painting was a long way from finished. It worried her.

"Of course, I lost touch with you all when you were about this age. How old would you be, darling? About ten? So clever of you to remember how you looked then. Oh, just look at Rupert! Had he left school by then?"

"Not quite. He was head boy that year."

"Hmm. The most exquisite moment in a young man's life. When he knows he's perfect and has never done anything to disprove it to himself. You've caught the look. Your mother was *so* proud of him."

"Yes, she was." Isobel's voice was neutral, colourless.

"And Simon. Such a poppet. And darling, you! What a divine little frock. Was it your favourite?"

"No," said Isobel, wiping a brush fiercely on her sweater, "I hated it. Mother and I had rows about it. She thought it made me look feminine. I just felt like one of those horrible dolls people kept giving me. All orangey pink nobbles under their soppy frills. I could never even speak coherently in that dress . . . I had to wear it when people came to tea. She made me curtsey . . ."

Isobel's grotesque pantomime of herself performing that dated courtesy as a child froze the nascent smile on Lucy's lips. The parody of self-conscious suffering was too accurately reproduced. Isobel was reliving some hideous, unforgiven moment from the past.

"I'm sorry Lucy," Isobel stopped abruptly, feeling the older woman's gaze. "Thinking aloud. When can I see a proof of the catalogue? And the guest list . . ."

"Soon, darling, soon. Really, there's nothing you need worry about there. Max and I take care of everything. That's what we're here for. Just you rest. The picture's lovely. I bet it's the first to go. Three adored and adorable children in an English orchard. Idyllic. Are you sure you won't come and eat with me at the Gritti?"

Isobel shook her head.

"Oh well. I suppose I could rustle up the appalling Yugoslav. If I gave him a bath first he might do. Tell me, darling, does he ever *talk*?"

"Oh yes. About his work."

"I was afraid of that. I know these artists, you see, darling," Lucy sniped. "An infinite capacity, most of them, for other people's boredom."

She went, concealing her disquiet, hoping Isobel wouldn't do anything foolish with that painting. With only twelve they couldn't afford accidents. No destructive displays of artistic temperament at the eleventh hour. For a moment there, she had seemed almost violent.

*   *   *

Two electric bars, thought Margaret Jefferson, was not an undue extravagance for Sunday. Not on a cold November afternoon.

She went back into the kitchenette to await the kettle's boiling, mentally checking the items on her tray. One slice of brown toast with honey, one buttered crumpet, Derby cup and saucer with silver spoon . . . silver pot warming. So vital to keep standards up when you were on your own. She reached for the caddy of Earl Grey. Another Sunday indulgence along with the Review section of *The Sunday Times* and a letter from Rupert saved up from the previous Wednesday. She would read that last.

She was almost tempted to put her bedroom slippers on to drink her tea but decided against it. A slatternly habit. Rupert would not approve. He was engaged to a film actress now . . . from Martinique. French. So elegant, the French. It wouldn't last, of course. Dearest Rupert was so exacting, as he had a right to be. No, he would be a long time finding his princess, Margaret was convinced. There was plenty of time .

She patted her son's letter before turning to the newspaper. What a treat. Two pages inside that envelope, at least. Much nicer and more private than poor darling Simon's interminable postcards. He had no gift for intimacy, Simon. Not like his older brother. No wonder he'd married a computer systems analyst who specialised in aviation safety. Three years and she wasn't pregnant yet. Not even worried about it. Said she earned far too much money to want to rush into babies. So grasping of her. Poor Simon. He must put his foot down before it was too late . . .

It was never entirely possible for Margaret to exclude thoughts of Isobel from her mind when she reflected on her children. She supposed every mother had her failures . . . If it wasn't for Sandro there would be no reason in the world to think of hers . . . The paper. She must read the paper before her tea got cold.

Making Fortunes in Modern Art, Margaret read. Not exactly up her street, she frowned, reading on. The first paragraph in bold type introduced the name of Larizzi Cooper to which she did not at first react. Several lines later, Margaret knew she was reading, amongst other things, about her old friend, Lucy. So pleasant to have influential connections . . .

. . . who with her partner, Max Cooper, well known to the New York market, will be introducing what both believe to be an epoch-making talent to international appreciation for the first time . . . The young, English-born artist, formerly Isobel Jefferson and widow of . . .

Margaret let the paper drop from her hands. She was not a woman who analysed her feelings. She merely felt them, submitting to their action without defence of reason.

So Isobel had managed to push herself in again. Sandro was her only grandchild . . . How like Isobel to exploit Lucy's kindness all those years ago – which had been a favour to *herself* – for her own ends. It was a deliberate taunt. Isobel was capable of that. Dangling her dubious success in her face like this . . . and her grandson. Of course, art meant nothing nowadays. Isobel could make infantile messes as well as anyone . . . No doubt that American hobbledehoy she lived with fed her vanity . . . Did Sandro speak English with an American accent. Rupert did. Such a pity . . .

It became clear to Margaret Jefferson that she could not sit idly by. She was no longer helpless. She must take steps. Her grandson needed her. As a responsible grandmother she was called upon to act. Where was Lucy's telephone number?

In Rome, Lucy's maid was unable to be of much assistance. She spoke no English. Just kept whining *Milano, Milano* over and over again. No matter. Application to international enquiries yielded results after a time. There was no number listed for the gallery Larizzi Cooper in Milan.

"Then try Rome," Margaret insisted, although a business number would be useless on a Sunday. She got the number, wrote it down and was left with nothing to do but continue reading the paper or Rupert's letter. The afternoon was ruined.

The letter from California did nothing to restore composure. It was full of the enclosed cutting from *Time* magazine and one from something called *The Art Investor's Diary*. Isobel and her exhibition.

Exhibition, thought Margaret jealously, was a laughably apposite word in connection with her daughter. An exhibitionist if ever there was one. Rupert had received an invitation and planned to go with his French girl. So good of him. All that trouble and expense for his little sister. She had no right to expect it of him. No right at all.

It never occurred to Margaret that Isobel was unaware the invitation had been issued in the first place. The address had been culled by Lucy on Max's behalf from the lists kept by Guilia Montenaro since Isobel's wedding. Brother or not, loved or otherwise, something young and glitzy from the world of Hollywood was a desirable addition to the social cocktail with which Larizzi Cooper planned to serve the press.

Rupert's own motives for attending the public launch of his sister's work had less to do with fraternal warmth than the attraction of borrowed limelight. Iz would make sure he got his share. Italy had a prestigious film industry to be courted.

Margaret, on the other hand, was keener than ever to join her family in Milan. Rupert and Sandro. What a thrill for the little chap to meet his famous uncle. Everything at last, was to come right. They would all be together again. The logistics of this encounter were vague in Margaret's mind. Isobel had no place in the imagined choreography. Her mother blanked her out.

Margaret renewed her efforts to locate Lucy the following day. The Rome gallery gave her the number of the Milanese branch. It was a new number. The place was undergoing renovation. Probably no one except carpet fitters, electricians and the like would be there. Was Madam a client?

"I am a friend of the *Contessa* . . ."

"Yes?" was the indifferent response to this. The *Contessa* had many friends. At the moment she was busy preparing for an exhibition of the work of a most important artist . . .

Margaret tried the Milan number anyway. A most important artist indeed. Isobel, forsooth.

"Ah, Lucy. Is that you? Margaret here . . . Margaret Jefferson. What's all this I hear about some sort of exhibition you're giving for my daughter? Really, it's so absurdly generous of you. The child hasn't really an artistic bone in her body but I suppose that doesn't matter these days . . ."

Caught on the hop, Lucy listened, finding herself disliking Margaret more with every successive syllable. As luck would have it, the men were uncrating Margaret's portrait as she spoke. It bore Isobel's signature in the bottom left hand corner. Three strokes forming a shield shape . . . a mask with the letter *I* inside. Max, who had insisted on there being a signature, liked this cryptogram. The initial of Isobel's name could be read three ways, as self identifying pronoun, as a graphic reduction of a face, eyes, nose and mouth . . . or simply as *I* for Isobel.

"Well," Lucy found her voice, "of course, I'll send you an invitation if you like . . . but I really don't think . . ."

The painting, Number Two, described as a portrait of the artist's mother, was hoisted into place against the dark green hessian walls. Lucy goggled at it as she realised the eyes could not be met.

Whichever way you looked at Margaret Jefferson's painted face, she was looking not at you, but over your shoulder. Isobel's shoulder. And yet the eyes were warm with love . . . for someone else. All at once, the meaning of this canvas was plain to Lucy. Before, she had been distracted by the clever likeness, the detail, the remarkable flesh tones . . . anything but the stark experience of privation which lay behind it.

"Look, Margaret," Lucy began to talk very fast. "It'll be a bore for you. Isobel will be very busy talking to people. Not your kind . . ."

"But I must come. Rupert will be there. We so seldom meet. He'll never forgive me if we miss this chance . . . And my grandson? I suppose Isobel will keep him up for the occasion. I miss him so much . . . It's in the evening, you say? Friday. I'll need some transport from the airport . . . I suppose Isobel has a car."

"No," Lucy cut across all this. Isobel was tied up all day. She had no car and even if she had could not be used as a taxi service. She was far too important. This was not a family occasion. "I can't stop you coming, Margaret, but don't you dare try spoiling this for her . . ."

"I think you forget yourself, *Contessa*," Margaret said sarcastically. "Remember, *I* am the artist's mother."

"How right you are," Lucy muttered savagely, putting down the telephone. "And soon the whole world will know it."

She went back to supervising the hanging of Isobel's canvases. Number Three was the doubleglazing slugs . . . Number Seven, the factory women queuing for their wages with Isobel's own back half seen in the middle ground. Money . . . and yet they all looked so frightened and despairing . . . Oh hell! One was missing. Where was Number Twelve? She should never have left Isobel alone with that painting. Three days to go and the artist had slashed a canvas. The biggest and the one with the readiest sale.

Max must be informed. He would go stark, raving mad.

*   *   *

Lucy was wrong on one count, bizarrely accurate on the other.

Max, who was leaving New York within hours of his partner's call in any case, took an earlier plane. Change at Rome for Venice. He was disturbed but not despairing. It was he who had soothed Lucy's worst fears.

"Yeah," he said. "So something's up. It usually is with this kid. Unscrew your knickers, Loo. It's not the painting. She'd rather cut herself than that. You gotta understand, Isobel don't have skin. She's got canvas. And she don't have blood. She got paint instead. Take it from me, babe. The painting's safe."

And so it proved. Max took a water taxi direct from the new Marco Polo Airport to Isobel's apartment. Rain was slashing down and the lagoon was choppy.

Sandro showed his mother's agent to her studio door. *Mamma*, the child shrugged, was in a mood. He and Brother Paulo were lying low. Visitors intruded at their own risk.

"So I gotta go in there and tame the lioness, eh?" Max ruffled Sandro's hair. A real cute kid. Cute enough to advise him, before running off, to ring for tea or anything else he wanted as *Mamma* would forget.

338

Lioness was apt. Isobel was pacing up and down her gilded cage in long, restless strides. The room, airily peaceful to the eye of reason, whisked the nerves with cyclonic pressure.

"Well, howdy," Max braced himself. "I was kinda hoping for an improvement in the weather out of the goddam rain . . ."

Canvas Number Twelve, he noted, was leaned against a table. Three great looking youngsters frolicking in a blossomy, sun dappled glade. It was undamaged but unframed. A bottle of solvent and a rag lay beside it on the floor.

"Oh, Mr Cooper," Isobel came towards him, her brow harrowed with distress. "I tried to ring you but I didn't know what to say. I expected you to come but not so soon . . ."

"Now, now, honey. Take it easy. So you cut it a little fine with the star item. Is this so bad? You show me the artist that doesn't fret over parting with a masterpiece . . ."

"I'm sorry." Isobel gripped the hair above her ears. "I know I promised twelve but it's not ready. You can't have it."

"Now you see here, honey," Max's features darkened, "I gotta have that painting . . . I got buyers lined right up . . . You got some whisky?"

Isobel ignored this request. "You don't understand. No one will want the painting. It's not complete. It doesn't resolve anything. It's meaningless."

Shit, Max thought. He rang the bell since his hostess wasn't going to. Artists could be fucking hard to love.

The catalogue price on that canvas was fourteen thousand dollars. It was crucial to Max's strategy. He planned to let it go at the marked price to get the ball rolling on the night. Most of the rest he intended to buy in. Notionally, that was, for himself. Purchaser undisclosed, naturally. When the red stickers appeared, the serious punters would move in.

To them, the red stickers would indicate one thing only. That the Isobel Bonetti commodity had hit a winning streak. And whilst they might well suspect that Max had bought the paintings himself, they wouldn't quibble at the increased price he asked as agent for the initial 'purchasers' . . . who would all, of course, be prepared to do a side deal.

With any luck at all, Max figured, the new owners would be ready to take a profit on their acquisitions within the hour. Larizzi Cooper, functioning as agents, would introduce new purchasers in return for commission. In all, Max expected to engineer a three to four layer transaction on eleven paintings. They were heavy investment stuff.

Only one, the one Isobel was being so goddam stubborn about

was a regular picture lover's buy. The rest, he reckoned, would finish up in galleries or private vaults. Not haunting family living rooms.

Taking possession of the whisky Isobel's housekeeper brought, Max explained all this. In the final analysis, art was business. And Isobel stood to gain substantially from the action scheduled for two nights hence. Seventy per cent of all monies realised, including a share of the commissions on third- and fourth layer sales. She may not realise it, but that was the actual effect of the agreement. Goddammit, hadn't she drafted most of it herself?

"Then we'll vary the agreement," Isobel helped herself to whisky. "I take sixty, you take forty. And I keep canvas number twelve."

The contest of wills raged on for hours. Commercial interest on the one side, artistic integrity on the other. Max was only trying to do his best for Isobel. She owed a duty to her audience.

All her paintings were about *something* . . . something to do with her. This one wasn't. Her face wasn't in it. Oh yes, it might be a technically correct representation of her immature features but beyond that, historic truth was missing. As a child she had always felt guilty about not being happy. As an adult she had realised the guilt had been misplaced. What she had sought to do was create a fusion between infant perception and future knowledge . . . It was supposed to be a happy picture. But the leaves, the trees, the hum and buzz of bees was all in vain without . . .

"You're crazy," Max interrupted. "You can't paint out the past . . ."

"No, it's the only time I tried. I have no right to foist failure on your customers."

They reached a compromise. Max caved in since night had fallen and he'd been ten hours without food. The painting would be displayed as planned with a 'sold' sticker on it. The purchaser would be Isobel herself. She was to buy her own work from the proceeds of the other sales.

Persuading Alessandro Montenaro to make like he'd bought the goddam thing himself should be a piece of piss. Or so said Isobel. He was a friend. Max wondered how Isobel's enemies made out.

"I'm hungry," said Isobel brightly. "Shall we have some supper?"

"Say," responded Max tartly, "reckon I could just pick at something light."

In Isobel's baroque dining room, there was a jointed roast hare under a silver cover, waiting on the hot plate. Another revealed a pile of crisp fried *polenta*. There were tureens of steamed vegetables, and to follow, grapes with cheese.

"Thank Christ," said Max devoutly.

They attacked the food, eating in silent concentration for some minutes.

"Tell me," Max enquired eventually, grunting with gastronomic satisfaction. "What's behind that thing you call the Nina painting? Canvas Number One. Great painting . . . but kinda spooky . . ."

Isobel told him, a recital which took some time. The painting represented a phobic aversion of hers which had its genesis in someone else's memory. From her own, she had taken a second print because she couldn't help it. Originally, she'd had no intention of allowing it to be seen . . .

Isobel moved the candelabra between herself and Max to see him better.

"Mr Cooper? Max . . . Are you all right?"

Very far from being all right, Max was slumped in his chair, breathing hard and waxen faced. He turned his eyes towards her as if from a far horizon. A second later, with a surge of effort, he tore the watch from his wrist, pushed up his cuff and bracelet. He leaned forward and thrust his arm at Isobel.

"Know what that is? Did your Nina have one of those?"

"Yes," Isobel faltered. "Very faint. At first I thought it was a birthmark . . ."

"Slaughterhouse number. Got mine cut out with the first money I earned. Rough job. I lost my parents in Dachau concentration camp."

Isobel dared not ask how. No more of this. Oh please, no more. Why had she told him anything about the Nina painting? Stupid, stupid . . . Would it never, ever be finished?

"I thought," she said carefully, "your father was a rancher . . . I'm sure . . ."

"Yeah," drawled Max. "Big spread in Wyoming. Thirty thousand head of cattle . . . Me? I grew up in the saddle . . ."

It transpired that Max had his own way of coping with a childhood he could not look back on. He had invented another. One he could talk about as vividly as if he had really lived it. The past, it seemed, *could* be painted out.

Isobel's waterman had gone off duty. She called a taxi launch and accompanied Max back to the Danieli. He had guzzled two-thirds of a bottle of whisky and at least one of wine. Drunk, he could barely walk. He would be better in the morning.

When morning came, a blustering, drizzling day, Isobel was still with Max. Sitting beside the bed on which he lay fully clothed, holding his hand. All night he had recounted episodes of the boyhood which had replaced the one he really had. Rodeos, barbecues, square dances, brandings . . . Every time Isobel rose to go, Max had clung to her and whimpered that she should not leave him. Now, at last, he was asleep, snoring loudly. Isobel pulled her fingers out of his.

"Max, Max," she nudged him. "I have to go now. Sandro . . . And I have to pack. The show's tomorrow. I have to buy a dress."

Max blinked and coughed himself awake. Dress?

"Jesus Christ, Isobel! Haven't you even got a cotton-picking dress?"

Max started gabbling. He had to get that painting crated . . . what had he been talking about last night? Oh yes. His childhood. Great place, Wyoming. Isobel should visit with him some day . . . She really shouldn't drink so much. A lot of artists went to hell that way . . . Did the kitchen guys here know how to compose a bacon, lettuce and tomato sandwich? He sure could murder one of those.

Isobel left, vowing she would never paint again. She wanted a bland and temperate life. Art had used her up too fast. After the show, it would all be over. She might, she thought with the confidence of youth, marry some bland and temperate man. A gentle, accepting chap like Ed. She still missed him sorely.

TWENTY-FOUR

T he artist was packaged for her presentation to the world by
  Giulia Montenaro.

Her visits to Isobel in Venice had been strictly rationed by her
husband, Alessandro, and rather cruelly, by Isobel herself. But
Giulia knew that her moment, too, would come. To whom else
should the task of Isobel's ultimate reclamation fall? Beatrice
Bonetti? Pah! What true mother had Isobel but she?

By the time Giulia's ministrations were completed, Isobel no
longer looked like a painter, and indeed, she no longer felt like one.
The creative current had passed safely through her, leaving her
dry and hollow.

In consequence, she was uncharacteristically docile before the
strictures of the hairdresser who had first lopped off her pigtail.

Forgotten her? How could he have forgotten her, he agonised,
raking through the unmanaged copse of Isobel's pale gold hair.
What had she been doing with it? Kitchen scissors? Domestic cleaning fluids . . . was she mad? Yes, she admitted meekly, she supposed
she was, a little.

Through all this, Giulia wrung her hands over Isobel's delin-
quency. Unthinkable, too, to leave her unsupervised for a second.
She might run away again.

"What about her hands?" Giulia implored the stylist.

He snapped his fingers at a manicurist who boggled at Isobel's
ragged nails with paint lodged in them. There was months of work
here, she gasped. Which wasn't bad, her client pointed out, when
you considered how many years of work they'd done.

The wearily defensive witticism cut no ice with Giulia. This was
not a time for joking. The purchase of a dress off the peg caused
endless problems. Any that fitted Isobel widthways were much too
short.

"Well, why not a short one?" Isobel asked, anxious to cause her
long suffering friend the minimum of trouble.

"Pah!" said Giulia and searched on with only hours to play with.
Isobel trailed in her wake, dazed by the clang and clatter of the
city. She had forgotten all this. The frightening size and speed of

wheeled traffic, the shattering deportment of the Milanese. Catching up with this was diverting. The nose, these days, was worn with a certain bellicose verticality . . .

"Pay attention, *Isabella*. This will do."

It did. A huge burgundy coloured velvet garment. Long sleeves, low, trapezoid neck and inches to spare on either side. Giulia got it and Isobel home to the Viale Regina Giovanna. She turned the dress inside out, chalked out new seam and dart lines . . . and machined them up. Then she cut the spare fabric away, got Serafina to press the slenderised result and dropped it over Isobel's head. Miraculously, it fitted. Giulia's eye was accurate. On which fact, Isobel commented appreciatively.

"I should think so," Giulia retorted. "Was it not I who spotted the beauty underneath the orphan ragamuffin? You, *carissima*, are not the only artist."

Direct of speech herself, Isobel overlooked the discomfort Giulia's caused her.

The diamond mask earrings and Giulia's South Sea pearls, borrowed for a second time, rounded off the rushed job on Isobel's appearance. With a plain girl, the *Principessa* declared, the whole thing would have been unachievable.

A dinner party followed, hosted by the Montenaros. The composition of the party, although pared down in numbers, bore a resemblance to the one Alessandro and Giulia had given for her nine years previously. An exigency of planning only, never intended to revive the past.

One ghost, however, dominated the pre-exhibition celebration meal. Its presence obtruded as soon as Isobel, the Bonettis, Montenaros, Lucy and Max Cooper foregathered at the same table at which Furio had first fallen in love with Isobel. Sandro, in his miniature dinner jacket, occupied his deceased father's place to his mother's right.

Seeing the young replacement link repairing the ruptured circle, was, to the Italian women, an emotional opportunity. Their men were not far behind. Sorrow sauced the pasta. During this briny interlude, Sandro left his seat to rush around the table consoling snivelling adults.

Why were they crying? Did Marzio and Giacomo know? Those young gentlemen shrugged and ploughed on manfully with their caviar stuffed *tortellini*. Max Cooper, sweating in his frogged, brocade smoking jacket, said 'Fucking Christ' a few times, while Lucy squirmed in controlled English misery.

"Sit down and eat your dinner, Sandro," Isobel ordered her son tightly. "We all miss your *Papa* tonight, that's all."

Carlo Bonetti caught his grandson round the waist and pressed a small leather case into his hand.

"Give that to your *Mamma*," he said, avoiding Isobel's glance.

The box contained a diamond solitaire, similar in size and style to the ring she'd sold to buy a house to shelter Furio's child. Dismayed by Carlo's misconceived gesture, Isobel leaned her elbows on the table, shading her face with her hands. She could forgive the past but Carlo could not give it back to her.

"Not one single tear," Giulia squeaked. "Don't you dare. She's got an hour's worth of Elizabeth Arden on her face," she confided to the assembled company.

"I like the ring," Isobel said gruffly, putting it on her right hand. "Thank you very much." Rehabilitated to a small extent in recent months, she was still not at her best in company.

Smiles broke out again fairly quickly and Sandro had many questions.

"*Mamma*," he said, "when we lived in England, did I have a *Nonna* and *Nonno* there as well?"

Lucy paled as Isobel hurriedly enquired what had happened to Giulia's maid, Rosaria.

"That woman, she insulted me," griped Alessandro of Sandro's English grandmother, and went unheard under his wife's reply to Isobel.

Rosaria had gone to live in Sicily, having married a man much older than herself from those parts.

Good, thought Isobel. Sicily was the home of curses and Rosaria belonged there. How Carlo would react to her ninth canvas depicting the maid's two-fingered malediction reflected in the bonnet of his dead son's Lamborghini on their wedding day, Isobel was afraid to think. If he recognised the scarlet shadow of Furio's features next to Ed's, he might be horribly distressed. The curse, of course, had been meant for her, but Furio and Ed had caught it. A virus of ill-wishing cultured in the metal of the car. She had been immune. Hard to explain all that.

It was not her business, Isobel decided, to protect anyone from her version of the truth. Art did not always flatter life. Anyway, it was all too late now. She had done what she had done. Steeling herself to the onslaught of personal and artistic judgement, Isobel was sure she'd overstepped the mark. Crafted twelve serious social misdemeanours. She was bound to have her nose rubbed in them.

She sat picking at Alessandro's own special cheesecake wrapped in a cloud of introspective gloom, preparing for rejection.

"Look at her," someone said. "She's about to be famous and she looks as though she's just read her death warrant."

345

As a pleasantry, it failed to recommend itself to Isobel. She glared in silence at the perpetrator. Poor, good hearted Beatrice who wouldn't harm a fly. Giulia smoothed the awkward moment over with unwanted second helpings.

Max got up excusing himself and Lucy. They must go on to the gallery now to approve catering arrangements and run a final lighting check. Isobel should arrive not later than fifteen minutes past ten o'clock.

"But you *must* have had a Mummy and Daddy," Sandro returned to his earlier question as Isobel reapplied her lipstick in Giulia's best guest room.

"Yes, darling. And I'll tell you about them some time. But not tonight. You remember Uncle Simon . . . who came to stay with us last year with his wife? They're coming to the show . . ."

"Why didn't they have dinner with us, then?"

*　　*　　*

Simon was attending another celebration. A family engagement party. No one observing the group around a table at Savini's a step away from the new Larizzi Cooper gallery would have recognised it as such. Certainly Josef Fischer who ate with his daughter at a table some feet removed, saw no conviviality there to envy.

A sensible-looking Englishman in a well-worn black dinner jacket with his equally sensible wife, wore expressions of determined affability. Opposite them slouched an American in his thirties, whose yellow locks brushed the shoulders of the sort of white jacket worn by Indian politicians. From time to time he caressed the glowing, damson coloured nape of his scantily clad companion.

"She's called Monique, Papa," Estella, who had been earwigging in the shameless way of twelve-year-olds, informed her father in German. "Don't you think she's beautiful? I guess the older lady's the hippy man's mother. She doesn't looked too thrilled with him, does she? I bet if she was a cat she'd have her back arched up and her tail all fat and fluffy."

Josef followed his daughter's glance and smiled. That's exactly how Margaret Jefferson looked. But he didn't recognise the woman whose hand he had fleetingly touched at Isobel's wedding reception. No more than the others present, bound for Isobel's show, recognised him.

There were plenty of these, however. Captains of global industries, curators of modern art collections, directors of pension funds, critics, gossip columnists, academics, *boulevardiers* . . . trend-setting riff raff of every kind and nationality. Free air tickets, flattery and

346

champagne lunches can do wonders. One in fifteen invited had accepted.

"Well," Margaret grated, watching Monique slalom insolently between the tables on her way back from the powder room, "I suppose we'd better go and give Isobel our support. I expect the turnout will be very small."

* * *

Standing alone for a moment amid the crush, Isobel wondered what to do next. Had Simon come yet? Should she talk to people or wait until they talked to her? Waiting, she decided, was safer. She couldn't go up to people and say 'Hello, I did the paintings.' It might embarrass them. It would embarrass her. And anyway, they knew. Max had given her the most fulsome introduction.

A lot of stuff about bright stars and new dawns as, one by one, the white, daylight spots went on. There had been a silence, *aeons* long. The brush of fabric as pushing people elbowed past each other to look closer at the catalogued enormities. Outraged expectations warred with admiration. The ice breaking remark was articulated by some wealthy amateur collector's wife.

"It's all so explicitly *personal*," she twittered . . .

A pathetic truism on which the experts could pour professional scorn. On the contrary, they assured each other, the work of this artist had universal implications. In fact, they talked a lot of contradictory rubbish, mostly on account of shock. Was there not rather a lot of shallow showmanship here? Lampoonery, pornography, a displaced sexuality . . .

Hearing that, Max purred with pleasure. Sexuality was always bankable. He scurried away to his office and his currency conversion charts, leaving this new-made market to talk itself up to fever pitch.

Largely ignored in the darkness of the gallery, Isobel felt the pang of sharp regret which every artist knows. She should have kept the curtains drawn across these windows on her mind. A striptease artist, she reflected, could at least put on her clothes again.

"Do smile, darling," Lucy darted through the crowd. "Did you see where I put those press releases? Everyone is so interested in you. Max could have sold Number Twelve twice already . . . Are you sure you won't change your mind? Circulate, darling. People want to see you . . ."

Obediently, Isobel edged around the tightly packed rooms, squeezing her way past animated groups whose eyes rested on her speculatively. How old was she? Where had she trained? Had she any other completed works in her studio? The gypsy theme would stand development . . .

Had she any plans, one man asked her in passing, busily annotating his catalogue, for the future?

"No," said Isobel, taking a champagne flute from a waiter's proffered tray. "None at all. Except I'd like to get married . . . I'm pretty fed up with painting."

The man looked hard at her, replacing the cap on his pen. Without another word he turned and thrust his way purposefully towards Max's office.

Then Pietro Arnolfi came. It hadn't been certain until this minute whether or not he would. All depended on his level of pain and medication. Seeing him now, approaching in his chair, wheeled by a male nurse across the Galleria floor, Isobel was taken aback by the change in him. The old man was bent double, his nose only inches from his knees. The male nurse, who kept bending down to speak to him, made Isobel aware in a quiet aside that the Signor couldn't move from that position.

How then, was he to see the paintings? Had he put himself to this grievous effort just to congratulate her? Not at all. Destroyed in body, Pietro was still supple enough in mind to overcome his near total disability.

Isobel squatted beside the chair to show her face and welcome her old teacher. He raised one trembling forefinger in greeting. The nurses went to fetch a plate-glass mirror, explaining as they placed it on the carpet that if their patient hunched forward in his chair, he could see the reflections of anything inverted horizontally above. He slavered at that moment and one of the nurses wiped his nose and mouth.

Lucy was summoned. The paintings, said Isobel, would have to be dismounted one by one and shown as described by the nurses. Lucy hesitated. She had not been warned of this. But seeing the look on Isobel's face and feeling the merciless force of the old man's intent, she commandeered the services of two able-bodied guests to display the paintings as requested in sequential order.

Not knowing whether he liked her work or not, Isobel talked of it as the canvases were brought, fluttering in her stomach. The tension was extreme . . . and not helped by the way all the other guests had taken to talking in whispery, churchy voices.

At the appearance of Number Eleven in the mirror, Pietro joggled his chair excitedly, causing his nurses to exchange nervous glances. His head turned a little, a tight nut, screwed round by a spanner. Could he speak? Very little and with great difficulty, said his nurses. His face, however, was working painfully. Isobel dropped to her knees beside him and put her ear to his lips.

"Death," Arnolfi dragged the word from himself, as if it were a rusty arrow embedded in his chest.

"Yes," Isobel replied. "It's Ed. You remember Ed. You came to see us in Tuscany. He died in a car accident."

"I'm glad, I'm glad," the old man scraped.

Nobody else heard and no one but Isobel could have known what he meant.

The painting, like a frozen cine film, showed Ed's image and that of his spaniel, repeated more than thirty times, diminishing in size until they disappeared into the neck of an ever brightening funnel of light. Sucked away from life. A reconciliation of speed with peace. And in the foreground, something intangible of longing. A beckoning also, to which of all the people in the gallery, only Pietro Arnolfi was in a position to respond.

They took him away then. Isobel touched his cheek with the back of her fingers and once again, he raised his own forefinger, whether in farewell, benediction or mere motor neurone spasm, she was never to know. He had been her first teacher; she had been his last pupil and in a sense, he had seen her through.

"This was a vision?" a bystander probed as Isobel watched the old man out of sight. Her throat was thick as she answered the well intentioned question whilst watching, simultaneously, her mother inspect her portrait on the far side of the room.

"I don't know," she said. "What *is* a vision? Something you see with your eyes . . . I saw this with my skin."

Cutting loose, Isobel began to make her way towards her mother. What it must have cost her to come here tonight . . . She was holding Sandro by the hand. They had found each other. Odd, Isobel thought of herself, that she should have produced something lovable of her own unloved substance . . .

"Oh darling, darling," Margaret turned to greet her at Sandro's nudge. "Your father would have been so proud," she fossicked in her bag. "All this money . . . People are saying such complicated things. You've made me seem so much better looking than I am . . . and the little pictures of you children on the pearls. Such a sweet idea," she said, dabbing at her eyes. "Sandro showed me. He's so big now . . . But I don't understand why my face is blue . . ."

There was no mention of the skulls. Isobel discreetly flicked off the spotlight which spasmodically revealed them.

Relieved that Margaret Jefferson had missed the point of her own portrait completely, Isobel allowed herself to be exclaimed over. She was older, she was thinner. Why hadn't she kept in touch

. . . so unkind of her. Wouldn't she have been better to wear flat shoes? So poor Mr Mazzerella had died, had he? Men in middle age were vulnerable to sudden death. Look at Daddy . . . When was Isobel coming home to settle? They had so much catching up to do . . . It wasn't too late to put Sandro down for his uncles' old school. Rupert, she felt sure, was making a tragic mistake. Isobel must talk to him. Sadly, these things never worked. The children always suffered . . .

Unable to digest more than half of this, Isobel just stood there. There should have been recriminations and there were none. Impossible to demand an accounting now. Her mother always cheated . . .

"Come on Grandma," Sandro tugged Margaret's arm. "Before all these other people eat the *dolce*. Look, there's my *Nonna* . . ."

"We'll see you later, darling," trilled Margaret girlishly. "This is all such fun. Do, *do* have a word with Rupert."

Rupert was outside in the fresher air of the Galleria concourse. Entwined with Monique's sable limbs, he was promoting himself to a group of journalists. Isobel spotted him and smiled. Nothing would ever change him, not even the ebon woman at his side. An arctic fox mated with a puma. Poor boy. He would be quite safe from Mummy, now. Monique from Martinique had ringed him round with voodoo.

Mentally, Isobel puddled blue with mulberry and peacock green. The black girl's flesh was a lake into which every colour drained. Nina's had done quite different things . . .

"Signora Bonetti," a woman with a notebook pushed in front of her. "Would you categorise yourself as a surrealist?"

"Yes. No . . . I don't know. Oh please, not now . . ." Isobel stopped herself. She mustn't be rude to people. Thoughts like these were a bad habit which led to painting and the neglect of life . . .

Max gave Isobel no opportunity to excuse this proposed abnegation of her art when he carpeted her in his office a few moments later.

"Are you out of your cotton picking mind?" he bellowed at her, scarlet faced. "I just had the acquisitions director of the Guggenheim Collection in here . . . He wants to back out of a deal for two canvases because you told him, you actually told him," Max pointed a fat, rigid finger at her, "that you had no future plans. No future fucking plans . . ."

"Well?" said Isobel.

"Boy, you English really crease me up. Cool as water melons and every bit as smart. Now get this, kid," Max hectored, "you're good, very, very good. But you're a future, see. Like a crop that hasn't grown yet. All we got out there is a forecast. I can't make a market on twelve lousy trial results . . . And you go and tell a punter there's nothing else to come . . . You gonna have me bust . . ."

Lunging forward, Isobel swept all the papers, pens and inkwell on Max's desk to the floor. Beside herself, she stamped her foot repeatedly. Tears spurted from her eyes in horizontal jets. It ought to have looked comically childish. But to Max's eye, it looked terrifying.

"Hey, take it easy . . ."

Isobel leaned across the desk and seized the dealer's velvet faced lapels.

"Shut up! Shut up . . . just shut up! I gave you what I promised. You haven't bought my life. I don't care what you've spent. I didn't ask you to . . . I've done all I can. It's finished now . . ."

"Hey, honey . . . We can talk about this . . ." Max looked down in alarm at Isobel's white, strong fingers. His shirt was sticking to him. Jesus Christ, she was really flaky.

Isobel hauled harder on the little man, his heels left the ground. "That's my life out there. All of it. It keeps on going round and round. Only it doesn't matter any more. Not to me, it doesn't. It's as if I was drowning. All I can see in front of me is a great white, wonderful space. That's where I'm going. And I can't wait. I'm tired, don't you see? Tired, tired, *tired*! I want . . . I don't know."

She let go of him suddenly. Max landed, groaning, on his coccyx.

"Shit." Isobel, who couldn't see him at that moment, was quite sorry she hadn't killed him.

"You really know how to excite a guy." Max's face, twisted with pain, emerged over the far edge of the desk. "So tell me, who's the bird-brain you're gonna marry?"

It took some desk thumping reminders from Max, of what she had said so lightly, earlier, before Isobel remembered. A ridiculous misunderstanding. She had nobody to marry. She'd only said she'd *like* to . . .

"'Cos let me tell you something, Isobel," Max smoothed his hair. "You start playing happy families and you're finished . . . D'ya know what this carpet cost me, huh? Genuine Isfahan . . . You gonna pay me for all this ink?"

"I . . ."

". . . Babies . . . baking bloody cakes and . . . Then you get in front of the canvas and what happens? Sod all. Fucking nothing. Trust me, I know. Artists . . . good artists . . . great artists, they're whadya call 'em? Hermaphrodites. They have to fertilise themselves . . ."

Isobel knew all this and said so. Who better?

"You're not listening to me. I've had enough. I'm lonely. I've talked to myself till I'm sick of myself . . . And I don't know how to talk to other people any more."

"I got the complete solution," said Max. "You can marry me."

He beamed and Isobel stared. The door opened, but neither one of them looked to see who it was.

"I suppose we could have a honeymoon on your ranch," Isobel tittered, panicked into savagery.

The pouches of flesh on Max's face seemed to wither, revealing the shadow of his skull. With infinite remorse, Isobel watched him go to pieces. He was like the cup she smashed in her mother's house . . . Irrevocable, wilful damage of which she alone was guilty.

"Excuse me," said Josef Fischer, standing in the doorway, "I hope I don't interrupt," his glance passed enquiringly between Isobel and her agent. "Your brother Simon told me where to come . . . It's my daughter, Estella . . . I'm so sorry, is there something wrong?"

"Shit," said Max gamely, heroically drawing the fragments of himself together. "Can I do something for you, feller?"

Finding herself once again in the dark hubbub of the gallery, Isobel felt the walls, punctuated with the landmarks of her life, begin to spin, blurring colours like a painted top.

Why was Josef here? Was he in love with her that he had to keep jumping out at her like this . . . like some gruesome Jack-in-the-Box? No, she decided. It was only that she represented a floating spar in the wreckage of Nina's life. His life . . . her life . . .

"Iz," Simon came swiftly to her side, "you look dreadful. Are you going to faint . . . It's the heat in here . . ."

"No it isn't," Sandro said sagaciously, emerging genie-like at that instant. "It's the people. *Mamma* doesn't like to talk too much . . ."

But Isobel was not excused from doing more of it. Estella presented herself with poise. She had questions. Incisive observations, too. And whereas Isobel would repulse any adult who bored or tired her, she would not knowingly snub a child. Even this one.

"You were my nanny, once, weren't you? When we lived in Milan . . ."

"Yes, sort of," Isobel replied. "Au pair. I wasn't with you very long."

"I spoiled a picture of yours, then, didn't I?"

"It doesn't matter. You were very small. And very pretty," Isobel stroked Estella's hair, still crimped but soft now as merino wool.

352

"That painting over there," Estella pointed. "It's my mother isn't it?"

"Yes," said Isobel reluctantly. "In a way."

"But it's about what happened to my grandmother . . ."

"You know about that?" Isobel looked down into Nina Fischer's daughter's steady gaze. How could they possibly have told her?

"Yes, I found out about it last year. They couldn't keep it from me any longer. I made my other grandmother tell me. She didn't want to. She got very angry and upset. But I think you have to know where you come from, don't you? All the sides."

"My son would agree with you," Isobel said slowly. "I'm very thirsty. Are you allowed champagne?"

They reverted, briefly, to the question of personal origins.

"But you were lucky," Estella cut through Isobel's doubtful musings, gesturing to where a large group stood around canvas Number Twelve. Margaret was holding court before it, basking in the painted charism of her children. "Your family was English."

There was pathos in the way Estella said that.

"I saw my mother, you know, in the clinic place. I made my father take me. She played with a doll he brought her. And then she sat cross-legged on the floor, the top half of her body leaned right over backwards. Anyone else would have fallen. There were tears running down into her ears but she didn't blink or move. They wanted us to go . . . the clinic people, but Papa refused. He spends an hour every month just looking at her. Sometimes she does awful things . . ."

"What things?" Isobel asked before she could stop herself.

"You know," Estella made a face. "Actions. Unhappy things. Why's that painting not for sale?" She nodded again at Number Twelve, keen to abandon a topic which, she could see, was beginning to agitate Isobel. The fiction of Alessandro's ownership had quickly been exploded. "Everybody loves it. That is you in it, isn't it?"

"Yes, maybe," said Isobel.

"If my mother'd had a life like yours," replied Estella, infinitely wistful, "she'd be here now with Papa and me . . ."

"No she wouldn't," Isobel countered with a flash of insight, "because I should not be here. It was your mother who made me paint." . . . Because her mother lost her head and because of that I nearly lost my mind. The mental encapsulation plopped into her consciousness with pat inconsequentiality. Just like an ordinary fact of life.

When half past midnight came, Isobel felt like an empty suit of skin. Ready to be folded and laid quietly on a shelf.

353

Giulia came to her in due course and cupped her chin.

"I'm going to take you home, *carissima*, and put you to bed. You have had a great success."

In the Viale Regina Giovanna Isobel lay awake thinking of Nina Fischer, her dolls, her actions and sculptural gymnastics. There was still something there, unfinished. Should she go and see her?

Breakfast, when morning came, was brought in on a tray by Giulia's new maid, closely followed by her mistress laden with bouquets. Most of these were from her own friends, some of whom had been present on the previous night.

"I thought this only happened to actresses," Isobel said wonderingly.

"It happens," Giulia remarked severely, "when occasion warrants, to any friend of mine."

The tributes were not all the result of corporate social action. There was an austerely decorated card of felicitation from Brother Paulo, flowers from her former neighbours in the crumbling *palazzo* overlooking the Ghetto bridge and, most touchingly of all, from the Ghetto community itself. All by advance arrangement with a florist in Milan. Sandro clearly, had been busy disseminating information.

Where *was* Sandro? The Bonettis had taken him home with them to the Villa Rondine. Alessandro, coming in a moment later carrying a sheaf of scribbled telephone messages, was able to shed light on the geographic dispositions of the rest of Isobel's kith and kin.

Mr and Mrs Simon Jefferson regretted their early departure on a morning plane. They invited Isobel to spend Christmas with them at their house in Stansted. They were sure the change would do her good.

Ungratefully, Isobel rolled her eyes and moaned.

"This is not a picturesque location?" enquired Alessandro, wickedly delighted by any defect in the Jefferson scheme of things. "But only think, *cara*, it says here, the house is sound-proofed and you are to have something called an *en suite* bathroom. Hah! You had much better come to us. Too much luxury will spoil you."

From the Excelsior Gallia, Rupert had also called. He and Monique were keeping their suite on for a day or two and supposed Isobel would join them for lunch, with or without Sandro, as it pleased her. Mrs Jefferson senior would be present. Alessandro offered no comment on this fact beyond an acidulous mime of Isobel's mother's most superior company face.

Margaret herself had rung to state that she would meet Isobel at Lucy's Milanese *pied-à-terre* in the Brera, where she had spent the night. They would have coffee together and discuss serious family business before lunching with Rupert and his, er . . . person.

"I give it to you exact," chirped Alessandro gleefully. "*Squisito*, eh? And in the afternoon, the *egregia* Signora wishes you to drive her out to the Villa Rondine, there to call upon the Bonettis and to visit her grandson. You see, *cara*, what a curriculum of enjoyment lies before you."

The list of options was far from over. Herr Josef Fischer had called, also from the Excelsior Gallia, and offered to delay his flight to Geneva if Isobel would consent either to lunch or dine with him and Estella. If this was inconvenient, he would depart at noon as planned, in the hope that she would respond favourably to a weekend invitation that the senior Frau Fischer would issue soon.

"To this you will not reply," said Giulia matter-of-factly. "He should not have been allowed to come here. And," she added, reddening, "he is impudent to telephone. Pah!"

Isobel, drinking her coffee, listened passively. She alone could incorporate all these mutually repellent elements in her life. As far as possible she must keep them separate. Like the ringmaster at the end of a circus show, controlling elephants, seals and tigers, parading in untouching but concentric rings.

To be noticed by the world at large, moreover, is not an unalloyed advantage. The boisterous ingress of Marzio and Giacomo brought a limp telegram with Arabic writing on the printed form. Opening it, Isobel saw it was from Mahmoud. She tore it across. Lucy must not, in future, give her address to anyone who asked for it.

From Dragan, there was nothing. A sadness. The separations of success are not like those wrought by quarrels. Nothing can repair them. Of this, Isobel naturally did not speak.

As Alessandro hugged her to him many times before leaving for his office, yet another telephone call was taken by the maid.

Mr Max Cooper wished to see the *Principessa*'s guest as soon as she was dressed. He was sending something called a 'limmo'.

This was unavoidable and Isobel trembled at the prospect. What would Max be, stripped of his life sustaining fantasy? Last night, even after her evil cobra strike, the graft had seemed to stay in place. If only Nina had one.

*   *   *

"Whadya mean, sorry?" Max wagged several banker's drafts. "We did good, kid. Sure, the profit's small . . . There've been expenses."

"I tried to tell you . . ."

"Sure, sure, I know. Too bad you felt that way. Loo fixed it. She got round the big-time guys and told them you'd a whole new series lined up but didn't want to talk about it. Superstition. That's okay."

They were talking about paintings, it seemed. Not, as Isobel had intended, marriage. Max, Isobel concluded, was made of solid rubber. He bounced back, undismayed by refusal or denial. But things could not be left hanging in the air like this.

"Look, about last night . . . What I said. About you wanting to marry me . . ."

"Yeah," said Max. "You and me . . . We'd'a made a great team. Pity."

"You see," Isobel went on painfully, "I don't love you . . ."

"Spot on, honey. I know that. You'd have been so damn miserable we could bet my bottom dollar on you painting real good."

"You really are a bastard, Cooper," Isobel snapped. "It's all you care about. You don't give a damn about me . . ."

"I love you, honey. I don't want to see you go to waste on some little, little guy who wants you to make him feel great before you paint . . ."

The telephone rang at that moment. Conversation in a language unrecognisable to Isobel ensued. It went on for twenty minutes, during which she made herself stand still before Max's desk. When it ended, the art dealer looked up at her with portcullises in his eyes. His experiment as a suitor was over. Wyoming and Dachau concentration camp were both struck cleanly from the permissible agenda. From Max there would be no absolution, and from Isobel, no excuses.

"You know who that was? I'll tell ya. Some guys in Tel Aviv. They want to buy your Nina painting."

Talking very fast, Max described the position of the Israelis. They were a government sponsored commission, supported by international Jewish finance, authorised to make an art collection for the nation. How could they have known of the painting's existence so soon? Easy. Telexes and telephones chattering overnight. News of a unique property soon spreads.

Bemused Isobel sat down while Max shouted for the file on canvas Number One. It had been sold several times last night. Finally, to a Seattle millionaire. Question was, would he part with it?

The painting still hung upon the wall. Its owner had flown out from Malpensa that morning. His purchase was to follow him as soon as shipment could be arranged. The Israelis, on the other hand, were offering a substantial premium in dollars.

"You're world class, baby. Didn't I tell ya? See the papers? You wanna do some interviews today?"

"Max," Isobel tried one more time, "won't you let me say . . ."

"No. You say nothing. If you want to do me good, you paint. Paint and I'll forgive you anything. That's the only thing you owe me."

To make the sole amends he would allow, Isobel promised to try and think of a new direction. It was unlikely to be soon. She had played out everything. To do some more, she would have to live some more. And there were friends, benefactors, too, to whom she had behaved hatefully. Carlo, Sandro, the Montenaros, Simon, Dragan even . . . they deserved something of her now, if she could discover what and how to give it.

"You got some kinda conscience?" Max sniggered cynically. "Don't let it run you ragged."

"I won't," replied Isobel dourly, buttoning up her coat. "It's just while I'm not painting."

There was some discussion about canvas Number Twelve and where Isobel would like it sent. Presumably to Venice.

"No. Would you hold it here for a while? I might want it sent to Stansted."

"Isn't that some runway stuck out in the goddam British tundra? Say," he narrowed his eyes suspiciously, "you haven't done a deal that cuts me out . . ."

"Of course not, Max. I might go and stay there with my brother. I could rework the painting in his house. It's just that I need some paler colours in my life."

Astonishing the American by kissing him fully on the lips, Isobel went then to meet her mother. Their talk would certainly be of colour, expressed, Isobel never doubted, in well bred pastel words.

Strap hanging in the tram, she read about herself in the inside pages of a seated passenger's newspaper. Two and a half columns in low-key type, listing, over far too many centimetres, the other people present at the show. *Not* the kind of coverage she got when she had kissed that kiss with Furio in the Ticinese nightclub nine years ago.

Isobel was miffed.

357

TWENTY-FIVE

Isobel's sojourn in Stansted was not an unqualified success, although in terms of social, emotional and environmental pallor it had everything to offer.

Accustomed now, to be welcomed without notice whenever she chose to visit the spacious, well staffed homes of the Bonettis or Montenaros, Isobel proposed herself to Simon's wife a month earlier than expected. In that hard working, shift dominated household, serviced by the sketchy attentions of a daily woman, there was consternation.

The younger Mrs Jefferson, Jennifer, as she was called, protested the impracticality of entertaining her exotic sister-in-law for such a length of time.

"Let's face it," she said, heating up her Carmen rollers in readiness for an eight hour stint, "I like your sister, Simon, but she's easily bored and makes no secret of it."

"Hmm," was Simon's placid response from the bed he'd just got into. "You generally know where you are with Iz."

"It's a bit much you know," his wife continued. "When we married nobody had heard of her for years. Yonks after that she turns up out of the blue and expects us all to go running round her . . ."

But Simon put his foot down, being more or less master on his own domestic flight deck. Isobel was his only sister, for whom, so far, the Jeffersons had done precious little. If she preferred to take a break with them in Stansted as opposed to with Rupert in Hollywood, then Simon for one was grateful that their old nursery alliance had stood the test of time.

"And what about this painting she says she's bringing? She wants to work on it. Decent of her to tell us she'll do it wherever the light is best." Jennifer stabbed the roller pins into her scalp.

"I'm sure Iz will do her utmost to be considerate," said Simon, rather doubting it.

"Hah! About as considerate as she is of that boy of hers. Leaving him with a tutor . . . I'll tell you what, Simon, my darling sister-in-law has a celebrity temperament. She only ever sees herself."

There was just a grain of truth in that. But Jennifer, along with a thousand million others, was not to know that there had been times when Isobel had not seen herself at all or that she perceived others with a hard edged, distant bird's eye clarity which transcended all normal sensitivity. A cyclical dysfunction in her human receiving equipment had made of her an artist.

*　　*　　*

Isobel arrived in a taxi full of propitiating pot plants and presented Jennifer with one of Ed's original Venetian studies.

"I thought you'd it like much better than anything of mine," she said humbly. "A touch gamey for your taste."

Jennifer was temporarily disarmed. Isobel, she acknowledged, had charm when she put herself out to use it.

To her brother, she gave one of her remaining Venetian revival paintings, framed and signed now with her cryptogram. It was one of the only three she'd had left on the day Carlo Bonetti found her.

"I'd no idea you could do anything like this, Iz," Simon cradled the little painting almost reverently in his hands. "Is it valuable?"

"Shouldn't think so," his sister giggled. "Not until I'm dead."

Privately, Jennifer wondered if Isobel wasn't a tad too sure of herself.

Forty-eight hours later, canvas Number Twelve arrived, stoutly crated, on the back of a carelessly driven lorry. The painting was stored, for the time being, in the garage, once Isobel had assured herself that the crate was lined with an impermeable envelope of tin.

"It'll be all right in there," the painting's creator approved. "I'm not ready for it yet."

Jennifer's heart sank as she saw the departing truck chew up her lawn edges. Then it was a matter of where Isobel was to arrange her painting things in anticipation of working when she felt inclined. She was assigned a small spare bedroom which faced north and had, by chance, the essential convenience of running water.

"Oh good," said Isobel. "A sink. But we'll have to take all the soft furnishings out of here, otherwise my mess will spoil them. We'll probably have to redecorate as well."

This was not the end of it. Although scrupulous herself about recording and paying for her telephone calls, Isobel could hardly compensate her hosts for the fact that their line was always busy.

Max rang . . . from New York, Milan or Rome. So did Lucy. Giulia seemed to follow suit every other day . . . for a chat. Sandro rang with gay abandon from the Villa Rondine and from Venice.

Was *Mamma* enjoying her holiday? He and Brother Paulo were enjoying knowing someone famous very much. (A Miss Guggenheim had left her card at the apartment.)

Isobel's housekeeper rang . . . questions to be referred to the Bonetti Accounts Department. Carlo himself rang. He had bought canvas Number Seven and wanted some small amendments making. Could Isobel paint out the features of this Mazzerella *tizio* and get rid of the maid's ugly cursing fingers? Then he would be satisfied. Margaret rang. She wanted Beatrice's number so that they could arrange an equitable division of Sandro's time over the Christmas holidays. And so on.

Isobel was sweetly apologetic about all this and offered to install another line with extensions.

"What? For a few weeks," Simon's jaw dropped open.

"Well, you need it, don't you?" Isobel replied sincerely.

She was necessarily left to her own devices for many hours in twenty-four as varying air transport schedules claimed her brother and sister-in-law. Fitting in surprisingly well with the routine of snatched meals and none, Isobel tramped the suburban avenues in an odd selection of her brother's clothes. She had, she said owlishly, a programme of planned thinking to be done. She might have refrained from adding that in Stansted there was nothing to distract her but being Isobel, she didn't.

First in the order of conscious meditation, was where in the world material for her next series of paintings, if any, was to come from. Max was right. She must certainly try and expand the only career she was fitted for. She was approaching thirty now, and the disciplines of formal business or any sort of training were not the kind to which Isobel could knuckle down in comfort. Absolutely not.

If only, she thought, lifting sodden leaves with the toe of Simon's overly large but comfortable new moccasins, she could come up with an interesting theme, all the peripheral details would fall into place. Where she was to live, for instance, and at what precise species of man she should set her cap. Perhaps a lover would be a better bet. One did have needs but one only had them when one wasn't working. Most men, unfortunately, had a way of expecting *meals* . . . and inconsequential chatter. A bit like Sandro. With Furio, providing them had been a novelty. And she'd had domestic help. And with Ed . . . Well, that was then.

How long would Carlo's financial support last? For Sandro it would, of course, be open-ended. But for her it was perhaps already over. And if it was not, should she continue to take it? The price, as in destroying her own works to suit her father-in-law's caprice, already looked too high. Soon there must be plain words spoken on these and other matters. At the Villa Rondine, there was a tendency to regard her as some kind of high caste Hindu widow who, having escaped the pyre, was expected to pass her days in an endless exercise of memorial purity. Ed was never mentioned.

Unless those unspoken Bonetti preferences were to be satisfied by default, there must be some exertion. Marrying Furio, after all, had not been a piece of cake. Even running away with Ed had called for a modicum of spirit . . .

Catching sight of herself in the plate-glass window of a bicycle shop, Isobel stopped dead. Who would want her anyway? She looked a sight. And always would, she reckoned, unless occasional politeness to a hostess required something in the way of smartness.

Passers-by did not share Isobel's assessment of her own attractions. Not a few glanced sideways at the tall young woman wearing a man's trilby hat. It was her expression as much as anything, commanding and remote. And her eyes, when she raised them from the pavement, were as entrancing as they were daunting. The colour of upland tarns in a rare, northern heatwave.

So thought a tall, spare man in a riding mac who watched Isobel in a florist's shop buying some chrysanthemums for Jennifer.

There had been a little stiffness about the way Isobel left her breakfast dishes in the kitchen sink. Where else she was to put them, Isobel couldn't and wouldn't think. Some flowers, she considered, would forestall any unwelcome suggestions Jennifer might have to make.

Stepping, therefore, into the florist's, Isobel went about the business of selecting eighteen blooms in white and apricot.

"Even numbers of Highland terrier faces, ping-pong balls and those bathetic daisy shaped things," Isobel crisply made her wishes known, "and some of that spotty dotty stuff. How much is it? It's far too much. I'll have to have it anyway."

In the midst of this transaction, she was discomfited to find herself observed minutely. Not dressed, not fit, as she put it to herself, for human consumption, Isobel frowned her disapproval at the starer in the riding mac. Ogling strangers wasn't done. In Milan, yes. In Stansted, no. This man, handsome if one cared for the medieval effigy style of feature, looked to Isobel as if he knew the difference. It was all the more deplorable of him.

His gaze refused to waver, even when Isobel widened her eyes and flared her nostrils as she had often seen her mother do. It was generally effective in putting people in their places. On this man it produced a faint, quirking smile. Insufferable.

As if she would allow herself to be picked up without make-up on. Or ever, for that matter. The season for casual encounters was, in her case, closed. As ought to be clear to any person of sense and breeding.

Isobel marched off with her flowers and thought no more about it. This morning she was confronting the question of Sandro's future education. English, Italian or both?

Other, unbidden thoughts wormed their way into Isobel's head. At the time they seemed to have no connecting thread. There was the large painting, still crated in Simon's garage. She hadn't even signed it, so deep was her discontent. Should she scrap it altogether? It was a lot of work to waste.

And there was Nina. Nina whose plural image was already making them both a name of note in art establishment circles. This, Isobel knew, was a truth which stood clear of Max and Lucy's hype.

Max himself had a place in all of this confusion but refused stubbornly to slot into it.

Isobel had the uncanny feeling that she was missing something. Patently absurd. She was wasting time in churning up this old ground and was getting nowhere.

It was not all soliloquy.

A day or two after the florist's shop incident, Simon took some leave in order to be with Isobel. Jennifer's shifts were organised so that she could at least join them in the evenings. There were friends and neighbours who wished to see them, not least because rumours of the Jeffersons' house guest's romantic background had leaked out. Assisted, it must be admitted by some proud blurtings of Simon's on a hop to Cyprus to pick up a consignment of citrus fruit.

The story, almost too fantastic to be taken seriously, was confirmed when a colleague working for the same air freight company idly picked up a glossy magazine in some continental airport, flicked the pages and found Isobel's name writ large. There were photographs of her and some of her paintings, too. Incredible. And there she was, mooching around in Stansted.

Invitations followed for the three of them, there being no trouble about a lone woman if she's an object of curiosity. A hostess who can never find a spare man for a pretty single girlfriend, can always drum up somebody for a halfway famous stranger. And failing that, as one said brightly to Jennifer on the telephone, they could always eat in the kitchen.

Catching the fag-end of that conversation, Isobel lugubriously deposed that in her own present apartment in Venice she had seen the kitchen only once. In the previous one, she had not had a kitchen. In other people's houses, these days, she was not encouraged to view the domestic offices.

Simon laughed uproariously with a nervous eye fixed on his fuming wife.

It was naughty of her, Isobel admitted inwardly, but she felt she was being or was about to be used. Fine, she thought, but she wouldn't come too cheaply. These people wanted something out of the ordinary to distinguish their dinner parties. They were going to get it.

*   *   *

Sitting at a succession of new, oval Regency dining tables, Isobel set herself the task of singing for her supper. It was, after all, jolly nice of people to ask her. In recognition of these occasions she wore clothes with Giulia's *imprimatur*. She intended, moreover, to be civil and answer every question addressed to her attentively. She doubted she could contribute much. Simon's world was different from the several she had known.

His friends and Jennifer's definitely knew their way about the world. But by Isobel's standards they had never lived in it. Stansted did not count. It was a transit lounge. The talk, such of it as Isobel could understand, was all of landing fees, turnarounds and stopovers. Difficulties with customs, cargo manifests and so forth. The group was tightly knit, their language esoteric.

A couple of times, Isobel found herself seated next to the flower shop man. His name (in fact, Bill Smith) was so deathly dull she couldn't remember it. She was given to understand by Jennifer, however, that he owned rather a large freight company with six newish aircraft and shares in several others. Isobel should consider herself greatly honoured, she was told. Bill Smith was thirty-eight, a confirmed bachelor and hardly ever accepted invitations.

Isobel thought it rather remarkable that he should ever receive any. The flower shop man never said anything beyond 'yes', 'no' and 'thank you'.

Was he bland and temperate? Not exactly, no. His presence at her side was large and warm. He shielded her, almost physically, from being bored or seeming boring. Presumably, Isobel reflected irritably, because he was more so. Attentive to her gustatory needs, he secured such condiments for her as he always rightly guessed she wanted.

"Mint sauce?" he muttered to her once, studying her plate. "No, I don't think so."

And indeed, Isobel had already taken redcurrant jelly.

That done, he let the conversation swirl around him, regarding

Isobel coolly whenever she was called upon to speak. On the whole, she found she didn't mind. He was like a sort of looming guardian. Although, perhaps, he needn't weigh all her words with quite such unnerving care.

"I don't know much about art," goofed a retired RAF technical officer on the third evening the flower shop man and Isobel were partnered, "but I like Russell Flint, myself. I managed to buy a couple of signed, limited edition prints of his when I was serving. They've shot up in value . . ."

"Have they?" responded Isobel crushingly. "How interesting. My agent is a strong believer in the commercial value of soft porn. And with all those tasteful draperies thrown in, I'm sure you can't go wrong. I wonder what an original would cost now?"

The ex-officer coloured and the topic was quickly changed.

"That was unkind," murmured Bill Smith, the flower shop man, without relaxing his concentration on the cheese, "and rather snobbish."

"Sorry," said Isobel contritely. The word was out before she could recall it. What right had this man to give her deportment lessons? She owed *him* no apology.

In spite of that, she found herself asking the RAF man questions he could answer at tedious length. She disliked him very much. Possibly because he reminded her of the clothing factory owner she had worked for in Plymouth. Another motor mouth. Even so, she sat submissively and apparently absorbed while he lectured her about what she scarcely knew.

"Thank you," said Bill Smith as he took Isobel's hand prior to departing.

Hating herself for knowing what he meant, and still more for dropping her eyes from his, Isobel went home fizzing with temper. It didn't help when she began to recognise those peculiar swooping feelings in the lower abdomen. Nothing that Alka Seltzer wouldn't soon put right. How dare he?

"Tomorrow," Isobel said lying in bed, "I shall *work*."

* * *

Bill Smith insinuated himself between Isobel and her purpose. He was a man who based his actions on searching but not dilatory appraisals, followed up by swift decisions.

He telephoned her at Simon's house, a proceeding which caused his secretary some frustration as the line was pretty constantly engaged.

"It's Bill Smith," he said.

"Who? I don't . . ."

"You probably refer to me, if you refer to me at all, as the man in the florist's shop."

"Quite," said Isobel, placing him at once, "I mean, I . . ."

"I have a cottage down in Devon. I wondered if you would like to be my guest there this weekend. The programme will include walking and talking. Please let my secretary know by tomorrow lunchtime." He gave her the number. "Goodbye, now."

That was talking the way Isobel liked it. Straight. But did she like the man? In order to discover, she thought she'd better go. Jennifer, doubtless, would be glad of the respite.

Ringing Bill Smith's office back directly, Isobel confirmed her acceptance. Others might have thought a period of dangling digni-fied. Isobel did not. She was not some flirty little girl. She must arrive by train and taxi, she told the secretary, as she didn't possess a car and hadn't driven one for ages. Reservations would be made on her behalf, the secretary said smoothly, and the details of times and any necessary changes communicated to Mr Smith's weekend guest in time.

Delivering Isobel to the station, Jennifer's manner was distinctly fluttery. Good heavens! Bill Smith. What a turn up for the books. No one she and Simon knew had ever even seen his Stansted flat, never mind his cottage. The hamlet in which it was situated was five miles from Plymstead Magna. As coincidences go, not much of one.

The cottage turned out to resemble a bun smothered in white fondant icing, snugly capped with thatch. Its tiny domain was firmly marked with a ring of black, spear tipped iron railings, and a gate which bore the legend: 'No hawkers, circulars, or Jehovah's Witnesses'.

At this same gate, Bill Smith greeted Isobel, paid off the taxi and took her suitcase. He shook her hand, hoped that her journey had been comfortable and that she'd brought some wellington boots with her. The fields he walked across were for the most part ploughed and muddy. It was the longest speech Isobel had ever heard him make.

"Come in now," he added. "It's cold and I have a fire."

So he had, a great roaring log affair in an inglenook, the dominat-ing feature of the cottage's only living room. On the hearth, a springer spaniel dozed. It thumped its tail once in cursory acknowl-edgement of the visitor. On a small oak table there was spread a magnificent afternoon tea, with a flask of whisky lined up beside a manly looking teapot. White porcelain with a line of charcoal grey and silver.

"Oh," said Isobel. "Thank you." A dumb thing to say, she

thought. The cosiness here contrived was not necessarily on her account. Although, of course, it was.

"You will want to wash," Bill said, the ghost of a self-deprecating smile curving his thinnish, clever mouth. "Let me show you."

Isobel followed him upstairs to a snowy bedroom with an ingeniously devised bathroom adjoining, fitted in beneath the eaves.

"It's all yours," he said, depositing her suitcase. "Come down when you're ready."

Grateful to him for demonstrating so tactfully the honesty of his invitation, that they should indeed walk and talk and that she would be put under no kind of amatory pressure, Isobel tidied herself with her eyes pricking. Was it the spaniel, she wondered. Or just this extreme of clean-cut kindness.

The talk went haltingly at first. Within an hour or two, however, the exchange of basic, two-way information increased its rate of flow.

Bill had been brought up in an orphanage in London and had joined the RAF as an airman in his teens. He had worked hard to get commissioned and win his training as a pilot. The day he'd clocked up a sufficiency of flying hours, he resigned the Service and applied for a civil licence. To have his own business had always been his dream. There had been some years of struggle and uncertainty, troubles with finance and unscrupulous competitors but he had won through at length to his current position of relative security. Some of his assets, now, he smiled laconically, actually belonged to him.

Isobel told her own story with as much economy as she could manage. It was long and it was lurid, or so it suddenly sounded as she listened to herself. Every time she faltered, Bill made some encouraging noise and Isobel went on until she arrived at Stansted and her state of present perplexity.

This was the springboard for more intimate revelations. Whilst trudging in the damp November air, Bill with a broken gun beneath his arm, Isobel with her mittened hands thrust deep into her pockets, and the spaniel running chaotically ahead, they probed each other with growing confidence.

"I didn't get married," Bill confided, "because in the beginning I didn't have time. Not if I was ever going to get where I was going. And then by the time I thought I'd better hurry up before all the best girls were taken off the market, I found my idea of what a best girl was had become unrealistically rarefied. I suppose I was just less adaptable."

There was no need for Isobel to reply to this with any explanation of her own single status. He already knew about all that . . . more, in fact, than Isobel suspected. Bill was a man who made enquiries and shrewd deductions from his findings. By marrying again, Isobel had a lot to lose. An unusual degree of freedom, periods of solitude he guessed were essential to her very health and, possibly, the lavish Bonetti financial provision. The sale of her eleven paintings had, he surmised, gained her a breathing space, not a lifetime's ease.

Isobel, for her own part, found it easy to think aloud about the stray ends of her life's experience and work. Her expressed thoughts came with a lucidity which amazed her.

"Isn't it true," she said, "that most ordinary medicine is discovered more or less by accident? You know, things like penicillin . . . What if my agent's idea of simply amputating his old childhood and giving himself a new one . . . like a kind of wooden leg, worked for other people too? Max doctored himself but supposing psychiatrists could do it by hypnosis? . . . Oh, what a bore I'm being. And probably very rude. Your childhood was no picnic."

"My childhood wasn't bad," Bill said, squeezing her elbow. "Go on with what you were saying. I'm interested."

They talked and walked some more, returning to the cottage at intervals to eat grilled meat and salad with moderate quantities of claret. On Sunday morning Bill got a rabbit, eagerly retrieved by his dog who was very impressed with her own prowess. Bill was impressed by the way Isobel skinned and paunched the animal. A legacy of Ed's tuition.

"I'm sorry. I just can't do the head . . . Could you . . ."

Knowing as no one else had ever done, the reasons for her distaste, Bill did it for her while she went in for a flurry of activity with a potato peeler. They had the rabbit, which was young enough to roast, for lunch.

In the afternoon, they went out into some woods. Full of meat and wine, they were quiet. A silence such as that which can exist only between the closest friends.

"Well, what do you want to do about it?" Bill said suddenly, striding ahead of her across a ditch.

Isobel was not about to ask what *it* might mean. Any kind of coyness would be an affront to both of them.

"I don't know," she said. "It depends on what you want yourself."

He turned to face her on the opposite side of the ditch and studied his feet for a moment.

"I would like you to marry me," he said, looking up.

Euphoria and relief in equal measure surged through Isobel's arteries. She had reserved too little of herself not to make it essential that he should want her, and not on approval either. This confirmation of her desirability to a whole and healthy man was welcome. In recent years she had begun to fear she was only a piece of production machinery constituted from the spare parts of a female wreck.

"But why me?" Isobel prodded, wishing, as any woman would, to have her uniquely desirable features enumerated to her. "You know I'm very difficult. Everybody says so." The note of prickly satisfaction here verged upon the smug.

"And you keep it up, don't you?" Laughing, he held his hand out to her. "I'll tell you why, my Isobel. Because I can never come to the end of you. The more layers I peel, the more I find. You grow outwards from the middle, like an onion. One woman for the price of an infinite, self-perpetuating number. What better investment could I make . . . ?"

"Would it have to be marriage?" interjected Isobel, stepping across the ditch. The image of the onion was appealing to her. "You know, the full thing . . . ?"

"If push comes to shove I'd rather have some of you than none of you," he answered, curling her into his embrace, "but I tend to go for as much as I can get of anything I want."

At that point, Isobel agreed to marry Bill Smith. It was what she had gone in search of, after all. To be normal like other people . . . And she could have this man, whom others had courted without success . . . A man, moreover, who knew more about her than any living soul and was big enough to realise that there might yet be more to know. Yes, had to be the logical answer. Doubts? You reached a point surely, when you were simply too old not to have them. Part of growing up.

"I suppose," said Isobel, "we'd better kiss. People do."

And Bill Smith, who made a thorough job of everything, made a thorough job of this. A staunch, blokeish sort of kiss with nothing louche about it . . . a piquant counterpoint to his faintly gothic looks. Sex with this man would equate to a hearty meal. Rounded, satisfying. Uncomplicated passion after which, thought Isobel, a person could sleep . . . or even paint.

"You shaved again," she said accusingly, noting that her face was not all red and scrapy. "You *planned* this."

"That's the way one runs an airline," he grinned, mimicking her own way of speaking without premeditation.

Isobel had never heard him joke before and liked the fact that it was she that had elicited this from him.

They walked, arms enlaced, out of that wood, engaged. It hadn't taken Isobel very long to find a mate.

"When?" she said to him after an evening before the fire when both were again quiet, exhausted with the great adventure they'd already had and awed by the one that was yet to be embarked upon.

"You must finish your work first," he said. He knew all about canvas Number Twelve. "Stay here, and I'll have it sent down to you tomorrow and anything else you want. I'll make things all right with Simon. If you're afraid to be alone, I'll leave the dog."

Isobel snorted. She was not afraid to be alone. Alone was what she had nearly always been. And other people's dogs had a great way of making you feel fifth-rate company. Ed's Messalina had been an expert. But as to finishing her work, as Bill put it, how did he suppose she knew how to do that?

"I think you do," he said. "Just go over everything you've said to me this weekend. Max, Nina and accidental medicine. And childhood."

Before leaving in the morning, Bill brought Isobel some tea. The first time he had come into her room. He would go and see Carlo in Milan. There were cards to be laid down on the table.

"No, please, not yet . . ." She stopped him. "When I've finished everything."

"All right," he said. "When you're ready. For the moment," he kissed her, "I'll deny myself the pleasure of showing myself off as the great Isobel's fiancé. I'll go around looking mysterious instead."

She might telephone him at any time but he would not disturb her. In his absences, likely to be frequent, his secretary would have instructions to attend to any needs of hers.

She might paint wherever in the cottage seemed suitable to her. He had some dust sheets somewhere. Walls could always be re-emulsioned. The man from the petrol station in the village acted as the cottage's caretaker and would help her with her painting's timber crating.

Sandro? His mother should speak to him each evening on the telephone in her normal way. She was borrowing a cottage in which to do some work. Until that was finished he should be told nothing more. Later, they would decide together how to handle Sandro.

Bill Smith directed Isobel in everything that she did not care to direct herself and in those things only. Where he could possibly have learned such manners, she never did find out. In the end she concluded that they proceeded simply from exceptionally high intelligence.

Kissing her before he went, he held her face in his long slim fingers, making her feel as precious as a mare's egg.

*　　*　　*

369

When canvas Number Twelve arrived, Isobel stared glumly at it for a couple of days. It was rather like, she thought, being marooned upstairs in the Parsonage with her homework. A day later she saw it differently. The error now was blinding in its obviousness.

Her own face must come out entirely. In its place she must paint Nina's. The frock would suit her better for a start. Nina had always been good at wearing patterns ... She needed that English orchard, with the safe, rose-brick parsonage walls rising behind the trees. What had Estella said? You were lucky to have an English family? It might not be too late to give Nina one ... the kind of wooden leg that Max had.

If anyone but Bill Smith could have read Isobel's thoughts at this time, they would naturally have thought her as mad as her intended subject. There was no scheme of treatment, however wild or radical, which could touch Nina Fischer now. She had been thrown down the deepest well, where no rope, ladder or sling can reach. A wooden leg of any sort could only, on the face of it, be a cruel irrelevance.

Isobel didn't care. Crankily perhaps, she believed that she knew more about Nina Fischer than anyone else alive. After all, she had come within a hair's breadth of sharing her mental prison. Right or wrong, it was what Isobel believed.

And as for childhood, did anyone ever get the right one? They were dealt out like institution uniforms. They fitted or they didn't. No swopping was allowed. But to give away a childhood one had long outgrown ... That might be feasible.

"Josef," Isobel almost shouted at him on the telephone, "have you *any* photographs of Nina as a child ... After she first turned up in Switzerland ... after, you know ... No, I can't tell you why. It's important. Send them. Or send me copy negatives ..."

Josef dithered, Isobel bawled and bullied. For pity's sake, she must have those photographs. Make commercial use of them? Publish them in a magazine? What *did* he think she was? He must trust her.

Battered into submission by Isobel's vehemence, Josef agreed to send her the only two there were in a family album his mother kept.

Isobel consulted the Yellow Pages, just recently invented, and ordered herself five pounds of modelling clay from a shop in Plymouth. She had never done any sculpture before, but it might help. A back-to-front, preliminary cartoon. From three to two dimensions. The petrol station man said he could collect the clay for her on the following day. Meanwhile, Isobel waited in a fever of impatience for the material and photographs to come. She had no other thoughts at all, not even of Bill Smith.

The clay came first. Isobel dumped it on the breadboard in the kitchen and formed it into a basic head shape helped by the butter knife. How could anyone bear to do this? It was loathsome. Like being a medical student or worse. She hid the head in the empty pedal bin until she could work further on it.

As good as his word, Josef sent the photographs, with many pleadings as to their care. They were small and faded brownish things. Nina was seen alone, full length in one, emerging with fifteen-year-old Josef from a swimming pool in the other. For the purpose, they would do. There was enough to indicate from what beginnings Nina's present features, or at least those Isobel remembered, had matured.

Bill Smith reneged on his promise to keep away, unable to resist temptation. It taught him a valuable lesson for the future.

He turned up just when Isobel had dissolved her own face from the canvas with a lye solution. The sight of this blank hole amongst all the surrounding, vibrant colour unsteadied him. He didn't know what he'd expected to see, but somehow, it wasn't this.

Civil to him, Isobel's words were what they should have been. But she seemed to Bill like something on automatic pilot. There was a Marie Celeste eeriness about her.

"How nice to see you," she said emptily. "Would you like some tea?" Then she couldn't find the kettle, which for some reason she had put inside the fridge. She warmed up enough to say she quite often did things like that when she was busy. No, no, of course he wasn't interrupting . . . much. Quite convenient really. She was between one stage and another.

Drinking the tea, Bill contemplated the canvas which had taken over his living room, trying in vain to come to terms with its aspect of freezing self-dismissal. Isobel herself was unaware of the impact it had on him.

Realising his mistake, Bill made off again within an hour of his arrival.

"Oh, are you going?" Isobel enquired with the barest inflection of formal regret. "What a pity."

"Can I kiss you?"

"Oh yes, please do," Isobel said. "You know how much I love you."

Her eyes, he saw, were uncommunicative as dried butter beans.

*   *   *

For eight days, Isobel ate what little she could find about the cottage . . . and it was very little. Bill Smith was a tidy man. She slept in her clothes on top of the bed under the eiderdown. She never made a fire, relying on an electric convector thing she found. It was a good job Bill didn't leave his dog she admitted to herself. The cottage was no place for one.

Jennifer rang. Was Isobel quite all right? She hoped her sister-in-law hadn't felt she'd outstayed her welcome . . .

"No, no," said Isobel. "I didn't feel that. I'm very, *very* busy. Could you please excuse me now?"

Giulia could have told Jennifer an awful lot about Isobel when she was painting. In English, frankly foul.

As the work approached completion, Isobel felt a soaring sense of potency. Nina made this picture live. Her hair and eyes contrasted supremely well with those of her two 'brothers'. Natural looking? Of course it wasn't. It looked excitingly ethereal. There was now a dryad presence in the orchard. The leaves and grasses stirred.

Other things had to be adjusted. The arms made thinner and the trunk fined down. The estimated height difference was fairly difficult to fudge.

On the last night, Isobel slept on the floor beside the painting. She wanted to see how it looked at the first blink of dawn, how it companioned her throughout the day. By nightfall she was as satisfied as an artist ever can be. Which is never, quite.

In the morning she rang Josef, told him what she'd done and why. He must contact the director of Nina's clinic. Isobel told him what to say. She had months of thought, and hundreds of hours of work riding on the outcome. Josef was not to try weaselling out of things. He was to stand no nonsense.

And Bill? That *was* his name. She had better to speak to him. Had those two days, nearly a fortnight since, really happened? That other day, when he came unbidden, she had forgotten.

Isobel ran upstairs and pushed open his bedroom door. There was a chest of drawers. She opened the middle one and found neatly folded sweaters. Pulling one out, she buried her face in it. Yes, this was Bill. She must have him now.

"Mr Smith is away at present," said his secretary. "Is there anything I can do?"

"No. No, thank you."

Isobel rang Sandro instead. He was not at home according to the housekeeper but accompanying his grandparents on their annual pilgrimage to the family tomb. A little later this year than usual. No, said the housekeeper, she had no number. Perhaps the Bonetti headquarters in Milan could help.

Isobel thanked her and rang off. Sandro, Furio's posthumous child had gone, an Italian, and a Bonetti born, where she could not follow . . . to view his father's body. A good thing, in a way, as she'd told Furio. But she could remember the husband of her brief youth only as he was. She was an outsider, after all.

TWENTY-SIX

"Nina, dear, come and look. Isn't this a lovely place?"

Patiently, Isobel led her back to the wall on which the clinic janitor had mounted the enormous canvas. She'd been at it now for hours and hours.

From time to time, faces appeared at the observation window in the door. Pleasantly professional faces wearing sceptical expressions. Everything had been tried with Nina Fischer. Even electric shock treatment in the early days. What could amateur interference do?

But the director had given his permission and that was that. Signora Bonetti was more likely to wear herself out before she wore out Nina. Like many schizophrenics she had the staying power of an ox.

Back and forth they walked, Nina shuffling and reluctant, Isobel gentle and remorseless.

"It's your home," Isobel went on, glancing up at a nurse and shaking her head, warning her against entering. Last time Nina had been brought near the painting there had been a second's hesitation before she turned from it. A heartbeat's pause but still, a pause. It was a step. Infinitesimal, but with any luck, not a false one.

"The orchard . . . Don't you remember it? It's apple-blossom time . . ."

The strict chronology of the thing didn't matter. Is or was. In fact, it mustn't matter. The idea, as much as anything, was to make time stand still for Nina in a place other than the one she now inhabited. Nina emitted a low, guttural sound in her throat. Isobel froze. Was this the beginning of response?

"Look, the petals are falling now. Nearly over. The leaves are coming. And here are your two brothers. They grew up and went away. But you stay in the garden. They love you very much. Sometimes they come to see you . . ."

And yet again, Nina turned away.

"We're going to walk up to the house, are we? Oh! I see. We're going to the stream instead. Perhaps we'll see a frog," Isobel improvised, careful not to let her weariness show. Endlessly, she painted extensions to her picture with no material but words.

She had been granted a week in which to test her theory. Subject, that was, to there being no deterioration in the patient's condition. Isobel had a room in the clinic and a direct outside line. She gave nightly reports to Josef. Discouraged herself, she encouraged him. It was the fourth day already.

Her first sight of Nina had exceeded all Isobel's worst imaginings. Her hair, that wonderful conflagration, was white. Dead and dry as ashes. The refined features Isobel had so envied, sagged and yawed. And the emerald eyes had faded to a pale, dust flecked beryl. Not noticeably well nourished, Nina's body now was a meagre sack of lumps.

Feeding her was a slow, messy, frustrating business. Sometimes Nina pushed the food violently away, like an angry baby in a highchair. Still, Isobel insisted on doing it herself. Taking her to the lavatory and putting her to bed. Changing her soiled clothing when it was necessary. She never stopped talking about the painting and Nina's place in it until the deranged woman slept. When she woke, Isobel was called immediately.

Nina was bored now. Or fatigued. Who could tell? She pulled away from Isobel, and straddle legged, dropped into a chair. She began rocking to and fro. This invariably went on for a long, long time.

"Oh we're on the swing, are we?" Isobel said. "It's been on that apple tree branch for ever such a long time. Rupert used it when he was young. And it wasn't put there for him. The chains squeak, don't they? I like the sound. They say how safe they are, however high you go, however low you fall. 'I'm safe, I'm safe, I'm safe.' If you swing up high, Nina, you can see your bedroom window."

That night, the director begged Isobel to desist.

"Miss Jefferson . . . Signora, no one can doubt your altruism or your sincerity. To work so many hours with a patient, unaccompanied and unrelieved, would represent an heroic sacrifice . . . a feat of colossal strength, even in the most dedicated professional nurse. Your gift of the painting is munificent but . . ."

"Am I harming the patient?" Isobel cut in.

"No, I don't believe so. I see no outward sign of increased distress. But it is of you I think. The strain . . . And the disappointed hopes Herr Fischer must inevitably entertain. Better now, I think, than later . . ."

Adamant, Isobel carried on. Her own courage was diminishing. For the first time in years, she prayed. Make it work. Don't let me give in.

Towards the end of the seventh and last day, there was a change. Nina began to linger near the painting and quite quickly after that to explore it with her fingers. She made crowing, gurgling noises. Almost, Isobel dared to hope, like a delighted infant.

"That's our dog, Timmy. He's supposed to sleep in the kitchen but you let him come on to your bed. Mummy doesn't like it, does she? But Simon always says it's not your fault. Timmy finds his way up to your room in the middle of the night . . ."

"Timmy," Nina said. Quite distinctly. Isobel could have wept with gratitude. She watched the observation window until a nurse came, summoning her with finger crooked.

"Please, get the director. Quickly, please. Tell him to watch what happens from outside."

The director was convinced. Not that the technique was working as Isobel hoped it would, but that it was bringing about a change of some sort. Nina's deep apathy was lifting.

"If you can stand it, Signora, I will answer for my patient. You may have three days more."

The director also spared her the trouble of ringing Josef that evening. He would do it, he said, himself. And give a responsible, clinical report on what he, as a psychiatrist, had actually observed.

Isobel was glad that Josef would hear her faith given official vindication. Time and energy were precious, too. Every hour now, without rest, she must work to prove herself and rescue Nina.

She slept beside her on a camp-bed that same night. God only knew what went on with Nina in the blackest hours. She found out. Nina woke several times and commenced her rocking movement . . . or masturbated. Once she wet the bed. Isobel found some spare linen in a press and changed it, talking all the time.

"There," she said. "We all have accidents, even when we're ten. It's all right now. Timmy's here. Ssh. Don't tell Mummy. The window's open. There's a wind tonight. Can you hear the swing chains squeaking. 'I'm safe, I'm safe . . . all safe.' Let's go and look, shall we? Out of the window."

A chink in the curtains at the real window revealed a waste of slushy snow, yellowed by the security lights. But inside, Isobel was increasingly hopeful; it should be, for Nina, a perpetual early summer.

Leading Nina from her bedroom into the sitting room adjacent, where the painting hung, Isobel drew her to it. Of course, the orchard should be dark, it should be empty of people and it should be seen from an elevated angle . . . But it seemed good enough to Nina.

"Timmy," she said throatily. Isobel led her back to bed. Timmy was waiting. He couldn't get to sleep without Nina.

Three more days and two more nights of this.

The staff had to get involved. They needed to know the topography of Nina's new existence. The stream lay away to the south of the picture and formed the parsonage territorial boundary at that end . . . in Nina's bedroom. The stables were east . . . by the window. The house stood north of the orchard itself . . . which was awkward because it meant walking through the wall. The door was near enough for Nina's purpose.

The patient became fractious if her attendants got any of this wrong. And the names. Simon was her favourite brother. Rupert was always taking things if you didn't watch him carefully. The bees belonged to Daddy.

Josef also came. He had to cancel a business trip to do so. He too had everything to learn afresh about his wife. Unfortunately, he found it difficult to concentrate. He kept turning round to Isobel and thanking her.

"Don't talk to me," she said. "Talk to Nina. Ask her where she put her doll."

"Rupert took it," Nina answered the question before her husband spoke. "Very naughty. I shall tell Mummy and she'll be cross with Rupert. Simon," she addressed Josef directly. "Play with me."

Whole sentences in English. There was a note in Nina's file as to when she last expressed herself intelligibly. Three years ago, in Polish. An obscene proposition to the clinic's hairdresser. And until now, nothing else.

They ran a brain scan. Stress levels were right down. The clinicians understood these things. Isobel understood something they could never hope to.

Occasionally, astonishingly, she saw Nina's golden apples smile transform her ruined features. Only it was the real thing now. The smile she must have had before. Not the travesty of that treasure she had come by in the concentration camp.

The director said he'd seen some remarkable things in his time but this approached a miracle. A cure, it wasn't. There were some practitioners of psychiatric medicine who might condemn it as an inexcusable manipulation of the patient's derelict mind. But Nina's new and tranquil interest in whatever life she lived now, spoke volumes in defence.

"That's speaking as a doctor," he smiled. "As a man, I'm lost for any words but 'thank you.'" He took Isobel's hand and kissed it.

Josef began half a dozen speeches but was unable to get past the first few syllables. He kept breaking down. Isobel put her arms round him and held him till she felt the shudders leave him.

Estella? Where would she fit in? Nina, Isobel guessed, would find a place for her daughter in the orchard. Perhaps as an alter ego.

"Little girls always have imaginary friends."

Packing her things to leave, Isobel regretted only one thing. She had never signed the painting on the front and had never, since she decided to give it to Nina, intended to. It should be Nina's absolutely, without reservation, whilst she lived. She was its author as much as Isobel herself.

Despite this resolution, however, Isobel was jealous of her reputation in the more distant future. She set store now by her identifying mark, as she would never have thought to do as recently as eighteen months ago.

She had planned to compromise by placing her cryptogram on the reverse side of the canvas. It was clear, however, that the unwieldy painting could not be moved. Nina's security depended on it remaining always where it was. At least for the moment. Who would be brave enough to say at what point the picture had transferred its essence from the wall to Nina's mind?

Nobody, Isobel guessed. Not even she. She would have to be content with the smile on Nina's face. That was the only signature which canvas Number Twelve would, in all probability, ever have.

Waiting for her taxi in the director's study, Isobel recalled her father's maxim. No gift is really worth the giving unless it stings a little.

*   *   *

Meeting her at Heathrow, Bill Smith found his fiancée very quiet. She was pale and answered him in monosyllables. He didn't press her to divulge what had passed in Switzerland. She would do that when she was ready.

"Here," he said, settling her into his car. "I've been busy while you were away. Look at this."

'This' was the estate agent's particulars of the parsonage house at Plymstead Magna. The agents were acting for the Church Commissioners. The house, the preamble said, a fine example of a small Queen Anne mansion, was surplus to ecclesiastical requirements.

"Or in other words," Isobel grunted, "no clergy family can afford to live in the place. I know we couldn't." The words, so practical and everyday, served as well as any others for a preamble to what she knew she must say.

"Bill, there's another thing. I really can't marry you. I'm so sorry."

She watched him anxiously, but he looked straight ahead, so that only his profile showed. Isobel braced herself to carry on. There was no reason why he should make this easy for her.

"It's not because I don't ... Oh, you must know I do. It's because it simply wouldn't be fair to you ... You'd be unhappy. You'll think me very ... I don't know, boastful, I suppose. But I don't know another way to put it. I'm not like other people. Never was, really. And if I was, I just don't think I can ever be again. Don't want to be ..."

"You needn't put yourself through all this," he said, inserting the ignition key. "I knew this could happen. I half expected it the day I blundered in on you when you were altering the painting ..."

"Oh? When was that?" Isobel was interested.

"Don't you remember at all?" He told her what had happened.

"Mmm," she fibbed cautiously, "I think I do, vaguely. Was I very, very rude?"

"Not at all. Not rude. Just not at home to visitors. Where will you live?"

"Venice," Isobel said unhesitatingly. "It's the right place for me. Weird, like me. Out on a limb ..."

"And very, very beautiful. May I come and see you?"

"Oh, yes!" she exclaimed. "As often as you want to ..."

"No. Only when you want me."

"Suppose I want you often?"

"Then I shall come often," he released the handbrake.

"Won't you ever say 'no'?"

"Unless I can't help it, no, I won't. I'd better see what there is to be had in the way of small private jets. If I'm not to keep a wife in style, then I'll need something swish to visit my mistress in, won't I?"

"I don't deserve you, do I?"

Permitting a twinkle to enliven his granite grey eyes, Bill Smith told her he'd let her know after the first five years or so.

"Shall I tell you about Switzerland?" Isobel asked as the car sped away from the airport.

"I wish you would," he glanced at her. "But only if you're sure you want to. Did it work?"

"Yes," said Isobel. "It did. But I couldn't sign it. I'm pretty peeved about that. I think it may turn out to be my best."

EPILOGUE

Carlo would hear nothing about discontinuing his allowance to Isobel. His duty to her, he said, would last as long as he did. The apartment was retained both as studio and a home for her and Sandro.

She felt she ought to put him in the picture *vis-à-vis* Bill Smith but Carlo waved these admissions down. He never, he said, interfered with the private and social lives of members of *la famiglia*.

This was quite untrue. Carlo was soon in possession of a comprehensive dossier regarding his daughter-in-law's lover. He found it entirely satisfactory and merely made the bodyguard he had added to his grandson's establishment aware that, in case of need, Bill Smith was a man to be counted on. A pity he couldn't be hired on a permanent basis.

A developer bought the old parsonage house at Plymstead Magna and turned it into an 'exclusive residential complex'. With some assistance from all her children, Margaret Jefferson purchased the sunny suite of rooms formed in the old coachman's quarters above the stables.

She is fully occupied chairing the Parsonage Residents' Committee and bullying the team of volunteers who keep the church spic and span. Few people know who her daughter is, as it doesn't occur to Margaret to mention the connection. Isobel's triumph faded rapidly from her memory. Nobody in Plymstead Magna, however, is ever left in any doubt as to who Margaret's husband was.

Simon visits his mother from time to time. Isobel, who has never been invited, doesn't. Rupert is no longer quite the object of veneration that he was.

Sandro, who has increasingly few illusions about his English grandmother, is content to take his uncle's place on his twice-yearly visits to Plymstead Magna.

About the time Margaret moved back to the Parsonage, Isobel began to work again. The new series arose out of a visit from her older brother Rupert and his wife, Monique. Both 'resting' at the time, the Rupert Jeffersons were offered three per cent by Isobel in return for her Creole sister-in-law's modelling services. Never dreaming that anything would ever come of it, Rupert said that a free crash in his sister's Venetian pad was okay man.

Those paintings, studies of Monique, voluptuous as ripe, purple plum flesh against the white Venetian light, trailing her fingers from a gondola, wrapped in red brocade, or lounging with a white Pekinese (borrowed) on her naked thighs, brought Isobel popular renown. There is something to be said, after all, for tasteful erotica.

The art establishment sniffed but Max, Lucy and Isobel rubbed their hands. Critical acclaim is all very well but no one can eat it. Applause in the bank is solid sustenance.

Over the years, the three per cents brought Rupert and Monique a worthwhile income. There were literally hundreds of thousands of prints taken, neither signed nor numbered. In England, they were sold in W. H. Smith and Boots. They could be picked up on junk stalls in Ootacamund or Mexico City.

Rowella Teague had one on the living room wall in her sheltered council bungalow. She never knew it had been painted by the girl who'd been sacked by her last employers. To her, the printed cryptogram meant nothing.

But that came later.

As the preliminary work on the Monique series progressed, Bill came and went at Isobel's frequent request. For much of those days he found himself tagging on to Sandro and Brother Paulo or frittering time in bars with Rupert. It was Monique herself who made this tolerable to him.

"You can kill yourself if you want, *chère*," she would say when the sun drowned itself bloodily in the lagoon, "but I'm going to join the boys at Harry's Bar. You're gonna lose that fabulous man."

"No," Isobel replied once to this, cleaning her brushes thoughtfully, "I shan't lose him." She didn't add that nobody else was going to excavate Bill Smith's navel with her tongue. That was a secret desire of his which he had confided in her alone. And Isobel liked fulfilling it. More especially, she liked the transfiguring, irradiating effect it had on him ... and her. No, nobody else had done that before. And no one, Isobel told herself, was going to get the chance.

Anyway, she needed his unwitting contribution to the Monique paintings. He infused an extra layer of sensuality which emanated not from the model but the artist. Sometimes she left Bill in the middle of the night to go to her easel. And on some of those occasions, Sandro came and sat with her. She found she didn't mind this. He was her familiar, the person with whom she had shared the most intensely creative period of her life.

"Will this make Aunt Monique as famous as Nina Fischer?" he asked her once.

"More, in a way. But not for as long."

Isobel knew that this was not her greatest work. That had been done already, once and for all. Her next series, not quite as popular, was derived from memories of Sandro as a small boy, skimming the canals of Venice. However, the originals sold well and were much sought after by private buyers and galleries.

The mask cryptogram was often discussed by owners of Isobel's paintings. You could always tell it was her because although the bottom leg of the *I* might curl up or down, the top one (some people called it the eye-line) was invariably, mathematically straight. Worth mentioning, because the cryptogram had once been forged on a work by an inferior hand. Brought to her attention, Isobel denied all knowledge of the painting.

She couldn't repudiate the one which brought Leadbetter and Murgatroyd, the double-glazing franchisees, crawling out of the woodwork.

They had been depicted, in the first Isobel series, as slugs sliming up between two layers of glass, seen from the anterior angle. The human faces were unmistakable to them and their lawyers. They sued, or attempted to, when one of them spotted a photograph of this painting which formed part of a retrospective exhibition of Isobel's work.

The matter turned on whether or not there was any copyright on human physiognomy. The would-be plaintiffs had not sat for these portraits. Was there any proof that they *were* portraits at all? The subjects had aged. What courts had jurisdiction? The case collapsed under the weight of a cheque from Carlo. But not before the affair had hit the world headlines. True, it was a quiet time for hard news.

Isobel was awarded an honorary degree in Fine Art by first Venice and then Padua University. Inevitably, she was also drawn into the circle of Venetian resident, Peggy Guggenheim, before the eccentric American collector's death in 1979. Two of Isobel's paintings acquired by Peggy's collection on the night of her first show hang intermittently in the Palazzo Vernier just across the Accademia Bridge. The Trustees would like to have the Nina painting but every approach to the Israeli commission who own it gets the brush off.

"Never mind," Isobel once consoled at a cocktail party, "I've got another of the same subject which is even better. One day, it will come on the market."

She would not be drawn further and regretted saying as much as she had done.

To this day, Isobel retains many of her peculiarities. She will not drive a car, stand in a queue, allow the use of disinfectant in her house or tolerate heady flower scents. Sepsis is maintained where necessary with a ferociously expensive product used for sterilising baby's bottles. It is odourless. Bill has spent many a fruitless hour sniffing bottles at perfume counters. Each time he comes away empty handed. Everything has flowers in it. Women are supposed to like them. Seawater and drains remain to be exploited by the perfumery trade.

To ensure they have time together, Bill and Isobel have resorted to one of those year-planner charts. At first, Isobel couldn't see why arrangements couldn't be slipped a month or two either way. Gradually, Bill got her into a rhythm.

This works well for Isobel who associates every new series of paintings with a particular series of encounters with her lover. Tokens of these creep mysteriously into the detail. What can a butterfly, climbing out of an ear as if from a chrysalis, mean? Art critics have quarrelled about it in learned journals. Journals which make uniquely stimulating pillow books for Isobel and Bill.

Dragan continued to paint tourist portraits on the Riva degli Schiavoni until the summer of 1985. Until, that is, the day his still on Torcello exploded when the Yugoslav had gone across to manufacture more hooch. It was days before Isobel heard about it. She paid for the funeral, despite the fact that he had not recognised her existence since she left Venice to attend her first exhibition. After all, she had swallowed a fair bit of his moonshine.

Mahmoud bin Hamid al Sur was never seen again in Venice. Or anywhere else for that matter. Sandro, who often talks over the lost years with his grandfather, once told him of the incident at the Danieli. Quite grown up now, and spending more and more of his time in Milan, he enjoys spooking his mother with proposals as to what his grandfather might have done with Mahmoud. Intriguingly nasty ideas. Carlo, retorts Isobel, is quite capable of anything Sandro can suggest and more. A villain, they both agree, with a heart of pure uranium. Keeping him alive is a constant concern.

Isobel's little costume jewellery business trundles along making a modest annual profit. The proceeds are donated to a charitable trust set up for victims of the holocaust and their descendants to the fifth generation. In 1988, Estella became the executive manager of the fund.

Once a year, Isobel goes to see Nina Fischer. They hold hands all day and talk in a language exclusive to them about the orchard at Plymstead Magna. Their mutual tenderness induces a tip toeing reverence in the clinic staff, some of whom falsely believe the mechanisms of this relationship to be delicate, whereas in fact they are extremely robust.

Nina herself, inhabiting as she does a permanent, stress free paradise of childhood, may live another forty years. Isobel, only twelve years her junior, and on whom the pleasures and pressures of adulthood inexorably pile, may not survive her subject long enough to see her greatest work publicly acknowledged.

It may yet fall to Estella, Nina's daughter, to declare the painting's origin. As yet, it remains unsigned by the artist.